BROKEN HEARTS,
FENCES,
AND OTHER THINGS
TO MEND

BROKEN HEARTS,
FENCES,
AND OTHER THINGS
TO MEND

KATIE FINN

SQUARE
FISH

FEIWEL AND FRIENDS
NEW YORK

SQUARE
FISH

An Imprint of Macmillan
175 Fifth Avenue
New York, NY 10010
macteenbooks.com

Square Fish books may be purchased for business or promotional use.
For information on bulk purchases, please contact the Macmillan Corporate
and Premium Sales Department at (800) 221-7945 x5442 or by e-mail
at specialmarkets@macmillan.com.

Library of Congress Cataloging-in-Publication Data Available
ISBN 978-1-250-06305-2 (paperback) / ISBN 978-1-250-06057-0 (e-book)

Originally published in the United States by Feiwel and Friends
First Square Fish Edition: 2015
Book designed by Ashley Halsey
Square Fish logo designed by Filomena Tuosto

10 9 8 7 6 5 4 3 2 1

For Emily van Beek

History repeats itself. First as tragedy, second as farce.
        —*KARL MARX*

CHAPTER 1

The Wednesday afternoon that it all started, I was thinking about how great my life was going.

Actually, to be totally truthful, it didn't start that Wednesday. It started earlier than that—five years earlier. But I didn't know that then. I was just wandering around the aisles of the Putnam, Connecticut, Target with no idea what was coming, like the blond girl heading down to the basement in horror movies. I was blissfully unaware that disaster was looming, and thrilled with the way everything was working out.

After all, I had made it through my sophomore year with decent grades—including a passing grade in Chemistry, which was in itself a minor miracle. (I'd been against Chemistry since the first class, when I noticed the safety station at the back, complete with chemical shower and eye-wash station. These things didn't seem to be necessary in Algebra.) School was over for the year, and the whole summer was stretched out in front of me. I had a wonderful best friend. And most important of all, I had an amazing boyfriend. Everything was perfect.

Well, except for the fact that I'd made the very grave mistake of wearing, to Target, a red tank and khaki skirt. I'd forgotten that all the employees there wear red shirts and khakis. And so every few minutes people were coming up to me and asking where they could find the toothpaste, because they thought I worked there.

"Okay!" I said, tracing my finger down the items on the list. "Let's get started." I smiled across the aisle at Teddy Callaway, my boyfriend. Of all the things that were currently good in my life, Teddy was number one. We had started dating my second week of ninth grade at Putnam High School and had been together for the past two years. Teddy was older—eighteen to my sixteen—and would be starting his senior year in the fall. He'd been sophomore *and* junior class president, and had been elected senior class president for the coming year. He was consistently being featured on the front page of the local paper, the *Putnam Post*, looking serious and humble, as a result of all the service groups he had started and all the good he was always doing for the community. And Teddy's altruism was actually the reason we were at Target together. We were leaving in a week to do volunteer work in Colombia, and we needed supplies.

Teddy swallowed hard, cleared his throat, and said, "Gemma?"

"Yes?" I asked as I looked down at the list and tried not to wince. When Teddy had first told me about this volunteering program, I had assumed it would mean doing things like planting gardens and maybe teaching children to sing, until my best friend,

Sophie Curtis, pointed out that I was actually thinking of *The Sound of Music*. I hadn't realized until I got the application forms that this program involved things like building houses and digging latrines. The five-page list of supplies included items like work gloves and first-aid kits (extra gauze) and antimalarial pills. But I wasn't going to let that dissuade me. I had been on board to go on this trip ever since Teddy told me about HELPP (Humanitarian Education Learning through Progressive Programs).

Well, technically, I had been on board once it was clear he was going with or without me. My parents had only agreed to let me go after I'd shown them the literature, proving that there would be supervision and that guys and girls stayed in separate cabins. I needed them to agree, because it seemed there were actually a lot of costs involved with volunteering. We'd had to pay for the program, something my dad hadn't been too thrilled about. He said that if I really wanted to learn about construction, he would happily let me work on the addition to his house, and for free.

But I pressed hard to be able to go, because this way Teddy and I wouldn't have to spend three weeks apart, even if we were staying in separate cabins and digging separate latrines. We hadn't been apart for that long since we got together, and I didn't see any reason for us to start now.

"Okay, we need gauze," I said, grabbing some from the shelf and dropping it into my basket. "And . . ."

"Gemma," Teddy said again, a little more loudly this time. I looked down at the list and saw what he must have been pointing out, and dropped in another roll, trying not to think what we would need gauze for. I glanced over at Teddy and noticed that he looked a little pale.

"Are you okay?" I asked as I looked for the Band-Aids. In the two years we'd been together, I'd learned to read him really well, and I could see that he had something on his mind. Possibly he'd been wondering the same thing about the gauze as I had. After all, we were usually on the same wavelength.

And, okay, if we sometimes weren't on *exactly* the same wavelength, I let him think that we were.

It was actually how we met. I'd spent the first week of my high school experience wandering the halls, bewildered, going to the wrong classes in the wrong classrooms, sometimes not realizing this until the class was over. My sense of direction had never been great, and Putnam High, with two thousand students, was huge compared to my middle school. I had been getting through the first week by basically clinging to Sophie like a bivalve. One day after school, I'd somehow gotten lost in the warren of classrooms and was just looking for a quiet one to duck into so that I could text Sophie and see if she could come and find me. It wasn't until I'd shut the door that I realized I wasn't alone.

"Hi," a voice from the front of the room said. I blinked, surprised, as a guy who looked older than me hopped off the desk he was sitting on and walked forward. "Are you here for the Warbler meeting?"

I just stared at him. The guy standing before me was incredibly cute, with bright blue eyes and blond hair that was a touch long, a lock of it falling over his forehead. He had such an air of confidence and authority about him that I felt a little dazed.

When I realized he was waiting patiently for an answer, I nodded, even though I had no idea what he was talking about. "Yes," I said, hoping he would tell me what this meant. I was hoping the Warblers wasn't some kind of a cappella group, as I had a terrible singing voice. But this was the most dazzling guy I had encountered in a while, and I would have said anything to get to stay in his presence. "I am."

"Great," he said, nodding. "I'm so glad you care about this. Too many people at this school are apathetic."

"I know," I said fervently, as though I hadn't been one of those people until a few seconds ago. "But it's something I've always been committed to."

He looked at me appraisingly for a moment, and his smile widened. "It's nice to meet you," he said. "I'm Teddy."

I later found out that the Warblers was a group dedicated to protecting the environment of the Marsh Warbler, a rare species of bird that wasn't even found in Connecticut. But that didn't matter, because after a while I really did come to care about the Marsh Warbler, even if I also secretly thought it was kind of ugly. Because as far as I was concerned, it had brought me and Teddy together, and so I would always have a soft spot for it.

Teddy and I became a couple almost immediately after that. And overnight, I went from being an anonymous freshman accidentally attending the wrong classes to Teddy Callaway's girlfriend. I was no longer just Gemma Tucker, not particularly special or memorable. I had an identity. His causes (and there were, I soon found out, a *lot* of them) became my causes. His friends became my friends. Teddy was my first boyfriend—though not my first kiss, which was a fact he didn't necessarily know. He'd been in my life so long now, and was such a part of it, that I really couldn't imagine it without him.

I smiled at him across the aisle, and he gave me a weak smile back. He opened his mouth like he was about to say something, when a harassed-looking woman, pushing a toddler in a cart, rolled into the aisle. "Where are the paper towels?" she demanded of me.

"Sorry," I said, wishing for the umpteenth time I'd worn blue that day. "I don't actually work here." She glanced at Teddy, and at my own basket of items.

"*Clearly,*" she said, rolling her eyes and pushing her cart away as she muttered about shoddy work ethic these days.

"Oh," I said, leading the way to the gardening aisle to look for bug repellant as Teddy trailed behind me. "Sophie and Doug wondered if we wanted to see a movie this weekend. I told them yes, okay?"

Sophie and I had stayed close, moved out of our bivalve stage, and my best friend had morphed into a class-A heartbreaker by the end of sophomore year, leaving besotted guys and a string of exes in her wake. Doug was her latest victim, but he'd actually lasted a whole month, which was a record for Sophie, who tended to cycle through boys in two-week increments. I'd said yes to the movie without checking with Teddy, because when you've been together as long as we had, some things were assumed, like the fact we'd always have a Saturday-night date. It was one of the million reasons I loved being with him. I didn't have any of the anxiety and stress that I saw Sophie going through with all her various boys. Instead, I had Teddy, who was constant and brilliant and wonderful.

"Gemma," Teddy said, shaking his head.

"I know," I said quickly. "Doug is kind of a meathead. And I know you think he's insensitive to the plight of the, um, worker. But they promised we could pick the movie this time, so I thought about that documentary you wanted to see. The one about the . . . plight of the worker?" I mumbled the last part. I could never remember the details of the documentaries Teddy wanted to watch. All I knew was that they were never the ones I wanted to see, which were mostly about penguins.

Teddy shook his head again and took a big breath. "Gemma . . ."

"But we don't have to have dinner with them again! It can be just the two of us. What do you say?" I picked up a citronella candle in a glass jar and gave it a cautious sniff.

"Gemma."

"We can go to that raw vegan place that just opened, and—"

"Gemma!"

I stopped talking when I realized I'd been interrupting, smiled at him, and thought, one last time, about how wonderful our summer together was going to be. How everything was falling into place. How great my life was.

Teddy looked at me, right into my eyes. He seemed to be struggling with something, and let out a long breath before speaking. "I . . ." He paused, then took another breath and said in a rush, "I think we need to talk."

"We are talking," I said. Then the impact of his words—and the tone of his voice—hit me, and I noticed again how pale he looked. The world seemed to wobble for a second, and it was like I was suddenly having trouble catching my breath. "What . . ." I started, haltingly, hearing how shaky—how scared—my voice sounded. "What do you mean?"

"Gemma," he said, his voice choked, "I think we should break up."

I dropped the candle I'd been holding, and the glass shattered into pieces at my feet.

CHAPTER 2

"**A**nd then what happened?" Sophie asked from her seat at the kitchen table, eyes wide.

It was two days later, and Sophie had shown up that afternoon, bearing tissues and chocolate and her "life coach"—otherwise known as *Cosmo*—clearly believing that I would be in a desperate, sobbing state. Which couldn't have been further from the truth. I was fine. This was just a temporary situation, and as soon as Teddy realized he'd made a mistake, we'd get back together. It was as simple as that. In the meantime, I was baking.

I'd always liked to bake, but I'd gotten much more into it over the last two years, and had started providing the refreshments for Teddy's various clubs and meetings and protest marches. Baking calmed me down, and I liked the order of it—the idea that when you mixed certain ingredients together, chemical change occurred, and you ended up with something else. And ever since I'd come back from Target, baking was the only thing that had appealed to me. If I wasn't baking, I found that I kept reaching for my phone, either to check if Teddy had called or to start to call him and try to find out what he'd been thinking. And since I knew that neither of these were good options, I'd been keeping myself—and my hands—occupied. My mother and stepfather, clearly understanding that I was on a tear, had been staying out of my way in the kitchen. And so far, I'd made three kinds of muffins, four kinds of cookies, a coffee cake, and an iffy batch of snickerdoodles. I had just put my double-chocolate-chip cookies into the oven when Sophie had shown up at the door, despite me texting her repeatedly that I was fine and that she didn't need to come over.

"Gemma?" Sophie prompted.

I looked up from the flour I'd been sifting for the next batch—white chocolate macadamia nut this time—and tried to focus on my best friend. Sophie and I had looked a lot alike when we were younger—it was uncanny, actually; people were always asking us if we were sisters, which we loved—but puberty had changed all that, and Sophie had gotten curvy while I'd gotten tall. We both still had brown hair and freckles, but Sophie tended to cover hers with makeup, and her hair was cut in a stylish, choppy bob while mine was kind of long and shapeless. We no longer looked like the doppelgängers we'd been when we were kids, especially after I broke my nose last year. When the doctor fixed it, he shaved off the bump that had always been in the middle. He just assumed I wanted it that way, but I actually missed it, especially when I saw the identical bump still on Sophie's nose. It seemed to have more character than my perfectly straight nose now did.

Setting us apart even further at the moment were our outfits.

I was wearing jeans and an oversized pink T-shirt that had once belonged to my stepfather but that I'd appropriated years ago as an apron. SALMON FESTIVAL! THE KICK-OFF OF SPAWNING SEASON! was emblazoned across the front.

Sophie, on the other hand, was decked out in her go to summer style—flip-flops and a sundress that hugged her curves, her sunglasses pushed up through her hair like a headband. The only things we currently had in common, looks-wise, were our necklaces. We'd splurged on them together last year. Sophie wore a gold *G* charm on a chain around her neck, and I wore a gold *S* on mine. We thought they were much better—and more unique—than traditional best friend necklaces. The two of us had promised never to take them off, and I knew it was a promise I'd keep.

"What?" I asked, trying to get myself to pay attention. "What did you say?"

"I just wanted to know what happened next," Sophie said, leaning across the table. "After Teddy said he wanted to break up and you dropped the candle."

"Oh," I said, as I set the flour aside and started measuring out the white chocolate chips. I really didn't see why I had to go through this whole recap; when Teddy called—which he would, of course, any minute now—it would all be moot. "Well, then this manager came up and handed me a broom and told me that the candle was going to come out of my pay."

"No," Sophie said, shaking her head. "What happened next with Teddy?"

I looked away and started chopping the macadamia nuts. "He

just said that he thought we were getting too serious too young, and that we should slow down."

Sophie snorted. "That's a new one."

I knew what she meant. Slowing down was something Teddy had never seemed to want before. Quite the opposite, in fact. He was always telling me that it was crazy we hadn't slept together after two years and never seemed impressed by my argument that Marie Antoinette and Louis XVI didn't sleep together for *seven* years, even after they were married.

But it wasn't like this had even come up recently. Things between us had been great . . . or so I'd thought. I'd spent the last two days—when I wasn't measuring out nutmeg and softening butter—trying to figure out why Teddy would have done this. It was a mistake, of course, and it would all be resolved soon, but *something* must have happened to make him think we needed to end things. I'd finally come to the conclusion that maybe I'd taken our relationship for granted, and maybe expected too much of his time when he was so committed to different projects.

But this was at least understandable, since Teddy and I had gotten together just as I'd finally begun to accept my parents' divorce was actually going to last. My mom had gotten engaged to my stepfather, my dad had moved across the country, and just when everything in my life seemed to be changing, forever and for the worse, Teddy was a constant, something I could hang on to. And so maybe I'd just held on a little too hard. But I would change. I knew this wasn't the end; we were still going to Colombia together, after all. Soon, we'd get back together and everything would be like it was before, except better, because we both would have grown and matured from this experience. Everything was going to turn out okay. But in the meantime, I had cookies to frost.

"Okay!" Sophie said as the timer *ding!*ed and I pulled the cookies out of the oven. I set them on the table as she opened her dog-eared and annotated *Cosmo* and tapped her finger on the page for emphasis. "So this article says that, post-breakup, the worst thing you can do is get into a new relationship too soon. It says you need to be in a mourning period for at least half the length of the relationship. And since you and Teddy were together two years, that would mean . . ." She tilted her head to the side, clearly doing some mental arithmetic. "A *year*?" she said, frowning down at the magazine. "No, that can't be right."

"This is irrelevant," I insisted, as Sophie reached for one of the just-out-of-the-oven cookies. "I don't need a mourning period. Teddy just needs to cool off. Like those cookies," I said, just as Sophie took a gigantic bite.

"*Haaaagh,*" she yelped, fanning her mouth.

"Exactly," I said, pointing to her, glad to have a visual metaphor to back up my idea. "But as soon as he cools down a little and can see things rationally, he'll see he made a mistake."

Sophie just looked at me as she took a big drink of water. "Oh, man," she said after a moment, shaking her head. "You're *so* much further gone than I thought." Before I could ask her what she meant by that, she set the magazine aside, stood up, and forcibly removed the butter from my hands. "Come on," she said, turning off the oven and herding me toward the door. "I think you need to get out."

Half an hour later, I looked at Sophie across my pizza slice and sighed. "I don't understand why we're here." Sophie had taken me to Putnam Pizza, the most popular pizza place in town. We were in the restaurant; there was a take-out-only window next door. Sophie hadn't told me where we were going; if I'd known, I might have changed out of my Salmon Festival apron-shirt. I'd suggested we just get slices to go, but Sophie had practically dragged me into the restaurant, and then ordered my favorite pizza for me—pineapple-sausage-pepperoni, which everyone else hated, including our waiter, if his expression when he wrote down the order was any indication.

"We're here because you needed to stop baking and get out of your house," Sophie said as she bit into her extra-cheese slice. I just shook my head, not wanting to tell her that this was actually not helpful, since now that I was away from my high-speed mixer, my hands kept reaching for my phone, every time I illuminated the screen sure I would see a text from Teddy, apologizing. "Also," she went on, looking significantly at my untouched slice, "I thought you could use some real food. I think the sugar might have been going to your head."

"What's that supposed to mean?" I asked as I took a bite of my pizza.

"Well . . ." Sophie said, sliding the *G* on her necklace back and forth a few times. "You said that the breakup with Teddy was a mistake."

"It was," I agreed immediately. "And probably just a misunderstanding. He's going to call me soon. I know it. And then everything will be okay."

"The thing is, Gem," Sophie said, leaning closer, "would it be . . . you know, such a bad thing if you guys stayed broken up?"

I just stared at her, trying to make what she'd just said make sense. "Of course it would," I finally replied. "What do you even mean?"

"Not that Teddy's not great," Sophie said quickly. "He's really, you know, committed to all that stuff he cares about. But maybe this is actually a good thing."

I couldn't even think of what to say to this; the idea that I wouldn't want to be with Teddy was crazy. My boyfriend—I refused to even think "ex"—was amazing. He wasn't just a do-gooder because he thought it would help him get somewhere—he genuinely cared about all his causes and tried to make the world a better place, and I always hoped that some of it would rub off on me. I knew Sophie would have said this was ridiculous, but she didn't know the terrible things I'd done when I was eleven, the summer I'd spent in the Hamptons. I had hurt my dad, and a girl who'd believed I was her friend, and I'd done it deliberately. Teddy gave me something to aspire to, and made me a better person. We were the perfect couple, which was probably why we'd been named Perfect Couple in the yearbook last year. We had to get back together. Anything else was just unthinkable. I shook my head. "You don't know what you're talking about," I said firmly. "Obviously this isn't a good thing. But it's only temporary. Teddy will call, and then he'll—"

"He might not need to," Sophie said, her eyes on the door.

I turned around to see what was behind me, what she was seeing—and it was like everything shifted into slow motion for a moment, and all the colors became brighter, the world changing into just an all-around better place to be. Teddy was walking away from the take-out window, holding a pizza box with two cans of soda on top, wearing that yellow Occupy Putnam shirt I loved so much. I stood up so fast that I knocked my water glass over, but I didn't care. I just needed to get to Teddy as quickly as possible.

"Gem," Sophie said, grabbing onto my hand to stop me as she simultaneously tried to mop up the table with her napkin. "*No.* I don't think you want to do this."

But I shook her off and ran for the door, then took the steps down to the parking lot two at a time. "Teddy!" I called, and he stopped halfway across the parking lot and turned around.

He squinted at me, then took a few steps closer. "Gemma?" he asked.

"Hi," I said, closing the distance between us, feeling more like my old self with every step I took toward him. It was like I'd been deprived of oxygen this whole time and hadn't realized it. But now, finally, I could breathe again. Things made sense again. I was with Teddy.

But Teddy didn't look like things were equally clear to him, for some reason. He mostly looked uncomfortable as he shifted his weight from foot to foot. "Hi," he said uncertainly.

"It's so good to see you," I said. It had only been a few days, but I could feel myself looking eagerly at the face I was used to seeing daily. It was like he'd somehow gotten cuter since I'd last seen him. How had I never appreciated that dimple in his left cheek before? It was taking all my self-control not to fling myself into his arms, but I restrained myself. Teddy had never really liked public displays of affection, and anyway, we'd be kissing as soon as we cleared this misunderstanding up.

"You too," he said, his voice strained. He glanced to the parking lot, where I saw his Prius was parked. He looked back at me and swallowed. "Listen, Gem," he said. "I'm really sorry about what happened in Target. I shouldn't have done it like that."

I nodded, but could feel the smile on my face freeze a little. It wasn't the *place* that had bothered me; it was the fact he had broken up with me at all. I waited for a moment so that he could tell me he also regretted making a terrible mistake by suggesting we end things, but Teddy just looked down at the ground.

"Listen," I said, figuring that I should just jump in while he gathered his courage. "I was just thinking about . . . you know . . ." I took a big breath and continued. "About you and me . . . maybe . . . getting back—"

"Yes!" Teddy said, cutting me off, but I had never been so happy to be interrupted. "Me too. I was going to call you about it."

Relief flooded through me; it was practically a physical sensation. Because even though I hadn't wanted to think about it during my baking frenzy, a tiny voice in the back of my head had been whispering—louder, the more time went on—that maybe Teddy had meant what he'd said to me in the gardening aisle, that it hadn't just been a momentary flash of crazy brought on by the fluorescent lights. "Really?" I asked weakly, feeling myself smile genuinely for the first time in forty-eight hours.

"Yes," he said, nodding. "Getting back your deposit for the program. I called the office and they said it wouldn't be a problem."

I just stared at him. "Deposit?" I managed.

"Yeah," he said. "I talked to them a few days ago. They said you'll just have to call to get it refunded."

"A few days ago?" I whispered, feeling whiplash from this turnaround. Teddy had called a few *days* ago? Before he broke up with me in the gardening aisle?

It brought reality crashing down on me. It wasn't just a momentary impulse. He wasn't going to change his mind. He'd made calls first to find out about deposits. Which meant the people at the HELPP offices had known about my breakup before I had. Because of course we weren't going to dig latrines together now. This was real.

Teddy Callaway had broken up with me.

"Yeah," he said. "So if you call them . . ." His voice trailed off.

I just stared at him, feeling my throat start to constrict. We were over. And I couldn't even understand why. "Teddy," I whispered, my voice wavering. I could feel myself on the verge of tears.

Teddy frowned, and I saw a look of regret pass over his face. And maybe—was I just imagining it?—doubt. He took a step closer to me. "Gemma," he said, his voice gentle. "I—"

BEEP!

Teddy jumped, and I looked over, startled, to the parking lot where the honk had come from. I followed his gaze to his Prius.

Which was when I noticed that it wasn't empty. There was someone sitting in the passenger seat, someone with their head turned away from me, but someone wearing a tank top, hair up in a long ponytail.

My stomach clenched, and it had nothing to do with the one bite of pizza I'd eaten. There was a girl in the car.

It clicked into place that Teddy was holding two sodas, one of which was ginger ale, which he never drank. He was bringing a soda to a girl with a ponytail. He was *dating* someone else already?

I was suddenly very aware that I hadn't put on any makeup, that my hair had been tossed into a messy ponytail, and that the shirt I was wearing was covered in flour and featured the word "spawning."

I looked down hard at the parking-lot asphalt, wondering if I could somehow get it to open up and swallow me whole.

"Anyway," Teddy said. He turned back to me, and the more vulnerable look that had been on his face only a few moments ago was gone. His expression now was closed off, all business. "I should go. But take care, okay, Gem?" He reached out like maybe he was going to touch my shoulder, but then must have changed his mind, because he pulled back his hand and gave me a thumbs-up instead.

I watched him walk away as long as I could before my vision got blurry. Out of the corner of my eye, I saw Sophie hurrying up to stand next to me. "Gem?" she asked. "What happened?"

I just watched the car drive away, catching one more glimpse of the girl in the passenger seat, and a flash of what looked like a tattoo on the back of her neck. Then the car disappeared from view, and Teddy was gone—probably forever.

"Gemma?" Sophie was saying, sounding worried. "Are you okay?"

I did know the answer to that, and shook my head. The love of my life had broken up with me. He'd just rejected me in a parking lot. He was already seeing some girl with a neck tattoo.

My whole summer was wrecked. And it was only the beginning of June.

CHAPTER 3

I really thought that things couldn't get worse.

They did.

In fact, it seems that thinking "things can't get worse" is an invitation for things to get much, much worse.

Immediately after returning from Putnam Pizza, I had gotten into bed and hadn't really gotten out again. I'd left a sobbing message on my dad's phone, trying to tell him about the deposits, but I guess not getting my point across, because when he called back, he clearly thought that I had either fallen down and hit my head, or totaled the car. I surrounded myself with my laptop, boxes of tissues, and pictures of me and Teddy.

In retrospect, it seemed totally understandable that Teddy would have broken up with me. He was older, smarter, and a better person than I was. And it was clear to me, as well as to the editors at the *Putnam Post,* that he was destined for great things, whereas I would just be the foolish high school girl who let this brilliant guy slip away. I could practically see the tiny mention I would have in his future biography: *Gemma Tucker—not good enough for the future Nobel Prize winner. She has never since done anything of note.*

So I spent my days in my room, crying, mostly curled into a little ball. And whenever I took a break to catch my breath, or drink some Gatorade (my mom had been leaving it outside my door, because she was worried I was going to get dehydrated), I realized that there was a piece of me that had been expecting this to happen from the beginning. I had been waiting for the moment that Teddy would find me out, the moment he'd realize I'd been faking—that I wasn't as good a person as him, that I didn't care about my carbon footprint as much, and that I thought the Marsh Warbler was ugly. After all, the whole way we'd met was based on a lie. And Teddy was brilliant—of course he would have figured it out eventually.

When I wasn't looking at pictures of us and crying, I was watching movies that were making me cry even harder, even ones I thought were safe, like *Ghostbusters*. Sophie stopped by once a day, bearing an iced latte for me, to try and coax me out of the house. It never worked, though, and usually she just ended joining me on the bed and staying for the day's second viewing of *The Notebook*.

I just really didn't see any point in returning to the outside world, because I couldn't imagine the situation ever improving. Also, if I ventured out, I might encounter Teddy and his neck-tattoo girl. But things were safe in my bedroom. So for the foreseeable future, I was staying put.

The only bright spot was that Sophie didn't have any gossip to report. People had been shocked by our breakup, but nobody had heard anything about Teddy dating someone new. So I figured that it might be bearable, and that I could just learn to live in this brokenhearted state. I had tissues, and daily iced latte deliveries. It would be okay.

And then, the morning of my third day of bed-living, my door opened and things got worse.

"Hi, Gem," my mom said, knocking as she opened the door, which, in my opinion, defeated the whole purpose of knocking. She gave me the kind of look people had been giving me lately, a mix of sympathy and fear, like I was a particularly pathetic-looking time bomb. "How are you?"

"Hello there, Gemma," Walter, my stepfather, said, coming into the room behind my mom and giving me his sympathetic frown.

"Hi, Walter," I muttered. Despite the fact that I'd known Walter for five years, we had never quite moved past the polite-awkward-small-talk phase. When things got really desperate, we talked about the weather.

And it wasn't like Walter's job provided tons of conversation fodder. He was a salmon expert, and had once been a competitive fly-fisher, because apparently there is such a thing. Now he just advised people on salmon. My mom, a real estate agent, met him when he was looking for a house with a basement big enough for his fly-fishing trophies and a pond so he could practice casting. When I was eleven and my parents separated, I had refused to believe that it would last. But it had, and as a result I'd had to listen to talk about salmon for the last five years.

"You know how sorry we are about you and Teddy," my mom

said as she perched on the edge of my bed. I could tell that something encouraging was about to follow. That was one of the dangers of being a realtor, I'd learned—you were always looking to sell someone on the bright side. "But maybe it's for the best!" she continued in the tone of voice she used when explaining that one bathroom would bring a family closer, and that, in her opinion, closets were overrated.

"Yeah," I muttered as I closed my laptop and picked a loose thread from my quilt. I couldn't see how having my heart shattered into a million pieces was for the best, but I didn't want to argue the point. Especially in front of Walter.

"But the thing is," my mother said, settling herself more fully on my bed, like she was preparing for a longer chat, "we need to talk about the summer."

I frowned. "What about the summer?" My dad had told the HELPP people I wasn't coming and had gotten most of his deposit back. And now that I no longer had any commitments, I was pretty much planning on continuing to spend the summer exactly where I was.

"Well," my mother said, "we thought you were going to be in Ecuador, darling. So we made plans."

"Colombia," I corrected, looking from my mom to Walter. "What plans?"

"We're going to Loch Faskally," Walter piped up from the doorway. "It's prime spawning season in the Highlands." I flinched slightly, as I always did whenever I had to hear my stepfather use the word "spawning," which was far more frequently than I would have ever believed possible.

"You're going to *Scotland*?" I asked, taking a guess, since that was the only place I'd ever heard of that had lochs.

"Yes," Walter said, taking a tiny step into the room, looking animated, the way he only ever did when talking about fish. "The laird asked me personally. We're staying in the castle as his guests."

"So, you see, you really can't stay here alone, Gem. And while we'd love for you to come . . ." My mother let this sentence trail off, with a small shrug. It appeared I was not invited, even though I really wouldn't have minded hanging out in a castle all summer. But I guess you really can't just call up lairds and ask if your stepdaughter can come along, especially if she has no interest in fish.

"Fine," I said, flopping back against my propped-up pillows. This whole conversation was exhausting me. "I'll go stay with Dad." My father was a screenwriter who lived in Los Angeles. When he'd been married to my mom, he was a struggling novelist who wrote freelance articles to get by. After they separated, though, he moved to L.A. His former college roommate, Bruce Davidson, had become a big-time Hollywood producer, and he offered my dad a rewrite job on a terrible movie about time-traveling turtles. And while I thought even the rewritten version of *Time Crawls* was still pretty bad, Bruce was thrilled, and my dad had a new career. I saw my father on holidays, and usually for a few weeks in the summer anyway. It might be a nice change, staying with him in California. Hanging out with my dad always meant that we saw a lot of movies and ate lots of pizza, two things that sounded very appealing to me at the moment.

"Good," my mom said, smiling like she was happy things had

been settled so easily. "Why don't you call your dad and figure out when in the next few days you want to head out there? And then Walter can drive you."

This made me sit all the way up. There was absolutely no way I was going to drive across the country with Walter. We'd run out of things to talk about before we left Connecticut. "Drive me to the airport," I clarified. And also, I was the tiniest bit stung that she seemed to want to get me out of the house so quickly. She could have at least *pretended* that she wasn't quite so eager to see me gone. I mean, really.

"Oh, no," my mom said, standing up and smoothing down the quilt where she'd been sitting. "Your dad's in the Hamptons this summer, working on a movie for Bruce. So it's just a few hours away!"

I froze, even as my mom talked on, about logistics and plans and what I should pack. I hadn't been back to the Hamptons in five years. It was where everything had gone down that summer, and I had avoided it ever since. It had always felt, to me, like the scene of the crime.

"Gem?" I looked up and realized my mom was looking at me expectantly.

"What was that?" I asked, trying to focus on her.

"I just asked," my mom said, her smile getting a little forced. I could tell she wanted to wrap this conversation up and consider the issue handled. Walter wasn't even pretending to pay attention anymore; he was looking down at his phone, no doubt playing Bait and Switch, the fishing game he was addicted to. "If you would call your dad and let him know the plan? And then we can confirm your dates."

I was on the verge of telling her I didn't think I could go to the Hamptons after all, and she'd just have to call up the laird and tell him I was coming, when my mom's phone rang. "I have to get that," she said, looking down at the screen. "Work. Gem, just let me know when you've talked to your dad, okay?" She hustled out, saying hello in her realtor voice as she left, Walter trailing behind, all before I'd even decided if I was going to be able to go back there.

I reached up and pulled open my curtains for the first time in days. What I'd done the summer I was eleven was the worst of me, a time I never liked to think back on if I could avoid it, and I wasn't sure that being in a place that would remind me most strongly of my biggest mistakes was the best idea.

But it *had* been a long time ago, I realized as I squinted out at the sun. And I had no reason to think that any of the Bridges—especially Hallie—had ever returned to the Hamptons, particularly after what had happened. And I really, really didn't want to spend the summer hearing about fish.

I looked around at the mounds of tissues that surrounded me and realized I was getting sick of wearing nothing but my pajamas. It actually had gotten a little tedious, spending all this time in bed. Plus, according to Sophie and WebMD, I might be in danger of developing rickets. It would probably be good to get out, and if I was away in the Hamptons, there would be no danger of running into Teddy and neck-tattoo girl. And at least if I had to live with this broken heart, I could do it at the beach.

I weighed my options one last time, trying to see if I was really going to be able to do this. I decided that I was, lay there for one minute longer, then rolled out of bed and headed off to call my dad.

⚬⚬⚬⚬⚬⚬

"**S**horter," Sophie commanded as I glared at her from underneath my curtain of sopping-wet hair as my stylist, whose name was Sigrid and who I wasn't entirely sure understood English, opened her scissors with a terrifying snap.

"Not shorter," I said quickly, grabbing my hair, just to make things clear. Sigrid rolled her eyes and stalked to the other side of the salon, where she flopped down into a chair, somehow managing to look tragic and Swedish as she did this. However, a moment later, I saw her look around furtively and pick up her copy of *Once Bitten,* the very controversial and highly erotic vampire-love novel that had been burning up the bestseller charts for months now. My mom had forbidden me to read it, but there was no need—there was no *way* I was reading it after I saw that she had a copy hidden in her closet. I mean, gross.

"Gemma," Sophie said to me in her warning voice, and I turned back to her.

"Sophie," I returned in mine.

Things had moved very quickly after I'd learned of the Scottish plan and called my father. I had managed to get out of driving to the Hamptons with Walter when I realized it would take us three hours to get there. I'd convinced my mom to let me take the train instead and arranged for my dad to pick me up at the station. I'd told all my regular babysitting clients ('sitting had been pretty much the way I'd gotten all my disposable income since I was about twelve) that I wouldn't be available for the rest of the summer. I'd stocked up on flip-flops, canceled the flight to Colombia, and returned all the gear I'd gotten for the trip (well, technically, I asked my mom to return it, since the thought of going back to Target was still too traumatizing).

My dad was happy I would be spending the summer with him, and my mom and Walter were happy that they wouldn't have to convince a laird to take me in. The only person who wasn't pleased with my summer plans was my BFF. Sophie had taken great exception to the fact that I was now deserting her for the whole summer, especially since I'd spent the bulk of the last week refusing, for various reasons, to leave my kitchen and/or room. So when she'd pressed me to take a late-afternoon train, so that we could spend my last day in Putnam together, I'd agreed without even suspecting an ulterior motive.

Which was foolish, because it was how I found myself sitting in an all-white salon with a frightening Swedish hairdresser. Sophie had a theory that you needed a makeover after a breakup. She thought that you had to do something right away to separate yourself in a very clear way from the person you'd been when in the relationship (it probably didn't help that Sophie adored makeovers and that both her parents were shrinks). In her opinion, the more serious the relationship, the more significant the makeover had to be. This meant that after most of her own breakups, Sophie simply changed her nail polish color or bought a new lip gloss. But because Teddy and I had been together so long, and because I still wasn't quite able to say his name without bursting into tears, Sophie decided that drastic measures were needed, and had booked me an appointment without my knowledge or consent.

"You need a change," she said, sitting in the swivel chair next to mine. "I'm telling you. You'll feel better once you do it."

"I don't think short hair is the way to go," I said, brushing some droplets off my face. Sophie had hustled me into the salon with such skill and stealth that I hadn't even realized what was happening until my hair was being washed.

"Okay, maybe not short," she relented, giving herself a push and spinning around once in her chair. "But a change. A *real* one. Okay, Gem?"

I stared back at my reflection and saw only who I'd been for the last two years—Teddy Callaway's girlfriend. Maybe a change wouldn't be the worst thing in the world. "Okay," I said, taking one last look at myself. Sophie motioned Sigrid over and I let out a breath. "Let's do it."

≈≈≈≈≈≈

Two hours later, a stranger stared back at me. The hair that had always been light brown was now a bright auburn. My one-length, slightly shaggy hair had been cut to just beneath my shoulders, with long, sideswept bangs. I looked nothing like myself. I certainly didn't look like the girl who'd been dumped in the gardening aisle of Target. Or the girl who'd been dumped again in the parking lot of a pizza place. I ran my hands over my new bangs as Sigrid finished up.

"You find new man with this hair," she pronounced as she gave a final snip. Sophie had told her the whole story of my breakup as I'd gotten my color applied. Sigrid hadn't been that impressed with Teddy, starting with his name. "Like the bear?" she'd asked. "No. Is no good." I'd tried to explain that Teddy was a nickname for Edward (which he never went by), but this hadn't seemed to make a difference. After hearing the story, she'd said something in Swedish, then pronounced me better off without him, telling me that I was too young to settle down, that there were plenty of herring in the sea.

Sophie had headed out to get us drinks as I was finishing up, and as I walked to the register to pay, I couldn't help taking little glances at my new self in the mirror. Maybe Sophie was on to something after all. I certainly felt better than I had since the Target trip.

"Love it!" Sophie shrieked as I stepped out of the salon. "Turn around." Rolling my eyes, I obliged, and she bounced up and down in her flip-flops, grinning at me. "Didn't I tell you?"

"You told me," I said, picking up one of my new red locks and staring at it. "You were right."

Sophie smiled wide at that; it was one of her favorite phrases to hear. "For you," she said, handing me a plastic cup from Stubbs, the local coffee chain. I saw she'd gotten me an iced soy vanilla latte, extra vanilla, my summer standby. *Sophie* was scrawled across the cup in huge letters. On her own plastic cup—lemonade with raspberry syrup—her name was also written, along with three hearts, a smiley face, and a phone number.

"Thanks," I said, taking my cup from her as we walked to her car. "You heartbreaker, you."

She glanced down at the phone number. "Oh, that." She smiled as she beeped open her car. "He *was* pretty cute."

"What about Doug?" I asked, settling myself in the passenger seat and immediately flipping down the visor mirror to continue to look at my hair.

"Ugh," Sophie said as she started the car and headed away from the salon, toward Putnam's main train station. The appointment had taken so long—it seemed that turning your hair a different color was a very time-consuming process—that I no longer had time to go home and get my bags. So Sophie was driving me to the station, and my mom was meeting us there with my suitcase. "Doug is getting on my nerves lately. He's starting to be a drag."

I shook my head and smiled at this, already seeing Sophie's summer romance playing out, Doug being ditched for this barista. Since I'd only ever dated Teddy, I'd had no experience with relationship drama, and frankly preferred it that way.

"What am I going to do all summer with you gone?" Sophie sighed as she turned into the station parking lot, double-parked illegally, and killed her engine.

"I was going to be gone anyway, Soph," I reminded her.

"I know." She sighed. "But just for a few weeks. Not the *whole summer.*"

On impulse, I suggested, "Why don't you come and visit?"

She brightened at that. "Really?"

"Sure," I said blithely, even though I hadn't checked with my father or Bruce. But I was sure it would be fine. All Bruce's houses seemed to have more rooms than anyone ever actually used. I saw my mother's car pull into the station, and winced, as I always did, when I saw the FISHERMEN LIVE IN THE REEL WORLD and GO AGAINST THE CURRENT bumper stickers Walter had put on. "That's my mom," I said, getting out of the car.

Sophie got out as well and met me around the back. "Call me tons," she said.

"I will," I promised, giving her a tight hug. "Thanks for . . ." I gestured to my hair, but hoped she knew it included this whole week and the years of friendship before that. "You know."

"I do," she said as she climbed back into her car and started the engine. "Say hi to your dad, okay? And have fun. Forget about what's-his-name. Make out with someone!"

She practically yelled this last statement, and several people walking to the train platform turned and looked at me. I just gave her a small wave as she grinned and sped out of the station parking lot.

I walked over to where my mom was standing by her car, looking around, my quilted duffel at her feet. I waved, but she only glanced in my direction for a second. "Mom!" I called, but again, she turned to me for only a moment before looking away again.

What was going on? "Hi," I said, when I was right in front of her.

My mother turned to me, her expression blank and polite, before she did a double take and recognition dawned. *"Gemma?"* she asked, sounding incredulous. "I didn't even recognize you!"

I brushed my new bangs back self-consciously. "Is it really that different?"

My mother just looked at me for a moment longer, then shook

her head. "It looks great," she said, and I couldn't help wishing she had led with that. "It's just . . . a change." She reached out and touched a lock of my hair. "You look like a whole new girl," she said with a smile.

I heard the sound of the train, and looked up to see it rumbling down the track. "I'd better go," I said. "Have fun in Scotland."

My mother gave me a quick hug, then handed me my bag. "You have fun too," she said. "I'll bring you back a kilt. Or some lox!"

I tried to look enthusiastic about these possibilities as I waved at her, then hurried up the steps to the platform. I boarded the train, iced latte in hand, and walked back until I found a half-deserted car. As I stowed my bag in the overhead rack and settled into a window seat, I thought about what Sophie had yelled to me, that I should make out with someone. I hadn't had the time to set her straight, and now I thought about texting her to tell her it wasn't going to be an option. Because while I might manage to have some fun this summer, I certainly wasn't going to be making out with anyone.

That was one thing I was totally sure of.

CHAPTER 4

I noticed the guy just after we stopped for the second time.

He was sitting across the aisle from me, also in the window seat, head turned toward the window. He had a pair of white earbuds in, and his head was moving slightly in time to the music he was listening to. He seemed like he was around my age, and though I couldn't see his face—not even his profile—it struck me that the back of his neck was really nice.

A second later, I came to my senses. What was I thinking? I had *just* been dumped and my heart was freshly broken. What was I doing looking at other people's necks? I was beginning to think that Sophie had been on to something with her mourning period theory. I was not going to think about boys for at least a year, if not longer. I couldn't even imagine wanting to date someone new. I turned away from the guy and focused my attention out at the scenery passing by the train windows.

When we made one of the last stops before the longer stretch that would take us to the Hamptons, a very large and very loud family got on the train, the mother loaded down with mono-grammed canvas bags and screaming children, the father ignoring the ubiquitous NO LOUD CELL CONVERSATIONS signs and yelling into his phone. When they approached, the nice-necked guy got up and offered them his row, which the family took, the mother looking almost absurdly grateful as the father screamed something into his phone about the Tokyo markets.

The guy picked up his backpack and duffel bag and looked across the aisle to me, and the two empty seats in my row.

"Hi," he said, setting his bag down on the aisle seat. I noticed now that he was *really* cute, the kind of cute seen more often in ads for orange juice and family smartphone plans than in real life. He had light brown hair, cut short, and eyes that looked greenish, but that might have just been because he was wearing a pale green T-shirt. He had dark eyelashes and eyebrows and though it was hard to tell because I was sitting, but it looked like he was a few inches taller than me, which meant he was pretty tall.

"Is this seat taken?" he asked, and I noticed that his voice was nice, deep but not scary Batman-deep.

"Nope," I said, hoping he hadn't noticed me staring. "Just let me make some room for you." I stood up and shifted my bag over on the luggage rack.

"Don't worry about it," he said, standing behind me and pushing his bag into place. "I'm—"

Just then, the train stopped suddenly. I was thrown off balance, and had managed to steady myself when the train sped up again. I fell back—and landed right on the lap of the guy.

"Oh my god." I felt my face get hot as I tried to understand what was happening. Somehow, I was sprawled across this guy's *lap*. "I'm so sorry, I didn't—"

"No, it's fine," he said, though I could see he was turning red too. I tried to push myself off him, but just as I did, he half-stood, and my hand landed on his thigh. His *upper* thigh.

"*Oh* my god." I half-stumbled, half-fell back on the middle seat and then scooted myself over to the window. I wanted to make it clear that I wasn't some kind of weird train harasser who used sudden stops to touch the legs of random cute guys. "I'm so sorry about that. I'm so, so sorry."

"It's fine," he said, but I could see that he was still blushing. "Are you all right?"

"Yes," I said. "I just . . . fell harder than I was expecting to."

He gave me a don't-worry-about-it smile, and I realized there was something about him that seemed familiar. I couldn't quite place him, but figured that maybe he was one of my friends' Friend-verse friends, someone I'd seen tagged enough in their posts that I recognized him, even though we'd never actually met. I picked up my latte—it had been resting on the tiny ledge by the window, and had not, miraculously, spilled—and took a deep restorative sip.

"Great name," the guy said, nodding at my cup, and I realized he was reading the *Sophie* that was written there.

"Thanks," I said. "But it's not—"

"Tickets!" the conductor yelled as he made his way down the aisle. The guy then had to explain he'd already given his ticket, that he had been sitting across the aisle, then moved, which the conductor seemed to think was some massive train transgression, but he finally left without making the guy pay again.

"Sorry about that," the guy said when the conductor had departed. "I'm Josh, by the way."

"Hi," I said. "It's nice to meet you." I ran my hand across my new bangs and was suddenly grateful to Sophie for dragging me to the salon. Not that I was interested in this guy, but it was just nice to know that my hair currently looked better than it ever normally did.

"You heading to the Hamptons?" he asked.

"I am," I said. I was about to tell Josh we would be in East Hampton when I realized that Bruce might have moved in the last five years. He'd certainly gone through at least three wives. "But I'm not exactly sure where."

Josh smiled. "Same here," he said. "My sister is already up there, but the house is new—I have no idea what neighborhood it's in." He stowed his iPod in the side mesh pocket of his backpack, like he wanted to keep talking, despite the fact I had already proven myself to be very uncoordinated. "Have you been to the Hamptons before?"

"Well . . ." I started. I should have probably been prepared for this question, but it caught me off guard. "Um, once," I said. "For a summer when I was a kid. But not since then."

"Same here," he said again. "Not even for a whole summer, in my case. But I remember I liked it."

"Yeah," I murmured as I looked out the window so that he wouldn't see my expression. Guilt was hitting me like a wave, and I was wondering, again, if I'd made a mistake in agreeing to go back. I had a sudden flash of a memory I usually tried to keep buried—me, staring through the car window at Hallie, her shoulders slumped, her face tearstained and puffy, all the while knowing that it was my fault, that I'd done things I couldn't take back.

"So you're from Connecticut?" he asked, shaking me out of this memory. "I, um," he continued, looking down at his feet, and I saw the tips of his ears were turning red. "Noticed when you got on."

"Oh," I said. *Oh.* I felt a fizzy feeling in my stomach, something I hadn't felt in a very long time, not since Teddy and I first began dating. But just as soon as it had started, it went away. I wasn't interested in this guy. He wasn't Teddy, and it was as simple as that. "Um, yeah. I'm from Putnam. Are you from Connecticut too?"

Josh shook his head. "I came from Massachusetts," he said. "I go to school there. Clarence Hall."

I raised an eyebrow. Clarence Hall was a boarding school a few hours from Putnam. Sophie had once dated two guys there at the same time, and it had ended in a spectacularly bad fashion. I'd given Sophie endless grief about it, telling her that deception never led to anything but heartache, and she must have listened to me, because after that, she stuck to dating one guy at a time, even if they did sometimes overlap at the end—Sophie wasn't the greatest at being on her own.

"Impressive," I said.

"I don't know about that," Josh said with a laugh. "I'm mostly there because of the lacrosse team."

"Extra impressive," I said, before I could stop myself. But I couldn't help it—the cutest guys at Putnam High played lacrosse. Since Teddy had opposed pretty much all sports for various ethical reasons—and I had too, in support of him—I'd never really known any lacrosse players well, just secretly admired them from afar.

Josh laughed at that, and I realized I liked the sound of it—a generous laugh without any meanness in it. The conductor got on the scratchy PA system and announced the Bridgehampton stop—and I realized that was the one I was supposed to meet my dad at. "Sorry," I said, getting to my feet very cautiously as the train slowed. "That's my stop." I reached for my bag from the overhead rack, but Josh was already leaning over me, lifting it up like it weighed nothing.

"Mine too," he said as he lifted up a red-and-black duffel with CLARENCE HALL printed on the side and swung one bag on each shoulder.

"You don't have to do that," I said, as it became clear he was going to carry my bag for me.

"Not a problem," he said. But when he reached down for his own backpack, I grabbed it before he had the chance.

"I've got this," I said as swung it over my shoulder and picked up my purse. He nodded, and we made our way up the aisle, where I saw at least three women and one guy reading copies of *Once Bitten*. We reached the doors right as they opened, and stepped off the over-air-conditioned train and into the warm summer night.

As the train pulled away behind us, I noticed that it was just starting to get dark outside. The air smelled familiar—fresh and clean, with the faintest scent of salt water and ocean behind it. The parking lot had a few cars idling in it. I looked around for my father, which was made a little more difficult because I had no idea what he'd be driving out here. But at any rate, nobody waved or honked at me, so it didn't seem like he was here yet.

Josh looked around as well, but didn't make a move toward any of the cars. The last idling car picked up its passenger and left the parking lot, leaving just the two of us and the occasional chirps of the cicadas.

"We may be stranded," he said cheerfully. It didn't seem like the prospect bothered him all that much.

"And we don't even know where we're headed," I said, shaking my head in mock seriousness. "We're in trouble."

"Well," he said, with a slightly nervous smile, "maybe if we ever get where we're going, I could call you sometime. I don't know a ton of people here."

"Oh," I said, and my brain suddenly went into hyperdrive. Was he asking me out? Because then I'd have to tell him that I was in a mourning period, couldn't even think about dating. But then it was like the second part of the sentence sank in . . . he didn't know many people. He wanted to be *friends*, I realized, relieved. And I had a feeling I might be able to use a friend, since the only people my age I knew here were Bruce's kids, and I wasn't even sure they would be around for the summer. "Sure," I said, giving him a quick smile. "That'd be great."

Josh pulled out his cell phone, which looked like the very newest model, and paused, just staring at the screen for a moment. "Sorry," he said. "I just got this, and I'm still figuring it out." But after a moment, he located the right feature, and he punched in my numbers as I recited them. A second later, my phone rang. I pressed the button to save the contact, and then looked up at him.

"What did you say your last name was again?"

He smiled at that. "I don't think I did. But it's Bridges."

My own smile was extinguished as suddenly as if someone had dumped a bucket of cold water over me—which was actually pretty close to how I was feeling at the moment. "Josh . . . Bridges," I repeated, hoping against hope that maybe he'd tell me that his real first name was actually something I had never heard paired with Bridges. Hershel or Donovan or Fred.

But Josh just nodded. "You've got it."

I tried to tell myself it was just a coincidence. After all, Bridges was a common enough name. It didn't necessarily mean he was the Josh Bridges I'd known briefly, the one who was Hallie's brother. He hadn't been around much that summer, so I hadn't spent a ton of time with him.

Which, I realized with a sinking feeling in my stomach, was pretty much what he'd told me himself about his first visit to the Hamptons. "Oh," I said, weakly, trying to get my bearings.

The quiet of the night was shattered when an open Jeep sped into the parking lot, tires kicking up gravel, the song that had been playing on the radio nonstop recently—a song about how it would be the *summer, summer, summer to remember*—turned up loud. There was a girl driving the car, a girl who looked my age, with long blond hair.

No, I thought as hard as I could as she killed the engine. *Please no.*

"Hey!" she called across to us. "Joshie!"

My thoughts still spinning, I handed Josh his backpack, and he set my duffel at my feet. I was trying to tell myself not to panic, that this was all just a coincidence. It didn't mean that this girl was his sister. I mean, this could have been his girlfriend.

"Come *on,* loser!" the girl yelled.

Maybe it was his girlfriend and they had a very strange relationship.

"That's my sister," Josh said, and the last of my illusions were crushed. "Coming!" he yelled toward the Jeep, but I saw to my horror that the girl had parked the car and was heading toward us. It was her, it had to be, but I still couldn't quite believe it until she walked up the three steps to the platform and was standing in front of me.

Hallie.

The girl who I tried never to think about, but who nonetheless came into my head whenever I thought about the worst things I'd ever done. The girl who I'd been crueler to than anyone else, ever. The girl whose life I had tried to ruin—and had come damn close—five years before.

"Hey," she said, bumping him with her shoulder, then shrieking when he picked her up in a sudden bear hug, then dropped her when she was still a few inches off the ground. "Stop," she said, but she was laughing as she whacked his arm. "Ready to go?"

"Sure," Josh said as he shouldered his bag. Hallie looked right at me then, full on. I saw confusion and then shock pass over her features as she looked closer, frowning.

"Sorry," she said, not taking her eyes from me, and I noticed her voice was the same, raspier than you'd expect, like she'd been a lifelong smoker, even at eleven. And though she didn't look just like she had when we were kids, it was unmistakably her. She had the same eyes, green and almond-shaped. Her hair was a slightly darker shade than the bright blond I remembered, but it was still long and curly, and it flowed over her shoulders and down her back.

I registered in a far-off, panicky way that she hadn't taken her eyes from me, and I could practically hear her brain whirring as she leaned closer to me, studying my features. She narrowed her eyes and a terrible, sick feeling overcame me. It was as though I had just found myself in one of my worst nightmares. "Wait a second," she said, her voice cold. "Are you . . ."

"Where are my manners?" Josh said, smiling at me, clearly not picking up on what was happening—namely, that I was probably about five seconds away from getting my butt kicked. "This is my sister, Henrietta. Hallie," he corrected quickly after seeing the murderous glance she shot him. "Hallie, this is Sophie . . ." He paused, looking at me expectantly.

"Curtis," I said automatically, because that's just what I always said after Sophie. "But wait," I corrected quickly. "That's not my—"

"Sophie," Hallie repeated. I saw her eyes flick down to my *S* necklace, the name on the cup in my hand, then to my hair and back to my face. "Sorry," she said. The confusion—and fury—that had been in her expression just a second before were now fading away. "I thought you were . . ." She shook her head. "I guess not. Never mind."

"No," I said, but so faintly that even I could barely hear myself. "I'm not . . ."

"It's so nice to meet you," she said with a big smile.

Nice to meet me. *Nice*. To *meet* me. These words reverberated in my head. I knew that brave—and sane—people would have used the moment to explain that, actually, we'd met before, we knew each other quite well, and she was justified in her hatred of me.

But I couldn't help thinking about all the things that were suddenly falling into place. My hair was an unrecognizable shade. My nose was straight. And there was the simple fact that I looked really different now than I had at eleven. I hadn't recognized Josh, after all. Hallie didn't know that I was Gemma Tucker. So maybe I didn't have to be her. This could be an opportunity to set things right with Hallie. And I knew I'd never get a chance if I told her who I really was. I found myself touching the *S* on my chain, sliding it back and forth once before I smiled back at her. "It's nice to meet you too," I said.

"So you two met on the train?" Hallie asked, looking from me to Josh.

"She kind of just fell into my lap," Josh said, deadpan, and despite everything else that was happening, I found myself smiling at this.

"Do you need a ride somewhere?" Hallie asked, just as a low-slung purple sports car jerked and sputtered into the parking lot. I could see my dad behind one of the lowered windows, glasses askew and hair rumpled. He looked exactly the same, which meant he could give me away in a heartbeat. My pulse was suddenly racing.

"No, I'm okay," I said quickly. "I'm good."

"See you, Sophie!" Josh called, and I noticed that they didn't look in the direction of the sports car—and was thankful for the fact that my dad's head was turned away as they climbed into the Jeep. Hallie sped out of the parking lot as fast as she'd pulled in.

My dad pulled the car in front of the platform, opened the driver's-side door, and, with some effort, hauled himself up out of it. All Bruce's cars were either tiny convertibles or enormous SUVs that looked like they were better suited for some sort of military operation than a Starbucks run.

"Gemma!" my dad called, waving.

"Hi," I called back, then looked around in a panic, to make sure that Josh and Hallie were gone, worried they'd heard my dad and my cover was blown.

The coast was clear, but a moment later, the true consequences of this sank in.

Oh god. What had I done?

CHAPTER 5

"It's good to have you here, Gem," my dad said as we both buckled our seat belts and slammed the car doors. We'd gotten dinner at the Upper Crust, which my dad swore had the best pizza in the Hamptons. And after we'd finished off a shared pie (my dad was the only one who would ever share my pineapple, sausage, and pepperoni pizza) I was inclined to agree with him. "I'm glad it worked out for you to come."

"Me too," I said as the lights dimmed with a subtleness that seemed to indicate just how ridiculously expensive the car was. It was like it was trying to ease you into the darkness gently. In the slowly fading light, I could see that my dad looked like he always did—slightly overgrown sandy hair, glasses with the lenses perpetually smudged, wearing his uniform of jeans and untucked button-down. But I couldn't help notice, this time, deeper lines around his eyes and much more gray in his hair. I tried to tell myself that I only noticed these changes in my father because I didn't see him very often. Probably if I only saw my mom a few times a year, I'd be thinking that she looked really old too. But even so, it bothered me a little.

My dad started the car, then winced when it made a terrible screeching sound. "Sorry," he said, as the car jerked forward, seemed to stall, then jerked forward again. "I haven't driven a stick shift in . . . well . . . ever."

"So does Bruce still live in the same house?" I asked as we sputtered down the road, the gears screeching, probably doing huge amounts of damage to the really expensive engine. I looked out at the scenery passing by, but wasn't sure I recognized anything. It probably didn't help that it was totally dark out.

We had spent the summer at Bruce's house the last time I was in the Hamptons, and I was looking forward to staying with him again, since his houses were huge and professionally decorated, and the kitchens were always stocked with trendy snacks and artisanal soda. I don't think my dad liked it quite as much. Though he and Bruce were old friends, they had become more like just colleagues in recent years, which meant that when we were in his house, my dad was basically on vacation with his boss.

"Same as what?" my dad asked as he managed to make it through an intersection successfully. "As when you were here before?" He glanced over at me, and I nodded. "Oh, no. This one is more like a cottage. Tasteful and understated."

That didn't sound anything like Bruce. "Really?"

My dad sighed and shook his head. "No, not really." He pulled onto a less-busy road, and I pressed the button to roll down my window and breathed in the cool, sweet-scented night air.

"Where are we headed?" I asked.

"It's a neighborhood called Quonset," he said. "According to Bruce, it's going to be the next Montauk."

"What does that mean?"

My dad just shrugged. "I've learned never to ask." He unrolled his own window and glanced over at me at a stoplight. "I have to say, I like the hair, squirt."

"Yeah?" I asked as I played with my bangs. I still wasn't used to it, and when I caught a glimpse of myself in one of the mirrored frames in the pizza parlor, I had done a double take. "It's mostly Sophie's doing."

"Well, I think it suits you." Not that I had ever taken fashion or beauty tips from my dad, but I still appreciated this. "Listen," he said as he signaled and turned down a gravel driveway so long I couldn't even see the house from the road, "I may not be able to hang out with you this summer as much as I would like."

"Work?" I asked, feeling like I already knew what the answer was.

"Yeah," he said with a grimace. "The studio's not happy with *Time Flies*." In addition to the other scripts my dad wrote—or rewrote—he still worked on all the time-traveling-animal movies, which had become a franchise, complete with celebrity voice actors.

"What animal is it this time?" I asked.

My dad winced again. "Penguins."

I just stared at him. "But penguins don't fly."

He sighed. "And with that, you've just recapped the last three months of arguments I've been having with various studio executives."

I tried not to smile, but I found I couldn't help it. I sometimes wondered if my dad had been happier when he was writing books nobody read, instead of writing movies everyone saw.

"Anyway," he said, "we're going to be back and forth to L.A. a bit. But I'll be around whenever I can. Do you think you'll be okay here if I'm gone?"

The house finally came into view, and I felt my jaw drop. It was an absolutely enormous mansion, gray-shingled and sprawling. I could see a glimpse of the water to the side of the house, and in front of it, a pool. "You know," I said as my dad pulled in front of the garage and killed the engine as the car gave what I swear was a relieved sigh. "I think I'll be fine."

≈≈≈≈≈≈

"**Y**ou're here!"

I had just stepped inside when I heard this greeting, and looked across the foyer (which could have easily held my bedroom back home) to see Rosie, Bruce's longtime assistant, smiling at me. With her cocoa-colored skin and model's height, she had always looked to me like she should have been in front of the cameras, not working for an irascible producer behind them. She gave me a quick hug, then stepped back and looked at me at arm's length. "Haircut? I like it," she said, without waiting for me to respond. "Bruce is about to get on a conference call, but I'll bring you by quickly—I know he'll want to say hi."

"I'll put this in your room, Gem," my dad said as he lifted my bag and headed for the staircase.

"Thanks, Dad," I called. I followed Rosie across the marble floor, looking for any evidence that Bruce's kids were there as well. "So is Gwyneth around this summer?" I asked. "Or Ford?"

Rosie gave me a sympathetic smile. "Sorry, kid," she said. "They're both in Hawaii with their mom. But I know they're going to try and come at some point."

This was better than nothing, I figured. Gwyneth was a year younger than me, and Ford was a year older. Since I'd grown up seeing them both a few times a year, I knew them pretty well, but my friendship with Ford had always been complicated by the fact that he'd been my childhood crush, who had morphed into my regular crush. Thankfully, he didn't know this. And since he lived in California, and I'd been with Teddy for the last two years, it had never really been an issue.

I followed Rosie down a long hallway, both walls covered with framed movie posters. That was one thing I knew I could count on: Whatever style Bruce's house was currently decorated in, it would be filled to the brim with movie memorabilia. Movies were Bruce's life as well as his livelihood, and it was the whole reason his children had the names they did. Ford came about during a particularly difficult negotiation with Harrison Ford. In a desperate move, Bruce promised he'd name his soon-to-be-born son after the movie star, something that Ford's mom hadn't been too happy to find out about. And on top of that, the movie had fallen apart after only five days of shooting. Gwyneth had gotten her name in a similar fashion, when Bruce was desperate to get Gwyneth Paltrow to sign on to a film that was on the verge of losing financing. He thought that she would be impressed by his naming his daughter after her, showing his dedication to getting her for the movie. But apparently, it just freaked her out, and she dropped out of the project as a result. Which, to me, seemed like an outsized reaction from someone who named her own children after biblical prophets and fruit.

But it was too late to change Gwyn's name at that point, and though it had never been confirmed, I had a feeling that trying to trade his kids' names for professional success might have been a contributing factor in Bruce's first divorce.

Rosie led me through to the kitchen, then stopped short, causing me to narrowly avoid crashing into her.

"Bruce," she said with a sigh to the open silver refrigerator door. "What are you doing?"

"Mmmph," the door said. It swung closed and revealed Bruce Davidson, feared Hollywood producer, holding a half-eaten burrito and looking guilty. "What?" he said, his voice defensive. "I was just—oh, hey, Gemma. Get in okay?"

"Bruce." Rosie reached out her hand. "Gimme." Bruce looked abashed and handed over the burrito.

"What's going on?" I asked, though I had a feeling I knew. Bruce was short and had a tendency to plumpness. He was constantly seeing different nutritionists and going on crazy diets he always broke. The last time I'd been in L.A., he'd been eating "low-impact"—he couldn't eat anything that was cooked or hadn't fallen naturally to the ground without picking or harvesting. He'd lasted almost a whole week on that one.

"Bruce is eating like a caveman, for reasons that make sense to him," Rosie said, as she contemplated the burrito, then took a bite herself.

"Paleolithic," Bruce mumbled.

"Caveman," Rosie said with a roll of her eyes. "It means, basically, you can't eat anything our ancestors—who had tiny brains, might I add—couldn't pull from the ground or kill with a stick. And they certainly didn't eat burritos, so . . ." Rosie took another bite, and Bruce sighed.

"I'm going to find Paul," he said, referring to my dad. "He should be on this call too. Glad you're here, Gem. Help yourself to whatever. And let's make a plan to go running."

"Definitely," I said with a smile. It was a running joke—so to speak—between us. It had started a few years ago, when I was visiting my dad in L.A. and Bruce was on an exercise kick. We had talked a lot about going running together, but all we had ended up doing was going to get doughnuts while they were still hot.

Bruce gave the burrito one last look, then shuffled out of the kitchen, yelling for my dad.

"Okay," Rosie said, turning to me. "Want the five-cent tour?"

There was nothing five-cent about the house, I soon realized as I trailed Rosie from room to room. It just went on forever, one beautiful, clutter-free room stretching into the next one. The whole house had clearly been decorated by someone who had taken the concept of a beach house very literally—it was mostly done in blue and white, with glass jars filled with sand or shells on every available surface. But when we reached a group of rooms toward the back of the house, things started to seem more like Bruce and less like his decorator.

"Bruce's domain," Rosie told me as she pointed to the three rooms at the end of a hallway. There was a screening room, which Rosie told me had just been installed so that he could watch rough cuts at home, his office, and what she called his "brag room"—a room that seemed designed just to woo actors and intimidate other producers. It was basically just a couch and two chairs, and the rest was all Bruce's memorabilia and posters and the awards that he'd collected over the years.

This included, in the very center of the room, a pedestal for Bruce's pride and joy, the Spotlight award he'd gotten a few years ago at the British version of the Oscars. There was even a small spotlight that shone directly down onto it, making the glass gleam. Ford had confided to me that he'd found out at the afterparty that the award had actually been meant for Marcus Davidman, the acclaimed documentary filmmaker, and not Bruce Davidson, producer of time-traveling-animal movies. But apparently the English filmmakers who were presenting the award were too polite to correct the mistake, and Bruce was none the wiser.

After the tour of Bruce's domain, Rosie started to show me the upstairs bedrooms, but gave up when we both got tired of walking so much. So the tour finished up in the guest room that would be mine for the summer. It was done in blue and white, much like the rest of the house—white wicker dresser, blue painted headboard, white sheets and pillows. There was a half-filled jar of seaglass on the bedside table, next to a small vase of fresh flowers. But best of all was the view, which looked right out on the water. I could see the waves crashing and the moonlight spilling onto the dunes.

"This is great," I murmured as I took it all in. It really was—certainly better than being at home, and most likely better than being in some crumbling castle in Scotland. I had a strong suspicion that castles didn't have air-conditioning.

"Glad you like it," she said. "Yell if you need anything, okay?"

"Sure," I said, smiling at Rosie as she headed out. "Thanks." I had a feeling that even if I yelled at the top of my lungs, nobody would hear me in a house this big. But at the moment, I really didn't seem to mind.

I crossed to the bed, where my dad had left my duffel, and was halfway through unpacking when there was a knock at the door. I opened it and saw my dad on the other side, because, unlike my mother, he clearly understood how knocking was supposed to work.

"You all settled in here?" he asked, peering around. His jaw dropped when he saw my view. "You've got it much nicer than me, kid. I think my window looks out at the garage."

"Maybe Bruce thinks you won't be working if you're looking at the scenery."

"Maybe," my dad murmured, eyes on the water. "Still."

"So is, um . . . Mrs. Bruce around this summer?" I asked. I could never keep straight the names of Bruce's wives—they all seemed to be named after Western states or gemstones.

My dad shook his head. "He and Dakota divorced this spring."

"Oh," I said, trying to sound sympathetic and surprised, when in actuality I would have been surprised if she were still around.

"And speaking of," my dad said, clearing his throat a few times, "I was sorry to hear about you and Teddy."

I nodded, feeling as I did the wave of sadness that always threatened to clobber me whenever I thought about Teddy. But it occurred to me a moment later that I hadn't thought about Teddy in at least a few hours, which was bizarre, since he had occupied so much of my brain real estate for years. I chalked it up to traveling, and the events of the day. "Yeah," I said, hearing my voice wobble a bit on the word, but not as much as it might have done the week before. "Thanks."

My dad nodded, cleared his throat again, and stuck his hands in his pockets. My father and I rarely talked about our personal issues, and as a direct result, we weren't really very good at it.

"What about you?" I asked hesitantly, feeling just how awkward this conversation was. "Are you, um, dating anyone in L.A.?"

"Oh," my dad said, looking startled by the very idea. "No, nothing like that." He gave a little shrug. "You know me."

I did. But I also couldn't help looking at the lines around my dad's eyes again. He was getting older—I didn't like to let myself see it, but it was true. And it occurred to me that soon he might be too old—or at least too used to being on his own—to meet anybody. He had only been serious about one person since he and my mom split. And it was all because of me, my doing entirely, that he was not with that person.

"Anyway," he said, giving me a quick hug and then ruffling my hair like I was still five, "you should get some sleep. I'm glad you're here, Gem."

He left then, and I tried to go back to unpacking, but gave it up after a few minutes of just refolding the same white shirt while staring into space. I pulled out my phone and saw I had a text from Sophie. She had ended up seeing the barista after all, and would have details for me in the morning. Since she added a winky face to the end of this sentence, I had a pretty good idea what these details involved. I thought about texting back, but stopped when I realized all that I would have to explain to her to get her up to speed. Suddenly, it seemed like the events of the day—my haircut, meeting Josh, realizing who he was, seeing Hallie again—were too big to be contained in the house, massive as it was.

I headed down the stairs, feeling like I should have taken a compass, or a map, to guide myself back to the kitchen. Luckily, I didn't have to worry about being quiet, even though it was after ten. Bruce—and as a result, my dad and Rosie as well—kept West Coast time even when in New York, so that they would be around to talk to people in California well into the night.

The kitchen was quiet, no sign of Bruce trying to sneak non-caveman food. So there was nobody to have to explain to as I pushed out through the back door, walking past the darkened pool house, then the pool, lit with underwater lights. I kicked off my flip-flops and dipped a toe in as I passed. It was just slightly heated, the perfect pool temperature. I walked down the steps that led to the dunes, then out the gate and onto the sand, the path lined with beach grass, finding my way by moonlight. In no time, I was at the water's edge, the moon huge above me, the beach deserted and all mine.

I sat on the sand and looked out at the water. I was back in the Hamptons. I was staying in a new place, with a new haircut. I was infinitely wiser and more experienced than I had been the last time I'd been there.

But it was becoming abundantly clear that the mistakes I'd made—and the people I thought I'd left behind—hadn't actually gone anywhere.

CHAPTER 6

That summer seemed ill-fated right from the start.

On the last day of fifth grade, my dad picked me up from school. This wasn't so unusual, since the afternoons were prime house-showing times for my mom. Normally my dad was writing, but he had been suffering from writer's block recently—something that, even at eleven, I was sure wasn't helped by my mom commenting on it, with loud sighs, at dinnertime.

The only clue I had that something out of the ordinary was happening was when he took me from school directly to Gofer Ice Cream and told me I could get whatever I wanted. This raised my suspicions immediately. My father had recently gone on a health kick, declaring refined sugar to be of the devil, and the thing that was interfering with his creative process. So I could barely taste my vanilla cone with rainbow sprinkles because of the way my dad was looking at me—desperately, and not just for my refined sugar. It was like he wanted to watch me having one last happy memory before everything crumbled. Needless to say, this made me lose my appetite, and I threw away most of the cone before it had even started melting.

My mom was waiting for us when we got home, and for the first time I understood what an ambush felt like. She and my dad sat me down at the kitchen table, one of them on either side of me. They told me that they were separating, that they weren't getting divorced, they just needed to take some time apart. But they still loved me, and always would. They went on to say other things—about logistics, and how I would spend the first two weeks of the summer with my mom, and the rest of it away with my dad, who was going to teach a writing workshop in the Hamptons. But I wasn't really listening to any of this. Instead, I was holding on to the one sentence that was all I wanted to hear—*it was just a separation, and they weren't getting a divorce.*

My dad left for his workshop, and I spent the next two weeks with my mother, in denial and trying to pretend that my dad was just away on a business trip, like my friends' fathers—the ones who didn't work at home in sweatpants—sometimes took. And as I took the Jitney, the Hamptons-bound bus (wearing an annoyingly visible MINOR sticker on my sweater that meant I had to sit up front behind the driver the whole way), I decided I would pretend that my dad and I were on vacation together, just the two of us. And I had a plan that I'd worked out as we'd driven across Long Island—I would use the next two months to subtly remind my dad about how great my mom was and how much fun we had as a family. And by the end of the summer, I knew, they'd both miss each other and realize they were being stupid, and would get back together. And we'd never even talk about the separation again, except in passing sometimes, remarking on how silly the whole thing had been.

We'd gotten settled in at Bruce's house, and had been in the Hamptons a few days, when my dad and I went out to dinner with his co-teacher—she was also a writer, whose debut novel had just been published—and her kids.

The timing was perfect, since I was starting to get a little bored hanging out by myself all day. My dad had thought Bruce's kids were going to be around for me to spend time with, but since Bruce was busy with a movie, they were spending the summer with their mother. So I was thrilled when we arrived at our table at the beachside fish restaurant, The Crabby Lobster, and my dad introduced me to Karen Bridges, and her kids, Josh and Hallie.

Josh left a few days after that for some intensive sports camp, and then it was just me and Hallie. Since both our respective parents were working all day, the two of us were thrown together a lot. And I found, after we'd spent a few afternoons at the beach, getting sunburned and prowling for snacks, that I really liked her. She was fun, always up for anything, and had a sly sense of humor that she used to great effect, usually to make fun of grown-ups to their faces and get away with it. She never insisted on having her own way, and was even willing to share my pineapple, sausage, and pepperoni pizza. And unlike Sophie, who could sometimes be overly bossy, insisting on getting her own way, Hallie was more laid-back, happy to roll with things.

We spent most of our time at the beach or riding bikes around downtown together, eating more ice cream than either of our parents would have been happy with. I told her my secrets—my longstanding crush on Ford, the boys at school who I liked who didn't know I existed, and the ones who did know I existed, but who were always the wrong ones. She confided in me in return, telling me about her huge crush on Cooper Sullivan, the kid who lived two doors down from the tiny house the Bridges were renting for the summer. She confessed that she was hoping he'd be her first kiss. Because my dad had told me, I knew that Hallie and Josh's father had died when they were both younger, but Hallie didn't seem to want to talk about it, so I didn't bring it up much. I was thrilled that our parents were getting along, since it meant that Hallie and I got to hang out more and more. Soon, it just became normal that my dad and I had dinner most nights with Karen and Hallie, the two of us leaving to watch a movie or play a board game as soon as our parents started getting into one of their epic talks about literature, which could go on for hours.

Whenever I think about that June when we became fast friends, everything seems to be golden and sun-drenched, kind of perfect, the way it only can be when you know a storm is looming on the horizon.

Everything came crashing down on the last day of June. Hallie and I were at the beach; our parents were teaching, and we'd already decided to bike downtown and get burgers for lunch. We'd just been in the water, so I was lying on my towel, letting the sun dry me off, and everything felt peaceful and good.

"Saltwater taffy?"

I opened one eye and saw Hallie offering the box to me. She'd discovered saltwater taffy recently at the candy store downtown and had become obsessed with it. She was really generous, and as a result, I'd quickly maxed out on the stuff.

"No thanks," I said, and Hallie shrugged and unwrapped a pink one, popping it into her mouth. "But I should remember to get some and bring it back to my mom." My mother loved it, and whenever we went on beach vacations, she came back with boxes of it. "Of course, my dad will probably do it himself when the summer's over."

I noticed that Hallie had suddenly gone very still. I pushed myself up on my elbows. "What?" I asked. I reached over and took a piece anyway, a green one. That was the thing about saltwater taffy—you thought you didn't want any, but after you'd been staring at it long enough, you found you couldn't help yourself.

"I just . . ." Hallie started. She shook her head and then went on, more slowly. "What do you mean, your dad's going to bring candy to your mom?"

"Just what I said," I mumbled, struggling to talk around the taffy. "When the summer's over and he comes home."

Hallie smiled quickly, like she thought I was joking about something. When she realized I wasn't, her smile disappeared. "But," she said, confused, "why would your dad bring your mom candy? They're getting divorced."

I felt a roaring sound in my ears, like the ocean had suddenly invaded my head. "No, they're not," I said, wondering what Hallie was talking about, and why she thought she knew anything about this. "It's just a temporary situation, for the summer."

"No," Hallie said, with an assurance that turned my stomach a little. "My mom told me."

"And why would your mom know anything about this?" I asked, baffled as to why Karen had suddenly entered this conversation.

"Because she's dating your dad," Hallie said, as though it should have been obvious, like it was a fact that everyone knew.

I just looked at her for a long moment, then pushed myself to my feet. "I have to go," I said, pulling on my sundress and stepping into my flip-flops, picking my towel up from the sand. I didn't believe her—*of course* I didn't believe her. But I also didn't know why Hallie would lie. And even though I tried not to, I couldn't help thinking back to just how much Karen had been around this summer. But it didn't mean anything. My dad was just being friendly. And Karen must have misunderstood.

"Wait," Hallie said, scrambling to her feet. Her face was pale, even under her sunburn, and she looked stricken. "Gem. I'm really sorry—I thought you knew. I thought your dad would have told you. . . ."

"I have to go," I said, not wanting to see her expression any longer, since it was so very sure of something that couldn't possibly be true. I hustled to my bike, dumped my towel in the basket, and biked as fast as I could toward the Hamptons Writing Workshop.

I'd only been there a few times, but I knew where my dad's office was. The office, I realized with a twist in my stomach, that he shared with Karen. I decided I didn't care if he had a class. I'd just wait until he was finished, and then I'd be able to see firsthand—when he would, of course, immediately deny it—that there was nothing to Hallie's story.

The receptionist must have been at lunch, because the front desk was empty, and I was able to just walk straight into the main building, the classrooms surrounded by offices that hugged the perimeter. I reached my dad's door and saw that it was ajar. I pushed it open slightly, and stepped one foot inside the office. I saw my dad and Karen, sitting across from each other at their desks, which were pushed together, Karen writing something, my dad reading.

I felt myself let out a sigh of relief. Hallie had no idea what she was talking about. They were just working together, that was obvious—

My dad reached across the table, picked up Karen's hand, and kissed it.

As I watched in horror, she smiled without looking up from her book. It was clear this wasn't the first time it had happened.

I backed away from the office, then turned and ran into the lobby and out the doors, not stopping until I reached my bike. I had the same feeling I'd gotten during the spring play, when one of Sophie's dance moves had gone wild, and she'd accidentally punched me in the stomach. This felt the same way—like all the wind had been knocked out of me, leaving me confused and gasping and trying to figure out what had just happened.

I skipped dinner that night and went to bed early, even though I didn't sleep a wink.

I was hurt and angry—but mostly, I was humiliated. Hallie had known about this, and I hadn't. It had been an open secret that everyone else was aware of except me, who stupidly believed that my dad and Karen were just good friends, and that was why she was always around, having dinner with us every night. It seemed so obvious now, and I wondered how long Karen and Hallie had been laughing at me, the oblivious one who clearly didn't know what was happening with her own father.

Like a movie I didn't want to see but couldn't seem to turn off, images from the last month were flashing through my mind, things I should have noticed from the very first day. Like the fact my dad's writer's block was totally gone, and he'd started working on a new novel, all about finding second love later in life, with the love interest a woman named Kara. The way he'd light up whenever Karen called or stopped by, and the way that all his sentences seemed to start with "Karen said" or "Karen did" or "Do you know what Karen told me?"

There was the way that he'd started to act like he was Hallie's dad, too. Like when I'd asked him to buy me a journal at Southampton Stationery, he went ahead and bought an identical one for her, even though she wasn't there and hadn't asked for it.

While Karen was a perfectly nice person—before finding out about this, I'd even liked her—that didn't mean that I wanted her to be the reason my parents didn't get back together. After all, they had told me in the beginning of the summer that they weren't getting divorced, and this was *just temporary*. Which meant Karen was a definite obstacle to that. How could my dad do the serious thinking he and my mom both told me they'd be doing if he was dating Karen? I knew things between my parents might not be perfect or go back to normal right away, but I also knew that they would have no chance if Karen was still in the picture. Which meant she needed to be removed from the picture.

I decided that something had to be done.

It was something that, under normal circumstances, I wouldn't even have been able to imagine. But these weren't normal circumstances. Was I supposed to just sit by and watch Karen wreck any chance of my family staying together?

I wouldn't be able to do it. But someone who was the mean version of me—like in old TV shows, when someone's evil twin showed up, usually wearing a goatee and an eye patch—could. So I started to think like a person who was the opposite of me, someone who wouldn't have a problem being mean on purpose.

I knew firsthand from a summer of hanging out with Hallie how close she and her mom were. I had a pretty strong feeling that if Hallie was miserable, Karen would leave and take Hallie with her, and my dad could forget all about Karen and come back home.

Since I wasn't sleeping anyway, I turned on my light, pulled out my green notebook, and started to write down plans.

I was going to make Hallie miserable.

The first idea I had involved Cooper, her crush. All the things Hallie had told me suddenly seemed less like friends sharing secrets and more like ammunition that she'd easily handed me, never thinking I might use it against her.

I knew that Cooper was obsessed with gummy candy—and with motorcycle stunts, though I couldn't think how that would help me, so I stayed focused on the candy. I didn't think that Cooper would be able to recognize Hallie's handwriting, but just in case, a few days before I put this plan into action, I told her about handwriting analysis. For a while there, Bruce had been developing a movie called *Love/Letters*, about calligraphers in love. The movie had fallen apart (even at eleven, this hadn't surprised me), but there was all kinds of research still in Bruce's office. And one of them was a handwriting analysis that could predict character traits. I told Hallie about it, trying to make it sound enticing and really fun, and since she was game for almost anything, she agreed.

We both wrote out *Amazingly few discotheques provide jukeboxes*, which was a sentence that contained every letter in the alphabet, and then examined our handwriting samples, comparing them to the charts in the book. I barely listened as Hallie read out what was predicted for both of us—she was logical and practical, I acted impulsively with little follow-through, we both were curious and open to the world around us—because I was mostly concerned with making sure I got ahold of Hallie's paper when the analysis was done. And when she wandered off to the kitchen for a snack, I saw my opportunity, folded up her paper, and tucked it into my pocket.

That night, I carefully traced Hallie's letters onto a note.

Cooper . . . meet me tonight at sunset for a sweet treat!

Then I let out a long breath. I was really going to do this.

* * *

"What's this?" Cooper asked me when he'd read the note. I'd told Hallie that I was going to video chat with my mom, and couldn't hang out with her that morning. She had been understanding—ever since she'd inadvertently dropped the dating bombshell, she'd been extra-nice to me. I had tracked Cooper down in the spot where I'd seen him riding—but mostly falling off—his skateboard.

"It's from Hallie," I said, trying to sound casual about it. "She just got this huge bag of gummy candy and wanted to give it to you."

Cooper's eyes lit up. "Really?" he asked. "That's awesome." Then he paused and frowned at me. "So why didn't she just tell me?"

"She's running errands with her mom today, and wanted to make sure you found out as soon as possible. You know it's better when it's fresh." I tried to sound blithe as I lied over and over, glad that I'd practiced what I would say to these questions on the bike ride over.

Cooper nodded thoughtfully. "That is true," he said. "Okay. Cool."

"Write her back and tell her," I said, thrusting a piece of paper and a pen—both of which I had ready—at him. "So she knows I passed on the message."

Cooper raised an eyebrow. "She won't believe you?"

I shrugged, trying not to look like my brain was whirring furiously. "I, um, always forget," I ad-libbed quickly. "So she doesn't trust me anymore."

"Okay," Cooper said with a shrug. He took the pen and paper, then paused. "Wait, where are we meeting?"

"You should put that in the note," I said, hoping it didn't sound like I'd planned this. "Just write *Meet at sunset at the bike rack. And sign your name.*" The bike rack near Hallie and Cooper's houses had become the de facto meeting place of the summer.

Cooper wrote quickly on the paper, then handed it back to me. "Done," he said. He looked at me hopefully. "Is it a lot of candy?"

I smiled at him. "It's definitely worth the wait."

<hr />

Hallie read the note, then looked up at me, her cheeks already going pink. "He really gave this to you to give to me?"

I made myself smile at Hallie as I sat next to her on her beach towel. I'd told her that I'd run into Cooper on my way to the beach and he'd trusted me to give her the note. "Not only that," I said, leaning forward conspiratorially. "I think he's going to kiss you. He asked me if I thought sunset was a *romantic* time."

"Oh my god," Hallie said, her voice high and excited. "Gemma, can you believe this?" She pulled me into a tight hug, and I had to swallow hard.

Was I really ready to do this? Was I really going to be able to deliberately hurt someone I liked and thought of as a friend? Someone who trusted me?

But then a moment later, I remembered seeing my dad kissing Karen's hand, the way he held doors open and chairs out for her. The time I'd overheard him on the phone, telling Stu, his agent, that he couldn't remember the last time he'd been this happy.

This was all the push I needed. I hugged her back.

Four hours later, Hallie and I were walking to the bike rack, Hallie nervously smoothing down her hair. We had spent the rest of the afternoon getting her ready. Now her blond curls had been coaxed into a fishtail braid, and she was wearing a light application of Cruel Summer—one of my favorite lip glosses, which I'd given her for the occasion.

"Oh my god," she said, twisting her hands together. "Do I look okay?"

"You look great," I said honestly.

"Thanks," she said. She bit her lip and looked to the bike rack. Cooper wasn't there yet, and I just hoped he'd show up and things would go as planned—otherwise, I would have some explaining to do.

"Look," I said, pointing in the opposite direction, where Cooper was making his way toward us. "Call me later," I said quickly, backing away, out of sight. "Tell me everything!"

"Will do," Hallie said, giving me a nervous, excited smile.

I waved and jogged away like I was heading home, but then doubled back and, crouching low, hid behind a nearby parked car, where I could see and hear everything that happened.

"Hi, Cooper," Hallie said, and I could hear her trying to sound like she was playing things cool, but not really succeeding.

"Hey," Cooper said. He crossed his arms over his chest. He looked at Hallie, who smiled back at him. After a moment, he cleared his throat and asked, "So are we going to do this or what?"

"Um," Hallie said, and I could see her smile falter a little. "I guess. I just thought . . ."

"What?" Cooper asked, sounding genuinely perplexed. "I mean, are you going to give me the sugar?"

I saw Hallie take a step back, her cheeks flushing bright red. "That's not exactly the way to ask," she said, her voice getting frosty.

"Sorry," Cooper muttered, looking taken aback. "I didn't think it was such a big deal, you know?"

"Well, it is to me, okay?" Hallie asked. But I could see she was calming down a little. She gave Cooper a smile and took a small step toward him, then another one. Cooper frowned, looking alarmed. Hallie had just closed her eyes and tilted her head to the side when he jumped back, causing Hallie to lose her balance and stumble forward.

"What are you doing?" Cooper asked, blushing bright red. "You're such a freak, Bridges. I don't want your sugar anymore!"

He turned and ran away, shaking his head as he went. I watched Hallie pick herself up and brush the dirt off her hands, biting her lip hard, the way she did when she was trying not to cry.

I turned away and, still ducking low, ran home as fast as I could, not wanting to see any more.

⚜⚜⚜⚜⚜⚜

Hallie called me, crying, just after I made it back inside. She told me the whole story, and I tried to sound sufficiently surprised and outraged. When she'd finished, I told her that maybe Cooper really *did* like her, but he had just lost his nerve at the last moment.

"Maybe," Hallie conceded, her voice still hoarse.

"So," I said, trying hard to sound casual, "you're probably going to want to leave now, huh? I mean, it'd be too awkward to see Cooper all the time, right?"

There was a pause on the other end, and when Hallie spoke

again, her voice was clearer, and she sounded less on the verge of tears. "I'm not going to leave," she said. "I can't let him *win*."

As she said this, I suddenly remembered something I'd noticed when Hallie and I played board games: She was ruthless when it came to winning, especially when she felt she'd been wronged, like when my dad had taken Park Place without her noticing.

"But . . ." I started, about to say something about how if she left, *she* would be winning. Somehow. I hadn't worked out all the logic yet. But Hallie interrupted me, shaking her head.

"I'm just never going to talk to him again, ever. And you can't either, okay? Promise?"

I promised, but as I hung up the phone, I couldn't help feeling that my plan had fallen short. Hallie was upset, but not enough to make her want to leave and take her mother with her.

So I just decided that I would do something else. Something bigger. Something that would work, and make Karen and Hallie leave for good.

I began writing down ideas and plans in the green notebook from Southampton Stationery. I detailed the first attempt with Cooper, and tried to sort out why it hadn't worked, and jotted down ideas for future sabotage.

But it wasn't like I was doing this free from remorse. Sometimes I would look up from my notebook, with its detailed plots and counterplots, realize what I was doing—coldly planning to hurt someone—and suddenly feel my guilty conscience rise up and threaten to clobber me. But then a moment later, I would picture my mother and me, sitting alone at our kitchen table, and the Christmas card that my dad and Karen would send out, with a picture of the two of them and Josh and Hallie, with me nowhere in sight. And this was enough to bring the evil-twin side of me back and strengthen my resolve to do what needed to be done.

So I let the air out of the tires on Hallie's bike. I sprinkled sand in her ice cream and made sure to put onions, which she was allergic to, on her hamburger. I left Karen's prized (and very old and therefore very valuable) copy of *The Count of Monte Cristo* out in the rain, in Hallie's beach bag, so it would look like she'd done it.

But none of this accomplished anything. My dad fixed Hallie's bike, she threw away the ice cream, and was only sick for a few hours after eating the hamburger. And though Karen was upset about the book, Hallie didn't get in real trouble.

I had a feeling I had to do something bigger—something *significant*—to make Hallie unhappy enough that Karen would want to go.

I told Karen that I wanted to help with throwing Hallie's twelfth birthday party, and we organized the celebration together. She helped me oversee the planning, the decorations, the Evites that were going out to all the summer kids we'd become friends with. What Karen didn't see was that I changed the date on the invitation right before they went out. When the day of the party rolled around, it was just me and Hallie and our parents sitting in our reserved lane at the bowling alley. The area was festooned with streamers and balloons and piled high with snacks, favors, and a huge strawberry-vanilla cake, but we were the only ones there.

As it was happening, I felt increasingly bad, my stomach churning with guilt as I watched Hallie biting her lip to keep from crying and the way Karen kept giving Hallie all these fake-cheerful explanations for why nobody had come.

I hoped that this would do the trick, sure that Karen would take her daughter and leave, but as the days passed, there was no sign of it.

I knew that things had reached a critical moment when my dad took me for ice cream at Sweet & Delicious, not seeming to understand that I now associated him buying me ice cream with him giving me terrible news. This time, he ate his own cone as he told me he and my mom were thinking about continuing their temporary separation after the summer was over, and that he was thinking about getting an apartment in Brooklyn. I sat there with my own ice cream untouched, knowing what this meant. Brooklyn was where Hallie and Josh and Karen lived.

I realized, as I watched him eating his ice cream, that I had been going about this all wrong. I should have cut out the middleman and just tried to get rid of Karen from the outset.

The opportunity presented itself later that week, when my dad hosted a party at our house. Technically, it was Bruce's house, but Bruce had barely been around the whole summer, as he'd been dealing with a movie that was shooting in Iceland and was beset with problems. Both the director and the star were always quitting or threatening to quit, there were crew mutinies, a reindeer stampede, and an unfortunate incident when all the stand-ins had gotten trapped on a fjord.

My dad seemed to want to take advantage of the fact that we were staying in a mansion in the Hamptons, and had planned a big-deal dinner party. He had invited the other teachers at the workshop, and a number of important publishing people—agents, editors, and critics—were coming up from New York City. And the most important guest of all was my dad's agent, Stu. My father told me he thought this dinner would be good for Karen's career, and that he'd been talking up her work to Stu, hoping he'd take her on as a client.

I worked out the plan for the party in detail, writing everything out in my notebook, not wanting to get anything wrong. I had a feeling that this would be my last and best chance to stop what was happening with my dad and Karen, before I suddenly had a stepmother and two stepsiblings and the chance of my dad coming home again was just a pipe dream. So I laid out the particulars of the biggest plan yet, the one that I was sure would change things.

I just didn't realize how right I would end up being.

◦◦◦◦◦◦

As the day of the party neared, my dad got more and more caught up in the preparations. He was sending copies of Karen's book to the critics and editors who would be attending, in addition to trying to sort out the catering and the decorations.

All this meant he'd pretty much stopped paying attention to what I was doing. At my urging, he'd bought me a game that I'd installed on his computer, Olympia and the Olympians. It was designed to be educational about the Greek myths, but actually just made me incredibly bored—except for when eagles sometimes tore people's livers out, it mainly seemed to be about people stuck in revenge cycles and never learning anything or stopping them. But it was very useful because it allowed me access to my dad's computer, so that he wouldn't be suspicious when he saw me using it. Because when I was on his computer, I wasn't playing Olympia and the Olympians. I was reading through my dad's e-mails, particularly the ones to Stu.

The night of the party arrived, and I was maybe more nervous than my dad was. Hallie and I were both attending the dinner, and it seemed to be going really well. There was lively conversation around the table that I mostly ignored, as it was all publishing gossip, but I could tell from the noise and laughter that it was a successful dinner. Karen was flushed and giddy with the attention she was getting, Hallie was basking in her mother's glow, and my dad was sitting next to Karen, smiling, looking happy and proud.

I waited for my opportunity, and when my dad went to the bathroom, I excused myself as well a moment later and dashed for his study. I pulled out my notebook from where I'd hidden it in the desk drawer and consulted it for the notes I'd taken on my father's correspondence with Stu. I turned on the computer, pulled up my father's e-mail, and entered Stu's e-mail address. I typed a message as fast as I could.

Stuart,

This is a difficult e-mail to write. I didn't want to say anything at dinner, but I felt I needed to tell you, mano a mano. I don't think you should work with Karen, even though we discussed the idea last Wednesday. Though she wants it, I really don't think it would be a good idea for you to have both of us as your clients. I don't think it's fair to you to be put in the middle like that.

And furthermore—and I hate to say it—her work is not original. Please don't work with her without thinking all this through carefully. After all, you have your own career to consider.

All my best,
Paul

My heart was hammering as I typed these lies, and I paused, lifting my fingers from the keys before hitting Send. Was I really going to do this?

I heard the toilet flush, then the sound of the water running, and I hit Send before I could question this any further. I deleted the message from my father's sent mail folder, closed out his e-mail, shoved my notebook back in the drawer, turned off the lights, and dashed from the room.

Hallie was waiting outside the door.

I gasped. "Hallie!" I said, trying to get my bearings, trying not to look like I was panicking. "What . . . are you doing here?"

"I was looking for you," she said. Her eyes strayed behind me to my dad's study and I shut the door quickly. "What were you doing in there?"

"Nothing," I said, willing my brain to think faster than it currently seemed to be capable of doing. "Just . . . needed to get away for a second. You know." I shrugged and smiled at her, but Hallie didn't smile back. She just looked at me for a moment longer, her head tilted slightly to the side, as though she was trying to figure something out.

"Girls?" I heard Karen call from the dining room, and I had never been so happy to be called back to the table. I hurried past Hallie, not meeting her eyes, and took my place next to my dad.

My dad and Karen were in the middle of telling a story together, trading off sentences, all about one of their students in the workshop, and the table seemed to be listening, rapt. Stu, though, was not engaged, and his eyes were glued to his Black-Berry screen. He frowned as he read what was presumably the e-mail I'd just sent, then turned to my dad, but my dad was looking over at Karen at the time and missed this.

Stu looked down at his BlackBerry again, then tapped the critic next to him and showed her the screen. She was soon whispering to the editor on the other side of her, and before long, it was clear that nobody was listening to Karen's anecdote, which fell flat when nobody laughed at the punch line.

The party broke up almost immediately after that, even though it was still early and dessert hadn't even been served. Stu left not meeting Karen's eye, and giving my dad only the most cursory of good-byes.

After the party, I found myself pacing around my room. I couldn't help but think that this time, I'd gone too far. But I realized that it probably wasn't too late to pull this back. I could go tell my dad what I'd done, and he could call Stu and tell him the e-mail was from me. He'd be mad at me, but it might be worth it. I took the stairs down to the kitchen two at a time, ready to confess, but stopped short in the doorway when I saw my dad standing by the kitchen counter with Karen, their backs to me, his arms wrapped around her.

"I think it went fine," he murmured, rubbing her back. "I'm sure everyone was just tired. You were great, as always."

"You think?" Karen asked. As I looked on, feeling my stomach clench, my dad bent down and kissed her.

I turned around, but not before the image had burned itself into my brain. I thought about my mom, all alone in Putnam. And as I walked back to my room, my doubts had vanished. I hadn't gone too far—this was what needed to happen. Karen needed to go, or we'd never be a family ever again.

≈≈≈≈≈≈

The next day, Stu told Karen he was no longer interested in working with her.

I was thrilled that one of my plans had finally worked, and I waited eagerly for it to cause a rift between my dad and Karen. But instead, it just seemed to make trouble between my dad and his agent. I was eavesdropping outside my dad's study the next afternoon and heard him on the phone to Stu. "What e-mail?" I heard my dad yell, and my breath caught in my throat. For just a moment, it felt like my heart stopped. But thankfully, they didn't linger on this, and it seemed like the conversation moved on—until a second later, when my dad slammed down the phone and stormed out of his study, not seeming to notice me lurking in the doorway.

I figured that the plan hadn't worked and I decided to chalk it up to the weirdness of adults and move on to the next idea.

Which was when things moved beyond my control.

Without warning, Karen's publishing house canceled her next contract—and when pressed for a reason, would only say that there had been questions about her artistic integrity.

My dad and Karen were baffled by this until the publishing blogs started to pick up a rumor that she had plagiarized her book.

The rumor gained traction, especially when a blind item was published about its origins—that it had come from a fellow writer who knew her work well. This writer had told his well-regarded agent, who had passed on the information to a respected critic at a Hamptons literary dinner party. It wasn't hard to figure out that this other writer was my dad, the agent was Stu, the party was ours—and the fault was mine.

I truly hadn't understood that this would be the result of my e-mail. I'd wanted Stu to help create distance between my dad and Karen—not to damage her career. When I wrote that her work wasn't original, I was just using the phrase I'd heard my dad use whenever he wanted to put down a fellow writer, usually one who had just received a good review. I hadn't realized it was code for being a plagiarist.

Over the next week, I watched in horror, feeling increasingly sick, as things for Karen went from bad to worse. Bloggers were going out of their way to find passages in her novel that were similar to other books. Every day, it seemed like a new sentence was found, a new passage that was close to something else, no matter how thin the evidence. Bookstores were returning her book in droves. She was a cautionary tale on the publishing websites. Her career as a novelist was over.

Karen had refused to speak to my dad ever since it came out that he was the one who'd started all this, and she and Hallie stopped coming by the house. And I came downstairs for a drink of water one night to find my dad hunched over the kitchen table, his face pale and dotted with stubble.

"Hey, kid," he said, and I heard just how tired his voice sounded. "Can't sleep?"

I shook my head and stayed where I was. I didn't want to join him at the table. I was afraid that if I did, I would confess, it would all spill out of me—everything that I'd done.

"Me neither," he said. He rubbed his eyes and I felt a sudden stab of guilt, knowing that I had caused this. "I should tell you something, Gem," he said, looking over at me as I shifted my weight from foot to foot and didn't meet his eyes. "I fired Stu." I opened my mouth and closed it again, at a loss for words. "I'm not going to finish the book," my dad continued, looking down at his hands. "I'm done with novels. I don't want to be a part of a business that would treat someone this way."

I just stood there, feeling myself shiver, even though it was a warm night. I tried to, but I couldn't get my head around it. My dad not writing was like my dad not having eyebrows, something I couldn't even fathom. What he'd just said threatened to upend everything I had ever known as normal. And it was *all my fault*. My stomach churned again and I wondered if I might be the first eleven-year-old in history to develop an ulcer.

⚬⚬⚬⚬⚬⚬

The last time I saw Hallie that summer was a few days later. I was sitting in the car as my dad stood by their house, holding a box of Karen's things he'd brought back to her. Karen, her face drawn, packed up her car. As a result of all the controversy, she had been fired from the summer writing workshop. Hallie was sitting on the front steps, her head down. My dad was trying to talk to Karen, but she just shook her head and walked back inside, slamming the door behind her. My dad followed her into the house, carrying the box, and then it was just me and Hallie, separated by a car window.

It occurred to me that I was finally getting what I had wanted, what I had been working for, all summer—Karen and Hallie were leaving. Things were over with her and my dad. I waited to feel happy, victorious . . . but nothing happened.

And just like that, it was like the evil, goateed version of me vanished, and I was left to see clearly the ramifications of what I had done. And I didn't feel happy about it. I didn't feel anything except sick with guilt and filled with remorse. This wasn't at all the way that I had wanted any of it to happen—or how I thought I would feel when it did. As I looked at Hallie, her face pale and her shoulders hunched, I finally realized the extent of what I'd done to her, and to Karen.

Hallie looked up and met my gaze, and I could see that her eyes were puffy. I reached for the door handle, then paused. What would I say to her? What *could* I say?

I opened my mouth, but then closed it again. Hallie looked right at me for a long moment, then turned her head away. I knew this was my chance to apologize, but how could I even begin? Also, I knew if I did confess, I would be in *so* much trouble. But should I just own up, now that I'd realized how empty this victory felt? Before I could make a move, my dad pushed open the door and walked down the steps between us, his face pale and his eyes red. He gave Hallie a quick hug, then got into the car.

He started the engine and backed down the driveway, and I felt like I was fleeing the scene of the crime. Hallie glanced back at us, and she seemed incredibly small, sitting on the steps of her rental house. She looked at us—it seemed like she was looking right at me—until we turned the corner and she disappeared from view.

I knew what I'd done to Karen and Hallie—but it wasn't until a few days later that I saw what I'd also done to my father. The happy, ice-cream-eating, novel-writing guy was gone. He now only left the house to go teach his workshop classes, spending the rest of the time either in bed or staring out the window.

His computer sat untouched in the study, which made it easier for me to go in and take back my notebook. But when I opened the drawer where I'd hidden it, the notebook wasn't there.

I didn't let myself panic at first, just made myself methodically search the desk, then my room, even though I knew the notebook wasn't there—I'd shoved it into the desk after sending the fraudulent e-mail. I knew I had. Inside the notebook was every detail of a summer's worth of plots to make Hallie miserable. Every terrible thing I had done was inscribed in it.

So where was it?

I suddenly remembered my dad carrying the box of Karen's things to give back to her. He might have found the journal and thought it was Hallie's; after all, it was the same as mine. Had I just accidentally told her everything I had done to her this summer? Had I just inadvertently confessed everything?

I tried to fight back my rising panic and tell myself that it didn't matter. The damage was done—did it really make a difference if Hallie knew it was me who was behind it?

As I shut the drawer of the desk, I made a promise to myself. I would apologize to Hallie and Karen. And I would work as hard as I could to keep this monstrous, evil side of myself—a side I had never before fathomed the existence of—at bay. And that somehow, someday, I would make things right.

I looked up at the moon over the beach and hugged my knees to my chest. Much as I might have wished for one, the story didn't have a happy ending. When I returned to Connecticut, I found out that my mom had met Walter over the summer, and they were already pretty serious. As soon as I heard my mother going on about Pacific breeding grounds and the different kinds of casting techniques, I had a feeling there was no chance my parents would get back together. I was right, and their divorce was finalized by Christmas.

Karen's name was cleared, slowly, as bloggers began to retract their earlier feeding-frenzy claims of plagiarization. But she never published another book.

And though I hadn't believed him at first, my dad, true to his word, stopped writing novels. He moved to Los Angeles that fall and began his new career as a screenwriter specializing in movies about time-traveling animals.

The extent of what I'd done—and how many lives I'd inadvertently wrecked—still kept me up nights.

I started letters—to Hallie, to Karen, to my dad, all full of remorse and apologies—but never sent them. I tried to begin the conversation with my dad a few times, but it soon became very clear that he didn't want to talk about the Bridges, or that summer, and started to get upset whenever I brought up either of them.

I spent the first few years actively searching for information about Hallie and Karen online, always hoping that good news would appear—that Karen had started writing again and gone on to bestsellerdom, that she and her kids were happier than ever. But nothing ever came up. As far as I could tell, scouring

Google with my heart sinking, she never wrote anything else or even held another teaching position.

I also couldn't find out much about Hallie. She showed up on Friendverse when everyone joined, of course, but her profile was private and I could get only the most cursory information from it. I tried to tell myself, as I looked at her profile intermittently over the years, that she looked happy. That maybe I hadn't caused irreparable damage after all.

I never told Sophie about it, and when I started dating Teddy—who was pretty much the embodiment of goodness—I couldn't help but hope that some of it would transfer to me, and keep the evil side of me away for good. But mostly, I tried not to think about what I'd done. And memories of the Bridges, and that summer, had only come up intermittently, and in my darkest moments.

Until today.

But as I looked out at the water, I realized that I was getting a second chance. It was an opportunity to make up for what I'd done. After all, Hallie wouldn't see me as Gemma Tucker, the girl who had been cruel to her, deliberately, over and over again. If Hallie had read the journal, I knew she would never give me, *actual* me, a chance to make things right. She wouldn't believe me for a second. I wasn't even sure if she'd be willing to listen to me explain how sorry I was.

But if she saw me as Sophie Curtis, friendly stranger, it could be the opportunity that I needed. I would get to show her that I was a good person. And then I would finally be able to apologize.

I pushed myself up to standing, brushed the sand off my hands, and walked back to Bruce's house, feeling a lightness that I hadn't felt for a long time. Even though it was five years later, I was finally going to make things right. And if it didn't work, I'd be in the same position I was now, but at least I'd have tried.

And after all, what did I really have to lose?

CHAPTER 7

"**N**ame?"

I froze as I reached for my wallet. I was at Quonset Coffee, where I'd gone after hanging around the house for the last two days. Since Bruce had dismantled his espresso machine (cavemen, after all, got their energy from escaping near-maulings by woolly mammoths, not cappuccino), I had finally been driven into the world by my need for an iced latte. But I hadn't expected to be so immediately confronted with the realities of the situation I'd landed myself in. I tried to take a subtle look around the coffee shop, to see if there was anyone I recognized, as that would determine how I should respond to this question.

The bored-looking barista sighed. "Name," she repeated, louder this time, her marker poised over the cup and eyebrows raised. *"Nombre?"*

"Um . . . I guess . . . Sophie," I finally said after a moment's consideration, the name feeling unfamiliar in my mouth. The barista rolled her eyes, scrawled the name on the plastic cup, and rang up my drink. I paid and then stepped aside to let the other customers in the tiny wood-paneled store make their way up to the register, wondering for the hundredth time in the last few days if this was really such a good idea.

The trip to the coffee shop was my first time out on my own since I'd arrived in the Hamptons. I had hung out with my dad, when he could get away from Bruce, who was reporting the demands of the studio executives, who always seemed to have new, increasingly terrible notes to give. I caught up with Rosie, and went "running"—also known as an early morning bagel trip—with Bruce. This was surprisingly fun, as he was developing a movie about a teenage girl and seemed to see anything I could tell him about my life as hugely important.

But mostly, I did my best to conceal my true identity and tried to figure out how to become friends with Hallie. I even had files on my computer (I had learned my lesson about writing things in notebooks that could go missing) labeled BECOME FRIENDS WITH HALLIE and SOPHIE CURTIS 2.0. I had written down everything I could remember about Hallie from when we were eleven, like the fact her favorite cake was vanilla with strawberries and that she could hold her breath underwater for almost a minute.

I made my Friendverse profile private, with crazy security controls, and deleted my picture from my profile, so that basically you couldn't see who I was, or even what I looked like, unless you were already one of my closest friends. Then I got Sophie—the real one—to do the same. I tried to tell her why, but I'd called when she was in the middle of a makeout session with her barista (why she always answered her phone during makeout sessions was a constant mystery to me), and I don't think she understood why I needed her to lock her profile and remove any picture that might come up in a Friendverse search. But when I checked the next day, the picture on her profile was of a jumbo-sized frozen yogurt, so I knew that at least part of my message had gotten through.

But unfortunately for my become-friends-with-Hallie plan, it looked like she had taken the same precautions as I had. Her profile was super private, and I could see only the smallest wisps of information about her. She still lived in New York, though now it looked like she was in Manhattan and not Brooklyn, and she went to one of the fancy private schools. She was taken—the Friendverse terminology for being in a relationship—though it didn't identify by whom.

My Google searches of her also turned up no relevant information. Josh popped up pretty frequently, always related to some sports triumph at Clarence Hall. But there was almost nothing on Hallie. I even tried searching "Henrietta Bridges," but without any luck. I realized this might not have been so unusual for Hallie—very little showed up when you searched for me, mostly because both my parents were convinced that if I had too much of a presence online beyond my Friendverse page, Internet predators would show up at the door. But surprisingly, there was also very little about Karen. She hadn't written any books beyond the first one, which was now out of print. It didn't seem like she'd remarried, but the Manhattan address and the private schools certainly seemed to indicate the Bridges were doing better money-wise than they had been when I'd known them . . . though I realized, with my eyes burning from too many hours staring at the computer, that I had absolutely no idea what had happened with them over the last five years. Maybe both Hallie and Josh were at school on scholarship. Maybe some rich uncle had died and left them a fortune. Maybe Karen had found a second career in investment banking. I had no clue, and it appeared that I certainly wasn't going to glean anything from Hallie's bare-bones profile.

After staring at her profile for two days and getting no real answers, I was tempted to call Ford and see if he could hack into it. Bruce's son was a computer genius and went to some whiz-kid school in Silicon Valley during the year. I knew that it might be possible for him to gain access to Hallie's profile, but I stopped myself before I even reached for the phone.

Since the whole point was to win Hallie's trust, I didn't think I should be simultaneously spying on her electronically. But unfortunately, this meant that all I had to go on were the most basic of facts about her life and what I could get from the profile picture—Hallie in a yellow T-shirt, smiling at someone just out of frame.

And though I had Josh's number, I hadn't called him yet. Knowing that he was Josh Bridges, and not just some guy with a nice neck who I'd met on the train, made the possibility of being friends with him more tricky. Also, now that I'd met Hallie again and assumed my best friend's identity, my priorities had shifted and I knew I had to focus on trying to make things right with Hallie.

"Sophie!" the barista yelled. When I didn't respond to this, she waved the drink at me, and I snapped back to attention, reaching for it.

"Right," I mumbled, as I collected my drink and a straw. "Thanks." I headed out into the afternoon sunlight. Not wanting to take a chance with either the tiny sports car (I had as much experience driving a stick shift as my dad did) or the SUV that could comfortably seat a baseball team, I had decided to go by bike. My dad had bought a used one for me at Beachside Bikes, and from there I'd ridden down the street to the coffee shop. It hadn't taken very long—the downtown was small, basically just one street lined with stores and restaurants. After checking that my bike hadn't been stolen by local Hamptons thugs, I wandered up the street, looking at the beach boutiques that had their sale racks out on the sidewalk, trying to find anything that looked wearable.

"Gem!" I turned instinctively at the sound of my name, then froze. Hallie was walking down the street toward me, holding a small girl with each hand. She nodded at me, and I nodded back, even though my heart was racing. Had someone just called my name—my real name?

"Hey, Sophie," Hallie said easily, with a smile.

I gave her a shaky smile in return. "Hi," I said. "How are—"

"Gem!" The girl holding Hallie's right hand yelled this, pointing right at me, and I realized she was the one who'd spoken before. I just blinked at her, wondering if she was one of those psychic kids that I had seen on *Psychic Kids*. How did she know my name?

"No, Isabella," Hallie said, bending down so she was more at her level. "That's *Sophie*."

The girl just frowned at me, clearly not impressed with this explanation.

"Sorry," Hallie said with a shrug as she straightened up. "She's become obsessed with that old cartoon show—you know, *Jem and the Holograms*? I guess you remind her of the lead singer."

"Oh, right," I said, as I tried to laugh in a carefree manner, hoping she couldn't see just how freaked out I'd been. But after a second, I remembered that Jem had *pink* hair. Like, neon pink. And this girl thought I looked like her? I brushed my bangs back, suddenly a little unsure about this color choice. "Sure."

"Anyway, this is Isabella, and this is Olivia," Hallie said, lifting up the hand of the other girl. "We were just going to get some ice cream."

"Oh, cool," I said, bending lower so that I was at the girls' level. They looked like twins, around six, and I felt myself relax a little. Whatever else was going on, I was totally comfortable with kids. I had always been good with them. "What are your favorite flavors?" I asked. I leaned closer, like I was sharing a secret with them, and whispered, "I like vanilla with rainbow sprinkles."

I smiled, but the girls just looked at each other, then back at me, their expressions skeptical and a little disdainful. It was hard to tell behind her pink heart-shaped sunglasses, but I was pretty sure Olivia rolled her eyes at me.

I straightened up, a little unsure. I'd never gotten that reaction from kids before, but maybe these two were just the exception. Or maybe in the Hamptons, you were already jaded and over it by six.

"So," I said to Hallie, "are you . . . I mean, are they, um . . ." I had been about to ask if she was babysitting—which I'd assumed—but I suddenly realized that, for all I knew, Hallie might have gotten some siblings or stepsiblings in the last five years.

"I'm babysitting," Hallie said with a laugh. "Our neighbors sometimes ask me if I can watch them."

"Got it!" I said. I smiled at the girls again, and they just stared back at me, stony-faced.

"Are you getting anything?" Hallie asked, and I realized she was looking past me to Sur la Plage, the bathing suit boutique I was standing in front of.

"Oh," I said, following her gaze into the shop. It looked like a really fancy store, and frankly, I'd never understood spending a lot of money on swimwear, since between chorine, salt water, and sunblock, it seemed like your suit was going to get wrecked pretty quickly anyway. Bruce's second wife had not seemed to share this philosophy, and had spent her time by their pool in Malibu fully made up and decked out in jewelry, never once going anywhere near the water. "No, just window-shopping."

"Well," she said confidentially, taking a step closer to me. "This place is great. I just got two bikinis from here."

"Cool," I said, deciding to keep my opinions on pricey bathing suits to myself. "I'll have to give them a try."

"Ice cream," Isabella whined, tugging on Hallie's arm.

"Sorry," she said, giving me a tiny eye-roll as she started to move away with the girls. "But it was nice to see—"

"I'll walk with you," I said hurriedly, falling into step with them. "If that's okay." After spending the last few days trying to engineer this, the opportunity to get to know Hallie better had practically dropped into my lap, and I didn't want to waste it.

"Great," she said, dropping the girls' hands and letting them walk on ahead of us. "You probably don't want any, though." She nodded at my plastic cup. "Since you have your coffee."

I nodded, relieved beyond belief that I'd given the barista the right name. "Yeah," I said, making sure to turn around the cup so that the *Sophie* faced out. "I'm all set."

We walked in silence for a moment, and I kept sneaking little glances over at her, still not quite able to believe this was happening. Here I was, after all these years, with Hallie Bridges. And there was no lingering tension or awkwardness between us. She was almost exactly my height, so I was able to get a clear view of her by just turning my head slightly to the right, and I pushed down my sunglasses so she wouldn't see me staring.

Her hair was down again, and she was wearing shorts and a T-shirt that looked much-washed and read LENIN AND MCCARTHY. It was a band that Sophie really liked, but I'd never gotten into, since it had always seemed a little overly hipster to me. There were, like, twenty band members, and I was pretty sure that one of them played the lute.

In contrast to the informality of her T-shirt, Hallie was carrying a designer tote bag and was wearing stacked espadrille wedges, also designer. And of course people didn't stay the same—I certainly looked and dressed differently than I had when I was eleven—but I was having trouble reconciling the girl next to me with the Hallie I had known, who had refused to carry a purse and seemed to live in her ripped cutoffs and Keds.

"So do you live around here?" she asked, her voice friendly but polite—the kind of voice you used when talking to a stranger.

"We're staying not too far," I said. "In Quonset."

"Oh, cool," she said. "We're in Southampton, but I just love this area. And plus, the girls like this ice cream parlor." She stopped walking, and I realized we'd arrived at a storefront that looked very familiar. It was Sweet & Delicious, the same place my dad had taken me at the end of that summer, when he'd hinted that he'd hoped our future would involve the Bridges family. My sense of direction hadn't been good even then, so I had no idea I'd even been on this street before. From what I could see through the window, past the HELP WANTED sign, the décor inside looked the same—wrought-iron tables and chairs, the same red-and-white color scheme.

Hallie handed the girls some money, and they practically threw themselves into the shop, causing the bell attached to the door to ring violently. "Remember when we used to be that way?" she asked, turning to me.

I just stared at her, trying my best to keep my expression neutral, even as alarm bells started to ring in my head. "Um," I started, searching her face for any kind of clues and telling myself to calm down. She didn't know it was me. She *didn't*.

"Well, maybe you weren't like that," she said with an easy laugh. "But when I was their age, I was a total sugar fiend."

"Right," I said, and I could feel myself start to relax. She had meant "we" in the general sense, not "we" as in Hallie and Gemma. I really needed to stop being so paranoid. "I know what you mean."

"So listen," she said, leaning in a little closer. "My brother keeps talking about you."

"Oh," I said. I blinked, trying to process this. It was flattering— that is, unless what he'd been telling Hallie was all about how I'd landed in his lap and then groped his thigh. "Really?"

"Really," Hallie said. She looked at me closely, her expression growing a little more protective. "Do you have a boyfriend?"

I literally had to bite my lip to stop myself from reciting what I was so used to saying, what I'd been saying without a second thought for the last two years of my life—*Yes, I do. I'm dating Teddy Callaway.* "No," I said. The loneliness of that syllable struck me, making me swallow hard. Even though I was no longer in Putnam, I was still constantly reaching for my phone to call or text Teddy something, before I would remember that we were over. And then I felt the loss of him—the loss of the us that we'd been— all over again. "No," I repeated, clearing my throat and hoping my voice didn't betray what I was feeling. "I just . . . got out of a relationship, actually."

"Oh, I'm sorry to hear that," Hallie said. "Was it a bad breakup?"

I flashed back to the Target aisle, the shattered candle, the piles of cookies, the inability to get out of bed for several days. And once again, I couldn't help but wonder exactly *what* had caused it. I still didn't know Teddy's reasons for breaking up with me, and so was left with the lingering, uncomfortable feeling that I hadn't yet gotten a satisfactory explanation. "It was pretty bad," I said with what I hoped was a smile and not a grimace.

"God, breakups suck, don't they?" she said with a roll of her eyes, and I laughed.

"They really do," I said. "What about you?" I hoped this sounded casual and not like I already knew the answer to my question because I'd Friendverse-stalked her. "Do you have a boyfriend?" I asked as the bell above the shop door rang again, and the twins came out, both moving more carefully than before, each with a multiscoop cone.

"Hallie has a *boyfriend*!" one of the girls—I'd now lost track of who was Isabella and who was Olivia—sang out, causing Hallie's cheeks to turn pink.

"His name is Ward," said the other twin with great authority as she took a bite of her cone. "And he's away for the summer."

"Thank you," Hallie said, steering them to one of the open outside tables. "And what did I tell you about listening to other people's private conversations?"

The girls just giggled, and Hallie turned back to me. "I do, in case they didn't answer your question fully."

"That's great," I said, and despite knowing it from her Friendverse profile, I actually wasn't surprised. There was a feeling you sometimes got from girls with boyfriends, a kind of calm assurance, and Hallie certainly had it. I knew, because I'd once had it too.

"Yeah," she said, blushing a little more. "It's new, but it's going pretty well so far . . . who knows?" One of the twins shrieked, and I saw there had already been one ice cream casualty—a rainbow scoop was now off the cone and melting on the table. "I'd better handle this," she said. "But listen, do you have plans tonight?"

"No," I said immediately, and then wondered if that made me sound too much like a friendless loser.

"Great!" Hallie said, not seeming to pick up on this, or if she had, not seeming to mind. "Then you should come to this party. One of Josh's Clarence friends is throwing it. It'll be fun! Give me your number and I'll text you the address."

I rattled off my phone number, feeling a little amazed at how easily this was all coming together. I'd expected to have to search to find Hallie, and then to have to work to get her to want to spend time with me. I hadn't expected to bump into her, and then for invitations to hang out to follow this easily. But Hallie had always been friendly, I remembered now, much better than I had been about walking up to kids and asking if they wanted to hang out or go get a snack.

My phone rang a moment later, and I pressed the button to save the contact, immediately typing in *Hallie Bridges*.

"It's Bridges—" she said, then paused and glanced down at my phone. "But I guess you already knew that?" She looked up at me, surprised.

"Yes," I said quickly. "Josh told me when I, um, met him." I knew this was the truth—it had been the moment I practically felt the world drop out from under my feet—but I still panicked for a moment that I'd somehow given myself away.

"Great," she said. "And remind me again, it's Sophie . . . ?"

"Curtis," I said, hoping I sounded like I'd said this name a lot, as I watched her type my best friend's name into her phone.

"Perfect," she said, saving the contact. The girls shrieked again, and I now saw that there were two scoops down on the table.

"Duty calls," she said. "But I'll see you tonight!" She hurried over to the table to try and contain the meltdowns (of twins and ice cream) that were taking place.

I walked back to my bike, drinking my iced latte as I went, feeling like things were falling into place. This would be good. I would get to know Hallie better and be as helpful and nice to her as I could during the party. I wasn't sure how I was going to achieve this—by bringing her snacks or something?—but I figured that at the very least, it would give me an opportunity.

By the time I got back to Bruce's, I'd felt my phone buzz with two texts, and as I pulled it out, walking my bike up the driveway, I saw that they were both from Hallie.

Hallie Bridges
2:19 PM
Party tonight at 88 Turtle Pond Lane.
See you at seven!
Hallie Bridges
2:35 PM
Hi you—dress code for party
is semiformal—dresses, coats, ties.
See you then!

Okay. Semiformal. I could do that. I let myself into the house, keeping my fingers crossed that the last Mrs. Davidson had left some of her clothing behind when she moved out.

A few hours later and a (hopefully) fashionable twenty minutes late, I stood on the doorstep of 88 Turtle Pond Lane. Bruce's last wife hadn't left behind anything that I would have been willing to wear in public, but luckily Gwyneth had a few things still hanging in her closet, presumably left over from the summer before. Gwyn and I wore the same shoe size, but I was a good four inches taller than her, which meant that the dress I had on was pretty short on me. But I figured it was better than nothing. I hadn't brought anything dressy with me, since I hadn't thought there would be a need for it. But Gwyneth—or rather, her closet—had come through, and as I rang the bell of the house, I glanced at my reflection in the glass panes on the side of the door. I had figured it would be better to be slightly overdressed than underdressed. The dress was purple and one-shouldered, fitted, and admittedly a bit shorter than the dresses I normally wore, but I figured that it would be okay—it was summer, after all. I'd also borrowed a pair of her shoes, made by a designer whose name I'd seen in magazines but had never encountered in real life. The shoes were beautiful, covered with hot-pink silk, and I'd been walking carefully to try and keep them looking as pristine as I'd found them. I'd blown out my hair and was wearing far more makeup than usual. As I stared at my reflection now, I decided that I looked like someone who had dressed correctly for a semiformal party.

Nobody was answering the bell, so I went to knock, and to my surprise, the door swung open. "Hello?" I called as I took a few steps inside, balancing carefully on Gwyneth's heels, which were a few inches higher than I was used to.

I didn't see anyone, so I made my way—carefully, since the house seemed to be decorated entirely with things that looked like valuable antiques—into the living room and then kitchen. As I stood and looked around this stranger's kitchen, I suddenly felt very aware of my party-crasher status. It hit me that I didn't even know the name of the person who was throwing this party. I pulled my phone out from the black silk clutch I'd borrowed from the former Mrs. Davidson (I had a feeling she wouldn't mind) and was about to text Hallie and see where she was, when I heard voices and music coming from the back of the house.

I realized that the party was probably in the backyard, and rolled my eyes at myself for not thinking of that sooner. I walked through the kitchen to the side door that was half ajar, smoothed down my skirt, and stepped out onto the patio.

I felt the smile freeze on my face.

There were probably twenty people there, but everyone was in bathing suits, and most people were either in the pool or standing around it.

I realized, to my horror, that I was in a formal dress. And this was a pool party.

CHAPTER 8

I stood there, rooted to the spot, realizing that people were slowly becoming aware of me, the bizarrely overdressed girl lurking by the edge of the pool. They probably thought I'd gotten lost on my way to the prom. I began to back away slowly. I hadn't seen Hallie or Josh yet, and I could make my escape now and just pretend that I'd misplaced the address, or gotten a sudden case of rickets, or something.

"Sophie?"

I turned and saw Josh pushing himself up and out of the pool, and my wardrobe mistakes were temporarily forgotten as I took in the sight of him, dripping wet in just his swim trunks. Dear lord.

"Hi," I said, trying to force myself to look at his face and not his abs, but it was a struggle. I saw now that Sophie and I had been right; the boys on the lacrosse team were every bit as hot as we imagined them to be. Josh's shoulders were broad, his arms were muscular, and he was already golden and tan, even though it was just the beginning of the summer. His surfer-style swim trunks were sitting low on his hips, and it was like his stomach muscles had each been painted on. Since Teddy hadn't believed in exercising for vanity when so many people were enslaved and forced to exercise in labor camps (I think—sometimes I lost track of all the things that Teddy was against, and the reasons why), seeing really in-shape guys up close and personal wasn't exactly something that I was used to.

Josh ran his hand over his hair, which looked almost black when it was wet, and shook the droplets away from me. "Hi," he said. He smiled like he was glad to see me, but there was definite confusion in it as well. "You look great. But . . . um . . ."

"Yeah," I said, and was now fully back to feeling mortified after the enjoyable but brief distraction provided by Josh's triceps. I tried to laugh in what I hoped was a carefree manner, but don't think I quite pulled it off. "Right. I, um, thought this was more of a formal party."

"Well," he said, "I am wearing a *suit*." He grinned, and then a moment later, turned red. "Like a bathing suit," he hastened to explain. "It was a joke."

"No, I got it," I said, a little surprised. It was just an unexpectedly dorky side to someone who looked like he could have been featured shirtless and holding a puppy on the cover of the Hollister catalog. But I liked it. I was about to say something to that effect when Hallie rushed up to us.

"Sophie," she said, her voice strained. Unlike her brother, it didn't look like Hallie had gone into the pool yet. Her curly blond hair was dry, and so was her suit, a cute, retro-style polka-dot bikini with a ruffled sweetheart neckline and high-rise bottoms. "I'm so glad you came!" she said, then she looked down at my dress again. "But . . ."

"Right," I said, deciding on the spot that after I made my second explanation, I was leaving, getting in Bruce's monstrosity of an SUV and driving back home, where nobody would feel the need to point out that I was wearing the wrong thing, just in case I hadn't noticed that already. "I got your text," I said, suddenly realizing that this was actually her fault, that I had proof I'd really been given the wrong dress code. I fumbled with the snap of the clutch and pulled out my phone. "About how this was semi-formal?"

Hallie frowned. "What? I sent you a text telling you it was a pool party." Josh looked between the two of us, and I hoped he didn't think that I was a crazy person who just liked to dress up way too much. Not that it mattered what Josh thought of me, of course. I was in a mourning period, after all. But still.

"No," I said, bringing up the text and showing it to her. "Otherwise, I wouldn't have . . . worn any of this."

Hallie motioned for me to give her my phone, and she gasped, covering her mouth with her hand when she read it. "Oh my god, Sophie," she said, looking back up at me, stricken. "I'm so sorry. This was meant for my boyfriend, about a Fourth of July party. His last name is near yours, and I must have just selected the wrong contact."

I nodded as I took my phone back. I realized now that it actually did explain the "Hi, you" greeting, which I had thought was a little strange. And it did say "see you then," not "see you tonight."

"Hal," Josh said, shaking his head.

"I know!" Hallie said, and I could see that a bright red spot had appeared on each cheek. "I'm *so* sorry, Sophie. And this means I should probably text Ward, too, otherwise he's going to show up to the party on the Fourth in a bathing suit."

"It's fine," I said, trying to keep my voice light, like this was just going to roll right over me. "It's just an innocent mistake." I dropped my phone into my bag and took a step back toward the house. "But it was nice to see you guys anyway."

"Wait a second," Hallie said. "You can't leave. You just got here."

"Exactly," Josh chimed in immediately.

"But . . ." I said. I glanced down at myself, then past the Bridges siblings at the other kids at the party, most of whom were still giving me sidelong glances. "I'm just not sure that I should stay, I mean, it's a pool party. . . ."

"It's not a problem," Hallie said. "I wasn't sure what I was going to wear tonight, so I brought two options. You can just wear my other suit, and give it back to me whenever. It's brand-new, never been worn."

"Wow," I said. "That's really nice of you, but . . ." I had a feeling that even if I changed, I would still be That Overdressed Girl.

"Oh, please stay," Hallie said. "I feel so bad about this. At least let me make it up to you."

"You should stay," Josh said, and I saw Hallie glance at him, surprised, before looking back to me. "Really."

"Okay," I said, figuring that probably nobody else at the party would even remember what I'd shown up in. After all, I was here to befriend Hallie, so who cared what anyone else thought? And Hallie wanted me to stay. It was a no-brainer. "Sure."

"Great," Hallie said with a relieved smile. "Come on, Sophie."

I walked with her across the lawn and back into the house. She walked through the downstairs like she knew exactly where she was going, and I trailed more cautiously behind, all too aware of my heels and the profusion of antiques that surrounded me. I followed her up a staircase and to a guest bedroom that had clearly been used as a dressing room for the night—beach bags and purses and nonbeach cover-up clothes were tossed on the double beds and piled on the floor.

"Here you go!" she said, pulling a bikini out of her canvas bag.

"Thanks!" I said, trying to sound enthusiastic as I took it from her. The bikini looked like it was the same style as the one she had on, but with red and white stripes instead of blue polka dots. I glanced at Hallie and realized we were probably around the same size, though it looked like she was probably a little curvier than I was—though this, unfortunately, wasn't that surprising. "I'll just change," I said, as I crossed the room into the attached bathroom and shut the door behind me.

I looked away from my reflection, no longer pleased with my semi-formal look, now that I knew it had been the absolute wrong thing to go with. I changed quickly, and was happy to find that the suit fit pretty well. The top was a little big, but things got better when I adjusted the straps, and I really didn't think that anyone else would notice.

I folded up my clothes into a little bundle, held the shoes carefully by the heels, and stepped back into the guest room, where

Hallie was sitting cross-legged on the floor and scrolling through her phone. She looked up at me and smiled. "You look so cute!" she said. "Seriously, that looks better on you than it ever did on me."

"Not at all," I said as I dropped my clothes and shoes on the floor by the nearest bed. "But thanks so much for lending it to me."

"I wasn't going to leave you stranded in a party dress after it was my fault you were wearing one," she said. Her glance fell to where I'd left my clothes. "Those shoes are amazing, though. Sure you don't want to consider wearing them with the bikini?"

I laughed at that. "I think I'll just go barefoot."

Hallie laughed too, then snapped her fingers as she looked at the suit. "Just let me do one thing." She reached out and grabbed the dangling tags. The barcodes were still on, but the prices had been torn off; I'd noticed when I'd put the suit on. She gave the two tags a hard yank, then tossed them in the trash.

"Ready?" I asked, adjusting the straps and wishing I hadn't spent quite so long blow-drying my hair.

"Wait a sec!" Hallie said. She leaned forward and looked at me closely. "Are you going to go swimming?"

"Probably," I said. I had just assumed that I would. Maybe it was because of Bruce's second wife, but I just didn't understand girls who wore bathing suits and then refused to actually get in the water.

"In that case," she said. She grabbed her canvas bag and pulled out a makeup pouch, then tossed me a pack of makeup-removing wipes. "To avoid the dreaded raccoon eyes," she said.

"Thank you," I said gratefully, pulling one out, having suddenly had a vision of myself coming up out of the water with eye makeup—and I had put a *lot* of it on tonight—running down my cheeks. "So," I said as I swiped off in a second what had taken me nearly an hour to achieve, "you said your boyfriend's going to be here on the Fourth?"

"Yes," Hallie said, practically lighting up. "If all goes according to plan, that is." She held up her hand. "Fingers crossed."

"It must be hard," I said, "to have him gone."

"It is," she said with a sigh. "Especially because it's so new. Not exactly the best time to take a break from each other, you know?"

I didn't. Teddy and I had been almost an insta-couple, and we hadn't really been apart since we met—that is, until he broke up with me. But I nodded anyway. "Right."

"Plus," she said, glancing at her phone again before setting it down, "the stuff that matters, you fight for."

I didn't know how to reply to that since, while I knew exactly what she meant, my version of it had involved trying to make her as unhappy as possible. I finished taking off my eye makeup, and she nodded.

"Better," she said. She pushed herself to her feet and gave me a smile. "Ready to take the plunge?"

***

An hour later, I was no longer feeling like people were staring at me, or that anyone remembered me as the person who'd clearly come to the wrong party. And anyway, my dress faux pas was quickly eclipsed when the guy who was hosting the party—Hallie introduced me to him briefly; it turned out his name was Todd—did a belly flop so intense (and apparently painful) that he'd spent the rest of the party recovering on a lounge chair.

I sat on the edge of the pool, my legs in the water. Hallie was standing off to the side, talking to a guy in a red baseball cap with a blue lobster embroidered on it who didn't really seem to fit in with the rest of the partygoers—at any rate, I noticed that he'd been on the edge of the group all night, and seemed to talk to only Hallie.

I was feeling much more relaxed than I would have believed possible, especially because when I'd first started talking to people, I was terrified someone would call me on my lie. I kept waiting for someone to start laughing, or call me out, or just scoff and say, *"You're* not Sophie Curtis. *Who are you trying to fool?"* But the more I talked to people, the more I relaxed into my new identity.

It wasn't like I was acting like a different person. I had decided that would be much too confusing, not to mention potentially dangerous, in terms of getting caught, if I forgot or mixed up the identity that I'd created. So I was basically being me, but with Sophie's name, and blurring the biographical details when necessary. And luckily, the conversations I'd been having with the other partygoers had all stuck to the superficial, so it wasn't really like I was even saying anything I wouldn't have said anyway, aside from my name: *I'm from Putnam. I'm staying in Quonset. Yep, that was me in the heels—I thought it was a different party.*

Hallie was still deep in conversation with red baseball cap guy, but she looked over at me every now and then, like she was making sure that I was okay. I had nodded and smiled back at her, but with a lump in my throat. In a way, it made me glad to see that it seemed Hallie was still a good person, a good friend. That somehow I hadn't stamped that out of her. But it also made me regret, yet again, what I'd done to her that summer.

"Hey."

I turned to my left and there was Josh, now wearing his T-shirt, unfortunately, sitting right next to me.

"Hi," I said, reaching up to adjust my straps, suddenly very aware of just how much of me was exposed in this bikini, modestly cut as it was.

"It's like you're a different person," he said, and I stared at him, forgetting how to breathe for a moment. "You changed," he added, and I just blinked at him before I realized he meant the bikini.

"Oh, right," I said, laughing a little too loudly. "Yeah, Hallie came through for me."

"That sounds like her," Josh said. "She'd give you the shirt off her back."

"Are you guys close?" I asked, realizing that this was an opportunity to get to know Josh better, and to get more info on Hallie. And plus, I was genuinely curious.

"Hmm." Josh hesitated a moment before answering, kicking at the water with one of his feet. I found that I really liked that he was thinking about his answer. I knew Teddy would have just started speaking immediately. Teddy tended to answer people in paragraphs, not sentences, something that had utterly dazzled me when we first met. "We are," Josh finally said, each word sounding carefully considered. "Kind of. I mean, she's my sister and I love her. I know she'd do anything for me. And believe me, I'd do the same for her. I'm a very protective big brother. If anyone ever hurts her, I'm going to make them pay." He glanced over at me, and I did my best to smile at this, and not let him see that it felt like I'd just broken out in a cold sweat. "But we haven't lived in the same house in a while—I started going to Clarence Hall in seventh grade, and I'm usually away at sports camps during the summer."

"Not this year?" I asked.

He lifted up his knee. "Tore my ACL in the spring. I'm on rest and recovery for the summer."

"So it sounds like you're really into lacrosse," I said, and Josh shrugged.

"I mean, when I started, it was because I was good at it. I guess I never thought about if I liked it or not. And I was getting scholarships to go to camps, and then to school. And even when we didn't need those anymore, it was kind of just . . . what I did." He looked over at me and gave an embarrassed laugh. "I guess I've never really had to think about it before."

"Well," I said. I swirled my own feet underneath the water, then moved them away when I realized how close they were to Josh's feet. "I don't think you have to let yourself be defined by your past." As I said it, I realized I was hoping for that to be true for me as much as for him.

He smiled at me then, a smile that was equally happy and

surprised. "I like that," he said. He looked at me closely, like he was really seeing me, and I looked away quickly. I had a feeling that extended eye contact wasn't part of correct mourning period behavior. "What about you?"

"What about me?" I asked, already feeling myself get nervous. *And which me?* I wondered.

"What's your thing?" he asked, then shook his head, and even in the moonlight, I could see that he was blushing. I realized, all in a rush, that he was embarrassed. This cute, amazing-bodied lacrosse player just thought he sounded stupid and regretted his choice of words. He'd made a cheesy pun earlier. I suddenly felt bad for having slotted him into the jock category, just because he hadn't started any organizations to protect endangered birds, as far as I knew. But I was in the habit of comparing everyone (especially every boy) to Teddy and then watching them all fall short. It was like I hadn't left room for the idea that a jock could also be a little—endearingly—nerdy.

"I mean, what are you into?" Josh continued, regrouping a little. He gave me a serious look and then asked, totally deadpan, "Lacrosse?"

I laughed, surprised, and saw Hallie look away from the guy with the baseball cap—she was still talking to him—and glance over at us. "No," I said, and I turned back to Josh to see that he was smiling too. "Not lacrosse. Just . . ." I thought back to how I'd spent most of my free time in the last two years: joining in with Teddy at his different protests and causes, taking up his interests as my own, never really having to form my own opinions. I was about to start telling Josh about the plight of the Marsh Warbler and the struggle for freedom of the people of Georgia (the country, not the state, which had really confused me at first). But then I realized that these had always been Teddy's interests, not mine.

"I don't know," I finally said, hoping he wouldn't think that I was beyond lame, but feeling that way a little bit. "I guess I'm still figuring that out."

"Nothing wrong with that," Josh said, and from his expression, it didn't look like he was judging me for this, or thinking I was beyond lame. Maybe just the opposite, in fact.

"Hey, you two." I looked up to see Hallie sit down next to Josh.

"Hey yourself," Josh said. He looked around, exaggerating the gesture. "Where's your friend?"

"Josh," Hallie said, shaking her head.

"What?" Josh asked, teasing and faux-innocent. "You've been talking to the guy all night. And just after you were telling me how into your new boyfriend you are . . ."

"Stop," Hallie said, whacking him on the arm, her cheeks turning pink. "I was just actually being nice, and talking to Tyler because he didn't know anyone else here."

"Ooh, *Tyler*," Josh said, clearly warming to his theme.

"Meanwhile, the two of you are just here talking to each other," Hallie said, arching an eyebrow at me. "What about?"

"You," Josh said without missing a beat. "And Tyler. We like his nifty hat." I laughed at that, and Josh smiled at me. I smiled back, but a moment later became very aware that Hallie, though also smiling, was watching us closely.

I felt my smile drop away, and I looked down at my hands. What was I doing? Josh was nice, and funny, and had to-die-for abs, but I was going to be in a mourning period for a year, and I wasn't even close to getting over Teddy—I'd broken down into floods of tears the day before when I saw Bruce's perfectly sorted recycling bin. Also, I had just talked to Hallie that afternoon about how hard my breakup had been. And now it looked like I was flirting with her brother?

"I'm going in," I said abruptly, pushing myself off the wall and into the water, heading for the deep end. It was unheated, and the shock of the temperature shook me back to my senses a bit. I avoided the pool volleyball game/chicken match that was going on in the shallow end—I wasn't sure I needed to be brought back to my senses via a rogue volleyball to the face. I treaded water for a little, then floated on my back. I looked to the side and saw Hallie and Josh still sitting next to each other, heads bent close, talking. Hallie caught my eye, and I could tell by the way she gave a little guilty start that they'd been talking about me. Not wanting Josh to see me staring, I ducked under the water, letting my hair fan out behind me, and smoothing it down before I surfaced.

I took a breath, then went to adjust my shoulder strap.

Which was when I realized it wasn't there.

CHAPTER 9

I gasped and looked down. The shoulder strap had totally separated itself from the suit in front—I could see it floating along
in the water behind me—and the top of my suit, too big to begin
with, was on the verge of falling down.

I clamped it to my chest, starting to enter into full-on panic
mode. What was happening?

As I watched, horrified, the strap on the other side detached
itself from the back and seemed to shrivel in the water a little
before floating in front of me.

"Catch!"

I turned and saw the volleyball sailing through the air toward
my head. I yelped and ducked under the water, holding the top to
me as tightly as I could. I resurfaced, sputtering, with my hair
plastered down on my face—I was no longer able to smooth my
hair back, since that required the use of arms, and mine were
currently occupied—to see that everyone who had been playing

volleyball was glaring at me. "Um, the *ball*?" asked a girl who was perched on a boy's shoulders.

"Toss it here," another boy said—with a girl on his shoulders as well—sounding a little out of breath.

"Oh," I said, as I watched it bobbing a few feet from me. I looked around and saw that I was the only one in the deeper end. The rest of the pool was taken up by the volleyball players, and there was nobody else in between. There were also very few people hanging around the pool; Hallie and Josh were no longer sitting on the side, and it looked like the crowd was now mostly gathered around the food table. "Um," I said, hearing how out of breath I sounded. I was treading water to stay afloat, and it was getting hard. "I can't," I said, trying to move forward in the pool, where I could at least touch the bottom with my toes.

I suddenly felt water against my hip where it hadn't been before. I looked down and saw, to my horror, that the seams on the bikini bottom were pulling apart from each other. Why was this happening? I suddenly remembered Hallie giving the tags on both pieces of the bikini a hard yank. Had she accidentally torn the material as well?

I shifted one hand across my chest and moved the other to my hips, grabbing the fabric tightly with my hands. I also reversed course, away from where the people were. I had to tread water in the deep end, but it also meant that there would be fewer people to see me if I ended up skinny-dipping by accident.

Unfortunately, the volleyball players seemed to take this move to mean I was going back to get their ball.

"Come *on*," the girl yelled.

"Toss it here," the guy repeated, now definitely sounding winded.

I stared at the ball, now bobbing only a few inches from me. I might have been able to get it when it was just my top that was malfunctioning, but now I couldn't spare either of my arms. "Sorry," I said, realizing that this made me look like the biggest jerk in the world, but not seeing anything I could do about that right now. "I can't."

"Why not?" the girl asked, looking down at me from her height on the guy's shoulders.

"I have, um, a fear of volleyballs," I said, knowing I sounded crazy, but not seeing any other options. My brain was focused on keeping myself clothed at the moment, not coming up with rational excuses.

"What?" one of the guys yelled.

"I *can't*," I yelled back, feeling very much like I needed to collapse for a while, but couldn't, because I had to both tread water and try and keep my bathing suit on. My legs were seriously burning, and I wondered if I'd inadvertently invented a new form of cardio.

"I've got it," I heard someone say. I looked back and saw Josh, leaning over the pool and scooping up the ball. He tossed it to the players, most of whom took the time to glare at me before returning to the game. I knew that between the outfit I'd shown up in and my refusal to throw back a ball, it was looking unlikely that I'd be receiving another invite to one of Todd's parties.

"Thanks," I called up to Josh. "I was just . . ." I realized I had no idea how to finish that sentence, so I just let my voice fade away. "Thanks," I finally repeated.

"Sure," he said. He smiled down at me, and I tried to look nonchalant, like I was just treading water—while keeping my arms firmly clamped at my sides—for fun. "You all right?" he asked.

"Fine!" I said brightly. "Just, you know . . . getting some exercise. Did you know the government recommends an hour a day?"

Josh frowned at this, but he must have believed me—it might have helped that I was almost totally out of breath—because he gave me a nod and headed back to where the rest of the party was.

I treaded water over to the side of the pool and leaned against it to give myself a little rest. I looked at the volleyball game going strong, and tried to estimate just how long it would take for people to get out of the pool so that I could make my exit without worrying about accidentally flashing people.

Surely only a few more minutes. Ten, tops.

An hour later, my fingers were thoroughly pruned and I had never wanted anything as much as I wanted to be out of the pool and no longer having to worry about accidental nudity—something that, before tonight, had never honestly occupied much space in my thoughts.

The volleyball game had ended, but now two of the chicken partners were canoodling in the shallow end and occasionally shooting me murderous looks, clearly wanting me to leave as much as I wanted them to leave.

Luckily, I hadn't had to tread water this whole time; I'd figured out a system where I could perch on the ladder and still remain clothed. I had watched, from this position, as most of the guests had said their good-byes and left, until there were only a few people still standing in small groups talking.

"Sophie!" I looked up, hoping there hadn't been a delay in my response, to see Josh and Hallie standing at the edge of the pool. They were carrying their bags and wearing clothes over their bathing suits—clearly ready to leave the party.

"So we're heading out," Hallie said. Her voice was friendly but her expression was puzzled, and I knew she was probably wondering why I had come to a party she'd invited me to and then spent most of the time alone in the pool. She probably thought I was weird and unfriendly, and I couldn't help but feel this night had been a total disaster, even without the self-destructive bikini. I'd come hoping to get closer to Hallie, and I had a feeling that after my behavior tonight, she wouldn't want anything more to do with me.

"Great!" I said, trying to keep my expression cheerful, like I was just having so much fun leaning awkwardly against a pool ladder. "I'll see you around?"

"Sure," she said easily, but I couldn't tell if she meant it or if she was just being polite. She turned to leave, but Josh stayed where he was, looking down at me, his brow furrowed.

"Sophie, is everything okay?" he asked, his voice a little low, directed just to me.

"Just fine!" I said, brightly. But he looked at me, right into my eyes for a moment, and I felt my smile falter a little under this scrutiny.

"I'm actually going to stay a little bit longer," Josh said, turning to Hallie, who was pulling her keys out of her bag.

"Oh," she said. She glanced at me, and her eyebrows shot up, then back at Josh. But she didn't look displeased about this, I noticed. "Okay. Are you . . ." She paused and looked down at the keys in her hand.

"Sophie can give me a ride home, right?" Josh asked, turning to me.

"Um . . ." Giving him a ride would involve getting out of the pool, and I didn't see that happening anytime soon.

"Cool," Josh said, seeming to take this as a yes, and turning back to Hallie. "So I'll see you at home?"

"See you then," Hallie said, still looking a little thrown by this development. She gave us a wave, and I nodded back at her. She turned and left, glancing back once at us before heading into the house.

"Okay," Josh said, turning back to me and bending down so that he was closer to my level in the water. "What's going on? Nobody spends this much time in a pool unless they're trying to win some kind of a bet."

"Nothing," I said, abandoning my post on the ladder and going back into the water, so that I could move myself farther away from Josh. It's not that I was dying to start treading water again—my calf muscles were still burning—but I didn't want him to be able to see the state of my malfunctioning bikini. I suddenly realized that it would be much worse if accidental nudity happened in front of *Josh*, as opposed to just the random canoodling volleyball couple. "I just don't want to get out."

Josh just looked at me for a moment, then shrugged. "Then I'll get in," he said.

"No—" I started, but that was when Josh pulled his shirt over his head, and I was momentarily struck speechless. By the time I'd stopped being blinded by his abs, he was already in the water and swimming toward me.

"Is it a secret?" he asked, and one of his eyebrows quirked up. "Did you find money on the bottom or something?"

"No," I said, feeling myself smile but simultaneously trying to move away from him and make sure that the pieces of fabric I was clutching all stayed where they were meant to. "It's just . . ." I looked at him, treading water along with me, and realized there was probably no sense in even trying to hide what was actually happening. I sighed. "Okay, fine. My bathing suit is kind of falling apart."

A very intrigued and happy expression took over Josh's face. "Really?" I glared at him, and he arranged his features into a more contrite expression. "I mean . . . that's horrible."

"And I've just been waiting for those two to leave," I said, tilting my head in the direction of the volleyball couple, who still showed no sign of moving. "So that I can try and get out without anyone seeing me."

Josh just looked at me for a moment, and I was suddenly struck by how ridiculous this must look, the two of us bobbing up and down as we had a conversation while treading water.

I was about to apologize for this mess I'd landed myself in—I knew Teddy would have been mortified if I'd done something like this—when Josh smiled, wide. "This is great," he said. "It's like a spy mission."

I blinked at him. "It is?"

"Totally," he said, like it was obvious. "Okay, I'll try and get them out of here, and once they're gone, I'll go get you a towel or something so you can get out without anyone seeing."

"But what about you?" I asked. I was really quite concerned about the mechanics of getting out of the pool, and about the state of the few scraps of fabric that were still holding together. Because I had a feeling that when I got out of the pool, the weight of the water would pull apart the last few seams still hanging on.

"I won't look," Josh assured me. "I'm a gentleman." He said this without any sarcasm at all, and for some reason, I believed him.

"Okay," I said, and I was suddenly incredibly relieved that I was in this with someone else, and someone whose powers of plan-making hadn't been addled by inhaling chlorine fumes for an hour. "Let's do it."

Josh started swimming over to the shallower end, motioning me to follow him. I did the best I could to propel myself forward without using my hands, catching up with Josh when he stopped a few feet from the couple, who were now playfully flicking water at each other. "Hey, Sophie," Josh said in a voice that was clearly designed to carry. It was also incredibly fake-sounding, and it was pretty obvious to me that maybe Josh should keep his talents on the lacrosse field and not start trying out for school plays.

"Yes, Josh?" I asked, hoping I sounded a tad more natural. I was now in shallow enough water so that I could stand, and I had never been so grateful to touch solid ground. My legs were shaky from all this unexpected cardio, and it was enough to make me think I should start actually running with Bruce occasionally, as opposed to just fake running.

"Did you hear about that flesh-eating bacteria? The one they started finding in swimming pools?"

"Why, no," I said, glancing over at him, and when I saw his fake-earnest expression, biting my lip hard to keep from laughing. "Could you, um, tell me more about it?"

The couple looked over at us. The girl mostly seemed annoyed, but I noticed it looked like the guy was listening.

"Oh yeah," Josh said. "It's been happening all over the Eastern seaboard. You get it when you've been spending too much time in pools. And there are no symptoms . . . until it's *too late.*" Josh said this pretty much directly to the guy, who paled, then turned, splashed his way toward the shallow end, and ran up the stairs.

"Seriously?" the girl, now abandoned in the pool, called after him. She scowled at me and Josh, then flounced her way out of the pool as well.

"Part one successful," Josh said, swimming over to the side and pushing himself up and out of the pool, giving me a nice view of the very impressive muscles in his back. "On to part two."

Josh grabbed a striped towel from the basket by the lounge chairs and held it up by the edge of the pool so that it would block anyone from seeing me—though I noticed that there really weren't very many people still hanging around. There was one guy (it looked like it might have been Todd, the host) passed out on a lounge chair, but aside from that, the backyard looked pretty deserted. "Ready?" he called, and I could see that, true to his word, he was facing forward, not looking back me.

"Ready," I said. I cautiously moved myself farther into the shallow end, then walked up the pool steps, gripping on even tighter to the suit, because, like I'd suspected, the whole thing had gotten heavier once I was out of the water. I risked dropping a hand for just a moment as I snatched the towel from Josh and wrapped it around me. I had never in my life been so grateful to no longer have to worry about indecent exposure.

"Okay?" Josh asked, still facing forward.

"Okay," I said, coming around to the other side of him. "Thank you." I waited to feel incredibly embarrassed by this—needing a very cute guy to help me not accidentally flash people—but the humiliation didn't come. It felt, strangely enough, like we were a team. And since he didn't seem embarrassed, it was like I wasn't, either.

"Ready to leave?" Josh asked.

"I am," I said emphatically. No offense to Todd, but I would be happy if I never spent any time at his house or in his pool ever again.

"Cool," Josh said, grabbing his own towel and wrapping it around his shoulders. "Meet you out front?"

"Sounds great," I said. I started to head to the house, then stopped. "Thank you," I said.

Josh just nodded, not brushing this off or making a joke. "You're welcome," he said. "See you in five."

I made it upstairs with the towel wrapped tightly around myself and went straight for the corner where I'd left my clothes. I shed the remnants of the bathing suit, and dried off and changed back into Gwyneth's party dress, understanding as I did so that there was a reason people normally put on shorts or T-shirts after swimming, and not formalwear. But the dress was staying in one piece, so really, I wasn't going to complain.

Once clothed again, I examined the ruined suit, baffled. I still didn't understand what had happened, but I figured I would look at it more carefully when I got home, because right now, Josh was waiting.

I picked up my satin clutch and looked around the now-deserted guest room, realizing that my shoes were gone.

CHAPTER 10

"It's up there, on the left," Josh said, and I signaled and turned down a driveway that I probably would have missed unless he'd pointed it out, as it was tucked between two high hedges.

I headed down the driveway and pulled to the side, where there was a little paved turnaround, and put the car in park. I looked up at the house and felt my jaw drop. I couldn't see all of it, but from what was lit up by the SUV's headlights and the moonlight spilling onto the driveway, this was a pretty amazing house. It looked really big—almost as big as Bruce's—but it was done in a modern style, all glass and sharp edges and steel. My window was down, and I could hear the sound of waves crashing nearby, which meant the house was either on the water or very near it. "Nice place," I said, still staring at it. It really seemed like Karen must have become a start-up millionaire or a master jewel thief since I'd last known her. Because otherwise, I couldn't get my head around how a failed novelist suddenly had a mansion in the Hamptons.

"Yeah," Josh said, sounding a little embarrassed. "It's okay."

We hadn't spoken much on the drive. I'd been driving barefoot, which was a new experience, and had been concentrating on making sure that I didn't lose control of the pedals. Josh gave me directions, studying the map on his phone to make sure we were going the right way. Since he'd only been in this house for a few days, he was still learning his way around the neighborhood. And my mind had mostly been on my vanishing footwear. I had looked all over the guest room and the downstairs of the house, but my shoes (technically, Gwyneth's shoes) were absolutely nowhere. And since I was probably the one person who'd shown up in heels and not flips-flops, it wasn't like someone could have grabbed them by accident, thinking they were theirs. Which meant that someone had deliberately taken my shoes. Or Gwyneth's shoes, but it was the same idea. I had a pretty strong suspicion that it had been the volleyball girl in the shallow end, getting her revenge on me for the flesh-eating bacteria rumor.

"Thanks for the ride," Josh said. He glanced into the back of the car, which was far too big to make any rational sense, then turned back to me and said, deadpan, "Glad you had enough room."

I laughed. "I know, it's kind of crazy." I thought about explaining how it wasn't really my car, but then realized I'd have to go into the fact that it was Bruce's, and that might lead to questions about my dad, and realized I probably should steer clear of that area. "Thanks for the rescue."

"It was no big deal," Josh said, shooting me a quick smile. Silence fell between us, and as I felt the car rumbling underneath me, I was suddenly aware of how close we were, despite the largeness of the car. Even though we'd been in a pool together, and wearing much less than we were right now, there was something about being in a confined space that made me all the more aware that I was very close to a cute guy who, I now knew, also had an amazing body. It made me nervous in a way that being with him in the pool hadn't. I was about to tell him I should really be getting home, when he said, "It was actually kind of fun."

I raised my eyebrows, and he quickly said, "Well, I mean, obviously, not as much for you. But I don't know, it just kind of felt like . . . a challenge, or something."

"It's one I'd rather not go through again," I said.

"Totally," he said. "I just . . ." His voice trailed off, and he looked out the window. The engine's rumblings started to sound unhappy, like it didn't like just sitting in park for this long. Plus, maybe because it was the size of a small bus, my dad had warned me that the SUV guzzled gas. I turned off the engine, and the interior lights flared on briefly before slowly dimming, and I could see Josh illuminated for a second in profile, his tan skin and scattering of freckles, his hair drying a little funny from the pool water, with occasional pieces sticking up. "I don't know," he said after a moment, and it sounded like he was trying to figure something out as he spoke. "My ex-girlfriend was all about appearances. It was like everything always had to be perfect. But you—"

"*Really* don't have that problem," I said, trying to keep my voice light. Because, frankly, it was true, and once someone has to help save you from a disintegrating bikini, you've pretty much left any attempt at perfect behind. I glanced over at Josh, then turned so that I was facing him a little more, after making sure the party dress was staying in place. I'd heard something in his voice when he said "ex-girlfriend." It was like he was still getting used to saying it, and that was familiar. "Was it a recent breakup?"

"Yeah," Josh said. "Right as school was ending for the year."

"I, um," I started, then paused, not sure where to begin. I hadn't really had to explain my situation to anyone yet. I'd skated over the particulars with Hallie, and Sophie had been there when I'd realized it was actually over with Teddy, so she hadn't really needed additional info. I took a breath. "Me too. I mean, breakup, I had." I stopped, wondering why I'd just started talking like Yoda.

"Oh yeah?" Josh asked, turning more fully toward me, and leaning his back against the door. "Recent?"

I was about to tell him that it had only been a little more than a week, when I realized that it had only been about ten days since I'd accepted it was actually over, but Teddy had, in fact, dumped me before that. "About two weeks ago."

Josh winced. "That is recent."

I nodded, even though it didn't feel that way to me. It felt like there was a chasm between the life I'd led when I was Teddy Callaway's girlfriend, and things were good, and now, when I was all alone and I still didn't know why. Also, I was going under my best friend's name and concealing my real identity to two people, so as far as fortnights went, this one had been eventful.

"Let me guess," Josh said, in what I already recognized as his joking voice, "he also always wanted everything to be perfect."

"No," I said, wondering if it was somehow a betrayal to discuss Teddy like this—but simultaneously feeling like it was a relief to talk about him to someone who didn't already have an opinion on the situation. "He *was* perfect."

Josh looked at me skeptically. "Really?"

I nodded. Josh still looked unconvinced, but that was because he didn't know Teddy—didn't know about all his organizations and commitments, and his tireless work on behalf of the Marsh Warbler. "Really."

Josh shrugged. "Maybe this guy was," he said. "But it seems to me that perfect doesn't exist."

"What about your ex?" I asked, hoping I wasn't overstepping my bounds.

Josh let out a short, humorless laugh, the kind I hadn't yet heard from him. "That's just the thing," he said. "It was all an illusion. She wasn't who I thought she was. She was cheating on me, for one thing. So . . . not so perfect after all."

My breath caught in my throat. "I'm so sorry," I murmured. It was for what he'd just told me as much as his expression—the open, friendly one I'd seen on the train was now totally gone, and I could see the pain underneath.

Josh shrugged, like he couldn't care less, but he didn't quite pull it off. "It was hard," he said quietly. "But it was better to know, in the end. And I won't make that mistake again. I'm done with liars, and people who pretend to be something they're not."

I was about to agree wholeheartedly when I suddenly realized that I fit into both of those categories. I looked down at my hands—only now becoming unpruned—and suddenly wished I could tell him the truth about who I was. But a moment later, I came back to my senses, remembering Hallie, and what I was in the Hamptons to do. I looked back up at him and saw that Josh's expression was less troubled than it had been a moment before. And that he was looking right at me.

"It's good to talk to someone who gets it," he said.

"It is," I agreed, recognizing as I said it how true this was. Sophie, for all her experience with boys, had never been in love, never really had her heart broken. And though she was always there to listen, I wasn't always sure she understood.

Josh shifted in his seat, and a shaft of moonlight came through the windshield and landed across his face. I realized, again, just how close we were. I could have reached out and touched him. I could have smoothed down one of the little tufts of hair standing up on his head. The thought of doing either of these things was surprising enough that I leaned back quickly, moving away from him. A moment later, Josh sat back and unbuckled his seat belt.

"I should go in," he said. He rested his hand on the door handle and smiled at me. "Night, Sophie."

I made myself smile back at him, even though hearing my best friend's name was a reminder that things were not simple here, no matter that we had recent traumatic breakups in common. "Night, Josh."

He got out of the car then, waving once before going into the house. I waited until I saw he'd made it safely inside before starting the engine and heading home.

An hour later, I paced around my room at Bruce's, showered and in my pajamas. I had really wanted to avoid any more contact with water for a while, but after that much time in the pool, I positively reeked of chlorine, and was worried about the effect it might have on my recently dyed hair.

I wasn't sure what I was going to do about the shoes, but at least Gwyneth was currently out of town, and not here and wondering where they had gotten to. So I had a little time to figure out a solution there. The bigger problem was the bathing suit.

As I looked at the pieces of it, I tried to see where it had come apart. It still made no sense to me how this could have happened. If Hallie really had ripped the suit when pulling the tags off, it seemed to me that it would have torn right away, and wouldn't have only happened once I was in the water. I turned it over in my hands, and it was then that I saw a tiny tag sewn into the lining, which read: *All-natural, untreated fabric. To preserve garment construction and extend garment life, do not expose to chemicals (this includes chlorine).*

Well, that made a lot of sense for a bathing suit. But at least I understood why it had happened. Just as this question was answered, it hit me for the first time that this was not *my* bathing suit. That it had been on loan to me, and while in my custody, I had effectively wrecked it. I wasn't able to stop myself from groaning out loud. Here I was, attempting to get on Hallie's good side—trying to show her that I could be a good person, that she could trust me—and I went and destroyed her brand-new bathing suit. The fact that I hadn't done it intentionally was beside the point. Coupled with the rest of my behavior—like refusing to get out of the pool for an hour—I had the sinking feeling that I'd done more damage with her tonight than good. I looked at the pieces of the ruined suit and figured I would sort out what to do with it later. I didn't feel up to it tonight.

I set the bikini aside and got into bed, snapping off the light. I tried to lose myself in sleep, but whenever I closed my eyes, all I could see were flashes from the night, all embarrassing, starting with showing up in formalwear.

But then, there had been Josh, offering to stay, helping me. And our conversation in the car, in the moonlight. So maybe it hadn't been a total disaster.

I rolled over on my side, trying to put a positive spin on tonight's events, all those cozy clichés and sayings passing through my thoughts as my eyes closed and I drifted closer to sleep.

Tomorrow is another day. Things will look brighter in the morning. It's always darkest before the dawn.

But just before I drifted off, another, far less comforting saying flashed into my mind.

Karma's a bitch.

CHAPTER 11

I reached up into the cupboard for the vanilla, then added a teaspoon more to the frosting. I carefully stirred it in, then gave it a tiny taste to make sure I hadn't overdone it. It was the morning after the unexpected pool party, and the house was very quiet. Bruce, my dad, and Rosie all keeping West Coast hours meant that they slept late, and I was the only one awake. But when I'd woken up that morning, I'd had what seemed like the perfect idea for how to make amends with Hallie for wrecking her bathing suit. I would bake her what had been her favorite cupcakes when she was younger—strawberry with vanilla icing—and spell out on them I'M SORRY HALLIE. It was maybe a little bit of overkill for something that had technically been the bathing suit's fault, not mine. But I felt like I had to do something.

And plus, my cupcakes were pretty legendary. I'd baked a lot of them over the last two years, and they'd always been a hit at Teddy's meetings. I'd even perfected a raw vegan version that you almost couldn't tell wasn't the real thing, unless, of course, you'd had a cooked egg-and-dairy-filled cupcake in recent memory.

I paused in my stirring and rested the spoon against the side of the bowl. What Josh had said in the car last night about Teddy lingered with me this morning. He'd implied that Teddy wasn't perfect, that nobody was. At the time, I'd just chalked it up to Josh not knowing him. But now, I couldn't help wondering if maybe there was a tiny bit of truth in this. I'd thought of Teddy as perfect for so long that it almost seemed impossible to think of him any other way. But then I'd remembered the way that he'd scoffed at the cupcakes I'd tried to bring to his meetings at first, saying that they were frivolous and a waste of resources—that is, until he saw how much they brought in to help his causes and how popular they made the meetings. And I somehow knew that he wouldn't have been understanding about the bathing-suit disaster. He would have told me that I should have read the label before getting into the pool in the first place. Which was true. But still.

The pink cupcakes (my secret was putting pieces of real strawberries into the batter) were cool, so I started to ice them, trying not to think this way. Even though Teddy had broken up with me, it still felt like a betrayal. Instead, I concentrated on the letters, making sure the writing was legible and accenting a few of the cupcakes with little slivers of strawberries.

"Looks great!"

I turned and saw Bruce barreling into the kitchen, his iPad under his arm. "What's the occasion?" He peered down at the cupcakes. "Who's Hallie and what did you do?"

"Well—" I stalled, not really sure where to begin.

Luckily, though, Bruce didn't really seem to be waiting for an answer, and started flipping through his iPad. "Listen to this!" he said, as upbeat emo with far too many instruments filled the kitchen. "It's this band, Lenin and someone. You kids like them, right?"

"Well . . ." I stalled again, busying myself by rinsing out the bowls.

"Morning."

I turned around to see Rosie striding into the kitchen and heading straight for the coffeemaker. "Those smell great, Gem."

"Thanks," I said, transferring the bowls to the dishwasher. "I really—"

"But who's M?"

"What do you mean?" I turned back to the counter and saw that what had spelled out I'M SORRY, HALLIE now just spelled M SORRY, HALLIE. I looked at Bruce, whose mouth appeared suspiciously full. "Bruce!"

"*Mmmph*," Bruce said. He gave me a thumbs-up. "Good," he said, around what was clearly the cupcake with the *I* and the apostrophe.

"Since when do cavemen eat cupcakes?" Rosie asked pointedly, taking a sip of coffee. The lead singer started to wail from Bruce's iPad, and Rosie frowned. "Is that a lute?"

"Morning, all," my dad said, coming in and ruffling my hair as he passed on his way to the teakettle. "Did you have fun last night, Gem?"

"Kind of," I started. Since the night had contained the amount of embarrassing moments that I normally hoped to space out over a month, "fun" wasn't the word I'd use, despite how nice Josh had been about everything.

"Oh?" Bruce asked, brushing cupcake crumbs off his hands. "What did you do? Like, typical teen things? And what, exactly, were they?"

"Leave her alone, Bruce," Rosie said, giving me a smile. "If you want her to consult on this movie, you're going to have to compensate her. And she's not doing it for scale."

"What is this?" my dad asked, looking around the kitchen. "Did you bake these?"

"I did," I said. "These were cupcakes for a friend, until Bruce—" Out of the corner of my eye, I saw Rosie's hand dart out and grab a cupcake from the other side of the sentence. "Rosie!" I cried, hovering protectively over the remaining ones. Honestly, I had expected more from her.

"Sorry, Gem," Rosie said, taking a bite out of what I now saw was the *E* at the end of "Hallie." "But you can't just leave cupcakes out and not expect us to eat them. Your dad understands."

I whipped around to see my dad with a cupcake halfway to his mouth.

"Um," he said, cradling it protectively and taking a few steps back. "I just wanted to make sure the frosting was still good. That it hadn't, you know, spoiled. I'm watching out for you, kid." I looked down and saw that my dad had snatched the other *I*. The cupcakes now spelled MSORRYHALL.

"Oh, darn," Bruce said, moving closer until I glared at him and he backed off. "Do you need to make a new batch now, or something? Maybe chocolate this time?"

The emo wailing and the lute was interrupted by the familiar *chime* of Bruce's Skype, and a moment later, Ford appeared on the screen.

Startled, I took a step out of his viewing range. For most of our childhood, Ford had been a little short and chubby, taking after Bruce, and not his mom, who was a former Miss Hawaii. He'd also spent most of his time—when he wasn't surfing—playing with video games and reprogramming Bruce's laptop, which was pretty much the reason that he was a computer genius now and went to school with other computer geniuses. But in the last few years, Ford had grown tall and lanky, gotten rid of the braces, and swapped his thick glasses for hipster-cool square frames. It had been disconcerting for me to realize, when I'd seen him last year, that Ford was suddenly cute in a way the rest of the world, and not just me, would recognize. But I'd always had a crush on him, even before he morphed into a hottie. He had black-black hair, tan skin, and dark brown eyes, and he'd been my first kiss, on my birthday the year I turned thirteen.

"Hey," he said, "morning, Pops. Did I see Gemma dart out of frame?"

I leaned in and waved. "Hi, Ford." Ford's tan skin was already its summer golden hue, and though I couldn't see the message, it looked like he was wearing one of his signature you-have-to-be-a-tech-geek-to-get-the-punchline T-shirts. I noticed that his glasses looked new, the frames tortoiseshell, not black, and they brought out his eyes.

"*Aloha,*" he said, stretching out the vowels. Ford could adopt a flat, surfer-dude Hawaiian cadence when he wanted to, usually when he needed to lull people into not suspecting him of something he'd done.

My dad and Rosie leaned in to say hi, and I stepped away again and tried to look nonchalant, like I hadn't just been checking Ford out in front of his dad, and mine.

"So how are things going in the Hamptons?" he asked. "How's that cute baby ocean of yours?" Ford had been surfing his whole life, and didn't consider any of the East Coast's waves legitimate. When I'd told him that the beaches of Putnam were on Long Island Sound, and that we didn't even *have* waves, he had laughed for about five minutes straight.

"Things are good," Bruce said, leaning closer to talk to his son. "Tell me, do you and your friends like this band, Lenin and whatsit? Their manager owes me a favor."

Rosie shook her head. "You mean a favor beyond getting them to play your accountant's kid's bar mitzvah?"

Bruce waved this away and focused on his son. "So do you like them? I'm thinking about getting them for the sound track of this new movie."

Ford raised an eyebrow, just one, a talent I'd always envied. "Not that script you sent me to read," he said. "Dad, really? It was awful."

"I know," Bruce said, not even reacting to this. "But what about that band?"

Another *beep* sounded, and Rosie looked down at her phone, then sprang into action. "Bruce, we have a conference call in three," she said. "I'll get it set up in your office." She waved to Ford and tapped my dad on the arm as she passed him. "You might want to be in the room too, Paul. Just so you can hear that I'm not making these notes up to torture you."

My dad nodded and followed her out of the kitchen, eating the cupcake as he went.

"I'll call you later," Bruce was saying as he reached toward the remaining cupcakes and I slapped his hand away. "Tell your sister hi for me."

"Bye," Ford said. Bruce left the kitchen and Ford looked around. "Gem, you still there?"

I stepped back into frame and pulled up one of the kitchen stools to the counter, so it was like I was sitting across from him. "Here," I said.

"What's going on there?" Ford asked, leaning forward. "Did you make cupcakes?"

"Kind of," I said. I picked up the iPad and panned around so that he could see them better.

"What are the letters supposed to mean?" he asked.

"Nothing, now," I said, then remembered that Ford had a talent for anagrams. It was just the way his very logical brain worked—he was great at puzzles, patterns, mysteries. He'd actually told me once that it was the reason he was better at surfing than he deserved to be—he could see the mathematical properties of the curves of the waves in ways other surfers couldn't. Who knew if this was true, but the anagram thing definitely was—I had been dismayed when he told me that an anagram of Gemma Tucker was actually Make Cut Germ. And when I tried to make this better by adding my middle name, Rose, all I'd ended up with was Escargot Meek Rum. "Ford, what can I make these spell out?" I held him over the cupcakes, then set the iPad back down and looked at him hopefully.

He furrowed his brow in thought, and then a moment later, said triumphantly, "Marshy roll."

"What?" I wrinkled my nose. "What does that even mean?"

He shrugged. "You're the one who wrote it."

"I didn't," I protested. "Before everyone started eating them, it was supposed to say 'I'm sorry, Hallie.'"

"Well, that makes more sense," Ford acknowledged. "So what did you do? To this Hallie person?"

I looked down at the granite countertop and wiped up some crumbs. It would be really nice to tell someone what was going on. But I knew I wouldn't tell him for the same reason I'd never told the story to Sophie—I didn't want him to start looking at me differently. Once I'd made amends and Hallie had forgiven me, that would be the moment to tell the whole saga. But not before. "It's a long story," I said, looking back at him. "You know."

"So how's the crusader?" Ford asked, and I knew he was talking about Teddy.

"Oh," I said. "We kind of, um . . ." I took a breath. "Broke up." I braced myself for an onslaught of feeling, and though my heart did constrict a little when I spoke the words, it wasn't as bad as I'd anticipated. Maybe it helped that I'd had to go through it the day before with Josh.

Ford shook his head. "I never liked him."

"You never met him," I pointed out. I'd certainly talked about Teddy a lot, but since Ford shuttled between California and Hawaii, he and Teddy had never come face to face.

Ford shrugged this off. "Since when is that a requirement for disliking someone?" I smiled at that, and when Ford spoke again, his tone was softer. "I am sorry, though, Gem. You okay?"

I nodded and gave him a smile, and it didn't feel quite so much like I was faking it this time. I heard someone call Ford on his end, and he looked away, then back at me. "I gotta go," he said. "We'll talk soon?"

"Sure," I said. *"Mahalo!"*

Ford just frowned at me. "You know that means 'thank you,' right?"

"Right," I said, trying to cover. I only knew about four Hawaiian words, and according to Gwyneth and Ford, always managed to use them incorrectly. "That's why I said it. To thank you for the anagram."

"Right," Ford said, but I could tell he didn't believe me. He gave me a smile, one that still startled me a little with its cuteness. Ford had been in industrial-grade orthodontia for years—they'd called him the Shredding Headgear—and I still wasn't quite used to its absence. "See you."

"Aloha!" I called quickly before he signed off, glad that I'd gotten at least that one right. He waved and then a moment later, the call disconnected. I put Bruce's monogrammed cover back over the iPad and examined what was left of my cupcakes.

Not seeing any better options present themselves, I moved the cupcakes around until they spelled MARSHY ROLL. I looked down at them and sighed. It was better than nothing, and much better than throwing them out and starting over. I grabbed a Tupperware container and started to pack them up.

The Bridges' house looked even more impressive in the daylight. I could see now, as I pulled into the driveway and put the SUV in park, that the house *was* right on the ocean. I could hear the waves crashing, and see a glimpse of the shimmering water just past the side of the front deck.

I got out of the car, carefully holding the remaining cupcakes, and headed toward the front door. I'd called Hallie twice before heading over, but she hadn't answered either time. I figured I'd just leave the cupcakes by the door with a note if nobody seemed to be home, but now that I was there, I was questioning the wisdom of this plan. What if Hamptons vermin got to the cupcakes before Hallie did? I suddenly had visions of the house overrun by sugar-crazed raccoons. I had just raised my hand to knock when I heard someone call, "Hello?"

I turned around and saw Hallie, wearing shorts and a T-shirt, walking up from the direction of the water. Her hair had been straightened, and it looked even longer than it normally did, hitting almost the small of her back. She was holding an iPod in one hand and pulling her earbuds out of her ears. "Hi," I called.

Hallie's expression relaxed when she saw me. "Hey, Sophie," she said. She smiled and came to join me on the porch. She tucked her iPod in her shorts pocket, but not before I caught a glimpse of what she'd just been listening to—"Let's Lute Portland," Lenin and McCarthy's latest, the one Sophie had insisted on playing every time we drove anywhere together. "What's going on?"

"Sorry to drop in like this," I said, very glad now that I hadn't just left the cupcakes and ran, and not only because of potential raccoons. It was really warm out, something I hadn't had to face in either the air-conditioned house or car. But now, standing outside, I was aware of how hot and humid it already was, and I knew the cupcakes wouldn't have lasted long outside before the frosting would have started to melt.

"It's fine," she said, her eyes falling on the Tupperware. "Are those cupcakes?" She frowned. "What's marshy roll?"

"It's . . . a Connecticut thing," I said quickly. "It's like, the traditional Connecticut hello. You know," I said, making it all up on the spot and wishing I'd come up with a better explanation in the car. "Marshy roll to you!" I did a big, fancy wave, then immediately regretted it and dropped my hand.

Hallie's eyebrows shot up. "Oh," she said, sounding a little confused—and I didn't blame her. "Well . . . cool. This is so nice of you."

She leaned forward for a better look, and as I watched her sleek, heavy curtain of hair swing forward as well, I couldn't help but wince. "Aren't you hot with your hair down?" I asked. "It's sweltering out here."

Hallie shook her head. "I always wear my hair down," she said. She lowered her voice. "Want to know a secret?" She lifted up her hair to reveal ears that stuck out a bit from the sides of her head. "Elephant ears. They're so embarrassing."

"They're fine," I assured her. "Really."

"Said like someone with normal-sized ears," Hallie said. She dropped the hair, shaking her head ruefully.

I tried to remember if her ears had been anything she'd been worried about when we were younger, but nothing came to mind. They looked maybe a tiny bit large, but nothing to limit your hairstyles over. But maybe this was like how Sophie was convinced that her eyes were slightly uneven, something nobody else had ever noticed or been able to see when it was pointed out.

"These look great," Hallie said. "And . . ." She paused and looked closer, her voice rising a bit. "Are these vanilla frosting and strawberry?"

"Yes," I said, trying to sound nonchalant, so she wouldn't suspect I'd known about her dessert preferences ahead of time. "Made with fresh strawberries, too. Why?" I prepared myself to look shocked but pleased when she told me that I'd made her favorite cupcakes.

"I can't eat those." Hallie took a step away from the Tupperware. "I'm allergic to strawberries."

I opened my mouth. *No, you're not* was on the tip of my tongue, but I stopped myself just in time. I wasn't supposed to know, after all, that she'd once even liked this dessert. But . . . what? "Oh," I said, pulling in the cupcakes a little closer to me. "I didn't know."

"It's okay," Hallie said, her voice still a little high and stressed-sounding. "I break out in terrible hives, my throat starts to close. . . . It's pretty bad."

"God," I said, moving the Tupperware even farther away from her. "That's horrible." I had read somewhere that you could develop allergies at any time, but I had never before met anyone it had happened to. "Well, I'll just . . . take these home, then." I looked down at the rejected, already-starting-to-melt cupcakes with their nonsensical phrasing and realized the whole thing had been a bit of a washout. At least the cupcake-mooching crew back home would be happy about my failure.

"By the way, there was something I wanted to talk to you about," Hallie said, her voice growing more serious, and I immediately felt myself tense up. A second later, I told myself to relax. Hallie didn't know who I really was. Nobody did. Things were fine.

"What's that?" I asked, hoping my face didn't betray what I'd just been thinking, and trying to keep my expression neutral.

"This is kind of hard to talk about," Hallie said, playing with the ends of her hair and then looking out to the water before taking a deep breath. I could feel myself getting more nervous with every passing second. "It's about Josh."

"Oh." I immediately relaxed. "What about him?"

"I just noticed that he stayed with you at the party the other night . . . and then he mentioned that you guys talked when you drove him home. . . ." Hallie's voice trailed off, and I wasn't sure if I should wait for a question to follow, or jump in and confirm these facts. But a moment later, she went on. "I don't know if he told you," she continued, "but he had a pretty bad breakup recently."

"He mentioned it," I said, still not sure where she was going with this.

"I just don't want him to get hurt again," she said, and I noticed that her cheeks were flushed, like she was embarrassed to be having this conversation.

"Of course not," I started, and then the penny dropped. She wasn't just keeping me up to date with Josh's romantic past—she was telling me not to get involved with her brother. Not that I had been planning on getting involved with him, but to be warned away like this was a little jarring.

"I know I'm totally overstepping here," Hallie said all in a rush. "I mean, you said you just had a bad breakup as well. So you probably weren't interested in anything, anyway, and I might be way off base. I just . . . wanted to mention it."

"Right," I said, still trying to process this. "Of course."

Hallie smiled, like we'd just agreed on something. "Great," she said. "I'm glad we're on the same page."

I nodded, wondering why it was that I felt vaguely insulted and also a tiny bit disappointed. I mean, I had no intention of dating Josh. He was still reeling from his own breakup and probably wasn't interested in dating me. And Hallie didn't know me— that is, this version of me—well enough to have this be anything personal. But I couldn't help but remember that when Josh had said he was going to stay, she looked kind of pleased about it. Had something changed? Of course, I had seen her from the pool, without the best visibility, and I might have imagined it. But still . . .

"Oh, and I was going to call you about this," Hallie said, sounding much more cheerful, like she was happy to have that part of the conversation over with. "But can I get my bathing suit back?"

I was suddenly jerked out of the Josh fog and back to reality. How had I let the issue with the cupcakes themselves cloud what their original purpose was? They were *apology* cupcakes, no matter what they said now, and I should have just led with that.

"The thing is," I said, taking a deep breath. I couldn't help but wish I'd chosen to make some other flavor, because then Hallie would have at least had some sugar to soften the blow. "About that. It's—"

"I'm sorry to be a pain about it," she said. "Normally I would say keep it as long as you want! But I kind of need it this afternoon."

"Oh," I said, gulping for air a little. "Um . . ." I knew I just needed to step up and tell her that I no longer had a functioning bathing suit to give her, because it had disintegrated in the swimming pool, through no fault of my own. But as soon as I thought this, I could hear how ridiculous it would sound—like I'd wrecked her bathing suit and was now making up silly excuses for what had happened.

"The mother of the girls I babysit for gave me a gift certificate as a thank-you, and I wanted to show her what I bought," she continued, not seeming to realize that I was about to pass out. "And I'm sitting for them today. So would it be possible to get it this afternoon? I'm happy to come to you if that's easier. . . ."

"No!" I gasped. Then I said, all in a rush, "You were nice enough to lend it to me, the least I can do is bring it to you. No prob." As soon as I said this, I started to panic even more. Why was I promising this? I had no bathing suit to bring to her. What was I doing, saying no prob? It was *not* no prob. It was a big prob.

"Great," Hallie said, smiling. "And thanks for the cupcakes anyway. It's the thought, right?"

"Right," I echoed, my head still spinning. "You bet."

"See you later?" Hallie asked, I nodded. She waved and headed back around in the direction she'd come from, already putting her earbuds back in her ears.

I staggered to the SUV and got in, feeling shaky. Why had I promised to bring her back a swimsuit that was currently in pieces in my trash at Bruce's? Why hadn't I just told her the truth?

I didn't turn on the car right away, but just sat there in the sweltering heat, knowing the answer as soon as I'd asked myself the question. I didn't do it because I didn't want to let her down or make her life harder, yet again. I'd done enough to her when we were eleven, and now I had to destroy her swimwear as well?

But how was I going to get a replacement? Because that's what it seemed was going to have to happen, unless I wanted to gamble on the chance that my dad had secret sewing skills he'd never happened to mention to me.

It was incredibly hot in the car, and I lifted my hair off my neck to try and cool down a little. Maybe I would think better if I turned on the AC. Or maybe I could stop and get some ice cream. . . .

I gasped. Just like that, it came back to me—standing with Hallie and the twins outside Sweet & Delicious, Hallie telling me that her newest bikinis had come from Sur la Plage. Maybe there was hope after all. With a new sense of purpose, I turned on the car, pulled out of the driveway, and headed back to Quonset.

CHAPTER 12

"*Oui?*" As soon as I had stepped inside Sur la Plage, a tiny chime sounded, and a saleswoman with a thick French accent, dressed all in white, materialized immediately. "Can I help you, mademoiselle?"

I reached for my bag, crossing my fingers on the other hand. "I really hope so." I'd gone back to Bruce's, dropped off the cupcakes before they melted entirely, and picked up Hallie's suit so I could try and buy an identical version. Then I'd come downtown, and luckily found a parking spot near the bathing-suit store. It was nice and cool inside, done in white and green, with what sounded like French pop music playing softly from hidden speakers.

I pulled out the pieces of what remained of Hallie's suit and held them out to the saleswoman, who wrinkled her nose and took a small step backward. "I need to buy a replacement for this bikini."

The woman looked down at the bikini, and then shook her

head sadly. "Did you go swimming . . . in a *pool*?" she asked, practically whispering the last word, like it was vulgar.

"Well, yes," I said. "I had just assumed it was . . . you know, a regular bathing suit."

She gave me an almost pitying smile. "The name of this shop is *Sur la Plage*," she said. "It means 'on the beach.' In French," she added, as though maybe I hadn't put that together. "All our bathing suits are made of nothing but untreated, all-natural fabrics, and therefore are only intended for fresh or salt water. Not *chlorine*," she said, pronouncing the last word with disgust. "There was a disclaimer on the suit. We take no responsibility if you do not follow the guidelines."

"Right," I said, glancing down at the pieces of the suit again. "I saw that a little bit too late." The woman gave me a one-shouldered shrug. She clearly had no sympathy for me. And since she worked in a store that sold self-destructing bathing suits, maybe it made sense that she didn't even seem surprised. "Do you have another one of these that I could buy?" I had been secretly hoping that she would offer to replace it for free, but clearly that was not going to happen.

She motioned for me to hand her what was left of the suit, and looked at the sizes. "We may have a few left," she said. "Let me check."

She glided off to the back, and I crossed my fingers again that she had one—if she didn't, I was really, really in trouble. My phone buzzed in my bag, and when I pulled it out I saw that I had a missed call from Sophie, and I resolved to call her as soon as I finished with this.

Sophie and I hadn't really talked since I'd come to the Hamptons, just exchanging texts and voice mails and missed calls. Also, it seemed like things were getting hot and heavy with her barista, and Sophie tended to get really wrapped up in whoever she was dating for the first few weeks (or days, more accurately, as so many of her relationships had a short shelf life), so it wasn't that unusual to have not been in touch. But I'd also been avoiding talking to her, because I knew I'd have to explain what I was doing here—basically, pretending to be her. And since I'd given her so much grief over her Clarence Hall dating deception, I had a feeling I was facing a big *I told you so*. But despite that, I needed to talk to my BFF and get her opinion on all this. I made a mental note to call her back as the saleslady returned. "Any luck?" I asked.

She nodded and held up the suit, looking just like it had when Hallie had given it to me—new and beautiful and not wrecked and in pieces. "We had one left in your size," she said, walking behind the register, and I followed, feeling relief flood through me. Everything would be okay. I could get it back to Hallie today, and she'd never have to know that it wasn't the same one she'd given me.

"Great," I said, pulling out my debit card. I wasn't the greatest with saving money, and the haircut and color had put a serious dent in my bank balance. My mom had given me some money before I left, maybe feeling guilty that she was going to a castle and I was going to Long Island. But I was pretty sure I could handle the cost of a bikini.

"That will be three nineteen," she said as I just stared at her, not sure I'd understood, since I'd never heard of a bathing suit being that inexpensive.

"Three . . . nineteen?" I repeated hopefully.

"Oui," she said, looking down at the register and nodding. "Three hundred and nineteen dollars."

I felt the store start to tilt slightly, and I grabbed on to the shiny white counter for support. "For a *bathing suit?*" I blurted out.

She just sighed. "All our suits are made of nothing but untreated, all-natural fabrics. . . ." she started.

"Right," I said, nodding, not needing to hear the whole speech again. My head was swimming as I slid my debit card back into my wallet. That was more money than I had ever spent on anything, let alone a bathing suit. Especially someone *else's* bathing suit, for that matter. But I didn't see any alternative—this didn't look like the kind of place that would let you bargain. "Okay," I said, swallowing hard as I pulled out the For Emergencies Only credit card my dad had gotten for me. It had my name on it, but it was linked to his card and all the bills went right to him. I had never used it before, and knew it was not supposed to be used for things like shopping. But I didn't know what else I could do. I handed the card over, my heart racing. I would just tell him what happened, and then pay him back. Maybe he'd let me do it in installments.

The saleslady rang me up, cut off the tags when I asked her to, then pushed the white receipt across the counter to me. I signed the receipt, and she placed a copy, along with the suit wrapped in tissue paper, into a shiny shopping bag. *"Merci beaucoup,"* she said as she handed the bag to me. "Come again," she added, and I just nodded, not wanting to tell her that unless I won the lottery, there would be no way that was going to happen.

I left the store and headed into the bright sunlight, my head still spinning a little over the price and what I'd just done. I was pretty sure my dad would understand. But even though I knew he was making a better living now as a screenwriter than he ever had as a novelist, he still seemed to have a struggling writer's approach to money—that is, he was always reluctant to spend any of it.

But I figured I would deal with it when I had to. I headed in the direction of Quonset Coffee, feeling very much in need of an iced latte.

∘∘∘∘∘∘

"Gemma?" Sophie answered on the first ring, and I smiled, just hearing her voice, as I settled down on the bench outside the coffee shop and took my first sip of iced latte. "Oh my god, hi! How are you? Have you been . . ." Sophie asked, her voice suddenly slower and more concerned, "baking?"

"No," I said, deciding not to tell her about the cupcakes, because I didn't think one batch counted. "I'm okay," I said, realizing as I said it that it was true. Despite wardrobe malfunctions, vanishing heels, cupcake errors, and prohibitively expensive bathing suits, I was certainly doing better than when I had been sobbing over *Ghostbusters* and living in my bed. "How about you?"

"Well," Sophie said, and launched into a much-more-detailed-than-I-wanted description of her last makeout session with the barista—whose name was apparently Blake—which had in fact taken place in his coffeeshop, which seemed to me like it was probably violating all kinds of health codes.

"So what's new with you?" she asked, once she'd finished the makeout recap. "What's happening out there?"

I took a breath. This was the perfect time to tell her what had actually been going on, and the secret life I had landed myself in here. No time like the present—which was, incidentally, the title of the straight-to-DVD Christmas special in the time-traveling-animal franchise. "Actually, the thing is, Sophie . . ."

"Sophie?" I turned around, and clutched my phone as I saw Josh stepping out of Quonset Coffee, holding what looked like an iced tea.

"Hi," I said in a strangled voice, my thoughts racing. How much had he heard? Had he just heard me call someone else what was supposed to be my name?

"Gemma?" Sophie called loudly through the phone, causing me to clamp my hand over the tiny microphone. "Hello?"

"The thing is, Sophie," I repeated into the phone, eyes on Josh, "that's what I said to myself, that, Sophie, it's just . . . not a good idea. You know?" I asked, and was met with confused silence on the other end.

"Um. What?" Sophie said after a moment. "What are you talking about?"

"I'll call you back later, okay, um . . . you? And we'll talk?"

"Are you all right?" Sophie asked, sounding skeptical. I looked over at Josh and saw that he was looking at me with a slight furrow in his brow.

"Just fine! I'll call you later, BFF!"

"But—" I heard Sophie say, but I hung up quickly before she had the chance to ask me any more questions, or call me by my name again.

"Hi," I said, turning to Josh, hoping that none of that had seemed overly suspicious to him. "How's it going?"

"Good," he said. He nodded at my phone. "Everything okay?"

"Oh yeah," I said, hoping I sounded breezy and carefree, and not like I was still trying to get my pulse to normalize. "Just my best friend from back home. She's dealing with some drama."

"Ah," he said. He nodded down at the spot on the bench next to me. "Mind if I join you?"

"Not at all," I said, moving over a bit—though not too far—to make room for him.

"So," he said, giving me a smile and taking a sip of his iced tea, "you decided against formalwear?"

I laughed. "Well, the ball gown was at the cleaners, so I went with this ensemble," I said, gesturing down to my not-fancy-at-all cutoffs and tank top.

"I think it works," Josh said appreciatively, taking a sip of his drink.

Before I could respond, or process what he had meant by that, my phone rang, displaying SOPHIE CURTIS—along with my best friend's picture—on the screen. I turned over the phone immediately.

"More friend drama?" Josh asked.

I nodded, switching the ringer to silent and stashing the phone in my bag.

Josh shook his head. "I'm pretty much over that," he said. "I feel like I had more than enough of it last year."

I nodded, and I knew he was probably talking about his ex. Suddenly, I flashed back to the conversation we'd had in the car, in the moonlight. And even though it had been less than twelve hours, I realized that it was really good to see him again.

He glanced down at the shopping bag at my feet. "Don't tell me," he said. "Doing some retail damage?" He groaned. "You and my sister."

"Hallie shops a lot?" I was beginning to get that, from the fact that she'd brought two bathing suit options to the party, not to mention how well put-together she always looked, but figured that confirmation wouldn't hurt. And it was still just a surprise to me, since the Hallie I'd known had been indifferent to shopping and clothes in general.

"Well," Josh said with a shrug, "mostly this last year. My mom's always going on about it. How it's like she's become a different person."

I could certainly identify, but I wasn't about to tell Josh that. "I'll have you know," I said, realizing as I heard the teasing sound in my voice that I was getting dangerously close to flirting territory, "that this is just the bathing suit Hallie lent me. I wanted to return it."

"Oh," Josh said, and the glint in his eye was replaced by something more genuine. "That's really nice of you." He took a long drink of his iced tea. "I'm glad that you two get along," he said after a moment, his eyes on the ground. "Hallie hasn't had . . . the best luck in the past when it comes to friends. I'm glad that she's met you. You seem like a really good person."

"I'm trying to be," I said, my voice barely above a whisper. Was the bad luck Josh was talking about . . . me? Or had Hallie had even *more* bad friends, after I'd left her life? The thought made my stomach clench.

"Do you want to get something to eat tonight?" Josh asked suddenly. "With me?" he added after a moment, and I felt myself smile involuntarily.

"Um," I said. I realized, to my shock, that I'd wanted to say yes. It had been my first instinct. But Hallie had, only an hour before, warned me off dating her brother. Not that I even wanted to, or knew for sure that this was what he had meant—Josh probably just wanted to get dinner as friends. But I was in the Hamptons for Hallie. To make things right with her, not to go out to dinner with her brother. "The thing is . . ."

"Plans?" he asked, raising his eyebrows. "Hanging out in a different pool tonight?"

"No," I said, trying not to laugh. "I don't have any plans, I just . . ." I stopped when I realized I'd maybe insulted him, as well as making myself sound like a loser.

"What?" Josh asked, leaning a little closer.

"Um," I said. I tried to figure out how to start, and when no good ideas came to mind, decided to just jump in. "I saw your sister this morning. And she told me how she didn't want you to get hurt again . . . and how, um, maybe we shouldn't . . ." I felt my face heat up. "Not that I'm saying that you wanted to," I said quickly. "Or that that's what you meant. I mean . . . not. Totally. Which is great. It's just that she, you know, kind of . . ." I stopped speaking when I realized I was no longer using any verbs or nouns, or making any sense.

Josh frowned, which was a reasonable reaction. I barely understood what I'd just said, and I'd been the one to say it. "She shouldn't have said anything to you," he said. He shook his head. "I know she looks out for me, but . . ." His voice trailed off and he looked away.

"Anyway," I said, after a moment of silence had fallen between us. "It's really hot today, huh?"

"Do you want to have dinner with me tonight?" Josh asked, looking right at me.

"But . . ." I said, having to stop myself again from saying yes, despite everything stacked against it. "Hallie—"

"It's just dinner," Josh said. "Dinner between swimming buddies."

I felt myself smile at that, and said what I'd wanted to say, right from the beginning. "Yes," I said. "That sounds great." I hoped Hallie would understand. I'd told Josh her objections, and it was clear we were going as friends, and nothing more. Which was all I wanted, as well. Wasn't it?

"Good," Josh said with a smile. "Want to text me your address? And I'll pick you up at seven?" I nodded, even though I knew I should probably suggest meeting there, as this was verging into date territory. But maybe he was just concerned about his carbon footprint. And plus, it was a Wednesday—not the most romantic night of the week. "I'll see you tonight, Sophie."

I nodded again and tried not to enjoy the view too much as he stood and walked away, turning around once to give me a last fleeting smile.

Once he left, I sat back against the bench. It wasn't a date. We'd made that clear. But even so, it was my first dinner alone with a guy who wasn't Teddy in two years, and I was suddenly feeling really nervous.

I pulled out my phone and saw that I had three texts from Sophie, all seeming to grow in confusion and number of exclamation points. I decided I'd call her back later, from the privacy of my room, where I wouldn't have to worry about people hearing me call her by her name.

I felt like the sooner I got the suit back to Hallie, the better. Then I could try and process what had just happened with Josh, and get ready for what was clearly not a date tonight. I decided I would read Sophie's texts later, and texted Hallie.

Me

3:05 PM

Hi! I have your suit! Happy to bring it anywhere!

I sent this, and then before I could lose my nerve, I texted Josh Bruce's address. I knew it was a little risky—what if he ran into my dad and recognized him? What if Bruce called me Gemma and outed me?—but it certainly seemed better than having him pick me up at the Jitney station, or something. I would just be outside, ready and waiting for him at seven, at the end of the driveway if need be.

I was walking to my car when my phone buzzed with a text from Hallie.

Hallie Bridges
3:08 PM
Thanks so much—you're the best! I'm babysitting
the twins at Quonset Beach right now—would
you be able to bring it over
(aka hang out with me while I babysit ☺)?

I smiled at that, and texted back immediately.

Me
3:09 PM
Sounds great! See you there!

I let out a sigh of relief. I would get Hallie her suit back, and she would be none the wiser that anything had happened to it. And despite me making her potentially lethal cupcakes, she wanted to hang out with me. It might have been just because she was bored, but I would take it. I took a long sip of my iced latte and headed for the car, feeling like things were finally starting to work out.

CHAPTER 13

Quonset Beach in the daytime was every bit as nice as it looked from my bedroom window. I felt embarrassed, as I walked along the hot sand, holding my flip-flops, that I hadn't really ventured out here during the day yet. It was, after all, practically Bruce's backyard. It was low tide, and the beach seemed to stretch on forever. I took a deep breath of the salty sea air, then got down to the business of looking for Hallie and the girls.

As I scanned the sand, I couldn't help hoping that the girls would be occupied with swimming or sandcastle building or something equally absorbing, so that Hallie and I could actually have a chance to really talk, just the two of us.

I'd only been walking for a few minutes when I spotted them, Hallie sitting on the edge of a giant striped beach towel, which was covered in canvas bags and beach paraphernalia—sunblock, hats, beach toys. She was looking out at the water, her expression serious, and didn't seem to notice me, even as I approached and stood near her, shifting my weight from foot to foot.

"Hi," I said after a moment, and Hallie turned, her serious expression vanishing, and smiling wide at me.

"Hey!" she said. "Sit down." She moved over and made room for me next to her on the towel.

"Where are the girls?" I asked, and Hallie pointed ahead to the edge of the water, where they were digging what was actually an impressively large hole. "Wow," I said, looking at the pile of sand next to the hole, which was almost as tall as Olivia—or Isabella. "Are they trying to make a break for it?"

"I know," Hallie said with a laugh. "I was trying to show them the fundamentals of sandcastle construction, but they got really into the idea of a moat, and then just decided to keep digging. So I removed myself from the process."

"Probably wise," I said, and then had a memory so strong that I had to close my eyes against it.

Hallie and I are building sandcastles on the Southampton beach. She's the architect, I'm the manual labor, and it's such a beautiful day that I've decided to put aside devious plans for the afternoon and have just been hanging out with her. Hallie's the planner— she has a designer's eye and precision—and after I've knocked over four turrets by accident, my role is reduced to the person who hauls up pails of wet sand from the beach.

We sit in the sun and work all afternoon, only pausing when we need to join forces and repel the annoying triplets who live at the other end of the beach and are determined to wreck our hard work. We're united, and it feels good.

As the sun starts to set, we sit together on the sand and admire our creation. Well, technically it's Hallie's creation, but she insists

on giving me credit. "You provided the raw materials," she says,
pushing her tangled curls behind one sunburned ear.

"But I never could have come up with this," I say, staring at
her—our—sandcastle. It's huge, with three stories and two turrets,
and something she tells me are called porticos.

"My dad was an architect," she says quietly, and I look over at
her—she almost never mentions her father.

"I think he'd like it," I say, and I mean it. She smiles at me, and
then knocks me with her shoulder before the moment can get too
serious.

"Is that the suit?" Hallie asked, shaking me out of this rev-
erie. She was gesturing to my purse, and I blinked at her, my brain
still taking a minute to update the Hallie I had in my mind—the
knotty-haired tomboy—to the girl sitting on the sand next to
me, her hair long and sleek, designer sunglasses perched on top
of her head.

"Right," I said quickly, springing into action. The suit was, of
course, the whole reason that I was even there with her on the
beach, having this flashback in the first place. Trying to appear
nonchalant, I pulled the bathing suit of my bag. I'd left the Sur la
Plage shopping bag in the car, but kept the tissue paper wrapped
around the bikini, feeling like it added a nice touch. "Here you
go!" I said, handing it to her.

"Wow," she said, taking the tissue-wrapped package from
me, eyebrows raised. "You didn't have to do all this."

"Well, thank you so much for lending it to me," I said, hoping
that I sounded genuine. After all, it wasn't *Hallie's* fault that the
suit rebelled. She hadn't gone in the water all night, so she

probably didn't know about the suit's weird chlorine aversion. "Um," I said, trying for a casual tone, "when I was putting the tissue paper around it, I noticed that there was a tag inside. It said something about how these suits might be best in the ocean or a lake, not a pool . . . just so you know."

She just looked at me for a moment, head tilted slightly to the side, like she was surprised, or trying to figure something out. "Thanks," she said after a small pause. "I'll keep that in mind."

I realized after a second that she probably thought I was confessing to ruining her suit—which, technically, I had done, but which she wasn't going to know about, if I could help it. "But this one's fine," I said hurriedly. "It's as good as new! I just wanted you to know for the future."

"Thanks," she said, still looking at me a little strangely. I held my breath, hoping that I hadn't raised her suspicions.

"Listen—" Hallie started, when her phone rang, loud, from inside her bag. Her ringtone was the song that had been inescapable for weeks, the one about the *summer you'll never forget.* "Sorry," she said as she picked it up, giving me an apologetic smile. "Hi," I heard her say softly, and I turned my head away and pulled out my own phone so I wouldn't be tempted to try and listen in.

I saw that Josh had texted me back a smiley face and a message that he'd see me at seven. I also saw that I had two missed calls from Sophie, and I decided to head back to the house and call her immediately, now that I'd returned the suit.

"So," I said, brushing off my hands and starting to push myself to my feet. "It was great to see you, but—"

Hallie looked up at me, and it was no longer with an easy,

relaxed expression. She held up one finger, the universal signal for *can you hold on a moment?* I nodded, and she returned to her call. "Okay," she said, her voice tight and concerned. "All right. I'll be there as soon as I can." She hung up and just stared down at her phone for a moment.

"Is everything all right?" I asked, even though it would really, really seem that it was not.

"No," she said, looking back to me and shaking her head. "Not really. There's a bit of a crisis brewing. And I really need to get out of here. . . ."

"Of course," I said quickly, pushing myself to my feet and stepping off her towel.

"But I can't really bring the girls. . . ." she said. She looked out to the water, and then turned to me, biting her bottom lip. "Sophie, I'm so sorry to have to ask this, and you can totally say no. But would you be willing to watch them while I take care of this? It would only be for an hour. Two, tops. It'd be doing me a huge favor."

I also glanced to the edge of the water where the twins were, but only for a second, as I'd made my decision the second she asked me. This would be my opportunity to help to balance the ledger of wrongs between us. And she couldn't have asked me for a better favor. While these kids had seemed unimpressed when I'd first met them, I had no doubt I'd win them over. Kids loved me, and this would be a piece of cake. The girls and I would have a great time together, and Hallie would see that I could be trustworthy and responsible. And the very fact that she'd asked me at all seemed like a really huge step in our developing Sophie-and-

Hallie friendship. You wouldn't ask someone to watch your baby-sitting charges unless you thought they were a good person, right?

"Sure," I said, smiling at her. "I'd be happy to help."

Relief washed over Hallie's face. "Oh my gosh, thank you so much. You're saving my life. Girls!" she yelled in the direction of the water, and the twins glanced up from their hole, which now looked even deeper. You could only see the tops of their heads peering out from it. "Come here!" she yelled. The tops of the heads shook in unison, but Hallie yelled, *"Now,"* putting so much authority in her tone that it never would have occurred to me to do anything but what she said. The twins must have felt the same way, because without protesting again, they clambered out of the hole and started to make their way up the beach.

"So is there anything I should know?" I asked. I was used to being primed ahead of time with my charges back in Putnam—personality quirks, allergies, weird phobias, whatever. And it was generally easier to do this when the kids in question were out of earshot, because if they heard you, they'd start to protest loudly that it wasn't true, they did *not* have a fear of mangos.

"Not anything big," Hallie said, gathering up her own things and dropping the bikini into her bag. "Just don't let Isabella have nuts—she's allergic. And don't let Olivia have any sugar. She's not allergic, she'll just go crazy."

"Okay," I said, watching as the girls ran up from the sand, both incredibly dirty. As far as these things went, it actually sounded incredibly simple. I babysat one boy in Putnam who refused to eat anything but orange food, cut into hexagons. I'd started bringing a protractor with me when I sat for him.

"And anyway," Hallie said, and though she smiled at me, I could tell it was a little forced, and I knew she was worried about her other crisis—whatever it was—that she needed to get to, "I won't be long." I nodded, and I couldn't help wondering what it was that was taking her away. Something with her mom? Or her boyfriend, the one who was out of town? I really wanted to know, but didn't feel like I had the right to ask, especially since she'd been purposely vague about what this crisis was.

"What?" one of the twins asked. Now that they were both covered in wet sand they looked even more alike.

"We were digging," the other one said petulantly.

"And it looks great," Hallie said. "But I'm going to have to go away for a little bit, so I'm going to need you to be really, really good for Sophie. Okay?"

The twins turned and looked at me, identical expressions letting me know that they were still not impressed.

"Hi," I said, bending down so I was more at their level and smiling at them. "We're going to have a lot of fun."

The girls looked back to Hallie, skeptical, but if she noticed this, she didn't acknowledge it. "I expect good behavior like we've talked about," she said, looking at them both closely. "And if you do behave, maybe we can get ice cream, okay?" Neither twin responded, but Hallie nodded as though they had. "Good," she said. "I'll see you soon." She leaned over to me and whispered, "Thank you so much." Then she hurried up the beach, her casual walk soon turning to an almost-run.

"So," I said, turning to the girls, both of whom had their arms crossed and were scowling. "I love your moat. You two

want to keep digging? Want me to help? I'm really good at hauling sand."

They looked at each other and seemed to be doing that secret
twin communication that I'd heard about, because even though
neither of them was saying a word, it was like they were having
a silent conversation. And sure enough, after a moment, they
looked back at me and both shook their heads. "No," one of them
said firmly. "We're bored with that."

"Okay," I said, looking between the two of them. "So what do
you want to do now?"

"I'm hungry," one of them said in a voice that was coming
dangerously close to a whine.

"Are you Isabella?" I asked, trying to think of things we could
eat that contained no nuts.

"Yes," both twins said in unison, then dissolved into a fit of
giggles.

"Seriously," I said, trying to inject the same kind of authority
into my voice that Hallie had used, since apparently that was
effective with these two. "Which one of you is Isabella?"

"Me," they both said simultaneously, and started cracking up
again.

I let out a breath, not about to let them know they'd rattled
me. I'd learned early on that babysitting is basically a power struggle, and the second you let a kid know they've gotten to you, you're
sunk. And after all, did I really need to know which was which? I
could just make sure that they both avoided nuts. And sugar.

"I'm hungry too," the other twin said, and her sister nodded
and started squirming in a way I recognized all too well.

"I have to go to the bathroom," she whispered to me. I looked up the beach. There were dunes, fences, and beach grass, but it didn't look like there were any public facilities—or, for that matter, any place to get something to eat.

I looked around the beach as though it might hold the answers for me. Which, when my eyes fell on Bruce's house, I realized it kind of did.

"Okay," I said, clapping my hands together. "Gather up your things and follow me."

⁂

I'd texted Hallie as we walked, giving out Bruce's address for the second time that day. It made me even more nervous giving it to Hallie than to Josh. Josh, after all, had never met Bruce. But it was possible that Hallie might remember him. He'd mostly been in Iceland that summer, dealing with unexpected elk stampedes and trying to hold his movie together. But he had been around occasionally, passing through his own house sometimes when Hallie was over—though I couldn't remember now if they'd ever officially met. Even though I hadn't wanted to, I knew I had to tell Hallie where we were going. I didn't want her to come back to the beach and not know where we'd disappeared to.

But I didn't think it would be necessary for her to stop by the house at all. I had a feeling we'd be in and out of Bruce's and back to the beach in a matter of minutes, and I'd just send Hallie a new text, telling her to disregard the last one.

"Okay," I said, turning to the girls as we crossed the deck and

⊰ 172 ⊱

stood outside the glass doors that led to Bruce's pristine house. Though some of the sand had fallen off them during the walk to the house, they still didn't look like people I would have, under normal circumstances, invited inside my own house, let alone someone else's. "I need you to be *very careful* with things, okay?"

The girls just stared at me, and I decided to take this as a yes. I pulled open the door, and the twins followed me inside. "Rosie?" I called into the dark, cool house. While babysitting twins was nothing I couldn't handle, it always helped to know there was backup around. And I had no doubt that Rosie would be able to lend a hand in dealing with small children—after all, she'd spent the last few years babysitting Bruce.

But only silence greeted me, and even though Rosie wasn't there, it probably meant that my dad and Bruce were out as well, which might be a good thing at the moment, considering how messy these two were.

"All right," I said. I turned my back on the twins and closed the door, so that neither could fall into the pool. As I made sure the door was latched, I decided on the course of action until Hallie returned—a nut-and-sugar-free snack, and then an immediate return to the beach. "So here's the plan," I said turning back to them. But I was talking to the air. Both girls had disappeared, leaving only sandy footprints across the carpet.

CHAPTER 14

"Okay!" I said an hour later, trying as hard as I could not to sound as frustrated as I was. "How about we play a game?" The twins just looked at each other, then back at me, their identical blasé expressions still in place. It had been a very long hour, and one that was causing me to doubt my babysitting prowess. When they had first disappeared, I'd tracked them down in the kitchen, all too close to the knives, attempting to get something down from the highest shelf—and getting sand everywhere in the process.

I had immediately moved us to the TV room, where they had flopped onto the couch and basically refused to move or engage in anything. They didn't want to read a book or go back to the beach or watch TV. All they wanted to do was complain about how bored they were. And it was getting annoying. I was also checking my phone with increasing frequency, hoping that Hallie would text me and let me know she was on her way. I was all too aware that Josh was going to be picking me up in a few hours for what was clearly not a date, and I needed to get ready for it.

"No." One twin—I still hadn't been able to get them to tell me who was who—sighed.

"Nooooooo," the other whined. "Games are boring."

You're boring, I wanted to snap back at her. But I restrained myself. I hadn't yet sunk to insulting kindergarteners, and saw no reason to start now. "All right," I said, determined to be cheerful if it killed me. "How about—" My phone beeped with a text, and I pulled it out, happy to be spared from trying to convince them how fun it would be to vacuum the kitchen.

Hallie Bridges
4:45 PM
Hi! Things are taking a little longer to sort out than I thought.
Might be another hour, so sorry! ☹
Tell the twins I said to behave!

"Who texted you?" one of the girls asked, sitting up slightly and looking the tiniest bit interested for the first time all afternoon. "Your boyfriend?"

"No," I said, looking over at her, a little surprised by the question. "I don't have a boyfriend."

"Why not?" the other one asked.

"Because," I said, wondering why I was defending my love life—or lack thereof—to someone who still used a lunchbox. "It's a complicated situation. And . . . well, the thing is . . ."

"*Hallie* has a boyfriend," the other one said, a little pityingly. "And he's—"

"So if it wasn't your boyfriend, because you don't have one, who was it?" the first twin asked, leaning a little closer to try and see my phone's screen.

"It was from Hallie," I said. "She said she's going to be another hour, and that you both should behave." The twins just looked at each other for a long moment, but neither started freaking out about the fact they were under my care for another sixty minutes, which I took as a good sign.

"Listen," I said, leaning forward a bit. "I have a dinner to go to tonight. It's not a date," I added quickly, and they just nodded, clearly not expecting anything better from me. "So maybe you two want to help me get ready?"

"Yeah," one of the twins said, after a tiny pause, with a smile. "We could do that."

"I'm . . . not sure," I said, looking at myself in the mirror, a little worried. It was twenty minutes later, and I was regretting ever making the suggestion that they "help" me. I had thought it would be a fun project—when I was their age, I'd loved to play with my babysitters' makeup. But it was becoming very clear to me that Hamptons children were different. The twins rampaged through my closet, scoffed at most of my clothes, and then finally picked out an outfit for me that was maybe the most hideous thing I'd ever put on—my running shoes, which they'd excavated from the back of my closet, paired with a lime-green striped top and plaid shorts. I'd told the twins I loved the look, not wanting to insult them or hamper their creative spirit. But now that we were in the bathroom, and they had taken over my makeup and hair, I was feeling less generous.

I was wearing bright blue eyeshadow on one eye, green on the other, dark red lipstick, and bubblegum-pink blush. The ends of my hair were singed from when they'd gotten to the flatiron before I could get it away from them. I looked terrible, and it was getting harder to keep pretending I liked what they were doing.

"I'm hungry," one of the twins said, dropping the blush brush with a clatter onto the bathroom counter.

"Me too," the other one said. They exchanged a look and then dashed from the bathroom.

"Hey," I called, standing up to hustle after them—and promptly falling over and hitting the tile floor, hard. "Ow," I mumbled, rubbing my shoulder. I looked down and saw that probably when my eyes were closed to get mismatched eyeshadow applied, they had tied my shoelaces together. "Girls," I yelled after them as I tried to undo the knots, then gave up and just pulled my feet out of the shoes and ran downstairs.

I finally found them in the kitchen, both holding giant candy bars. "Where did you get those?" I asked, then looked behind them to a cabinet that was open. It looked like it contained what must have been Bruce's reserve of noncaveman food—meaning it was almost all sugar. "Oh, no," I muttered, thinking about what Hallie had told me about Olivia going crazy. Both twins grinned at me and then bolted from the kitchen.

⚬⚬⚬⚬⚬

"**S**ophie?"

"No." It was another hour later, and I was sitting on one of the kitchen stools, holding one of the twins—I still hadn't been able to get them to give up their true identities—by the makeshift leash I'd fashioned out of something called "trussing twine" that I'd found in one of the drawers. My back was to the cabinet that held Bruce's secret stash. I didn't know what Hallie was talking about with regard to Olivia, since *both* girls seemed to go crazy with the sugar rush.

They had been absolutely bouncing off the walls after they inhaled the candy bars, and I tried my best to corral them, running from room to room, catching priceless art before it crashed to the floor. I found myself waiting—and then hoping—for the inevitable crash. But maybe, like a watched pot that never boils, a much-needed sugar crash never arrives, since both of them had a huge excess of energy, all of which they seemed to want to channel into destruction.

They'd left grubby handprints all over the white walls, had almost flooded the laundry room when they'd started the washer, and had emptied the perfectly sorted and alphabetized spice containers all over the kitchen.

I had finally managed to catch one of the twins as she made a desperate grab for more Pixy Stix, and was now basically holding her as bait, since I knew her sister would come and look for her before too long, probably so that they could plot the downfall of their next victim or small industrialized nation. The girls, I'd found, were ruthless, creative, and indefatigable, like Batman villains, only smaller. My eyes were fixed on the kitchen clock and on my phone, as I watched the time when Josh was supposed to pick me up getting ever closer, and I still had no response from Hallie.

"But, *Sophie*—" the twin whined.

"Nope," I said. I looked down at my phone again, hoping that there would be a text from Hallie, one telling me that she was on her way, which would mean I would have plenty of time to take a shower, remove the horrible makeup, and put on something else—pretty much anything else would be a marked improvement. Getting cleaned up was extra-essential now, because in addition to the bad hair, makeup, and clothes, I was now covered in sand, suds, and spices, after trying to reduce the twins' messes as much as I could. There was a clump of tarragon that I hadn't been able to get totally out of my hair, it was making me sneeze intermittently.

The twin in front of me let out a long, put-upon sigh, the kind of which I was pretty sure I hadn't started giving to my elders until I was at least thirteen. "Well," she said, huffy, "can I at least play a game on your phone?"

I considered for a moment—since she would be right in front of me, I would be able to intervene if the phone was in danger of being broken. And, frankly, playing a game on my phone sounded just like the kind of quiet, occupying activity that I was very much in favor of at the moment. "Sure," I said, not letting go of the string as I reached for my purse and unlocked my home screen. I handed it to her, making eye contact the way Hallie had. "Be careful with it."

She gave me a nod, and I realized as I watched her zip through my pages of apps, that I probably didn't need to be worried about her damaging my phone. She had clearly been using one since birth and was already a pro. A few seconds later, I heard the familiar sound track to Grand Theft Flamingo, the game that involved trying to steal various exotic animals and sell them on the black market. After a few moments of no mayhem and no escape attempts, I could feel myself start to breathe a little easier. I made a mental note to be sure to tell Hallie that however much she was being paid, it should be doubled.

I had just started to relax when two things happened at the same time. The second twin poked her head into the kitchen, and my phone beeped with a text.

"Text message!" the twin holding the phone squealed as I made a judgment call and tried to move closer to her sister, so I could maybe keep both of them in the same room for more than a few seconds. "Wait, who's Gem-ma?" She pronounced it wrong, with a hard *G*, but nonetheless, it was my name. I could feel the blood drain from my face, and I realized whoever texted me must have included my name in the text.

"Nobody," I said quickly, turning away from the doorway and reaching for my phone.

"And it says the text is from Sophie," the girl continued, her brow furrowed.

"No, it didn't," I said quickly, hoping I didn't sound as panicked as I felt.

"Yes, it did," she replied, jutting her chin out at me.

"You don't know how to read," I reminded her. "That's who it's *to*. Me. Sophie. *From* my friend Gemma."

"*No*," the twin said stubbornly, but I grabbed the phone away from her before she could prove her (correct) point.

But as I retrieved the phone, I let go of the string, and the twin made a break for it. I cursed under my breath and ran after her, stopping short when I heard a loud crash and the sound of glass shattering, followed by silence. I put the phone in my pocket and ran toward where the crash had come from, my heart sinking as I realized it was Bruce's brag room.

I stepped into the silent room to see the girls staring up at me with identical guilty expressions. There was sand tracked all over the room and handprints on the glass cases. But most distressing was Bruce's Spotlight award, lying on the ground, the glass globe broken cleanly off.

"What . . ." I managed. I could feel my panic start to rise, in addition to my frustration. What was *wrong* with these kids? Were they child sociopaths, like I'd seen on *Child Sociopaths*?

"Sorry," they both muttered, and they actually did look sorry, and ashamed of themselves. I took a breath, preparing to give them a lecture anyway, when my phone beeped. I realized that it was probably Sophie again, and I chastised myself for being a terrible best friend. I'd never called her back that morning like I promised, or responded to her texts. But when I looked at the screen, I saw the message was from Hallie, telling me that she was on her way and would be there in a few minutes.

I let out a sigh of relief that the people down on Quonset Beach could probably hear. "This is what's going to happen," I said in a tone that didn't allow for any other suggestions. "You're going to leave this room very carefully and not step on the broken glass. And then we're going to get your things and wait outside. *Now.*" Maybe they heard in my tone that I was done messing around, because they complied and didn't even protest or try to steal any more candy.

I was able to mask the fact that Bruce's award had broken by resting the globe on top of the base. It balanced, and looked fine from a distance, but it wasn't a permanent fix, by any means. I knew I'd have to either tell Bruce his pride and joy had been broken on my watch, or figure out a way to repair it without him finding out, but I figured I would just sort that out later, when hopefully some brilliant solution would come to mind.

After I'd hidden the damage done to Bruce's award, it took a few minutes to gather up the twins' things while making sure neither of them went rogue again, but we were packed up and waiting out in front of the house before Hallie arrived, giving me a moment to try and do some damage control.

"So," I said as casually as I could muster, "I don't really want to tell Hallie about how you two misbehaved." Since Hallie saw these girls every day, they obviously didn't act like this around her. And I didn't want to make it seem like I was totally incompetent around small children, or make her feel bad that she'd asked me to do something that had turned out horribly.

"She won't care," one of them said immediately, and with great assurance.

"Bell!" the other said, glaring at her. She was clearly trying to keep her sister from getting into any more trouble by lying. And I now realized they'd given me the clues as to which was which.

"I think she will care," I said, and both twins immediately looked down at the gravel of the driveway, avoiding eye contact. "But," I said, dangling the word like a promise, "maybe I won't tell her."

The twin I now knew was Olivia, the one who'd been with me in the kitchen, looked up at me with suspicion. "Really?"

"Oh, sure," I said in what I hoped was a blithe manner. "And you don't have to mention that thing with the text I got." Olivia frowned and I added quickly, "I don't want Hallie to know I was texting."

"But you weren't," Olivia said. "You just *got* a text. From Sophie—"

"Look, there's Hallie!" I said loudly, cutting her off. Hallie's Jeep pulled into the driveway, and she killed the engine and hurried toward us.

"I'm sorry that took so long," she said when she reached us. She stopped and did a double take at my appearance, reconfirming what I already knew—I really, really had to change before Josh picked me up.

"It was fine," I lied. "Is everything okay?"

"I think it will be," she said. "I can't thank you enough. Did they behave for you?"

"Yep!" I said, breaking eye contact with her and brushing some stray rosemary off my hands. Sure enough, when I looked back up at her, Hallie's expression was skeptical. After a moment, though, this disappeared, and she smiled at me. I realized that she probably knew just what a nightmare these girls could be, but hadn't wanted to tell me before I agreed to sit for them. And it seemed like we were both just going to pretend that they had been angels.

"Go get in the car," Hallie said, nudging the twins in the direction of her Jeep. "I'll be there in a moment." Proving that they were willing to listen to Hallie and not me, the twins turned and ran to the Jeep without a word of protest. "Thanks again," she said to me. "I seriously owe you."

"You really don't," I said unthinkingly. I only realized what I'd said when I noticed Hallie still staring at me, brow slightly furrowed. "Because you lent me the bathing suit," I said, thinking fast. "So we're even now."

"Even so," she said. "If there's ever anything . . ."

A strange wheezing sound came from down the driveway, and I looked up to see, to my horror, Bruce staggering up it, wearing his new-looking workout gear, breathing hard, clearly having decided today would be a good day to go actually running, and not just for bagels.

"We're fine!" I said brightly, trying to usher Hallie in the direction of her car, so that I could prevent the two of them from interacting. Worlds were potentially about to collide, and I didn't like the look of it at all. Everything could be ruined, right here in the driveway. "Totally even. I'll see you around, okay?"

But Hallie was still looking at Bruce, alarmed, like maybe he was some very out-of-shape Hamptons burglar. "Do you know him?"

"Sure," I said, as I tried to herd her toward the Jeep. "Family friend. This is his house, actually. We're staying with him for the summer."

"Oh," said Hallie, and despite my best efforts to get her to leave before I would be forced to make the introductions, she was still looking at Bruce, frowning, like she was trying to place him.

"So I'll talk to you soon!" I said, stepping between Bruce and Hallie so she wouldn't be able to get a good look at him and possibly remember where she knew him from. "Bye now!"

"Bye," Hallie said. She finally looked away from Bruce, then gave me a quick hug, not seeming to care that she might get marjoram all over her shirt. "Thanks again," she said. "You're the best."

"No worries," I said, trying to sound light, speaking around the unexpected lump that had just formed in my throat.

Hallie got into her car, waving at me as she headed down the driveway. Bruce reached me as she pulled out of sight, bending double, resting his hands on his knees as he tried to catch his breath.

"Hey," I said, relieved beyond measure that I'd been able to avoid an encounter between the two of them.

"Hegggggeh," Bruce wheezed.

"So you went running without me?" I asked, and Bruce straightened up, wiping away beads of sweat from his very red face.

"It was Rosie," he muttered, in between large gasps of air. "Apparently she bet your father that I couldn't make it from downtown to the house without calling for help."

"Well, looks like you won!" I tried to sound as enthusiastic as possible, since it actually looked like Bruce might have won a visit to his cardiologist.

"Yeah," he muttered, walking past me, limping slightly. He turned back, hand on the doorknob. "Did I recognize the girl who was here before?"

"I don't know," I said, grateful that Bruce had phrased the question this way, since I had no idea if he recognized Hallie or not. I didn't think I needed to tell him that there was a very good reason he might have recognized her. Bruce pulled open the door, and I suddenly had a vision of him seeing the house in the state the twins had left it in. I said, all in a rush, "So I was babysitting earlier, and the house might be a little . . . disarrayed. But I'll clean everything up. I promise." I thought about adding that there was no reason to look at his award, that all was fine with it, but had a feeling that might fuel his suspicions, and so just gave him my best trustworthy smile.

Bruce just stared at me for a moment, and it looked like he was contemplating getting upset, but then he must have decided he valued his breath more for respiring than lecturing, and he nodded and limped inside.

I waited just a moment, and when I didn't hear any screaming about what a disaster the house had become, I knew it was safe to follow. I had just pulled the door open when I heard the sound of tires on gravel.

I pulled out my phone to check the time, my heart sinking when I realized that it was a minute before seven. And, sure enough, when I turned around, there was Josh, stepping out of a truck, carrying a small bouquet of flowers, coming to pick me up.

CHAPTER 15

I looked down at myself in horror and ran my hands through my hair in an attempt to get it to look less terrible. But even as I did this, I knew it would be no use. And I couldn't just flee, at this point. Josh had seen me, and I would look utterly bizarre—even more than I already did—if I turned and ran into the house.

"Hi," he said, coming closer, his expression becoming more confused as his eyes flicked down to my outfit and then back up to my face. "You look . . . um . . ."

"Hey, Josh," I said, giving him a big smile, deciding at the last minute to try and brazen my way through this. Even as it was happening, I was already regretting the decision, but didn't think I could turn back now. "What's up?"

"Um . . ." he said. He looked at my outfit again, and the corners of his mouth twitched violently. "Not a whole lot," he said, sounding like he was trying not to laugh. "What's . . . up with you?"

"Oh, you know," I said with a shrug, trying not to notice that as I did so, some cinnamon fell off my elbow. "Nothing much."

"So." He raised an eyebrow at me and I realized that we were in somewhat of a standoff, both of us pretending I was wearing something normal, each waiting for the other one to crack and ask—or explain—what was going on. "Are you ready to go?" I could hear the challenge in his voice, and I glanced down at myself and felt my stomach plunge. I could pretend nothing was wrong in the driveway, but actually go out like this? To a restaurant, with other people?

"Sure," I said, though I could hear my voice sounded unsteady. I looked down and saw that I was still in socks, since the twins had tied my shoelaces together. "Let me um . . . just . . . get my shoes." I turned toward the door and caught my reflection in the silver DAVIDSON MANOR plaque that adorned the whole middle third of it. Reflected back at me was proof of just how ridiculous I looked. I saw my shoulders slump.

"Sorry," I said, turning back to him, somehow feeling even more embarrassed now that I hadn't admitted what was wrong right from the beginning. "I can't do this."

Josh laughed, shaking his head. "I was wondering when you were going to break."

"I was babysitting for the twins as a favor to Hallie," I explained, wondering why I hadn't just led with this. "And they decided they were going to help me get ready. And then they kind of destroyed the house. . . ."

"I've met those girls," Josh said. "I believe it."

"Anyway," I said, "I'm really sorry. I planned on being ready, and on . . . not looking like this."

"Want to change or something?" he offered. "I can wait."

It was incredibly appealing—the idea that maybe the evening could still be salvaged, that maybe the twins' makeover and house destruction hadn't totally derailed the night. But then I thought about the house, and what a mess it was, and how much cleaning I had ahead of me, and knew that even if we did still get dinner, half my brain would be on the state of the kitchen and making sure I got home before Rosie saw it.

"Could we do it another night instead?" I asked. "I feel so bad about this. It'll be my treat."

"Well, I don't know if I can agree to that," Josh said with a smile. "But how about Friday?"

"Perfect," I said immediately, realizing only after I'd said it that getting dinner on Friday was veering dangerously close to date territory. And maybe because the focus was off my own out-fit, I noticed for the first time that he was dressed up, wearing khakis and a polo shirt, his short hair carefully combed. He looked even cuter than he normally did, maybe because I could see the effort behind it, the comb tracks still visible in his hair. I thought about how, until the twins derailed me, I had also wanted to put a lot of effort into getting ready. And a moment later, I wondered what this meant, since tonight was supposed to have been just a dinner between friends.

"Friday," he said with a nod. "I'm going to hold you to that."

I raised my hand. "No last-minute babysitting," I said, relieved that he was being so great about this. "I promise."

He smiled, then turned to go, but stopped after a few steps and walked back to me, holding out the small bouquet of flowers. "For you," he said.

I took a step closer and saw how lovely they were. It was a mixed bouquet, all bright summer flowers, oranges and yellows and purples. As I reached out to take them, it hit me that Teddy had never given me flowers. He'd told me once he was against the commodification of nature. But until my hand closed around the stems of this bouquet, I hadn't known how nice it would be to get them.

I expected Josh to let go right away, and was surprised when he didn't. I looked up at him, and realized how close he was, and how our hands were just a few inches away from touching. I noticed how good he smelled, like light, woodsy cologne and spearmint gum. My heart started pounding harder. We were close enough to kiss.

The thought was so startling that I stepped backward involuntarily, taking the flowers with me. After all, I hadn't kissed anyone besides Teddy in two years, and only Ford (and then only one time) before that. I knew that it was way too soon for me to be thinking about kissing someone new.

Also, what if I'd forgotten how to do it?

"Thank you," I said, looking down into the flowers and hoping he couldn't tell that I'd just been thinking about kissing him. "They're beautiful."

"They reminded me of you," Josh said, giving me a slightly embarrassed smile. He took a step back toward his truck. "I'll see you soon," he said.

"Soon," I echoed, smiling at him, hearing for the first time how the word sounded like a promise.

Josh pulled out of the driveway, honking once as he left. I

watched until his taillights faded from view, then headed back to the house, feeling like the day had already contained far too much drama considering that it wasn't even dark yet. I stepped inside and saw Bruce through the windows, pacing around the pool and yelling into his headset while some underling in Los Angeles undoubtedly cowered on the other end.

I took the fact that he was otherwise occupied as a good sign and threw myself into cleaning the kitchen. When it was more or less in order—even though the spices were significantly depleted—I tackled the laundry room, and then went from room to room with Windex and a roll of paper towels, trying to get all the handprints I could. By the time I finished, I was utterly spent and collapsed on the couch as Bruce came inside and walked past me, still talking on his Bluetooth. He gave me a nod as he continued back to his domain, which was when I felt my stomach plunge.

His award. I held my breath, only letting it out when Bruce went into his study and not into his brag room. I knew I could only get away with hiding the evidence for so long—Bruce was fond of showing the award to almost everyone who came by, which included encouraging them to hold it.

I pulled out my phone, knowing there was only one person to call. But would he think it was weird that I was talking to him again? I hesitated for only a moment before scrolling through my contacts and finding his name. The thought never would have crossed my mind if I'd still been with Teddy. And the fact was, Ford was pretty much the only one who could help me. He was not only one of the smartest people I knew, but also one of the most devious, and he knew how to handle his father. I let out a breath and made the call.

"Twice in one day," Ford said in lieu of hello, picking up on the second ring. "Do you need something else anagrammed?"

"No," I said, feeling myself smile. "Just your advice. There's a . . . bit of a situation here." I took a breath and told him about the Spotlight award and my temporary fix that wasn't going to hold up under any close inspection.

When I'd finished, Ford let out a low whistle. "It's too bad this didn't happen in L.A.," he said. "I would always blame an earthquake. Got me out of a lot of jams."

I somehow had a feeling that even Bruce wasn't going to buy the excuse that an earthquake had hit the Hamptons, and even then, just his house, and then only one portion of it. "Well," I said, "barring some apocalyptic weather, I'm not sure an earthquake is going to show up here anytime soon."

"Can you get it out of there without Bruce noticing?" Ford asked, his tone now all business. "Send it to me. I know a guy who knows a guy."

"Okay," I said, beyond relieved that someone had a plan other than just balancing the broken part on the base and hoping for the best. "But what should I tell him when he notices it's gone?"

"Tell him you wanted to get it polished," Ford said immediately. It was one of the reasons that Ford got away with the things he got away with—he was great at coming up with excuses on the spot. "To thank him for his hospitality. He'll totally buy it."

I could feel relief flooding through me. "Thank you," I said.

"Don't you mean *mahalo*?" Ford asked, and I could hear that he was smiling. "The one time you could use that word correctly, and you choose not to?"

"Just keeping you on your toes," I said. "But I really, really appreciate it."

"It's no big thing," he said. "And I talked to Gwyn; it looks like we'll be there around the Fourth. So I'll be able to bring the award back in person."

"That would be awesome," I said, before I did the math and realized that the Fourth was still two weeks away. I crossed my fingers that Bruce wouldn't get too suspicious before then.

Ford told me where to send the award, and we were just starting to discuss his dad's latest movie and how abysmal the script was when another call beeped in. "Gotta take this, Gem," he said. "But call if you need to, okay? Anytime."

"Sure," I said. "*Aloha.*" We hung up, and I was fully prepared to head upstairs and take longest shower of my life and then collapse, when I realized I'd left the car down at the beach parking lot.

Luckily, it was only a few minutes' walk from the house, or I really might have left it there for the time being. I was pretty sure it wasn't going to get towed, since I had a feeling it would be too massive for most tow trucks to handle. I got there just before the parking gates were being locked for the evening, and drove back to Bruce's feeling like I'd dodged a bullet, that at least I'd gotten one break this afternoon. As I grabbed my purse from the seat, I saw the Sur la Plage bag in the first row of backseats, and remembered that I still had to tell my dad about the fact I'd spent a huge amount of money on a bikini that I then gave away.

I figured that I might as well have the documentation ready to show him whenever he got home, and reached for the receipt in the bottom of the bag.

But it wasn't there, and it also didn't appear when I shook out my whole purse, and then went through every piece of paper in my wallet.

I remembered the saleslady placing the receipt in the bag, with the bikini. I no longer had the receipt, and Hallie had the bikini. Which meant it must have gotten in with the bathing suit, tucked in with the tissue paper that I hadn't removed. The receipt that had my full name on it.

Which meant . . .

I closed my eyes and sat back against the seat, but this didn't stop reality from intruding. I had just lost everything.

I had accidentally told Hallie exactly who I really was.

CHAPTER 16

Me

8:09 PM

Hey Hallie!

Just had a question for you.

No big deal. Everything's fine. Just text me
whenever you get a chance, okay?

Me

9:00 AM

Hey Hallie! Sophie again.

Just give me a call or text me if you
get a sec, okay? I have a question..

Me

3:12 PM

Hi Hallie! Just checking in again.

Call me if you get this?

I stared down at my phone, feeling myself getting more and more nervous. The night before, as soon as I'd realized that I'd left the receipt with the bathing suit, I had texted Hallie. I had been hoping to maybe get to the suit before she noticed the receipt was there—I hadn't worked out what I would say, exactly, but figured I'd sort it out in the moment. But I hadn't heard from Hallie. Not that night, and not all day today. This didn't seem like her, to ignore my texts and two calls, which had gone right to voice mail. And the more I looked at my phone, which was utterly silent, the more I was getting the distinct feeling that I'd blown this.

Hallie had found the receipt—of course she had. I would probably never hear from her again. And worse, what if she thought I was doing this—pretending to be someone else, then leaving the receipt there deliberately—in order to hurt her again?

I stared out at the pool in front of me. I was sitting on one of Bruce's lounge chairs, my phone, fully charged, resting next to me. I attempted to think of something—anything—else, but all I could see was Hallie's face falling when she unwrapped the tissue paper and realized that I had hurt her, yet again.

I pushed myself to my feet and started to pace past the empty pool house and around the pool like I'd seen Bruce doing countless times. But instead of trying to convince studio executives that the entire test screening audience hating the movie was a *positive* thing, I was trying to figure out how I'd managed to do the one thing I'd intended to avoid, the one thing I'd been trying to fix. It hit me that if I'd just told Hallie who I was from the outset, this would have been avoided. She would have been mad, and rightfully so, but she wouldn't have made a new friend who then turned out to betray her.

I stopped when I realized that I needed to leave. It would just be kinder to Hallie if she wasn't running into me all the time. I'd go tonight, and stay with Sophie until I could talk to my mother and figure out the plan to get to Scotland. I figured it probably wouldn't be so bad. They had bagpipes there. I didn't *totally* hate bagpipes.

All at once, I thought about Josh. I'd have to text him and tell him I couldn't have dinner with him, not to mention the fact that I probably wouldn't ever see him again. This hit me harder than I'd been expecting, and I realized just how disappointed I was.

As I turned and headed toward the house, I tried to tell myself that it didn't matter. I was in a mourning period anyway, and so what if we hadn't been able to have dinner together. It wasn't a big deal. The bigger deal was Hallie, and how I'd managed to wreck what I'd come here to fix.

I had just pulled the door open when my phone rang.

I hurried back over to it, and felt my heart start to pound when I saw it was Hallie calling. I took a breath and answered the phone, bracing myself for the worst. "Hello?"

"Sophie?" It was Hallie, sounding slightly out of breath, but like her normal cheerful self. "Hi! I'm so sorry, I was out of town with my mom and left my phone behind. I just got all your messages and texts. Is everything all right?"

I felt relief flood through me. It was all okay. She wasn't mad at me. She didn't know who I really was. "Fine," I said, and I could hear the relief in my voice. I sat down on the lounge chair on legs that felt wobbly. "Yeah, I was just . . ." It suddenly occurred to me that just because she hadn't found the receipt yet didn't mean that she wasn't *going* to. I might not be out of the woods just yet. "I was just wondering," I went on, more cautiously, "if everything went okay with the bathing suit?"

"You know, I haven't even unwrapped it," Hallie said, and I let out a long sigh of relief, holding the phone away from me so she wouldn't hear. "After the crisis the other day, it kind of got lost in the shuffle. Why?"

"Oh, no reason," I said, hoping I sounded calm and disinterested. "Just wanted to . . . make sure everything was okay with it. That's all."

"Oh," Hallie said, and I could hear that she was still a bit confused, probably wondering why I'd texted and called multiple times about this. I just crossed my fingers that she would let it go. "Well, as far as I know. I could check if you want—"

"*No!*" I yelled this without meaning to, then cleared my throat and lowered my volume. "I mean, no need. I'm sure it's fine."

"Okay," Hallie said, sounding more confused than ever. "Well, I have to get unpacked, but maybe we could get coffee or something soon?"

"I would love that," I said, meaning it, but also hoping that I could spin this into somehow getting to the package before Hallie opened it.

"Great," she said, and I could practically hear that she was smiling. I felt myself smiling back while still acutely aware of how close I had just come to wrecking this. "Talk to you soon!"

We said good-bye and hung up, and I leaned back against the lounge chair and looked out at the water. I was incredibly relieved that things hadn't been ruined with Hallie. But I was also—maybe more so than I had admitted to myself until now—glad I wouldn't have to say good-bye to Josh. Not to mention incredibly happy not to have to spend the summer surrounded by fish and bagpipes and kilts.

With this comforting thought, I headed inside, to see if there was any chocolate left in Bruce's secret stash.

◦◦◦◦◦◦

"I hope you like this place!" Josh said as we were led across the patio to a prime table, one with perfect views of the water and of the pink-and-orange sunset that was just beginning.

I gave him an enthusiastic smile back, but I couldn't help but feel a little thrown. It was Friday night, and we were at the Crabby Lobster, which apparently had stayed in business for the last five years. It was the place that my dad had brought me for dinner with the Bridges right after I'd arrived in the Hamptons. It was, in fact, the only place Josh and I had ever had a meal together, since he'd been along with his mother and sister that night. It didn't look like the décor had changed much, if at all; it still had a beach-shack charm to it. The tables outside were wooden, with red-painted benches, like picnic tables, and nautical bric-a-brac decorated the restaurant inside. As we took our seats across from each other and the hostess handed us our menus and hustled away, I found myself looking closely at Josh. Why had he picked it? Did he have any recollection of the previous time we'd eaten here?

"So you've been here before?" I asked in what I hoped was a casual tone.

"It came highly recommended," he said, looking slightly worried, like I was questioning his restaurant taste. "I've heard it's really good."

I nodded as I looked down at my menu, which seemed to feature mostly seafood in different fried, steamed, and breaded forms. So Josh didn't remember. It probably wasn't so strange that he couldn't recall coming here, once, five years ago. I remembered it because it was my introduction to Karen and Hallie, and because of everything that came later. But if that hadn't been the case, I probably wouldn't have remembered either. I certainly couldn't name every single restaurant I went to when I was eleven.

"Great," I said with another smile.

"I mean, Hallie's here all the time," he continued, and I saw that he still looked worried. "So she must really love it."

At the mention of his sister's name, my hands tightened around the menu. "Oh," I said. I looked down at it, noting with surprise just how many forms of chowder one could order, then, trying to sound breezy, added, "Did she say anything about me?"

Hallie and I had been exchanging texts, trying to make a plan to get coffee, and so it seemed like everything was fine between us—that she still hadn't found the receipt—but I was still waiting for the other shoe to drop. When Josh had come to pick me up—I'd been waiting outside, early, dressed and ready to go, to try and make up for the lack of all these things the last time— I'd searched his face for clues that his sister had said something about me, about who I really was. But I hadn't been able to see anything amiss. And if she had said anything, I doubted he'd be sitting across from me, looking nervous that I wouldn't like the restaurant that he picked. I looked up at him, but only saw a slightly baffled expression on his face.

"About you?" he echoed. "Like what?"

"Just . . . anything," I said. He still looked confused, and I let out a breath, feeling my heart start to slow. It seemed that I was still in the clear.

Josh shook his head. "No. Just that she was really grateful for the help when you stepped in as a babysitter the other day. She said to tell you hi."

I nodded, and felt myself smile, relaxing once again. I hadn't yet confessed to my dad about the suit I'd charged on his card, but I'd told myself that it was because he, Rosie, and Bruce had all headed into Manhattan for the weekend to take meetings with the New York studio executives. I had tried to pretend that I didn't want to stress him out before some important meetings, but deep down, I knew I was just avoiding having to confess. Also, on the day of his departure, I really didn't want him to think of me as irresponsible. I'd had to argue for twenty straight minutes to convince him that I didn't need a babysitter to stay with me while they were gone.

I glanced back up at Josh and caught his eye. He gave me a quick smile, and then we both looked away. A slightly uncomfortable pause followed, and we both took long sips of our water in sync. It was what I'd been worried about since he had come to pick me up earlier in the week wearing a nice shirt and carrying flowers—that maybe this was more than a dinner between friends.

And the fact that I'd wanted to spend more time getting ready—and then had spent at least two hours primping before he picked me up—was proof that this feeling wasn't just limited to Josh.

But I was in the Hamptons for Hallie. She had pretty much told me that she didn't want me dating her brother, and I wouldn't. I would just keep things platonic and steer the conversation into dull, unromantic waters. And maybe Josh and I would be friends. The only other guy friends I had were Ford, and I didn't think he counted, since I'd kissed him, and Reginald the vegan, who had really been Teddy's friend, and not mine.

"So," I said, after casting about for subjects that would make it clear we weren't going to stray out of friend territory, my eyes finally landing on the menu. "Fish. They're crazy, right?"

Josh raised his eyebrows. "Uh," he said. "I guess."

"Did you know that salmon can live in both fresh and salt water?" I asked, glad that all the fish facts I'd picked up over the years from Walter were finally useful for something. "Also, the longest migration on record for a salmon is twenty-four hundred miles."

"That is a . . . fact to know," Josh said, looking maybe a little concerned. "Are you, uh . . . into salmon?"

I couldn't help but laugh at his expression. "No," I said. "But my stepfather is."

Josh frowned, and I had a feeling he was going to ask for an explanation, but before I could tell the story of Walter and his ridiculous job—he called fishing "the world's *true* oldest profession," despite the fact my mom was always begging him not to—a tall guy in a red baseball cap slouched up to the table.

"'Sup," he said in a bored-sounding voice. "Welcome to the Crabby Lobster. I'm Ty, and I'll be your server for tonight. What can I get you?"

I blinked at him. I thought there was something about him that was familiar, but nothing was clicking into place.

"Sophie?"

After a moment, I looked at Josh—I still hadn't quite gotten the hang of responding to that like I would if it were actually my name—and realized that both he and Ty were staring at me, waiting.

"Oh, right," I said quickly, as I gave up trying to place him, looked down at the menu, and ordered the lobster roll.

"Awesome choice," Ty said, nodding with satisfaction. "You?" he asked, turning to Josh.

"Um . . . the burger," he mumbled. "Medium."

Ty shook his head. "Dude," he said disapprovingly, before taking his order pad and leaving.

"You can't get a burger at a seafood place," I said when we were alone again. "I think it's against the rules."

"Yeah," he said with a sheepish smile. "I, um, don't like seafood that much. Or, actually, at all."

"But . . ." I said, looking around. Even if Josh hadn't remembered being here before, there was no way he wouldn't have figured out that this was primarily a seafood restaurant, between the name and the décor and the fact that the sign in the parking lot had told us to PARK HERE NOW, SEA FOOD SOON! "Then why are we eating here? We can go someplace else. But," I added, "we might have to pay for the stuff we just ordered."

"No," Josh said, and I was actually kind of relieved. I'd really been looking forward to my lobster roll. "I just wanted to take you someplace good. It didn't matter that this wasn't my kind of food."

"Oh," I murmured. "That's really nice of you." It truly was, and it took me aback. I couldn't help but wonder if Teddy would have done that for me. *Of course*, was the immediate answer that flashed through my mind. But a moment later, I still found that the question was lingering. Teddy and I had mostly gone to vegan restaurants, and our restaurant choices had always been dictated by his current ethical dietary needs. I suddenly knew, without even being able to say how, that he would never have taken me to a restaurant he didn't want to go to, just to make me happy. It wouldn't even have occurred to him.

"So your parents are divorced?" Josh asked, bringing me back to the moment at hand. "You mentioned a stepfather. . . ."

I nodded, feeling the tiny stab I always got in my chest whenever I had to answer that question. It was certainly easier now than it had been right when my parents had made their separation official, but that didn't mean I could talk about it without feeling anything. Despite the fact that so many years had passed, talking about it still felt a little raw. "About five years ago," I said. "I live with my mom during the year." I held my breath after I said this, hoping he wouldn't ask any follow-up questions about my father.

"It's just me and Hallie and our mom, too," Josh said. "My dad's . . ." He looked at me, then away. "Not in the picture," he finally finished, with a note of finality.

I nodded, but I couldn't help feeling a little disappointed. I certainly wasn't going to tell him that I knew about his father—because while Gemma Tucker knew, Sophie Curtis would have no idea—but I was a little hurt he didn't trust me enough to tell me the truth. Getting off the subject of our parents, though, seemed like a good idea, as there were far too many potential land mines we could set off if we weren't careful.

"So," I started, but at the same moment, Josh asked, "What does your dad do?"

"Oh," I said, looking down at the paper placemat that covered the wooden table. "He's a writer," I said, trying to keep my voice casual, hoping with everything I had that he wouldn't ask what kind, and what his name was. Josh nodded, but didn't ask any follow-ups, which I was grateful for, if a little surprised. "What about your mom?" I asked after a moment. Now that it appeared he wasn't going to press me on the details of my dad's writing, I was actually really curious about what Karen had been up to in the last five years, especially since the Internet was not being very helpful.

Josh glanced at me, and his face took on a slightly guarded look. "She's just . . . doing the mom thing," he said, looking away from me and out at the water. I got the distinct feeling somehow that we were both keeping secrets, talking in code. "It's a beautiful sunset," he said, pointing, and it might have seemed like he was trying to change the subject, but the sunset *was* absolutely stunning. "Actually," Josh said after a small pause. "That's not entirely true about my mom. She's—"

BEEP-BEEP-BEEP.

I jumped, startled, and Josh frowned as he reached into his

pocket and pulled out his phone. He silenced it, then looked down at it, shaking his head.

"God, I'm so sorry," he said. "I really don't know why this keeps happening. It beeps every time I have an e-mail."

"Was it something earth-shattering?" I asked, but Josh wasn't even reading the e-mail, and was just putting the phone back in his pocket.

"Not at all," he said. "It does it for every single one, and I can't get it to stop. I reprogram it every night, but it doesn't seem to stick."

"That's annoying," I said, all the while wondering if there was any way for us to go back to what he had been saying just before the interruption. I felt like I'd been on the verge of uncovering part of the Karen mystery. But before I could even try to steer the conversation back that way, Ty appeared with our orders.

"Enjoy!" Ty said, barely looking at us as he dropped the plates in front of us and hustled away, confirming my suspicions that even a subpar waiter was probably ashamed to be serving nonseafood.

"This looks great!" I enthused as I took in my lobster on a roll, slathered with mayo and served with a side of fries and coleslaw.

"This looks . . . okay," Josh said, clearly trying to sound up-beat as he stared down at his admittedly pathetic-looking burger.

"That's what you get," I teased him as I took a big bite of my lobster roll. It was delicious, and I hadn't realized how hungry I was until I started eating. I paused after my third bite and nudged the other half of the lobster roll toward him. "You want to try it?"

Josh shook his head. "I told you," he said. "I don't really like seafood. I never eat it."

"Have you ever even *had* a lobster roll?" I asked, taking another bite. "Because it really doesn't even taste like lobster. It mostly tastes like butter."

"Well," he said, considering, looking over at my plate. "I do like butter."

"Come on," I said, pushing my plate toward him until it rested against his. "I dare you."

Josh raised his eyebrow at me. "A challenge?" he asked, and I nodded. "You know, I never walk away from a dare," he said, a glint coming into his eyes. He reached over and picked up the other half of the lobster roll, then took a cautious bite.

"Well?" I asked.

"It's not bad," he said. He took another, bigger bite this time. "You were right. It's pretty buttery."

"See?" I asked, smiling. Josh offered me the rest of the roll, but I shook my head. "All yours," I said. "I'm just happy I was able to introduce you to the wonder that is the lobster roll."

"Well, I consider myself enlightened," he said, taking the final bite and then reaching over and taking a handful of my fries.

"Hey," I said, laughing, pulling the plate back toward me. I realized I was no longer worried about whether this was a date or not. I was just having fun. "I said the lobster, not—" I stopped short. My stomach had just lurched violently, and a wave of nausea crashed over me. I could feel perspiration beading on my forehead, and my heart was beating hard, but not in a full-of-excitement way. No, this was more like an oh-my-god-I'm-about-to-throw-up way.

I gripped the edge of the table hard and tried to take deep breaths. After yesterday, I had been worried about embarrassing myself again, but these worries had mostly been things like getting food stuck in my teeth and not realizing it until the end of the night. But now, as another, fiercer wave of nausea hit me, I realized I had a worry that certainly trumped it—a very real concern that I might throw up, in public, and in front of Josh.

I could hear him start to say something, but I couldn't really make out any words over the roaring in my ears. I closed my eyes tightly for a moment, just trying to breathe, hoping this would go away as soon as it had arrived. What was causing this? Had the lobster been bad?

"Sophie?" I heard Josh say this, and opened my eyes to see him looking concerned, leaning toward me, his expression worried. "Are you okay? What's wrong?"

"I think," I said, swallowing hard. I got dizzy suddenly and snapped my mouth closed, trying to breathe through my nose, not caring any longer if I looked weird. I just needed to get out of there. "I think I need to go home," I managed. I looked across the table at him, and in so doing caught a glimpse of my discarded lobster roll bun and half-eaten fries. Just the sight of them was enough to send my stomach rolling again.

"What?" Josh asked, looking even more worried—not to mention a little freaked out.

"I need to go," I blurted, all in one breath. I wasn't trusting myself to say too much. It was even worse now than it had been just a few moments ago. "We need to leave. Now."

"Now?" Josh echoed. "Are you—"

"I'm going to be sick," I said, standing up and pushing myself back from the table. I fumbled for my bag, and with shaking hands tried to extract my wallet, but Josh was on top of it, dropping some money down on the table. I walked across the patio, bent over slightly, just trying to tell myself to breathe, that this would be over soon. It had to, right?

As we headed out of the restaurant, I saw Ty leaning on the door frame, watching us go. I glanced back toward Josh to make sure he was still behind me (he was, looking more freaked out than ever), and when I looked back, Ty had vanished—probably to check that we'd paid and weren't skipping out on our bill.

I practically ran toward Josh's truck, yanking open the door before he had a chance to open it for me. He hurried around to the driver's side, and as soon as he turned on the engine, I unrolled the window, breathing in the fresh air.

"Um," Josh said as he pulled out of the parking lot, "do you need to go to a doctor or something?"

"Home," I managed, leaning even farther out the window and letting the cool air hit my face, which now felt like it was burning up. "Just take me home." Despite the breeze, I could feel myself sweating, and I ran a hand over my face and eyes. When I looked down at my hand, I saw that it was now covered in black, and knew I was probably rubbing off most of my carefully applied eye makeup. I closed my eyes. I could only imagine how bad I looked, but at the moment, I didn't care about that as much as I cared about getting home without completely humiliating myself.

"Should I drive slow?" Josh asked, and, with what felt like a lot of effort, I turned my head to look at him and opened my eyes. "Is this better for you? Or . . ."

"Fast," I said. I had started to feel clammy, and my pulse was racing, and I knew that I wouldn't be able to hold out for too much longer. "Drive fast."

Josh stepped on the gas, and the car lurched forward. I closed my eyes again and made myself keep breathing. It was just a few more minutes. I could handle it. I could.

"Do you think it was the lobster?" Josh asked from across the car and just the one word was enough to make my stomach heave.

"Don't say that," I muttered.

"What?" Josh asked, sounding genuinely confused. "Lob—"

"Yes, that," I muttered through clenched teeth. "Just . . . don't. Please?"

"Sure," he said, and I could feel us start to speed up, like he'd just stepped on the gas again.

Somewhere, in the part of my mind that wasn't focusing all its effort on keeping the nausea at bay, I could tell that I was making absolutely the worst impression possible, and that I had effectively ruined our night. But I could think about that once I was at home and a bathroom was within easy reach. I didn't have the capacity for it now.

I could feel the truck's tires were now crunching over gravel and I opened my eyes and saw we were finally back at Bruce's house. "Um," I said as Josh pulled around in front of the house. "I'm so sorry about this. . . ."

"No," Josh said. "It's okay, really." He ran his hand across his face. "Actually—" He killed the engine and the lights flared, letting me see that he no longer looked so good. In fact, he looked pale and clammy, and I could see perspiration beading on his forehead.

"I'm not actually feeling so well myself. Can I . . . um . . . come in for a second?"

I nodded, no longer caring about embarrassing myself, just needing to get inside as quickly as possible. "Hurry," I said. I got out of the car and ran for the door, Josh right behind me. I turned the key in the lock with shaky hands, then stepped inside, closing the door behind us and immediately starting to take the stairs to my room.

"Um," Josh called, swaying slightly, looking unsure—and sicker than ever.

"Follow me!" I yelled, and hustled up the stairs. When I reached the landing, I pointed to the guest room on the other side of the hallway from me. I wanted Josh absolutely as far as possible away from what I feared was about to happen, and soon. "Guest room," I yelled. "Bathroom's attached."

"Thanks," he called weakly, heading that direction. I ran toward my own room, made it inside, and slammed the door behind me.

CHAPTER 17

Me
11:09 PM
Hey. You okay?

Josh Bridges
11:11 PM
Not really ☹

Josh Bridges
11:13 PM
You?

Me
11:14 PM
A little better. But it would have been
hard to be worse.

Josh Bridges
11:16 PM
I hear that.

Me
12:19 AM
Left extra T-shirt and sweats
outside your door just in case.

Josh Bridges
12:21 AM
Thank you! These are great.

Josh Bridges
12:25 AM
They're just a little big.

Josh Bridges
12:26 AM
Also, is this a sloth on the T-shirt??

Me
12:28 AM
Afraid so ☺

Josh Bridges
12:45 AM
Feel like venturing out? I think I'm up for it.

Me
12:47 AM
Meet you downstairs in five.

By the time I descended the staircase, Josh was already waiting, sitting on the bottom step. I ran my hands through my hair as I took the last three steps to meet him and he stood and smiled weakly at me. "Hey."

"Hey," he replied. I looked at him and couldn't help letting out a small laugh. Josh was wearing what I'd found for him in the promotional bins in Bruce's office—a navy T-shirt and gray sweatpants, both size XXL. There was a cartoon sloth stretched across the T-shirt, and a meerkat took up one of the legs of the sweatpants. Both had been promotional tie-ins for *Time Stands Still*, the only movie in the series that didn't feature time travel. It also featured cartoon animals that don't move very much— meerkats, sloths, ostriches, possums. It had been the only one in the franchise to do badly, but in retrospect, I couldn't believe anyone had been surprised about this.

Josh looked much like I knew I did—pale and tired. What had happened once I'd made it into my room hadn't been pretty, but it appeared to be mostly over now, and I was trying not to dwell on it. I was also planning never to eat seafood—or pretty much anything else—ever again. It seemed like the worst of the food poisoning was over, and I was just praying that it wouldn't come back.

"It's a good look for you," I said, nodding at his ensemble, and he laughed faintly.

"Thanks," he said. "Um, why do you have these?"

"We're staying with a family friend," I said, after a tiny moment in which I'd considered how best to reveal the Bruce information. Truthfully, I had been worried about bringing Josh this far inside of my real life here at Bruce's. But everyone was away, there would be nobody there to call me Gemma and give up the game, and there really wasn't anything else to do. I was supposed to leave Josh, sick, outside? It wasn't even a possibility. And, frankly, I was feeling far too wiped out for subterfuge or coming up with excuses. It seemed safest to go with a vague version of the truth. "This is his house. He produces those movies."

"Oh," Josh said. He glanced around, suddenly looking worried. "Is it okay that I'm here?" he asked. He lowered his voice, even though he hadn't been speaking that loudly to begin with. "Are we going to wake someone up?"

"Don't worry," I said. "It's just me here. Everyone else is in the city for the weekend." In other circumstances, I knew this might seem somehow suggestive, like I was spelling out that we were in the house alone together. But I honestly felt so tired and gross that the idea of romance barely even crossed my mind, and at the moment I could not think of anything less appealing.

"Got it," he said. "Well, thanks for lending me these. I'll be sure to return them."

"I really don't think anyone's going to miss them," I said honestly. I crossed the foyer and Josh followed, holding up his sweatpants by the extra room at the waistband to keep them from falling down. When I reached the kitchen, I leaned against the counter, a little exhausted by the trip. "Want something to drink?" I asked as I pulled open the fridge door. "Or"—I winced before saying it—"eat?"

Josh shook his head. "Nothing to eat," he said firmly. "But maybe some water or something?" I took out two bottles of water, and then also pulled out a bottle of Gatorade so we wouldn't get dehydrated. Josh nodded when he saw the bottle. "Good call."

"Have you ever had food poisoning before?" I asked as I brought down glasses from the cabinet.

"Nope," Josh said. "You?" I shook my head and poured us both glasses of the bright-orange liquid. "But it must have been the lobster, right?" he asked, and I was glad that I could now hear that word without getting nauseous.

"I think so," I said, then realized what this meant. "Oh my god, that means that it's totally my fault you got sick too. I made you try it."

Josh shook his head and picked up the glass I pushed across the counter toward him. "You didn't make me do anything," he said. "I was just trying to impress you."

The phrase seemed to hang in the air between us for a moment, and I looked down at the countertop, not sure how to respond. "Well," I said after a second of silence, "I'm sorry anyway."

"I'm sorry too," Josh said. He gave me a small, rueful smile. "I was the one who took you there. I hope the Crabby Lobster knows they have a scathing online review coming their way." He glanced at the clock on the microwave, then back at me. "Is it okay if I stay a little longer?" he asked. "I'm not sure I'm up to driving home just yet."

"Of course," I said. I certainly knew what he meant—suddenly, just staying upright for this long was exhausting, and I didn't want Josh falling asleep at the wheel or something. "Stay as long as you want." I glanced through to the TV room and the leather couches there, and didn't think I had ever seen anything look as appealing. "Hey, you want to watch something?"

It soon became clear that Josh and I had very different taste when it came to movies. Bruce had a huge digital collection, and Josh was particularly impressed with the breadth of the action movies and all their attendant sequels. I didn't think I was up for seeing buildings blowing up repeatedly, or buses being driven recklessly across freeways, so I nixed all the ones that he suggested. Josh, in turn, didn't seem particularly interested in romantic comedies, or my favorite girl-power movies that featured multiple makeover montages. He claimed that he already felt sick enough without needing to add to it. As we were going back and forth about our choices, I couldn't help but think of Teddy again—how mostly, we just watched his depressing documentaries, and I never pushed to see the movies I really wanted to see, since I knew he would think they were frivolous.

Maybe I was just too tired and dehydrated to care what Josh thought about my choices, but I was pushing hard for my chick flicks, just as Josh was stubbornly holding out for his action movies. I had begun to fear that we wouldn't reach a consensus, when I stopped at *The Princess Bride*.

"Hey," Josh said, sitting up a little straighter. "I like that movie."

"Me too," I said, selecting it and waiting for it to load. I hadn't seen it in years, but was more than willing to watch it again—and plus, we'd agreed on something, so I was happy to go with it. All that scrolling past different titles was beginning to make me dizzy.

The FBI warning flashed across the screen, and I sat back on my couch a little more. The couches in the TV room were at right angles to each other, forming an L shape, and Josh and I were each on our own couch. As the opening credits rolled, I relaxed a little more, stretching out on the soft leather.

Fred Savage was complaining about not wanting to hear a kissing story when Josh's phone beeped. He picked it up, squinted at it, then typed out a quick text and set the phone back down on the coffee table, close enough that I could get a glimpse at the screen.

"Everything okay?" I asked, after trying not to be nosy and utterly failing.

Josh nodded. "It's my sister. I had to text her so she wouldn't get worried when I didn't come home, and I think she's just concerned."

I leaned forward a tiny bit, telling myself I was only stretching, even though I knew it wasn't the truth, because now I could see his phone, and that he had a number of texts from Hallie. Her texts seemed to get increasingly confused and worried. *What's going on? Where are you? Why are you sick? What did you eat?* The latest one was an offer to come by and pick him up, and I saw just before the screen went dark that Josh had replied that he was okay, and he was going to stay for a while. I felt a little flutter in my stomach when I read that, and it had nothing to do with the food poisoning. Because if Josh had wanted to leave, he could have, and he wouldn't even have to drive. But he was choosing to stay here, with me.

I looked over at him and saw that he was now lying down on

the couch as well, and our heads were both at the end of our couches where they met, which meant our heads were right near each other.

"I haven't seen this in a long time," Josh said, and I looked back at the screen and realized we were now in the fairy-tale world of the story, Westley and Buttercup at the beginning of their star-crossed romance. "It's Hallie's favorite, though. She used to watch it all the time."

"Oh yeah?" I asked. Hallie hadn't ever mentioned it when I'd known her, but maybe she'd gotten into it after the summer I knew her. That year, we'd mostly watched and rewatched *The Parent Trap*.

"Yeah," Josh said, but his voice was distracted, and his eyes were glued to the screen.

I looked there too and soon was lost in the story—love and princes and pirates and giants. When I'd seen it before, I'd mostly been focused on the romantic parts, not the revenge aspect of the story, Inigo Montoya's burning desire to find and punish the six-fingered man who'd wronged him.

"Here's what I don't get," Josh said when we were about an hour in. I turned my head toward him and it hit me again just how close together we were. I could have reached over and touched his cheek without extending my arm. But this didn't make me nervous or anxious, like my realization in the car after the pool party had. Maybe it was the result of stomach troubles, or that fact that it was almost 2 A.M., but mostly I just felt comfortable and relaxed, all the while still able to appreciate how good he could make a sloth T-shirt look.

"What don't you get?" I asked around a yawn.

"Westley and Buttercup," he said. "Even though he's going under another name, shouldn't she realize who he is? If he's her one true love and all?"

I could feel my pulse start to beat a little harder at the base of my throat, and I took a moment before answering, choosing my words carefully. "I don't know," I said. "I . . . think that sometimes people have reasons for not telling the truth about who they are. And does it really matter? When she realizes who he really is, she's okay with it." I crossed my fingers under my head, knowing full well that I was talking more about myself than Westley pretending to be the Dread Pirate Roberts.

"Of course she is," Josh said, his voice getting slower and more sleepy. "She loves him. It doesn't matter what his name is."

"So," I started. I suddenly felt much more awake, and was no longer paying attention to the movie at all, even though we were almost at the fire swamp, with the Rodents of Unusual Size, which had always been my favorite part. "You think that even though he's not telling her the truth about who he is, it's okay?"

"Sure," Josh said, and I looked over and saw that his eyes were drifting shut, his long eyelashes casting shadows on his cheek. "Of course."

I took a deep breath. I didn't know if it was the potential dehydration making me a little loopy, but I suddenly had a feeling that Josh would understand. I wanted to tell him, right then, who I really was, even though it went against everything that I had been planning. I suddenly wanted him to know the real me. "Josh," I whispered. "Can I tell you something?"

When he didn't respond, I sat up a little more and looked over at him. But his eyes remained closed, and I noticed that his breathing had turned slow and even. I knew I could have woken him up to tell him, but as the seconds passed, I lost my nerve. I turned the volume on the TV down slightly and lay down again, holding on tight to what Josh had just said. That it didn't really matter what you called yourself. So maybe when he found out the truth, he'd understand that some deception was necessary for a larger purpose.

I closed my eyes too, and just let the story wash over me—revenge and deception and true love and misunderstandings, everyone on their way to an eventual happy ending—until I fell asleep as well.

When I woke up, the movie was over and the TV was scrolling through its screensaver images, close-ups of flowers and insects and ocean waves. I sat up, stretching out a crick in my neck, and noticed that it was morning, early pale light streaming through the windows. I looked over at Josh, whose eyes were still closed. For just a moment—before this turned into creepy stalkerish sleep-staring—I took in the sight of him on the couch. His hair was sticking up, he had a crease on one cheek from the leather pillow, and the too-big sweatpants had slipped down slightly, revealing a strip of flat, toned stomach.

Josh opened his eyes, and I jumped, looking away and picking up the remote, pretending to be very interested in how it worked. "Hey," he said, stretching and giving me a sleepy smile.

I looked over, like I was surprised to notice him there. "Oh, hi," I said, in what I hoped was a casual, I-wasn't-just-staring-at-you tone.

"What time is it?" he asked, yawning.

I squinted at the clock on Bruce's entertainment system. "Seven thirty."

Josh sat up and ran a hand over his eyes. "I'd better get going," he said. "I'll just grab my stuff from upstairs." He headed toward the staircase, then turned back and glanced at the TV. "I guess I missed the Rodents of Unusual Size, huh? They were always my favorite part."

Josh left before I could respond to that, and I tried to tell myself firmly that it didn't mean anything. It was probably lots of people's favorite part. I picked up our discarded glasses and put them in the dishwasher, checked my reflection in the toaster, and was glad to see that I looked better than I had last night. This seemed encouraging, though the truth was, if I'd looked worse, I think it would have meant I needed to call a doctor, or the morgue.

I met Josh by the front door. He was carrying his clothes from the night before and still wearing the sloth shirt and meerkat pants. "Okay if I wash these and bring them back?" he asked.

"Seriously," I said, "take them. Nobody will even notice they're gone, I promise you."

"Okay," he said. He tossed his keys on his palm a few times. "Well . . . thanks for letting me convalesce here."

"Anytime," I said. I moment later, I reconsidered. "Actually, no. I hope this never has to happen again. In a good way."

"I agree," he said. "Stay away from lobster."

I laughed at that. "Right back at you."

"Well," Josh said. He gave me a smile, and I noticed that the pillow crease was still on his cheek. He looked a little pale, and I knew from the toaster that I did too. But I kind of liked it. It was like proof that we'd been through something, together. "Good morning."

I smiled back. "Good morning, Josh."

He pulled open the door, waving once to me before heading to his truck, which was still parked haphazardly from when we'd abandoned it and dashed full-out for the house. I shut the door behind him and then leaned back against it.

I closed my eyes for a second, turning over the events from the night (well, the nondisgusting ones) in my head. Somehow, things seemed different now. Like we'd moved on to something new from when he'd picked me up, which felt like a lifetime ago. I tried to tell myself that maybe this was what always happened when you shared a food-poisoning experience with someone, and then recuperated together watching an eighties movie. It just felt like, in the space of a night, something had shifted. To or from what, though, I wasn't sure.

But I didn't think my still-recovering brain would be able to come up with an answer that could be trusted. I pushed myself off the door and went to go look for some ginger ale.

CHAPTER 18

Two days later, I stood in the doorway of the sitting room that had been repurposed as my father's office for the summer. My dad was hunched over his laptop, muttering dialogue to himself, with the occasional elbow flap, which seemed like proof he was maybe getting a little too into this penguin movie.

I had spent most of the last two days inside, existing on ginger ale and saltines, working my way back up to plain bagels, though food in general still wasn't very appealing. When Bruce, Rosie, and my dad had returned, Rosie had taken charge and ordered me back to bed, even though I wasn't really sick any longer. But it was nice to be taken care of—even though Rosie's definition of caretaking included giving me lectures on how eating shellfish coated in mayo, outdoors, had just been asking for trouble.

Josh and I had been texting back and forth, but we hadn't made any plans to see each other again, and I was kind of glad. Reliving the night in the cold light of day, it had all seemed extra embarrassing, not to mention a little confusing, and I was glad not to see him for a few days, happy to hang around the house, where I knew all the food was safe.

But it was not lost on me that I seemed to be spending an awful lot of time this summer getting into humiliating situations and hiding in my various bedrooms to recover from them. It did bother me, however, that this was becoming a definitive pattern and it wasn't even July yet.

Since my dad seemed absorbed in his work, I knocked twice. I'd found a note from him under my door that morning, asking me to come and see him when I got up. I had a feeling this meant that he was late on the script, since when he was running behind, Bruce confiscated his phone, changed the Wi-Fi password, and refused to tell him what it was, so that he wouldn't have any distractions from his work.

My dad started and spun around in his chair, his expression relaxing when he saw me. "Oh, Gemma," he said, giving me a tired smile. "I thought you were Bruce, demanding a progress report."

"How's it going?" I asked, then when my dad winced, added, "You don't have to tell me if you don't want to."

"You know what, kid?" he asked, taking off his glasses and rubbing the bridge of his nose. "There are some days when I just want to toss this whole crazy business and write another novel." Since my dad hadn't even so much as mentioned going back to books in five years, I wondered just how bad this screenplay was. But before I could say anything—or figure out a noninsulting way to ask this—he motioned me inside. "Come in," he said. "I think we need to talk about something."

I felt myself freeze. These were never good words to hear from my parents, but especially from my dad, who never wanted to talk about anything significant. He'd left most of the heavy lifting, parenting-wise, to my mom. As a result of this, my dad and I got along great, mostly because we only talked about fun stuff— movies and trivia and gossip about the famous actors who gave voices to his sloths and turtles.

The timing of this also seemed particularly ominous. Had he somehow found out that I'd had a boy stay the night? Even though we'd just been on parallel couches, I had a feeling my dad would not be okay with it. I found my eyes darting upward to the ceiling. Did Bruce have some crazy security system installed or something?

And then I realized my dad might be talking about another, much bigger secret. Had he found out, somehow, what I'd been doing here this summer—pretending to be Sophie and trying to mend fences with Hallie? Getting involved with the Bridges once again? I had always planned on confessing to my dad what I'd done that summer—in theory, anyway—but didn't want to until I'd resolved things with Hallie.

I took a few tentative steps into the room. "Um, about what?"

"Two things," he said, turning in his chair to face me more fully. He sighed, his expression regretful. "We have to go to L.A. in a few days," he said. "We'll be there for a week or so."

"Oh," I said, nodding. While I was relieved it didn't sound like I was in trouble, I couldn't help being a little disappointed. Staying by myself in a house this big was only fun for a day or so, and then it just started to feel lonely. Also, between my dad's work and my focus on the Bridges, we hadn't been able to see each other much this summer.

"But we'll be back after the Fourth," my dad said, clearly trying to put a cheerful spin on this. "Will you be okay here on your own? If not, you can come with us."

"No!" I said, more forcefully than I'd meant to. "I mean, no thanks," I amended, as my dad had started to look insulted. "I'd just rather stay here. You know how I hate, um, packing." Truthfully, I had no issues with packing, but didn't want to leave things up in the air here. Even though I hadn't seen Hallie since the day of babysitting, she'd sent me a text saying she heard I was sick and hoped I was feeling better. I had gotten thrown off by the food poisoning and hadn't been hanging out with her as much as I would have wanted to. And I didn't want to fly across the country and derail any friendship momentum that might be building. Plus, Los Angeles in the summer always seemed excessively sunny, like the whole city was just showing off.

"I'll be fine," I assured my dad. "Really." I gave him a confident smile so that he wouldn't try and get me a babysitter, and I told myself it wasn't like I was going to be technically alone, since there were always people at Bruce's—housekeepers and pool people and gardeners and someone whose whole job seemed to be washing Bruce's car the second that he returned with it. "And we'll hang out when you're back, right?"

"Definitely," my dad said, giving me a tired smile. "I'll be finished with this monstrosity by then and on to the next thing."

I was about to ask him what the next thing was when Bruce stuck his head into the room. "Paul!" he barked. "Why aren't you—" He noticed me and his tone softened. "Oh, hi, Gemma. Stop bothering your dad, okay? He has to turn around this draft by seven."

"We're almost done, Bruce," my dad said. Bruce nodded and, though he still didn't look convinced, left us alone again. "So," my dad said, turning his attention back to me, causing my guard to go flying up again. "You've been having fun here, right, Gem? You've met some kids to hang out with?"

I nodded, wondering where this was going. "Yeah," I said slowly. "A couple of people."

"Anyone I know?" His tone was joking, but even so, my stomach clenched.

"Um, I don't think so," I said. "Just a brother and sister I met while taking the train here."

My dad looked away and sighed, then back at me. "Look, I want you to have a good time," he said. "But I think we need to talk about this." He turned back to his laptop and punched a few keys. I saw his credit card statement fill the screen and remembered that I'd never told him about the bathing suit.

"Oh, right," I said hurriedly. "I was going to talk to you about that."

"What is this place?" my dad asked, squinting at the screen. "Some kind of French restaurant?"

"No," I said. "It's . . . um . . . I bought a bikini."

My dad turned about three shades paler and gripped the chair arms for support. "A bikini?" He gasped. "You spent three hundred dollars on a *bikini*? Gem, I didn't even spend that much on my suit when your mom and I got married."

Bruce stuck his head back into the room. "Paul, that's just sad."

"Bruce," my dad said, rubbing his eyes again.

"Right," Bruce said, disappearing again—but, I had a feeling, not going far.

"I'm really sorry," I said all in a rush. "I should have told you." My dad just raised his eyebrows. "And," I added quickly, "not bought it in the first place. Of course."

"This card is for emergencies, kid," he said, sounding disappointed. I bit my lip, wanting to tell him that it *had* been an emergency—but knowing that I couldn't make him believe me without telling him everything that had been happening this summer.

"I know," I said in a small voice. "I'm sorry."

"Well, you're going to have to pay me back," he said. I nodded, trying to do mental addition of just how many hours I'd have to babysit to equal the cost of the bikini. "And this makes me think . . . I don't like the idea of you just hanging out all summer. I think you should get a job, Gem."

"Oh," I said. I had nothing against getting a job; aside from babysitting, though, I'd never had one before. "Well, can we talk about it when you get back?"

"Great idea!" Bruce called from outside the door, his voice muffled.

"To be continued," my dad said. "But while we're gone, look for some options, and then we can discuss. Okay?" I nodded. "Good," he said, clearly relieved that his parenting duties were over for the time being. He gave me a smile, then turned back to his computer and pulled the screenplay up.

Without even realizing I was going to ask it, I blurted out, "Dad, do you ever think about Karen Bridges? From that summer when I was eleven?"

My dad turned his chair to face me again. Based on his expression, this had been the last thing he had been expecting me to ask. "What made you think about her, Gem?"

I looked away and shrugged. "I don't know . . . maybe being back here again?" After all, it wasn't like this was actually untrue.

My dad took a breath, then shook his head. "That was a long time ago," he said, looking back at his laptop, making it clear that he was done with this conversation. A second later, though, almost more to himself than to me, he added, "And some things you just can't fix."

I headed for the door, but paused and turned back before opening it. "But the things you can fix," I said, "you should try, right?"

My dad looked at me for a long moment, then gave me a sad smile. "Yes," he finally said. "If there's a chance, I think you have to try. I think you have to do everything you can."

I gave him a nod, then stepped into the hallway, almost crashing into Bruce, who was lurking outside the door. "He's getting back to work," I promised.

"Good," Bruce said, flipping open his iPad cover and jabbing at the screen. "Because if we don't get the script in on time, it'll be— oh wait, that's not my calendar. Hold on—" A lute and a didgeridoo had started playing, and I had a feeling I knew exactly what band it was.

And just like that, I had an idea for something I could do.

"Hey, Bruce," I said, "still want me to tell you about teen stuff for your movie?"

"Of course," he said immediately. "Hold on, let me get the coast on the line." He pulled out his phone, but I jumped in before he could wake up and terrify someone in Los Angeles.

"I'm happy to help," I said. "But I was wondering if we could work out some kind of a trade."

"Ah," Bruce said, giving me an impressed look and shutting his iPad cover. "A negotiation. Maybe we should discuss it on a run?"

"If by a run, you mean bagels," I said with a nod, "then I'm in." Bruce gave me a *duh of course* look, and I smiled. "Okay," I said as we headed for the front door. "Here's what I was thinking . . ."

CHAPTER 19

Me

12:05 PM

Hey Hallie! Are you free tonight?

Hallie Bridges

12:09 PM

I think so . . . why?

Me

12:10 PM

It's a surprise. You just have to be free
from about 6 to 9.

Hallie Bridges

12:11 PM

I'm free! Just confused. Details?

Me

12:12 PM

Surprise means I can't tell you any details!

Pick you up at five?

And wear something semiformal.

Hallie Bridges

12:14 PM

Okay, now extra confused.

But see you at five, Sophie!

Me

12:15 PM

And that means semiformal for you, Hallie,

to the event we'll be attending

this evening, tonight. ☺

Hallie Bridges

12:17 PM

Okay, I deserved that ;)

Rosie looked over at me and raised her eyebrows appreciatively as she folded a shirt. "That's a favor and a half. How much
time did you have to agree to give him for this?"

I winced and picked up a pair of her heels, trying to see if
they'd fit me. I was already dressed and ready to go, but had some
time to kill before I had to pick Hallie up, and decided to spend it
hanging out with Rosie in her room while she packed for L.A. I
was wearing another dress I'd borrowed from Gwyneth, but had
kept my own shoes this time, just to be on the safe side. "Two
hours," I said. "With some intern in California transcribing what
I tell him about being a typical teenager." Rosie laughed, but I
couldn't help feeling that maybe I'd pulled the wool over Bruce's
eyes in this deal. I didn't think there were many teenagers who

were currently going under aliases and juggling multiple identities. And if there were, I needed to find them, so we could form a support group or something.

"Well, have fun," she said, taking the heels away from me and dropping them in her suitcase before I could try them on.

"I wish you didn't have to leave." I sighed, flopping back onto the bed and watching her lightning-speed packing. Rosie traveled so much, it was practically a military operation, and a marvel to behold.

"Just a week or so," she said as she folded a T-shirt into a tiny square. "And when we're back, Gwyneth and Ford should be here too, so if we have to leave again, you won't be all alone."

Well, that was something. I reached for another pair of heels to try before they got put in the suitcase, which was when I saw a very familiar red-and-black cover. "Rosie," I admonished as I picked up the copy of *Once Bitten*. "Not you, too."

"It's for work," Rosie said, blushing maybe a tiny bit.

"Oh, sure," I said, turning the book over to look at the back. There was no author photo, just the information that Brenda Kriegs lived on a remote island with her family.

"It *is*," Rosie insisted, taking the book back from me. I was about to ask how, exactly, it was for work when Rosie straightened up and cocked her head to the side. "Did you hear that?"

I looked up and listened. Sure enough, there was the sound of tires crunching on gravel. But this really wasn't so surprising, as it seemed like things were constantly being delivered to the house—scripts, packages, flower, bribes. "Probably just a delivery," I said with a shrug.

"That's what I'm afraid of," Rosie said, dropping the jeans

she'd just picked up and hustling out of the room. "Bruce has been getting food delivered, I'm sure of it."

I didn't disagree with her—if he had a secret candy stash in the kitchen, I had no doubt that he was finding other ways to get noncaveman food. But I didn't see why Rosie should care. Bruce cheated on his diets; it was just one of the universe's facts. "So?" I asked, following her out of the hallway and down the stairs.

"I want to catch him in the act," she said, taking the steps down to the foyer two at a time. "So I don't spend the whole plane ride listening to him tell the poor pilots and crew about how they all need to eat like cavemen too." Rosie reached the door and yanked it open before the bell had even rung. "Hi," she said, sounding surprised. "Can I help you?"

I made it down the last few steps and walked around to see who was there—and my heart stopped for a second when saw it was Hallie, in a dress and heels, standing on the doorstep with a shopping bag.

"Hi," Hallie was saying to Rosie with a big smile. "I'm here to see—"

"Hello!" I practically yelled, throwing myself in front of Rosie before Hallie could finish her sentence. "Hi!" Rosie looked at me curiously, and I babbled, "This is Hallie. She's a friend of mine. She's coming with me tonight."

"Oh," Rosie said, her expression relaxing. "Nice to meet you." At least I didn't have to worry about either one of them recognizing the other, as Rosie hadn't started working for Bruce until I was thirteen. "So how do you know Ge—"

"Rosie!" I interrupted loudly. I truly had not been aware of how often people said my name before I had to try and fend off every instance of it.

"Yes?" she asked, turning to me. She was frowning, maybe worrying that I hadn't quite recovered after all, or that the food poisoning had gone to my brain, or something.

"Didn't you have to get back to packing?" I smiled at her, but raised my eyebrows significantly, hoping that she'd take the hint.

She raised her eyebrows in return, and I knew she'd understood me. "Sure," she said easily. "You girls have fun tonight." She gave us a wave and then started up the staircase toward her room.

I turned back to Hallie. "Hi," I said, trying to ease the door closed behind me and hoping she wouldn't think it was weird that I wasn't asking her inside. But this was the reason I'd made plans to pick *her* up. I had been hoping, once inside her house, to find the suit and try and get rid of the receipt evidence once and for all. But aside from losing that chance, her being here was much too close for comfort. It was one thing for Josh to come inside Bruce's house when no one else was home, and we were both violently ill. But to have Hallie here was a potential minefield. My dad was still working in his office, just a few rooms away, and a glimpse of him could blow my whole cover. "Wasn't I supposed to come and get you?"

"I know," Hallie said with a shrug. "But I was ready early, and thought I'd drop these off!" She handed me the bag, and I looked down and saw that it contained the shirt and sweatpants I'd lent Josh, washed and folded.

"Oh, great," I said, taking the bag and tossing it into the house behind me, in the general direction of the stairs. The last thing I wanted was to leave her alone while I brought it to my room—or worse, had to explain why she couldn't come with me. "So we should leave. Like now, maybe?"

"I thought I heard a car!" I turned and saw, to my horror, Bruce emerging from his office and flinging the door wide. His face fell when he saw Hallie. "Oh," he said. "I guess you don't have my pizza?"

"Nope," I said quickly. "And we'd better get going." I had successfully prevented one Bruce and Hallie run-in and I didn't want to give them any opportunity to remember where they might have known each other from. I grabbed my purse, beyond grateful that I'd left it on the hall table, within easy reach. I'd intended to toss in a lip gloss before leaving, but I decided just to forget it. Where we were going, there was nobody that I would need or want to impress.

"So thanks for pulling the strings, Bru—you," I said. "See you later!" I had just stepped outside and was pulling the door shut when Bruce pulled it open again, frowning.

"Sorry," he said. "But this has just been bugging me." He pointed at Hallie. "Have we met before?"

"You met the other day," I jumped in quickly. "In the driveway, remember? When you were . . . running."

"Ah, yes," Bruce said, and I could see him color slightly at the memory. "Right. I'm Bruce Davidson."

I kept a smile frozen on my face, trying to look like I wasn't having an internal meltdown. Even if Hallie recognized Bruce's name, why shouldn't Sophie Curtis and her family be friends with Bruce too? Was he allowed to have only one friend, or something?

"I'm Hallie," she said, and I was incredibly grateful that she didn't include her last name. I doubted Bruce would remember Karen's last name, but I didn't need anything that might jog his memory.

Bruce gave her his producer's handshake, then smiled at me. "It's great to see you making friends," he said, and I couldn't help but wish he'd phrased that in a manner other than one that made me sound like a inept pariah. He turned to Hallie. "And how do you know Ge—"

"Train station!" I yelled, cutting him off before he could get to my name. "We met at the train station. Right?"

"Right," Hallie said, giving me a slightly confused smile.

"We should go," I said, a little desperately. The last thing I needed was for Bruce to drop a reference to "Gemma's dad" before I could stop him. "Bruce, we'll talk before you leave about that project, okay?"

Bruce nodded. "I'll get it on the calendar," he said. "In fact . . ." He looked back and forth between us, and his eyes lit up. "Since you're both here, maybe your friend wouldn't mind if I picked her brain too? It's for a movie I'm working on," he explained.

"Actually," I said, as firmly as possible, hoping to channel my inner Rosie, "now's not the best time, Bruce. We're going to be late. But—"

"Wait a second," Hallie said, turning to him, her expression doubtful. She looked from me to Bruce, like she was trying to figure something out. "Bruce. Davidson," she echoed, her voice flat. "Are you telling me . . ."

An icy feeling crept over me. It was over. Hallie had figured it out. I was about to be exposed, right then and there. And it wasn't the receipt, or some slipup of mine. It was all due to Bruce and a pizza. I closed my eyes and braced myself for the end.

"You're Bruce Davidson, the producer?" Hallie's voice had now risen a few octaves and decibels, but she sounded excited, not furious. I opened my eyes and saw that she looked dazzled.

"Well—yes," Bruce said, frowning at her. "Do you . . . know my work?"

"I'm a huge, huge fan," Hallie enthused. "I love your movies! I had no idea that you were staying with the Hollywood elite," she added, to me.

"Oh—right," I said quickly. "I enthused I just forgot to mention it." My heart was pounding hard, but with relief. Hallie hadn't put it together. She just knew Bruce's movies, which was a little weird, and liked them, which was even weirder. But clearly *someone* liked Bruce's movies, otherwise he wouldn't have been able to afford this house and his multiple alimony payments.

"I just loved *Ever and Always*," Hallie was gushing to Bruce. "I thought you were robbed at awards season."

"The awards in this country are so politicized," Bruce said dismissively. "The foreign awards are really the ones based on merit. In fact, a few years ago, in the UK, I won the Spotlight award."

At the mention of this award—currently with Ford in Hawaii

for repair—my stomach plunged again. "Um," I said, a little feebly.

"What an honor," Hallie said. "Is it as gorgeous up close as it looks in the pictures?"

"Better," Bruce said. He smiled happily, and I could tell he'd now completely forgotten about the pizza. "I actually have it here, if you want to see it."

"I would love that," Hallie said, giving me an *isn't this cool?* look that I tried my best to return.

"Great!" Bruce said. "Let's—"

"Um," I said, louder this time, "actually . . ."

"Bruce!" Rosie called. A moment later, she appeared at the top of the staircase, and shook her head when she saw us all still grouped around the door. "Your call started twenty minutes ago. Why don't you leave the girls alone?"

"Hallie here was just telling me what a big fan she is," Bruce protested.

"Really," Rosie said with a laugh. She paused and looked down when she saw both Bruce and Hallie nodding. "Really?" she asked again, her voice now heavy with disbelief.

"Apparently, I've reached the youth market!" Bruce enthused. "And—"

"Call," Rosie said firmly, cutting him off. "Now." She folded her arms and stayed put, not giving Bruce a chance to keep talking to us—or, even worse, to try and show Hallie an award that was currently MIA.

"Nice to meet you," Bruce said in a voice that sounded like he knew when he was defeated. "Any friend of—"

"Bruce!" This was Rosie, in just the nick of time.

"Coming," Bruce called as he gave us a wave and headed off to his study.

"It's so cool you know Bruce Davidson," Hallie said, turning to me.

"I guess," I said. "I mean, I've known him all my life, so it's really not that impressive to me." Also, when you've seen someone bribe delivery people and eat a cupcake in under ten seconds, it really prevents them from ever being impressive to you again. "But I'm surprised you know his work." After all, I wasn't sure I could name all movies Bruce had made, and there were posters of them decorating the house.

"Oh, totally," Hallie said with a shrug. "I'm a huge movie fan. And I have a really good memory, so if I see someone's name in the credits, it's pretty much locked in there forever. I don't forget *anything.*"

I swallowed hard. "Oh."

"So you said we should get going?" she asked, adjusting her bag on her shoulder.

"Right," I said, springing back into action. "Bye!" I yelled into the house, to nobody in particular, then stepped outside and shut the door behind me.

"Okay if I leave my car there?" Hallie asked, pointing to the Jeep parked in the driveway.

"Sure," I said, leading the way to Bruce's SUV. As I thought about the distance we'd have to drive tonight, I realized that maybe my dad had been on to something with wanting me to get a job. I might need one soon, if only to keep this thing filled with gas.

We buckled in and I pulled out of the driveway, feeling myself begin to relax the more distance I put between us and the house. That had been close, but I had prevented any major catastrophes.

"So," I said, turning in the direction of the highway that would take us back into Long Island proper, "thanks for returning that stuff. But I told Josh that he could keep it."

Hallie shook her head. "Josh is, like, the most honest person on earth," she said. "He never would have kept something that wasn't his. Things are kind of black and white with him that way." Hallie reached into her tote and pulled out a lip balm, but didn't apply it, instead just rolled the tube between her fingers. "About the other night," she said, her voice hesitant. "When Josh stayed over . . ."

She let the sentence trail off and I jumped in. "Because we were sick," I said quickly. "He didn't feel up to driving."

"So," she said, looking over at me, and I saw her expression was serious. "There was nothing else?"

"No!" I signaled to take the entrance ramp to the highway. "We were just having dinner as friends when we both got food poisoning. Nothing more. I promise." I could make this promise easily, because nothing else *had* happened, but was it entirely the truth? Hadn't there been a moment when I'd looked at Josh sleeping on the couch and seen him as more than a friend? Hadn't there been a moment between us when we said good-bye? I concentrated on merging, and tried not to think about the answers to these questions.

"Well," Hallie said, looking relieved and a little less serious, "I was so sorry you both got sick. I guess you can't trust lobster, huh?"

I hadn't realized Josh would have gotten that specific about the events of the night, and I felt myself inwardly groan a little. "So Josh really went into detail, huh?" I asked with a grimace.

Hallie looked thrown for a moment, then nodded. "Right, he did. I mean, I asked what he'd eaten so, you know, I could never eat there."

I smiled. "It's a good plan. Avoid the Crabby Lobster at all costs."

Hallie laughed and reached forward to turn on the radio. "Noted."

It turned out that Hallie and I had pretty similar taste in music, even though she was a little more into hip-hop and I liked the cheesy summer pop songs more than she did. But she was good driving company, telling me when I could merge and which lanes were clear when I needed to get over. And when we stopped at a gas station—it turned out we needed some after all—she emerged from the minimart with a bag of chips to share. She even took the role of the navigator, checking the map on my phone, since I'd long since given up trying to use the SUV's navigation system. It was military grade and gave coordinates in longitude and latitude, and was incredibly unhelpful—and kind of judgmental—when you made a wrong turn. I knew it was safe to give her my phone, since I had password-protected anything that might identify me as me—my pictures, e-mail, everything. I'd even changed the background to one of the boring generic ones that had come with the phone.

"Okay," Hallie said, looking up from the phone and squinting at the road. "I think you should make the next left."

"Great," I said, noticing that we were pulling into the North Hills Hyatt, which was exactly where we were supposed to be.

I avoided the valet and self-parked, and Hallie followed me into the hotel, looking increasingly confused. "Okay," she said, as she looked around. "So . . . we're going to a hotel?"

"I think it's this way," I said as I looked around for ballroom 2A. Sure enough, we rounded the corner and there was a giant sign decorated with a spinning red British phone box that read DROP IN TO SCOTT'S BAR MITZVAH!

Hallie turned to me, eyebrows raised. "Bar mitzvah?" she asked.

I grinned at her. "What," I asked, deadpan, as I took in Hallie's baffled expression, "not what you were expecting?"

"Hello," a frazzled-looking woman clutching a clipboard said as she came hustling up to us. "Are you here for the event?"

"We are," I said, taking a step closer to her. When Bruce had put us on this list for this party, I wasn't sure what names he gave, and I certainly didn't want Hallie to see *Gemma Tucker* printed there in huge letters. "Bruce Davidson's guests?"

"Ah," the woman said, scanning down her list. She paused, her pen hovering over the clipboard, and I let out a relieved sigh when I saw the list read only *B. Davidson 1* and *B. Davidson 2*. "Got you," she said. She looked behind Hallie, frowning. "And . . . will Mr. Davidson be joining you?"

"Nope," I said, trying to make it sound like this was totally normal. I started to head into the ballroom, Hallie behind me, when the woman held out two bright-red canvas bags to us.

"Gift bags," she said, as we took them. They were surprisingly heavy, which seemed to me like a good sign. "Enjoy your evening."

"Thanks," I said as I pulled open the ballroom door, and Hallie and I stepped inside.

As I looked around the ballroom, it was clear that the newly minted man, Scott, was very into the British show *Sergeant Which*. I only really knew it because Ford loved it, and half his obscure geeky T-shirts made reference to it. From what I could glean, it was about a brilliant ex-military detective who solved crimes while traveling through space in a magical phone booth. And yet, Ford refused to watch romantic comedies with me because they were, in his words, "unrealistic."

But the show was clearly the theme of this party. There were blown-up cutouts of the actors, a photo booth made to look like the red phone booth, and the show's theme song playing at full volume.

"Okay," Hallie said, sounding more confused than ever as she followed me to the seating chart, which had all the tables named after the Sergeant's greatest adventures across space and time. "So . . . do you know these people?"

"Never met them," I said as I saw that we were at table nineteen, the Battle of Gettysburg. I hoped that wasn't a bad sign as I negotiated our way around the side of the ballroom. It seemed like things were just getting started—no one was eating yet, the stage was dark, and the dance floor was empty. Apparently, the theme song, with its repeated list of time periods, was not inspiring people to get down.

"But . . ." Hallie said, still sounding lost, as we sat down at the mostly empty table—clearly reserved for overflow and last-minute RSVPers. "Um, what are we doing here? I like a gift bag as much

as the next girl," she said, peering into it. "But I just think it's . . .
ooh look, an iPod!" She picked it up, turning it over in her hands.
I noticed that it had a picture of a smiling kid—presumably
Scott—on the back, but I figured that was a small price to pay for
getting free electronics.

"Just wait a second," I said, glancing toward the stage and
seeing a very thin roadie hauling out equipment, then staggering backstage looking winded. "I think you'll see why we're here."

"But . . ." Hallie said again, looking around. "Should we really
be here? If you don't know anyone? I mean . . ."

The lights in the ballroom dimmed, and a huge group of people,
most of them carrying giant, unwieldy instruments, crowded
onstage. "Hi," a guy wearing a T-shirt and carrying a harpsi-
chord said into the microphone. "Congratulations to Scott!"

The ballroom burst into applause, and Hallie turned to me.
Her jaw had dropped, and she looked utterly shocked. "This
isn't . . ." she said faintly. "Sophie, you didn't . . ."

"We're Lenin and McCarthy," the singer continued. "Hope
you enjoy the set!"

Hallie turned to me, shaking her head in what looked like
happy disbelief.

I smiled at her. "Surprise."

CHAPTER 20

"That," Hallie said, "was amazing."

I nodded and picked up a slice from my pizza box. We were parked in the driveway, sitting in the giant back area of Bruce's SUV. The door was up, and the space was so enormous that there was more than enough room for both of us and two pizza boxes, plus a Diet Coke for me, a ginger ale for her, and a stack of napkins. We'd stayed at the bar mitzvah until the band stopped playing, and when they left the stage, Hallie and I had joined the crowd of thirteen-year-olds who lined up for autographs and pictures. We'd hung out a little after that and took pictures together in the photo booth, but when a seemingly endless line of relatives started approaching the mic to tell stories about "Scotty," we decided it was time to hit the road. Since we'd left before dinner was served, we stopped by the Upper Crust on the way back to Bruce's.

"It was fun," I agreed, taking a bite. Even as someone who didn't love their music, I'd enjoyed the show. The only thing that

I really regretted was that Sophie couldn't be there. She would have loved it. I had gotten the lead singer to say "Hi there, Sophie," into my phone and I'd recorded it, telling Hallie I wanted it as a souvenir for myself.

"No," Hallie said, shaking her head. "I mean, that was *incredible*. Thank you so much, Sophie."

"It was my pleasure," I said, meaning it. The cupcakes had been a bust, and while helping her babysit the twins was one thing, tonight felt like the first time I'd really been able to do something nice for Hallie. I'd been able to make her happy, and it felt pretty good. Much better, in fact, than making her miserable had done. "And after all," I said, raising my eyebrows at her, "you might have gotten a date out of it."

"Oh my god," Hallie said, laughing and covering her eyes. "I could not believe that kid." Halfway through the band's set, Scott's cousin Marvin had decided he was in love with Hallie, despite the fact that he couldn't have been more than twelve. He'd pestered her until his mom finally came and dragged him away, but when we were leaving, Hallie found that he'd left his number, e-mail address, and World of Warcraft player name in her gift bag.

"Maybe you should consider it," I said, deadpan, as I reached for another napkin. "It takes a special kind of guy to pull off a plaid tie."

Hallie just shook her head. "My boyfriend might have a problem with that," she said. "But it's nice to know that I'm a hit with the middle school set." She opened her own pizza box, but there were only crusts left.

"Want some?" I asked, angling my box toward her. I had two slices left, which I had been planning on sneaking to Bruce as a thank-you for getting us into his accountant's son's bar mitzvah. "I'm finished."

Hallie looked down into the box and her expression clouded slightly. "No," she said. "I'm . . . I'm fine." She closed the lid on her own box, taking her time getting the tab pushed in just right. When she turned back to me, her face was drawn. "Actually . . . I used to know someone who ordered their pizza almost like that. Someone who was pretty awful to me."

It felt like my heart totally stopped for a moment. I hadn't quite ordered my usual, pineapple, sausage, and pepperoni, because I'd gone to town on the appetizers we'd been served at the party and wasn't super hungry. I had ordered my pie with just pineapple and pepperoni. But that was a fairly normal pizza topping, right? Other people ordered that, didn't they?

After I stopped panicking that I'd given myself away, what Hallie had just said sunk in—she was talking about me. Eleven-year-old, pizza-ordering, life-ruining me.

"Oh?" I asked, concentrating on lining up the edges on my napkins so that they were all even. I didn't trust myself to look at Hallie without the truth showing all over my face.

"Yeah," Hallie said, and I could hear the pain that was in her voice. "Sophie, have you ever read any Tennessee Williams?"

This question surprised me enough that I felt like I could look at her and not totally betray myself. "Um, no," I said. I did know who he was, because Bruce's second wife had gotten him to finance a film version of *The Night of the Iguana*, starring her and set in a postapocalyptic wasteland, with zombies. My dad had wisely passed on Bruce's offer to adapt the script. "Not exactly."

"Well, we read *Streetcar* freshman year, and this character talks about how she just can't stand deliberate cruelty. She can't abide it." I nodded. I had a terrible feeling that I knew where this was going. "And this person . . . the one who ate pizza like that . . . they were just deliberately cruel to me. There's no other way to put it."

I took a moment before speaking. I wasn't sure I could trust my voice not to break, and it felt like someone had just punched me in the stomach. And the worst part of it? It was the truth. "Hallie," I said, making myself look at her as I said it, "I'm so sorry."

Hallie gave me a shaky smile. "You didn't do it," she said. "Anyway, it was a long time ago. You just think you're past something, and then . . ." She looked down at my pizza box and shrugged. "Anyway," she went on after a moment, in a voice that sounded determined to be upbeat, "I should get going. But thank you so much for everything tonight, Sophie. It was so fun."

"It was," I said, making myself smile at her, hoping that I didn't sound as thrown as I was.

Hallie climbed out of the back, and I followed, grabbing the pizza boxes and our gift bags. I handed Hallie hers, and she slung it over her shoulder. "Want to come to a party tomorrow?" she asked. She blurted this out, and sounded almost like she was surprised she was asking. "I mean," she added after a moment, sounding more like herself, "if you're free."

"Oh," I said as I closed the back of the car and turned to face her. "Sure, that sounds fun."

"It's just a small thing," she said. "A bonfire. Our house, around eight? No seafood, I promise."

I smiled at that. "Awesome."

"And if you were looking for a date . . ." Hallie rummaged in her bag and then held out Marvin's contact info to me.

"Ha," I said, and though I tried to keep a straight face, I soon couldn't help laughing for real, and Hallie joined in with me. I knew I was laughing partially out of relief—that even though Hallie was still hurt by what I'd done to her when we were younger, she didn't suspect me. She was still inviting Sophie Curtis to parties, and my pizza order hadn't ruined everything. Though the fact that pizza had been responsible for almost revealing my true identity twice on the same day was a little troubling. I resolved to hold off on ordering it for a while. Or at least a few days.

I waved at Hallie as she got into her car and drove away, beeping once as she turned down the mile-long driveway. I headed inside, glad that the house was quiet. I had no doubt everyone was still awake and working—after all, it was only eight on the West Coast—but everyone appeared to be in their own rooms, and not hanging out in the kitchen or watching movies, which I was grateful for. I wanted some alone time to think.

I left the pizza in the fridge for Bruce and headed upstairs, holding my shoes in my hand. When I got to my room, I tossed my bag on the bed, and lay back, staring up at the ceiling. It was becoming clear that I'd have to tell Hallie who I was, and soon. The longer I put it off, the more it felt like I was lying to her. And she knew now that I was a good person. So really, there was nothing left to wait for. But what would she say? What would Josh say?

Half the contents of my purse had spilled out when I tossed it on the bed, and one item caught my eye. I reached forward and pulled out the photo booth pictures Hallie and I had taken together. They read *Great Scott!* on the bottom, but I figured that could easily be cut off.

I smiled as I looked at them. There were four vertical pictures, and in the first one, Hallie and I were both looking in different directions, clearly not understanding how the thing worked. In the second, we were looking in the same place, but the picture was snapped before we could smile. In the third, we were both yelling at Marvin, who had just stuck his head into the booth. And the last picture showed us cracking up, our heads turned toward each other, Hallie's hand on my shoulder as she leaned on me, looking like two girls who had been nothing but best friends for a long, long time.

CHAPTER 21

"Your house is amazing," I said as I turned in a circle, gaping at the foyer. "It's . . . I mean . . ." I trailed off, at a loss for words.

I'd arrived at Hallie's bonfire early. Everyone else had left for Los Angeles that morning, and by the afternoon, I was already tired of being by myself in the house. So I'd left sooner than I needed to, and had forgotten the fact was that Bruce's car was surprisingly zippy for a vehicle that could seat twelve. When I'd arrived at the Bridges' house, though, only Hallie was home. As she let me in, she'd told me that Josh was out picking up some stuff for the party. I nodded at that, like it was just regular information. But even though I hadn't wanted to ask her when she'd invited me, I'd been wondering ever since if Josh was going to be coming, then chastising myself for wondering that, then wondering again.

Even without knowing for certain that he would be there, I'd spent a little extra time with my makeup and was wearing a shirt that technically belonged to Sophie, but that I'd appropriated a few months ago. It was, therefore, much tighter and more low-cut than anything I would have normally worn. I had also borrowed another pair of shoes from Gwyneth, stacked espadrille wedges. This might not have been the smartest thing to do, since the last shoes I borrowed from her had never turned up, despite the fact that I had made a practice of checking out people's feet to see if they were wearing hot-pink silk heels. But I decided to risk it.

I told myself that I only wanted to look good since I needed to replace the last image Josh had of me, when I was pale and sickly and just-woken-up. But even I no longer believed myself, which seemed like a pretty low point to have gotten to. The truth was, I wanted to see Josh. I wasn't sure what this meant for my mourning period, but I knew I had been thinking about Teddy less and less, and Josh more. I didn't know precisely how I felt about him, and had no idea how he felt about me, but it had been several days since I'd seen him, and I missed him. It was as simple—or as incredibly complicated—as that.

Since I was the first guest to arrive, Hallie was showing me around. And I was kind of glad that I was early, as the private tour allowed me to take in the absolutely stunning house. I knew it was impressive from the outside, but the inside was even more so, bigger than it looked from the driveway. It was beautifully decorated inside, everything going together but not overly matchy, art on the walls and the built-in bookcases filled with books.

"Thanks," Hallie said offhandedly. "We've only been here a few months, but we like it so far."

"So is your mom . . . here?" I asked, hoping I sounded casual, just like a normal partygoer hoping for a lack of parental supervision.

"No," Hallie said, her expression suddenly guarded. "She's not." She said it with a note of finality, one that didn't invite any follow-up questions. I just nodded, and when I didn't say anything, it seemed like she relaxed a little. "Want to drop your bag in my room?"

"Sure," I said, thrilled that Hallie had suggested this, hoping I would find an opportunity to get rid of the bathing-suit receipt without having to resort to subterfuge. I followed her up a flight of stairs and down a pristine, white-painted hallway. As we walked, I saw a professionally photographed black-and-white picture of Josh, Hallie, and Karen on the wall, but before I could get a closer look, Hallie was opening the door to her room, and I had to follow, or else make it obvious that I was gawking at her family portraits.

"You can just drop your bag anywhere," Hallie said, stepping inside her room.

"Thanks," I said, following her inside. Hallie's room was meticulously neat; another change from when I'd known her—she'd been a bit of a slob. There was a perfectly made bed covered with a blue bedspread, a white desk, and a blue armchair in the corner. There was an open laptop on the desk, the screensaver scrolling through pictures, and a stack of books on the bedside table.

I had just dropped my purse by the side of the bed when I heard the sound of a door slamming.

"Hal!" We both turned at the sound of the voice coming from downstairs. I realized it was Josh, and my pulse started to pick up a little. "I need some help with this stuff!" I could hear what sounded like a small crash, and then another voice saying something I couldn't make out.

Hallie rolled her eyes at me. "Coming!" she yelled back. She headed out of her room, and I followed, but as soon as I stepped over the threshold, I had a sudden attack of nerves. What would Josh say when he saw me? Would it be weird between us now that we'd spent the night sleeping in the same room? And then a terrible thought filled my mind: What if he didn't know Hallie had invited me? What if he was disappointed I was there? What if he'd invited some other girl to the party? Someone who wouldn't force him to eat seafood he didn't want, make him sick, and then not even let him watch *Die Hard*?

"Um," I said, stopping, looking around for something I could say to stall. Hallie turned back to me and raised her eyebrows. "Bathroom?" I asked.

She nodded back toward her bedroom. "Through there," she said. "See you downstairs?"

I nodded, and she headed down the hall, quickening her pace when another, louder crash sounded. I ducked back into Hallie's room and went into the bathroom, but just to apply some lip gloss and make sure my hair was behaving itself. I smoothed down my (technically, Sophie's) shirt, made sure my *S* necklace was straight, and then headed back out into the room. As I passed Hallie's bureau, I smiled when I saw that she'd propped her copy of our photo booth picture against her mirror.

I dropped my lip gloss back into my purse and looked quickly around the room, wondering where I would be if I were a bathing suit with a potentially damaging receipt inside. As I was looking around, I noticed something under the bed. Telling myself that I was just making sure my purse was properly closed, I dropped to my hands and knees to get a better look, and saw loose articles of clothing, pieces of paper, and magazines in a jumble. It looked like Hallie had just shoved everything under there to make the room look presentable—which was exactly what the old Hallie would have done. I was pushing myself to my feet when something else caught my eye—a small, tissue-wrapped object.

I realized to my immense relief that this was it. Knowing I didn't have much time before she started wondering where I was, I reached under the bed and pulled the bathing suit toward me, trying not to wrinkle the tissue too much. I pulled it open, lifted up the bikini—and out fluttered a tiny piece of paper. I grabbed it, and saw that it was the receipt I was looking for. And there was my signature—*Gemma Rose Tucker*—written neatly above the printed version of my name.

It actually made me feel a little sick to see, in Hallie's room, my full name right there, as clear as anything. I stuffed the receipt into my pocket, then quickly wrapped the suit back up and slid it back under the bed. Since things were jumbled under there haphazardly, it seemed less likely that she'd notice it had been moved.

I stood up, feeling incredibly relieved. I had gotten to the receipt before Hallie had seen it. My cover wouldn't be blown. Things were still good with me and Hallie. Feeling like I was now ready to join the party, I straightened my (Sophie's) shirt, doing a last check in the mirror on the door of what looked, from the crack it was ajar, like Hallie's closet. I turned away and headed for the door when it hit me that I'd seen something in there. I backtracked slowly, my eyes resting on what they'd caught a glimpse of—a flash of hot-pink silk.

CHAPTER 22

I just stood there, frozen, staring into the closet. My heart wasn't hammering hard—instead, it seemed like it was going the other way, slowing down, making me feel like I wasn't getting enough air. I just stared at the one segment of fabric I could see, as other items were piled all around it.

Had Hallie stolen my shoes from the pool party? Why would she have done that?

My brain was spinning with justifications—maybe she'd brought them back for me, to keep them safe. But then why wouldn't she have mentioned it? Or given them to me? Why would they still be in her closet?

And then a thought struck me with such force that it weakened my knees a little. What if Hallie knew who I really was? What if she'd figured it out? And she'd taken the shoes on purpose?

"Hey." I whipped around to see Hallie standing in the doorway, arms folded and eyebrows raised. "You okay?"

"Fine," I managed, even though it felt like my throat was too tight, and speaking was harder than usual. "I just . . ." I looked at her, taking in her concerned expression. It wasn't possible. Was it?

I looked back to the closet, then away again, trying to bring some order to my thoughts. My eyes fell on Hallie's laptop, where the screensaver was now showing her leaning against some-one—it looked like a guy, his arm wrapped around her shoulder. But before his face became visible, Hallie crossed to the laptop and closed the screen, tucking it under her arm.

"I came up to get this," she said. "Josh has some crazy idea about projecting movies against the house." She looked at me closely. "Is everything all right?"

"I . . ." I looked back into the closet. "I just . . ." I didn't want to say anything about my suspicions. Because what if I was wrong? But—and this was even worse—what if I wasn't?

"Oh, I wanted to show you this," Hallie said. She set the lap-top down on the bed and crossed to the closet. To my shock, she flung the door of the closet wide and reached down for the hot-pink object I'd been staring at. I held my breath as she lifted a clutch purse and turned around, showing it to me with a smile. "What do you think?"

"It's a bag," I said, feeling a little wobbly with relief.

"Yes," Hallie said slowly. "But I meant, what do you think of it? I was maybe going to carry it to a party on the Fourth. Ward's going to be there, and I want everything to be perfect."

"I think it's great," I said, totally meaning it. I gave her a smile. "Really." Now that there was an explanation—and a ratio-nal one—I felt stupid that I would have thought anything else.

And really, what did it say about me that I so easily leapt to these conclusions? Just because I had behaved badly, I assumed Hallie would do the same? When she hadn't been anything but nice to me this whole summer.

"Yeah," she said with a smile, turning it over in her hands. "I think it'll go." She tossed the clutch back into the closet, then picked up her computer. "Come on," she said, nudging me toward the doorway. "The party awaits."

I followed her down the hallway, my relief over the fact that Hallie hadn't found out the truth and extracted footwear revenge becoming replaced by nervousness over seeing Josh again.

Hallie led me across the foyer and into the kitchen, which was all gleaming surfaces and new-looking appliances. We went out a side door, and I saw there was a wide deck, with a table covered with drinks and bowls of snacks. There were steps that led directly down to the beach, and I could see, at the water's edge, a ring of stones surrounding a pile of sticks—what would become the bonfire.

There weren't very many people yet, and I remembered what Hallie had said about keeping it small. There were a handful of people I recognized from the pool party hanging out on the deck, and another small group standing around by the water. I was relieved to see that, this time at least, I was dressed appropriately for the occasion.

Hallie's phone beeped with a text and she looked down at it. "I've got to get the door," she said, heading back toward the kitchen. "But make yourself at home! Help yourself to the food!"

I nodded and made my way to the refreshments, looking

around for Josh while trying not to be obvious about it. I pulled a Diet Coke out of a cooler and had just popped the top when I heard a voice behind me say, "Hey."

It was Josh's voice, and I felt myself smile as I heard it, my pulse racing with a mixture of excitement and nerves. I turned around and there he was, looking somehow even cuter after an absence of four days, his hair tousled and a faint sunburn across his nose. "Hi," I said. Now that he was in front of me and not just theoretical, I felt my anxiety fade. What had I been so nervous about? This was *Josh*. I'd seen him with a pillow crease across his face, wearing meerkat sweatpants.

"How are you feeling?" he asked, and for some reason, the question didn't embarrass me.

"Much better," I said. "All recovered. You?"

"I'm great now," he said. "But I think you may have permanently prevented me from trying seafood ever again."

"No!" I protested. "You can't let one bad experience make you give up."

"What are you talking about?" Josh asked. "That's, like, the whole reason for giving up. When you have a bad experience, it's the universe's way of telling you not to eat seafood. And who am I to go against the universe?"

"That's not what the universe is saying," I said with great authority, and Josh threw his head back, laughing.

"Oh, it's not?" he said with a grin. "Please, Sophie. Enlighten me."

"Bridges!" A big guy with a very red face hustled up to Josh. "I think we're all set up down by the water. Just need some *fuego* and we'll be in business. I mean, you know, fire." He seemed to notice me then, and turned even redder, taking a step away. "Sorry, man," he said. "I didn't—"

Josh just shook his head in a way that made me think he was used to this guy saying these kinds of things. "Reid, this is Sophie," he said. "Sophie, Reid."

"Oh, hi," I said, remembering that on the drive to the restaurant, Josh had talked about his closest friend at boarding school. "Nice to meet you." Reid was taller than Josh, and big—not exactly fat, but big-boned. He had close-cropped auburn hair and blue eyes that he seemed to blink a lot.

"You too," he said, his face still a little red. "I didn't mean to interrupt, or anything."

"You didn't," Josh said firmly, grabbing Reid, who was continuing to edge away, by the shoulder and pulling him back toward us. "Reid's staying with us for a week."

"Yeah," Reid said, looking down at the deck. "My internship didn't really work out the way that I'd hoped."

Josh shook his head. "I still don't understand why you quit."

"I didn't *quit*," Reid said. "I was fired. For overwhelming incompetence. Remember?"

"Oh, right," Josh said, shooting me a small smile.

I smiled back and let out a long breath as Josh and Reid continued to banter. It was a beautiful night, my secret was safe, and Josh was looking over at me occasionally and smiling. Suddenly, I was in the mood for a party.

* * *

264

"**W**hat about that one?" Josh asked.

"Nope," I said firmly. "Too big." We hadn't been talking with Reid for long before Hallie had broken up our group, pulled Josh away, and moved the party down to the beach. She was really running the whole thing, I'd noticed—getting people drinks, putting out bowls of food, organizing everything. It was like she had a vision for the night and was going to see it through. Mostly, I was just trying not to be in the way, and doing what I could to help. So when she realized she needed sticks for roasting marshmallows, I volunteered to go look for some, and Josh immediately said he'd join me. Reid had volunteered too, but after Josh shot him a look, he sat down and said he'd changed his mind.

Josh and I were walking on the beach, both of us holding small handfuls of sticks. Josh was grabbing anything made of wood, not appearing to care if it was a twig or a massive branch. The sun was starting to set, casting the water and the whole beach in a pale pinkish-orange glow. I had left my shoes back at the house, and was walking barefoot on the beach, the sand warm between my toes.

"Here," I said, spotting a perfect marshmallow stick up by the dunes and grabbing it. "This is what we're looking for."

"Ah," Josh said, nodding. "I see what you mean." He reached down and picked up what could only fairly be called a twig. "Like this?" he asked, deadpan.

I laughed, even though I was trying not to. "That can be yours," I said, and Josh grinned at me. "Think we have enough?"

"Well, now that we have this one," Josh said, lofting his twig on his palm, "I think we're all set."

We both turned and started walking back toward the house. As it came into view, I was struck by how cool and modern it was, and how it stood out from the houses on either side of it. "Your house really is amazing," I said.

Josh looked at it for a moment and nodded. "Yeah," he said. "It was pretty much my dad's vision."

"Did he design it?" I asked, not even thinking about it. But when Josh stopped walking and turned to me, I realized what I'd just said. Oh, crap.

"What?" he asked.

"Um," I said, nervously. I couldn't believe I'd let myself slip up like this. Gemma Tucker knew that Mr. Bridges had been an architect. But Sophie Curtis would have no idea. "I just . . . didn't know if . . ."

"Did Hallie tell you about him?" Josh asked, his brow furrowed, like he was trying to put something together. "She usually doesn't bring him up."

"Well," I said, drawing out the word, trying to buy myself time. I was trying to decide if it would be better to say that Hallie told me and hope Josh wouldn't bring it up to her, or else just pretend I had been doing some recreational googling, when Josh spoke again.

"I'm glad that she can confide in you," he said, his voice a little softer. "That's sometimes hard for her." I just nodded, not really trusting myself to say anything. "He did design this house," Josh said, looking at it with a faint smile. "I didn't know my mom saved the plans all these years until she started building."

I nodded, trying to think of what I could say—like how sorry

I was—when Josh started walking again, and I fell into step with him. We hadn't gone very far when his hand, the one empty of sticks, brushed against mine, sending an electrical jolt through me.

I glanced over at him, but Josh was looking out at the water, and I figured it had probably just been an accident. But we took a few more steps, and his hand touched mine again, lingering a little longer this time.

My heart started to pound. It hadn't been an accident. Josh had just touched my hand. And that touch alone made me feel like every nerve in my body was suddenly wide awake.

A tiny voice in the back of my head was reminding me about Teddy, about the mourning period. But I was no longer listening to it. Forget about the mourning period. Teddy had broken up with me, and this was happening here, now. I let out a breath, let Teddy go, and before I could stop myself, reached out for Josh's hand.

My fingers just grazed his wrist, and Josh still didn't look at me, but I saw the corners of his mouth lift in a smile. And we walked like that all the way back to the bonfire, touching—but not quite holding—hands.

CHAPTER 23

"Okay, I've got one," Hallie said, leaning back on her hands and stretching her legs in front of her. "I've never . . . gone skinny-dipping."

I looked around the circle, at the faces illuminated by the firelight, and tried not to choke on my soda when Reid sheepishly popped a marshmallow into his mouth. We were playing I Never, which was technically a drinking game. But since most of us had curfews—not to mention the fact that nobody had been able to get anything to drink—we were playing it with marshmallows. If you had done the thing that was said, you had to eat one.

It was the end of the night, and the party had pretty much run its course. There were only a handful of us sitting around the bonfire under the stars—me, Josh, Hallie, Reid, and a guy named Brian who seemed to have quite the adventurous life, and as a result was currently looking a little green.

I was sitting next to Josh on the sand. I knew my lip gloss was in place, as I'd taken a surreptitious "bathroom break," which actually involved going inside, grabbing my purse, and reapplying. Josh had given me his sweatshirt once the sun went down, and I was already planning on not giving it back. It was a gray Clarence Hall hoodie, and it felt soft and much-washed. It was infinitely cozier than Teddy's sweatshirts, which had been stiff and scratchy, maybe because they had been made out of stuff—like hemp and flax—that you could also find in breakfast cereals. Josh and I were sitting close together, and even though we'd taken a step away from each other before we returned to the group, I noticed that Hallie kept shooting looks my way, like she'd somehow picked up on what had happened.

Out of the blue, I'd gotten kind of a weird text from Sophie as the bonfire was being lit. She'd asked me where I was, which made me worry what she'd gotten up to that night. To be funny, I texted her Hallie's whole address and added "(the Hamptons ☺)" after it. I hadn't heard from her again, so it seemed like my text was enough to remind her, however hard she was currently partying, that I was not in Putnam at the moment.

But that was the only thing that had even come close to disturbing the peace of the night. It just felt really magical to be sitting there, under the stars, the remains of a bonfire in front of me, close to a boy who I liked as a friend and maybe liked as more, his sweatshirt, which smelled like woodsy cologne and spearmint gum—like him—around my shoulders.

"Okay," Reid said, rubbing his hands together. "I've never . . . stolen anything."

I was about to sit this one out, when I looked down and saw the hem of Sophie's shirt. Not to mention the two pairs of

Gwyneth's shoes. I wasn't sure where the line between stealing and indefinitely borrowing actually was, but I felt like I'd been sitting out most of these, so I picked up a marshmallow and tossed it in my mouth. After a moment, I saw Hallie take a marshmallow as well. She gave me a small smile, and Josh nudged me with his shoulder.

"So what'd you take?" he asked.

I shook my head. "Nope," I said, smiling at him. "Not telling."

"Brian?" Hallie asked loudly, turning to him. "It's your turn."

"Nnnrgh," Brian said, looking greener than ever in the firelight. "I'll pass my turn."

"Okay," Josh said, glancing over at me and raising his eyebrows. "I've never kept a secret from someone." We all took a marshmallow on that one, though I noticed Brian didn't eat his, and groaned a little as he looked at it. Everyone in the circle looked at me, and I realized it was my turn to ask.

"I've never . . ." I started, thinking. Maybe this was my chance to indirectly apologize for what I'd done to Hallie. "I've never hurt someone on purpose," I said, taking a marshmallow as I did. I saw Hallie look at me, confused, probably wondering what I'd done. Little did she understand that she knew all too well what I'd done—because I'd done it to her.

And maybe she was thinking along those same lines, because it was her turn next, and she said softly, "I've never been hurt on purpose." She took a marshmallow then, and so did Josh.

"Whoa," Reid said. "This game got dark." Brian grunted in response. Maybe Hallie felt this too, because she stood up, brushing her hands off.

"Okay," she said. "Who wants s'mores?" She widened her eyes at me, and I knew this was my cue to go inside with her. She clearly wanted to talk to me about what was happening with Josh. I wasn't sure what I would be able to tell her, though, as I wasn't sure myself. Unless it turned out that Josh only gave his sweatshirts to girls he desperately wanted to date. That would help to shed some light on things.

"Be right back," I said to Josh as I pushed myself to my feet, grabbed my bag, and crossed the sand to catch up with Hallie.

As soon as we were both in the kitchen, Hallie turned to me, eyebrows raised. "So," she said, and I noticed her voice was high and a little strained. "Um, what's going on with you and my brother?"

"Nothing," I said automatically, but then thought about the zingy way I'd felt when our hands had touched, the way I'd been aware of every breath he'd taken next to me as we sat close on the sand. "Well," I amended after a moment, "I don't know. Nothing *has* happened, though."

Hallie just looked at me for a moment. "You're wearing his sweatshirt," she said.

"I was cold," I said, and she just nodded, but didn't confirm that this was Josh's one gesture of true love, which was actually a little disappointing. It would have cleared things right up.

"I just . . ." Hallie started, then yanked open one of the cabinets and took down a package of graham crackers. "I thought I told you . . . I mean, I thought you said that you weren't going to date him."

"And I'm not," I said quickly. "But . . ." I looked closely at her, and saw for the first time just how upset she really was. "I mean, would it really be the worst thing in the world?" I asked, my voice quiet, and I could hear the hurt in it coming through. Because as far as Hallie knew, I was just Sophie Curtis—why would she have something against it?

"No! God, Sophie, I'm sorry," Hallie said, turning away from me and pulling down a bar of chocolate and a package of marshmallows. When she faced me again, her expression was more composed. "I just really don't want Josh to get hurt," she said, in quiet, almost desperate voice.

"I don't want that either," I said, in total honesty.

"Do you really like him?" Hallie asked, looking at me closely.

I took a breath, about to deny it, say what I'd been saying to her and myself all along. But I found I couldn't. It was what I had realized on the beach. I was done pretending that I didn't have feelings for Josh, out of . . . what? Loyalty to Teddy? The sense that it was too quick for me to be interested in someone new? Instead of denying it, I just nodded. "I really do."

Hallie looked away from me, making a pyramid of the s'mores fixings, taking a moment before she spoke. "It's funny," she finally said. "But Josh said something to me earlier. About how . . . he thought you were a really good friend to me. And how he was glad that I had found someone that I could trust."

I opened my mouth and closed it, not sure what to say to this. I knew Josh had only told Hallie this because he thought she'd confided in me. But I didn't know how to set her straight without wrecking the moment. Was this her way of telling me that she was okay with the possibility of us? "Oh," I said.

"Who knows what made him say it," Hallie said with a shrug. "But . . ." She looked at me, then down again, like she was fascinated by the graham crackers' nutritional information. "I mean, he's right. You're a really good person, Sophie."

I felt my breath catch in my throat. It suddenly occurred to me that maybe this was the moment I had been waiting for, working for, this whole summer. Was I going to find a better opportunity? It was what I'd wanted before I told Hallie the truth—to get her to see me differently than the person she remembered. And I'd done it. Hallie and I were friends. She liked me and thought I was a good person. What more was I waiting for?

I took a breath. "Hallie," I started.

"Sophie," she said back, imitating my serious tone.

"I . . . should tell you something."

"What?" she asked, her expression maybe a little wary.

"I . . . the thing is . . ." Even as I thought about how best to put it, I could feel myself hesitating. What would happen once I told her? What would happen to our fledgling friendship? And— my stomach plunged at the thought—what would happen with Josh? Was I really ready to potentially wreck all this?

"Yes?" she asked.

I paused, still torn, not sure what I should do. But was I going to get a better moment than this? I took a breath and prepared myself to say it. "Hallie," I started again. "There's something I've been meaning to—" Before I could continue, though, my phone beeped with a text that sounded very loud in the quiet kitchen. "Sorry," I said, looking down at it.

Sophie Curtis

11:15 PM

Hi! I'm here!

I stared down at the phone, baffled. What was Sophie talking about? Was she outside my house in Putnam, expecting me to come down?

At that moment, though, I heard the sound of a car outside, getting closer, pulling into the driveway, and headlights flashed through the windows.

"Is someone here?" Hallie asked, frowning, as she crossed to the front door. "If so, they've totally missed the party."

I followed behind her, my heart starting to beat hard. There was an explanation for this. It wasn't—couldn't be—what I thought.

I stepped out of the house with Hallie and felt my stomach plunge at what I saw. There was a taxi idling in the driveway. And standing next to it, bags in hand, was my best friend.

Sophie Curtis—the real one—had just arrived in the Hamptons.

CHAPTER 24

I stared at Sophie as she paid the driver, trying to somehow make her presence here make sense. And then I remembered I'd texted her Hallie's address when she asked me where I was. And that she was about to totally blow the entire cover I'd constructed for myself.

"I don't think I know her," Hallie said in an undertone to me, as she stared at Sophie. "Maybe she has the wrong address? We're up the street from the Southampton Arms, people sometimes come here thinking it's the hotel . . ."

I licked my lips, which suddenly felt very dry. I could feel my heart beating faster and faster, and I knew I was starting to panic. This was more than I could handle. This was not trying to prevent Bruce or Rosie from saying my name aloud. This was worlds colliding on a whole advanced level and I wasn't sure I was up for it. It was like a grenade had just gently rolled up to me and was resting by my feet—not exploding yet, but about to, any second now. "I . . ." I started. "She's . . ."

"Hello," Hallie called, a question in the greeting.

The driver got back into the taxi and it pulled away and Sophie turned, squinting. I took an instinctive step back into the porch shadows, trying to buy myself time, even if it was only seconds.

"Hey," Josh said, coming up from the beach, around the side of the house, Reid behind him, chewing on what I assumed was another marshmallow. "Did I hear a car?"

I took the microsecond this distraction bought me to type the fastest text of my life.

> **Me**
> 11:19 PM
> YOU'RE NOT YOU. I'M YOU.
> OKAY??? BUT YOU'RE NOT YOU!!!!!!!!!!

Sophie's phone chimed with the text, and she looked down at the message, then squinted into the darkness, like she was trying to locate me. "Hello?" she called.

"Hi," Hallie said, taking a step closer to her, sounding confused but not unfriendly. "Can I help you?"

"Hallie," I said, as I stepped out onto the driveway to stand next to her, deciding that it would be better to take charge of the situation and salvage what I could from it, rather than watch as it blew up in my face. "This is . . . my friend. I just didn't realize she was going to be here. Or in the Hamptons at all."

Sophie's expression, which had registered happiness and relief over seeing me, suddenly did a 180 into confusion. "No," she said, looking from me to Hallie, baffled. "It was kind of a last-minute thing . . ." She turned to me. "This isn't your house?" she added, her voice quieter, and I could tell she was starting to get embarrassed.

"Well, any friend of Sophie's is a friend of ours, right, Hallie?" Josh asked, coming a little closer with Reid.

Sophie's eyebrows shot up at the mention of her name, and she glanced down at her phone again, then back at me, looking totally lost, and understandably so.

"Right," Hallie said, smiling easily. "Of course. Sorry you missed the party."

"Oh," Sophie said, still sounding as confused as I'd ever heard her, "that's okay." She gave me a desperate *help me* look, but I forced my expression into something neutral and friendly, and not what I was currently feeling, which more accurately resembled the skinny guy by the railing in *The Scream*.

"I'm Hallie," Hallie said. "You know Sophie, of course." Here she smiled at me, and I tried to return it, but I could practically feel the confusion coming off Sophie in waves. "That's my brother, Josh, and that's Reid Franklin."

"Hi," Sophie said. She gave Reid a double take, like she recognized him, but then turned back to me, giving me the kind of look a drowning person gives a lifeguard.

"And you are?" Hallie asked, smiling politely.

"Oh," I jumped in. "Well, that's my friend. That's, um . . ."

"Gemma Tucker," Sophie said, raising an eyebrow at me in triumph, like she was glad she'd finally figured out what was going on.

Oh. No.

It was like all the air had suddenly disappeared from the driveway for a moment, and I swear even the cicadas, which had been going full blast all night, stopped chirping for a minute. I closed my eyes, wishing that I'd gotten to speak first, or that Sophie had used pretty much any other name in the whole entire world.

"You're Gemma Tucker," Hallie repeated, her voice disbelieving. "Really." She raised her eyebrows at Sophie, who was now shooting me drowning looks again, like she knew she'd gotten something wrong but had no idea what it was or how to fix it.

"Yes?" Sophie said hesitantly, looking to me for confirmation.

Hallie just stared at her hard, and the words I had been planning to say—about how she'd misspoke, that this was my friend *Emma* Tucker, that this was all just a crazy misunderstanding, ha ha ha—died in my throat when I saw the way Hallie was looking at Sophie, like she was adding things up. I suddenly remembered the pictures of me and Sophie from when we were both eleven, looking almost like identical twins, hard to tell apart unless you knew for sure who was who. There was the bump on her nose that I no longer had. Her hair was still dark brown, the same shade it had been when we were both kids. The fact was, Sophie looked more like me at eleven than I did now. And as I took in what she was wearing—denim mini and tight striped shirt—I noticed, for the first time, that she was wearing her *G* necklace, the one that matched my *S*.

It was completely believable that Sophie was me, all grown

up. Which was, I realized, as I saw the look on Hallie's face, a very big problem.

"Gemma Tucker," Hallie said, her voice now a whisper. She was staring at Sophie like she was something out of her worst nightmares come to life. "Oh my god."

"Um," Sophie said helplessly, looking to me for guidance. "Um . . ."

Hallie turned to me, and I saw her face was flushed. "You're friends with Gemma Tucker?" she asked, her voice high and tight with emotion.

"You see," I said, wondering if there was any way I could still walk us back from this. "The thing is . . ."

"Hal?" Josh asked, coming to stand next to his sister. He was keeping a wary eye on Sophie, like he was worried she might charge at Hallie any moment, or something. "You okay?"

"I can't believe," Hallie said, her voice shaking, "that you have the nerve to come here. And then to pretend like you don't know me, like nothing happened, like you didn't . . ." The rest of her sentence was lost in a sob, and Hallie turned and ran for the door, yanking it open and disappearing inside.

Sophie looked at me, more lost than ever, but I couldn't do anything more at the moment than give her a helpless shrug.

Josh started to head inside after his sister, then turned back to me. "Sophie, I'm so sorry," he said, his brow furrowed. "It's . . . she's . . ." He looked at the real Sophie, shook his head, and turned back to me. "I'll call you tomorrow, okay? I'll explain."

I nodded dumbly, and he reached out and touched my shoulder for a moment before he followed Hallie inside. Reid stared at Sophie for a moment, like he was trying to place her, but then turned and followed Josh inside, leaving Sophie and me alone in the driveway.

"Okay," Sophie said, turning to me. "What the hell is going on?"

CHAPTER 25

"Let me get this straight," Sophie said, sitting up in her lounge chair and staring at me. "You've been pretending to be me this whole time? And now I have to keep pretending to be you?"

I took a bite of my sandwich and nodded miserably. "I'm afraid so." We were sitting out by Bruce's pool, where we'd gone after we'd essentially broken up the party.

I'd spent the trip home turning over and over what had happened in the driveway, and how Hallie's expression had changed when she'd heard my name. There was a piece of me that was beyond grateful I hadn't gone ahead and told her the truth in the kitchen, since that was the way she reacted. But I also felt like I'd lost the chance I'd been working for this whole summer—the chance to get her to see me differently. Now, instead of realizing that I was actually a good person, she just thought I was Sophie. And if the way she reacted had been any sign, she still hated me—maybe now more than ever, since she thought I'd blithely turned up on her doorstep and then pretended not to remember her or her brother.

These thoughts swirling in my head had made driving—let alone driving a massive car while trying to explain a fairly convoluted situation—a challenge, and after I'd sideswiped a neighbor's hedge and then narrowly missed a mailbox, Sophie suggested we wait to talk until I didn't have to multitask. When we got to Bruce's, we decamped to the lounge chairs by the pool, but soon felt that sustenance was required to keep going, and had raided the fridge. Luckily, before they'd headed to L.A., Rosie made sure the fridge was well stocked, and now I was eating a gourmet panini and Sophie had heated up some pad Thai.

"And now this Hallie girl hates me," Sophie continued, setting down her fork to keep track on her fingers, "because she thinks I'm you. But she likes you, because she thinks you're me."

"Well," I said, leaning back against my lounge chair and looking up at the sky for a moment. I took a second's worth of solace in looking at the stars. I bet things were really peaceful up in space, and very quiet, and nobody was pretending to be anyone else. "I've pretty much just been me, just with your name. I haven't been, like, appropriating your personality or history or anything."

"Is this why you wanted me to change my Friendverse profile?" she asked. "And take down my picture?"

I nodded. "I did try and tell you," I said. "But . . ."

Sophie nodded, and then looked away, her expression a little guilty—just like I suspected mine was. It hadn't escaped my notice that Sophie and I had been having trouble communicating—

which was pretty much the entire reason for the debacle that had taken place in the driveway. If we'd both been able to find the time to talk, it might have been avoided. It wasn't her fault, or mine, but it made me feel like there was real distance between us, for the first time I could remember.

"I know," she said, sliding the G on her necklace back and forth. "I've been out of touch. . . ."

"Me too," I jumped in. "I'm sorry."

"I'm sorry too," Sophie said. We sat in silence for a moment, and then she asked, "So is the you-being-me plan working? How have things been going out here?"

"Well," I said, about to say that they'd been going great. But then a montage of all the disasters and semidisasters of the summer so far suddenly flashed before my eyes. Showing up in formalwear to a pool party. The bathing-suit mishap and its expensive replacement. Gwyneth's stolen shoes. The babysitting fiasco and Bruce's destroyed award. The food poisoning. "They've been better," I admitted. "Things haven't totally been going according to plan."

Sophie shot me a sympathetic look, then picked up her fork again, but stopped with the noodles halfway to her mouth. "Should I save some of this for your dad?" she asked.

"No need," I said, but Sophie was already setting her plate down.

"Is it even okay that I'm here?" she asked, sounding uneasy. "I mean, I know you said I could visit, but I didn't check before coming. . . ."

"It's so fine," I assured her. "Really. It's just me here. My dad and Bruce and Bruce's assistant are all in California. But they wouldn't have a problem even if they were here."

"Oh, good," Sophie said, letting out a breath and picking up her plate again.

"But . . . why *are* you here?" I asked, hoping she didn't take that to mean I didn't want her there. I did—I just would have preferred a little more advance warning, that was all. "Did something happen back home?"

"Oh my god," Sophie groaned. "There is *such* boy drama." I was more than happy to forget my own drama, and listened, rapt, as she told me about the dramz back home. Things had fallen apart with Blake the barista, so she had hoped to get back together with her ex Doug until she'd gone to a party earlier that night and seen him there with some "Hartfield High hussy" and had gotten fed up with everything and decided to get out of town for a while. Hence the late train to the Hamptons and the cab to Hallie's.

"I'm so done with boys," she declared definitively. I nodded, but since I'd heard this many, many times before, I didn't put much stock in it. "But what about you?" she asked, raising an eyebrow at me. "What's up with you and that cute guy? I sensed sparks. . . ."

"Josh?" I asked, hoping she didn't mean Reid. Even though he seemed perfectly nice, he was someone I didn't exactly want to have sparks with.

"Yes," Sophie said, then frowned. "Although does that Reid guy look familiar to you? Because I swear I know him from somewhere."

"No," I said, but remembered the way he had looked at Sophie, like he had recognized her too. "But maybe you've seen him around Putnam? He knows Josh from boarding school, but I don't know where he lives the rest of the time."

"Maybe," Sophie said. She shrugged. "But anyway. Josh. Spill."

I took a breath, not really sure where to begin. "Well," I started. "Okay. I mean, he's really nice. . . ."

Sophie smiled. "Good! You need someone nice. And he's *really* cute, Gemma."

It was such a relief to hear someone call me by my real name that I almost gave Sophie a hug for saying it. "He is," I said, images of Josh coming unbidden into my mind—reaching for my bag on the train, being so nice when I looked like a mess post-babysitting, the way his eyes fluttered closed just before he fell asleep. However, a second later, reality intruded. "But I don't know if it could ever work," I said. "His whole thing is about trust. His last girlfriend really hurt him, she cheated on him and lied to him . . ."

Sophie looked outraged. "But you wouldn't lie to him!"

"I'm lying to him right now," I reminded her. I suddenly remembered the look that Josh had given Sophie when he thought she was me. There was *such* loathing in it. I pushed away my sandwich, feeling a little queasy. "Remember, he thinks I'm you?"

"Oh, right," Sophie said. She thought a minute, then shook her head. "But like you said, you're not *being* me. You're being you, just with a different name. It's not such a big deal."

I nodded. It was what I'd tried to ask Josh when we watched *The Princess Bride*, and even though he had said pretty much the same thing, I wasn't sure I could let myself believe it. "Maybe," I said, but without much hope. Sophie suddenly leaned forward, studying my face. "What?" I asked, worried I had panini crumbs all over it.

"You like him," Sophie said, sounding surprised. "I can tell. I mean, you *really* like him."

Since I'd had basically had the same revelation with Hallie just an hour before in her kitchen, there seemed to be no point in denying it now, and I just nodded.

"Wow," she said, nudging me with her foot. "That's great."

"Really?" I asked, leaning closer to her. "But what about the mourning period?"

Sophie waved this away. "Forget about *Cosmo*," she said. "If you find someone you like, you have to go for it. That's, like, a rule. And it's about time you liked someone new." She picked up her fork, but didn't eat anything, just pushed her discarded cilantro into a pile. She cleared her throat and then asked, "Um, Gem? What did you do to this Hallie girl? What was terrible enough to warrant all this?"

I looked at my best friend and realized that I had to tell her. But I also knew that I wouldn't be able to do it if I had to see the trusting look on her face slowly become one of shock and disgust. I stood up and nodded toward the beach. "Want to go for a walk?"

ophie and I walked the beach together, and I was silent at first, trying to gather my thoughts, rearrange all the pieces of a story I'd never had to tell to anyone before—a story I'd never even admitted out loud—into some kind of order. And even though Sophie could be the most impatient person on earth (I'd once seen her curse out her phone when a page wasn't loading fast enough), I didn't feel any of that from her now. I knew, somehow, that she'd walk with me for as long as it took to be able to tell her. The moon was almost full in the sky, but there were dark clouds passing it, cutting off its brightness every few minutes and throwing us into darkness.

I waited until one of these moment before I started speaking, haltingly at first, about that summer—about the separation, coming to the Hamptons, becoming fast friends with Hallie—and how everything had fallen apart with the revelation that our parents were together. I told her how my evil side seemed to take over, how I was soon doing things I never would have been able to imagine. When I got to driving away from Hallie and realizing that my dad might have accidentally given her the notebook, I heard Sophie draw in a sharp breath. But she didn't say anything, and I pushed on to the end of the story—to trying to find out about the Bridges, then meeting them here and pretending to be her. I took her through everything that had happened up until earlier that night.

When I'd finished, Sophie didn't say anything for a long moment, just looked out to the water. When she turned back to me, though, I could see in the moonlight that she didn't look judgmental or disgusted, like I'd been afraid of. Instead, she just looked sad.

"Gem," she said, shaking her head. "You should have told me this years ago. I can't believe you've been carrying this around the whole time."

I just blinked at her for a moment, not quite able to believe that this was her reaction to my darkest secret. "You mean . . . you don't think I'm a horrible person?"

Sophie shook her head so hard her dangly earrings jangled. "Of course not," she said. "I think that you were *eleven* and scared and doing the only thing you knew to do. In fact, I think it's called transference. I'll have to ask my parents, but . . ."

"Soph." If you didn't stop Sophie quickly when she got on a shrink-theory kick, you could be listening to jargon for hours.

"Right," she said. "Sorry. I mean, yes, it sounds like some of the stuff you did got out of hand. But you were a kid. And I think you're doing a good thing here, trying to make it right."

I gave her a half-smile at that. I was still a little amazed that this was Sophie's reaction. But telling her didn't make me feel like a huge burden had been lifted from my shoulders. I knew that I wouldn't get to feel that until I told Hallie the truth and she forgave me. "I hope so," I said. "I mean, I'm trying to do the right thing out here, and be a good person, but—"

"Wait," Sophie said, stopping short. She just stared at me for a moment, head tilted, like she was putting something together. "Oh my god, I get it now."

"What?" I asked, baffled.

Sophie made a vague, circular gesture with her hands. "The Teddy of it all! Is this why you were with him for so long? You wanted to be around someone who was a do-gooder? You thought that would make up for this?"

"No!" I said immediately, even though she wasn't that far off. This was the problem with having a best friend—they knew you *really* well, sometimes better than you wanted them to. "Of course that wasn't the only reason. Teddy's amazing. He's smart, and cute. . . ."

Sophie just shrugged. "He's okay. You could do better."

I shook my head at that. "Well, of course you have to say that. As my best friend, I think you're obligated. It's in the handbook."

Sophie smiled, and we started walking again. "I'm just glad you've moved on," she said. "With this Josh guy. It's a good thing."

I dragged my feet through the sand as we walked, thinking about this. Was I *really* over him? Did the fact that I was able to admit I had feelings for someone else mean that I was going to put Edward Callaway behind me for good? I wasn't sure.

But something in Sophie's tone had given me pause. It was a tone of voice I knew well—it meant she knew more than she was telling.

"Why is it a good thing?" I asked her. "If I've moved on?"

She stopped walking and looked down at the sand, drawing a crooked heart with her bare foot, then scrubbing it out with her toes. "It's just . . ." she started, then looked up at me. "If you weren't thinking about this new guy, I wouldn't tell you this."

"What is it?" I asked, feeling my heart start to beat hard.

"I think Teddy went on that trip you guys were supposed to go on together," she said. "To El Salvador?"

"Colombia," I said automatically. "Wait, what?"

Sophie nodded. "I was at the beach and ran into that weird vegan guy—"

"Reginald," I supplied, and Sophie nodded. Since I hadn't heard from Reginald once since the breakup, I had a feeling he'd picked Teddy's side, something I ultimately wasn't that upset about. All Reginald's shirts seemed to have messages on them about how great it was to be a vegan and how terrible it was that you weren't one too.

"Right," Sophie said. "Anyway, he was saying how he'd gotten a postcard from Teddy, and something about his volunteering . . ." She shrugged apologetically. "I wasn't really listening. I was mostly trying to get out of talking to him."

This was a common response to Reginald, but that's not what I was thinking about at the moment. Teddy had gone on the Colombia trip? He'd gone *without* me? When he'd talked to me about getting my deposit back, I only assumed that he was getting his back too.

"Oh my god," I said as a sudden, terrible thought hit me. "Do you think he went with her? That girl with the neck tattoo from the pizza place? Do you?" I stared hard at Sophie, who wasn't answering fast enough. *"Do you?"*

"So . . . not really over him then?" Sophie asked, looking at me carefully.

I opened my mouth and then closed it again when I didn't come up with any kind of answer. A breeze blew in off the water, and I felt myself shiver. The clouds were passing over the moon faster now, and it was staring to get chilly. "We should go inside," I said, glad that we weren't that far from Bruce's.

Sophie nodded and we walked up to the house together. When we'd brushed the sand off our feet and stepped inside, I closed the glass door, shivering once again as I looked out at the increasingly choppy water.

I made sure the door was latched before I turned and headed upstairs. Because from what I could see, it looked like there was a storm coming.

CHAPTER 26

When I woke up the next morning, the first thing I heard was the rain. It was pounding against my window, and as I opened my eyes and pushed myself up to a sitting position, I could see that it was almost totally dark outside. The ocean was rough and choppy, and the trees were swaying in the wind. The second thing I heard was my phone, which was ringing away on the bedside table.

I reached for it, then stopped when I saw Hallie's name—and the picture of her I'd taken as she posed next to the fake phonebooth—lighting up the screen. I wasn't sure I was awake enough to handle Hallie and keep my cover stories straight. The phone stopped ringing and I sat back against the pillows, relieved. I would call her later that afternoon, when I'd had some coffee and could think about what I was going to say to her, how I would explain the sudden appearance of my friend Gemma Tucker.

I had just had this comforting thought when the phone

started ringing again. It was still Hallie, and I knew she would think something was off if I kept ignoring her calls. My heart thumping, I answered the phone.

"Hi, Hallie," I said, clearing my throat after hearing how scratchy my voice sounded.

"Sophie, hi," Hallie said. "I hope I didn't wake you up."

"No, it's fine," I said, pulling the phone away from my ear and squinting at the time. It was almost eleven in the morning, so it wasn't like Hallie was calling at the crack of dawn or anything. "What's up?"

Hallie sighed, and said, "I just wanted to . . . apologize about last night. I'm sorry the party kind of fell apart at the end."

"No, it's fine," I said quickly, closing my eyes for a second. Hallie's voice sounded tired and thick, like she'd been crying, and most likely because of me. Again.

"I know this is a little bit of a strange situation," she said. "I don't know how much . . . what exactly Gemma has told you."

I paused before replying. The way Hallie had pronounced my name was awful. She'd practically spat it out. "We, um," I said, not really sure how much to admit I knew, "went into things a little bit last night."

"Well, I'm just so sorry to put you in the middle of all this," Hallie said, sounding sadder than ever. I was about to tell her that *I* was the sorry one, but before I could, Hallie took a breath, sounding like she was psyching herself up for something. "But that's not exactly why I called. Is Gemma there? Do you think I could speak with her?"

"Oh," I said, my mind racing. "You know, I don't think that

would be such a good idea. She's still sleeping. In fact," I said, getting a sudden inspiration, "I think she's actually heading back to Connecticut, like, this afternoon, so—"

"Hey!" There was a pounding on my door and I jumped. It swung open, and Sophie, her hair up in a face-washing topknot that also somehow managed to look chic, stuck her head in my room. "Are we going to get breakfast? I'm starving."

I was giving her all the *stop talking for god's sake now* gestures that I knew, but Sophie obviously didn't have her contacts in yet, as she just squinted at me. I knew I probably just looked like a gesticulating blob. "What?" she asked loudly, and I inwardly groaned.

"Was that her?" Hallie asked, her voice quiet, and I knew I couldn't really tell her that I'd had another friend magically show up on my doorstep in the last twelve hours.

"Yeah," I said. "Um . . . hold on a second." I pressed the mute button and scrambled out of bed. "It's Hallie," I whispered to Sophie, even though I knew Hallie couldn't hear me, and that I could just talk at a normal volume. "She wants to talk to you."

"Me?" Sophie asked, looking panicked.

"Well, she wants to talk to *me*." I mouthed this last word, as if Hallie would be able to hear it. "But she thinks you're me. So . . ."

Sophie backed out of my room and down the hall, and I followed. "What am I supposed to say?" she asked. "What does she even want?"

"I don't know," I said. "But I think the longer we keep her on hold, the more she's going to think something strange is going on."

Sophie looked down at my phone for a long moment, then took a breath and nodded. "Okay," she said, gesturing for me to give her the phone. "Is she going to yell at me?" she asked.

"I don't think so," I said, with much more confidence than I felt. "It didn't sound like it."

Sophie nodded and unmuted the phone, and I leaned against the wall, realizing that we'd stopped to have this conversation right in front of the framed *Nightmare of the Zombguana* poster. I turned away slightly from it, as the bright colors and tepid praise from bought-off critics—not to mention the zombie-iguanas— were really not helping at the moment.

"Hello?" Sophie asked, her eyes on me. "This is . . . Gemma." I tried not to wince when she said my name. It was, I knew, how I must have sounded when I called myself Sophie the first few times—completely unnatural. Sophie listened for a moment, then shook her head. "No, I'm not leaving," she said, shooting a questioning look at me a moment too late, and I realized Hallie must have asked her about what I'd said "Gemma" was planning to do— head back to Connecticut today. She listened for a long moment while I bit my fingernails, straining to hear and wishing I'd told Sophie to put the phone on speaker. "Okay," Sophie said. There was another long pause, and she nodded. "Sounds good. See you then." She ended the call and gave the phone back to me.

"That's it?" I asked, shocked that the conversation had been so brief, not to mention so free of yelling.

"Yeah," Sophie said, sounding a little shocked herself. "She wants to meet for coffee at noon. So we can talk things out. It didn't really sound like she was that mad, Gem."

"So you're having coffee with her in . . ." I checked my phone. "An hour." I was starting to get a fierce headache, and felt that the sooner I got caffeine, the better for all involved. "And you're going to go there pretending to be me."

"Should I not have said yes?" she asked, biting her lip. "I mean, I thought it would be weird to say no. I was worried that it might make things even worse."

I nodded; I couldn't argue with that. "Okay," I said. "Well . . . maybe this will be fine. We can see what she thinks about me, right?"

"Right," Sophie said. I could hear my best friend using the same voice I currently was—a cheerful tone on top of growing panic.

"It'll be fine," I said.

"Right! Fine!" Sophie echoed, even though it was clear neither one of us believed this.

Just then, there was a huge crash of thunder from outside that rattled the panes of the windows—which *really* didn't seem like a good sign.

"Come on," I said, giving up on all attempts at forced optimism. "We should get ready."

⸻

"**O**kay," I said as I turned the car into a spot across the street from Quonset Coffee and cut the engine. The wipers stopped and the windshield was instantly engulfed in rain. The weather had not improved, and in fact had gotten worse as the morning had gone on. I had found a giant golf umbrella in the garage, which we had needed just to cross the driveway to the car—and even then, we got drenched. "So . . . are you feeling okay?"

"Yeah," Sophie said, flipping down the visor mirror and fluffing up her hair. "I just want to get it over with."

"I hear that," I said. I was hoping that this would be fine, that I wasn't sending my best friend into the lion's jaws.

But I just wasn't sure what Hallie wanted out of this. Her request for a meeting with her former adversary was the last thing I expected. I couldn't make any sense of it, and it was with an increasing sense of alarm that I was sending Sophie in my place. I was also wishing that Ford hadn't made me watch the Godfather movies with him quite so many times.

Sophie flipped the mirror back up. "Is she really going to think I'm you?" she asked. "I mean, what if I'm in there and she starts talking about how she knows I'm an imposter? And then she throws her coffee at me or something?"

"She won't," I said, trying to sound as sure of this as possible, despite the fact I'd been worried about something very similar on the drive over. "And of course she's not going to say you're an imposter. She believes I'm you, so why wouldn't she believe you're me?"

Sophie bit her lip and nodded. "Okay," she said. She pulled out her phone. "Sure you want to do this?"

I nodded and took out my own. On the drive, we'd devised a plan so that I could listen in to the conversation. I would call her and she would just leave the connection open, with her phone in her purse, which would be as close to the table as possible. This way, if things got tricky—if Hallie asked Sophie about something that I would have known—I could text her the answer.

"Here we go," I said. I called her, and Sophie answered, then stuck the phone in her purse. "It'll be fine," I said, trying to sound much more sure of this than I felt.

"*Mercedem non sine periculo,*" she said. "It's the Clarence Hall motto," she explained. "I picked it up when I was dating Justin."

"And Jason," I reminded her.

Sophie waved this away. "Anyway, it means 'no reward without risk.' Appropriate, right?"

I nodded and forced myself to smile. "Thank you for doing this," I said. Sophie gave me a smile back, but I knew her well enough to see that she was really nervous.

"Here I go," she said, squaring her shoulders. Then she looked out at the rain and sighed. "Ugh."

"Take the umbrella!" I said, starting to reach into the backseat. "It's pouring."

"No," Sophie said, "I'm just going to run for it." She took a deep breath, then got out of the car and darted across the street. I had just lifted the phone to my ear when the passenger door opened and Sophie was back in the car again, half-drenched and dripping.

"You want the umbrella after all," I said knowingly. Sophie just shook her head, and I felt my heart leap. "She wasn't there?" I asked hopefully. "We got stood up?"

"I haven't gone in yet," Sophie said, talking fast and brushing droplets of water from her face. "It just hit me. Clarence Hall!

That's where I know that Reid guy from. He was Justin's room-mate." She frowned. "Or Jason's. I can't remember. But I *knew* I knew him from somewhere!" she said triumphantly.

"But . . ." I said, now worrying about more than this coffee date. "If you remember him, that means he might remember you, right?"

"Oh," Sophie said, her face falling. "Right."

"And he'd remember you as Sophie Curtis. Not as Gemma Tucker." I let out a breath as the ramifications of this became clear. Reid was staying with Hallie and Josh, and at any moment he might remember how he knew Sophie, including her name— which would make everything I'd built this summer come crash-ing down around me.

"So . . . what now?" Sophie asked. "Do I still have to get coffee with her?"

"I think so," I said. "And I'll . . . come up with something in the meantime."

"Okay," Sophie said, though she sounded very unconvinced. She looked outside, shuddered, then headed into the deluge once more. When I saw she'd made it across the street and gone inside Quonset Coffee, I lifted the phone to my ear.

"Hello," I heard Sophie saying. Even though her voice was muffled though the bag, I could tell that she was nervous. "It's me, Gemma. I mean, hi."

Hallie said something in response, and I pressed the phone to my ear harder, trying to listen. Someone hurrying down the sidewalk caught my eye—there were almost no pedestrians out, as anyone with any sense had stayed home. But this person looked familiar, and as I squinted through the sheets of rain, I saw that it was Reid.

I tapped on the windshield, but he just kept hurrying, umbrella-less, up the sidewalk. There seemed to be no choice but to get out and try to talk to him. Phone still to my ear, I grabbed the massive umbrella from the first backseat and stepped out into what I felt had to be classified as a tropical storm by now. I beeped the car shut and jogged up the sidewalk toward Reid, the rain lashing against my legs and soaking my feet, making me glad I'd gone with flip-flops.

"Reid!" I called, then realized that if I could hear Hallie and Sophie through the phone, they would also be able to hear me. Wishing I didn't have to, but not seeing any other choice, I ended the call and dropped the phone in my bag.

Reid turned and squinted at me through the rain. "Sophie?" he called.

"Hi," I said, then, taking pity on him, raised my umbrella over his head so that he was under it too. Even though it was an enormous umbrella, I was still closer than I really wanted to be to Reid, and the fact that he was leaning back as far as he could and still stay dry led me to believe that he felt the same way about me.

"What are you doing here?" I asked.

"Meeting Josh at the diner," he said, gesturing up the street to the restaurant that was still a good two blocks away. "I, um, thought it was closer than it turned out to be. And I didn't realize it was raining quite this hard."

"Oh," I said. Even without knowing the guy well, I had a feeling that things like this probably happened to Reid a lot. I searched his expression to see if I could tell he'd remembered anything about Sophie, but Reid just looked the way he had last night—cheerful but also slightly confused. And, right now, damp.

"So that was crazy last night, huh?" Reid asked after a moment.

"Yeah," I agreed, shaking my head, hoping he'd say more. "Crazy."

There was a slight pause, and I was about to take my umbrella and head back to the car—I was worried that Sophie might be running into trouble, and I wanted to text her to let her know I was still there even though I'd disconnected the call—when Reid cleared his throat.

"You know, it's weird," he said. "But you know that friend of yours? The one from last night? I could have sworn . . . I mean, she looks just like this girl that my roommate . . ."

Oh no. For a fleeting moment, I thought about denying the whole thing, but just as quickly, I dismissed it. If I wasn't going under Sophie's name, we might have been able to get away with pretending it was just a coincidence, "Gemma" looking so much like "Sophie." But all it would take was one text to Justin—or Jason—to double-check Sophie's name, and we'd be exposed. The only thing to do was to come clean. Even though I didn't see Josh coming up the street, I didn't want to take any chances. I grabbed Reid's sleeve and pulled us both, still under my umbrella, into the nearby alley.

"Uh . . ." he said, looking alarmed. "What's going on?"

"Listen," I said, keeping my voice low and talking fast. I lowered the umbrella, forcing Reid to bend down to stay under it, bringing him closer to my height. "You're right about what you think you're right about. But I just need you to not say anything to anyone about what it is that you think. Okay?"

Reid just blinked at me. "What?" he asked, a little helplessly.

"Just don't say anything to anyone about what you're thinking," I said. "Especially not Hallie or Josh. And I promise that I'll explain later, okay? Oh, wait, I don't have your number. What is it?"

"But . . ." Reid said, looking more confused than ever. "I don't . . ."

"Or e-mail?" I asked. Reid just opened and closed his mouth, and I sighed. "Come on, Reid. Your e-mail?"

"Um . . . Reid Franklin at Clarence Hall, edu. My name's all one word. But I don't . . ."

"Do you promise?" I asked, taking a step closer to him. "That you won't say anything about this to anyone?" I knew I probably sounded crazy, but the last thing we needed right now was Reid casually mentioning to Josh or Hallie that his roommate used to date a girl named Sophie Curtis, who looked nothing like me whatsoever.

"Okay," Reid said, his face turning red. I wasn't sure he was entirely clear on what he was promising, but that would have to do for now.

"Thank you," I said. I raised the umbrella up a bit, and Reid stopped hunching over so much.

"Sophie?"

I turned around and saw Josh, standing under a blue umbrella, his expression confused—but mostly hurt. "What's going on?"

"Nothing—" I started, when Reid jumped in.

"Nothing!" he said, loudly and too emphatically. "Totally nothing. We were just . . . talking. But I can't tell you about what. Not that it's anything bad, I just . . . can't tell you. Um, what's up with you?"

If Reid had intended to sound incredibly guilty, and like he was hiding something, I wasn't sure he would have been able to do a better job of it.

"Not much," Josh said, looking from me to Reid, like he was trying to figure something out. "I was just heading to the diner and saw you guys."

"Cool," said Reid, in what I'm sure he thought was a casual tone, but was actually incredibly suspicious. "Cool. Cool . . . beans."

I winced at this, but before I could say anything, my phone beeped with a text. I pulled it out of my bag, trying to shield it from raindrops, and glanced down at the screen.

Sophie Curtis
12:25 PM
Done with coffee! Where are you?

"Did you just get a text from yourself?" Josh asked, and I realized that he was leaning a little closer to me and had a perfect view of my screen.

I instinctually turned my phone over. "No," I said, forcing a laugh. "It's . . . Gemma. She grabbed my phone by accident this morning." I texted back that I was across the street, and dropped my phone in my bag, looking away from Reid, who was maybe doing the worst poker face I had ever seen.

"Oh," Josh said. "About that." He took a tiny step closer to me and Reid—though you couldn't get too close, as my umbrella was far too big to make any rational sense—and I noticed for the first time that he looked tired, his hair slightly more askew than usual and circles under his eyes, like he hadn't gotten much sleep the night before. "I wanted to explain about last night . . ."

"Hi!" I looked away from Josh to see Sophie dashing across the street to join us. I looked at her carefully to see if I could get any clues about what had happened during her coffee with Hallie, but she looked fine—untraumatized and not bearing any obvious psychological scars. And her white tank top was free of coffee stains, so clearly she'd been safe on that front.

"Hey," I said, gesturing to her. "Get under here. There's kind of room. . . ."

"Here," Josh said, his voice cool. He moved to the side of the umbrella and held it toward Sophie. "You can share with me if you want."

"Oh," Sophie said, as she stepped under Josh's umbrella and brushed her damp hair out of her face. "Thank you so much." I tried not to see how close together they were now standing, or how cute Sophie looked. I never looked good in the rain—my hair got plastered down in a way that made my head look huge. But Sophie got these cute little ringlets in her hair, and I noticed they were appearing now.

"Hello, *Gemma*," Reid said in a louder-than-normal voice. He really was a terrible actor. I made a mental note to tell him never to pursue the theatrical arts.

"So," Josh said. He was standing at the edge of his umbrella, looking at her, and apparently, to my relief, not taken in by how great her hair was currently looking. His expression was cold and unimpressed. "I don't suppose you remember me?"

"Um . . ." Sophie said. She glanced back at me, and I tried to nod my head as subtly as possible. "Yes?"

"It has been a while," Josh said, and his tone got slightly less frosty. "And we really just had dinner that one time."

"Right," Sophie said, nodding emphatically. "That one time. Dinner." She took a small glance back at me, and I gave her another tiny nod.

"And you do look a little different than you did back then," Josh said.

Josh couldn't be flirting with Sophie, right? He was just being polite.

"Just a little bit different," Sophie said, and I could hear the tiniest bit of playfulness creeping into her voice. I know she didn't mean anything by it; it was just natural instinct as far as she went. Sophie could flirt with the umbrella I was holding. But still. I widened my eyes at Sophie over Josh's shoulder, and she took a tiny step away from him. "Anyway," she said, looking to me. "We should go?"

"We should," I said.

"Great idea!" Reid chimed in, again much too loud. He shot me a look that I pretended not to notice as he stepped back into the rain and Sophie ducked out from Josh's umbrella and joined me under mine.

"Oh, Sophie," Josh said, and both Sophie and I looked over at him. Sophie looked away a moment later, and I just hoped Josh hadn't noticed. "Um . . . can we talk later? Once you get your own phone back?"

I nodded, relieved he'd brought it up. It felt like what had been maybe starting between us at the bonfire was getting lost in everything that had happened since. And Josh and I talking, just the two of us, sounded wonderful. "I'd like that," I said.

Josh nodded and Reid waved, and Sophie and I hurried over to the car. I left her the umbrella as I ran around to the driver's side and unlocked it. As we'd agreed on it beforehand, we didn't speak until we were back in the car with the doors closed.

"So how was it?" I asked as I wiped the droplets off my hands and started the car.

"Where were you?" Sophie asked as she buckled her seat belt and I headed for home, the windshield wipers already working overtime. "Hallie started talking all about some time we built sandcastles together, and I had no idea what to say!"

"I'm so sorry," I said. "I saw Reid, and thought I better go talk to him." I filled Sophie in on the fact that Reid had put her identity together. "And he's a terrible actor," I added. "I don't know if he's the best person to keep this secret."

"But we have to tell him the truth, right?" Sophie asked. "I mean, since he's pretty much figured it out anyway?"

"I guess so. I left him pretty mixed up, so we should probably e-mail him and straighten things out."

"Poor guy," Sophie said with a sigh as she flipped down her visor mirror. "But he's kind of cute, don't you think? Not as cute as Josh, obviously, but not bad."

"Mmm," I said. I paused at a stop sign, then turned to her, not able to take the suspense any longer. "So aside from the sand-castle thing, was it terrible?" I held my breath.

Sophie paused for a moment, looking out the window, like she was gathering her thoughts. "You know, it really wasn't," she said, sounding a little surprised. "I thought she was actually really nice about the whole thing. She apologized for the way she acted last night. She said I'd just caught her off guard. And then I apologized for what I did, like we talked about, and then she said she hoped that we could both move on."

I paused before pulling into Bruce's driveway and just stared at Sophie. "And that's it?"

"That's it," she confirmed. She shot me a relieved smile. "It looks like we were worried for nothing. Good, right?"

"Right," I echoed as I pulled into the driveway and put the car in park. "Good." While I was relieved that Sophie hadn't had a terrible coffee date, I was really, really surprised that Hallie had acted this way when confronted with the girl she thought was me. I had been sure that she would still be furious, sure that she wouldn't have been able to get past it easily. It had been all over her face that first day we met again, at the train station.

Had I been that wrong?

And—more worryingly—had I done all this for nothing?

"Hey," Sophie said, waving her hand in front of my face. "You okay?"

"Fine," I said. "Just . . . thinking."

We got out of the car and dashed for the front door. I closed it behind us, thrilled to be dry once again and planning on not going out until the weather was back to being what it ought to have been: hot and sunny and summery.

"I think Hallie's cool, actually," Sophie said as she kicked off her flip-flops. "She was really nice and funny. The whole apology part didn't take that long, so then we talked about boys. Did she tell you how her boyfriend Ward is out of town?"

"She mentioned it," I said as I kicked my own sodden flip-flops off. I knew, realistically, that it shouldn't have bothered me that Hallie was able to let this go so quickly. Just like it shouldn't have bothered me that she was apparently becoming friends with my BFF. Just like it shouldn't have bothered me that Josh was maybe being a tiny bit flirty with her. But that didn't change the fact that all these things were really, really bothering me.

"And she invited me to this Fourth of July party she's throwing at her house," Sophie said as she headed toward the kitchen. "She said it's going to be really fun."

"Really," I said, dropping my bag on the hall table and following her, trying not to sound as hurt as I felt. "She didn't invite me."

"Oh," Sophie said, frowning. "Well, I'm sure she will soon. Or Josh will, right?"

"Right," I said, trying to keep my voice upbeat. "Sure." The Fourth was in two days, so it seemed like time was running out on that front. I pulled open the fridge and took out two bottles of sparkling water. I held one out to Sophie, and she nodded, and I slid it across the table to her.

"So what should we do about Reid?" she asked. "I mean, if he's staying with them, he's probably going to be at the party too."

I nodded and picked up my phone. "I got his e-mail," I said grimly. "Time to do damage control."

Sophie took a long drink of her water, then shook her head. "You know, Gemma, I came here to *escape* all the drama."

I felt myself smile as I started typing the e-mail to Reid. "How's that working out for you?"

CHAPTER 27

I pulled open the door and was not quite able to stop myself from rolling my eyes. "Hi, Reid."

Reid was standing on Bruce's doorstep, nervously glancing over his shoulders. He was wearing a baseball cap pulled low over his eyes and a pair of sunglasses. His outfit was made even more ridiculous by the fact that, even though it had stopped raining, it was still overcast and cloudy out. Reid could have only been more obvious if he'd also been wearing a T-shirt that read I'M TRYING TO GO INCOGNITO.

"Hi," he said, keeping his voice low. "Is it safe to talk here?"

"It's fine," I said, opening the door wider and motioning him inside. "Come on in."

Reid had responded to my e-mail immediately, but told me he wouldn't be able to get away that day without raising suspicions. We'd arranged to meet this afternoon, as both Josh and Hallie were running errands for the party, and he didn't think they'd notice his absence. And here he was, on Bruce's doorstep, looking like he was trying to dodge the paparazzi. "I don't think I was followed," he assured me in grave tones, and I gave him a thumbs-up.

"Good work." I led him through the back and out by the pool, where Sophie had been all morning, mostly just shivering in her bikini and telling me whenever she thought she saw a ray of sunshine start to appear.

"Hi!" Sophie called, waving from her lounge chair. I noticed she'd put on a sweatshirt over her bathing suit, but hadn't zipped it. And as we walked across the deck to join her, Reid had a bit of trouble navigating around the lounge chairs and almost fell into the pool once, mostly because he hadn't taken his eyes from my BFF once. Sophie in a bikini tended to be distracting like that.

"Hi," Reid managed, sitting and only missing the lounge chair on his first two attempts. He opened and closed his mouth a few times, but it didn't seem like anything else was forthcoming. As I watched Reid take off his sunglasses and lose the ability to form sentences in Sophie's presence, I wondered if this was the best idea. After all, we needed him to be able to follow what was happening, and it looked like his IQ had just plummeted several crucial points. I was on the verge of asking Sophie to zip up her hoodie when Reid managed to pull himself together.

"So. Okay. Um," he said. He pointed at me. "You're not Sophie." He pointed at Sophie. "You are, right? I remember you from Clarence Hall."

"That's right," I said, happy that we were all finally on the same page. "The thing is, this all started with a misunderstanding." I took a breath and was about to launch into the story of the iced latte cup with Sophie's name on it when the doorbell rang. Figuring that this was just another one of Bruce's deliveries, I stood up. "I'll get that," I said. "Soph, can you fill him in?"

I headed around the side of the house and saw, to my surprise, Josh standing at the front door, nervously smoothing down his hair and checking his reflection in the Davidson Manor panel.

The sight of him—and this private glimpse I was getting—made me feel a sudden wave of affection for him. I realized we'd never had that talk he'd mentioned when we stood on the street under our umbrellas. It just seemed like suddenly there were too many land mines to avoid, and normal conversation had become impossible. But as I watched him now, it registered how much I'd missed talking to him, even though it hadn't really been that long.

"Hi," I called, and Josh turned around, startled.

"Hey," he said, dropping his hands and sticking them quickly in his pockets. "I guess I thought someone would answer the door."

"We were around back," I said, gesturing to the side of the house. "I heard the bell."

"Got it," Josh said, nodding. He looked behind me, to where Reid's car was parked. "Is Reid here?" he asked, his voice clipped, like he was upset about something.

"Um, yeah," I said. "He's out by the pool." Josh nodded and looked down at the ground, and I felt disappointment hit me as I realized that was probably why he'd shown up at the house. He wasn't here to see me, he was trying track down his friend. "Is . . . that why you're here?"

"No," Josh said, without looking up. "I came to ask you a question."

"Oh," I said. I took a breath, then let it out. "Okay." I resolved, then and there, that whatever he asked me, I would be totally honest with him. Even if it was about me and Hallie and who I really was, I would tell him the truth.

"Is something going on with you and Reid?"

That was not the question I had been expecting, and it was one that was not at all difficult to provide an honest answer to. "No," I said, a little incredulously. "Of course not."

"I just . . ." Josh started, then took a breath and continued. "I mean, I saw the two of you in the alley yesterday, and he's been acting really strange ever since—like he's hiding something. And then I come over, and I see that he's already here. . . ."

When he put it all together like that, I could see how it didn't sound good. "No," I said emphatically. "Nothing like that. He just . . ." I thought quickly, then decided to settle on something that was probably closest to the truth. "I think he likes So— *Gemma*," I corrected quickly, hoping Josh hadn't noticed this, "and he um, wanted me to see if she liked him too. And that's why he's here."

"Oh," Josh said, looking relieved. "Good."

"Yeah," I said, giving him a smile, hoping he'd bought it.

Josh glanced around to the back of the house, then shook his head. "I have to say, thought, I'm a little surprised. Reid doesn't usually act so impulsively."

"Right," I said quickly. "Well . . . um . . . maybe he's turning over a new leaf out here."

"Maybe," Josh said, sounding unconvinced. "I'm not sure it's such a good idea, though—Gemma and Reid."

I certainly didn't think it was, either, but couldn't exactly tell him why. "I agree," I said, and he just nodded. Silence fell and, suddenly, I was aware of just how many unsaid things there were between us. "So," I said after a moment, "was that the question you came to ask me? About my undying passion for Reid?"

Josh laughed. "No, that wasn't it. Actually, I wanted to know if you wanted to come to our Fourth of July party tomorrow. Apparently all the houses on our stretch of land do it; they call it the beach block party. It should be fun. Hopefully the weather will be better by then too. If it's a clear night, there's going to be fireworks."

I felt a smile take over my face. "I'd love to," I said. I was also a little relieved. The fact that Hallie had asked Sophie but hadn't yet asked me had been bothering me. But maybe she knew Josh was always planning on asking me himself. Either way, I was just happy to be going.

Josh took a tiny step closer to me, then stopped. He looked down at me, and I could see the flecks of gold in his green-brown eyes. And just like that, I had a flashback to the beach, to the shocks that had gone through me when we touched. Was he asking me to the party as his date?

Maybe Josh was having a similar tangle of thoughts, because he broke eye contact with me and took a step away.

"Tomorrow?" he asked, as he began to back away toward his truck.

"Tomorrow," I said, nodding at him. Once again, I heard the

promise in the word. I waved as his truck headed down the driveway.

Even after his taillights had disappeared, I stayed where I was, bare feet on the gravel, just thinking. I had promised more than just to attend the party when I'd echoed his *tomorrow*. Because right there, in the driveway, I made a decision.

Tomorrow night, I would tell Hallie, and then Josh, who I really was.

CHAPTER 28

"**A**re you sure about this?" Sophie asked.

We were standing in front of the hall mirror, giving our party outfits final looks. I'd told her my plan the day before after I'd finally gotten Reid to leave. Sophie had explained the situation to him while I'd been talking to Josh, and it was clear Reid wasn't going to say anything to anyone—mostly because he was utterly besotted with Sophie. She seemed to be tolerating it, but not necessarily reciprocating the feeling, and after Reid spent another whole hour hanging out by the pool, mostly just gazing at Sophie adoringly and laughing at her jokes, I'd told him we needed our privacy. I'd explained my plan to her, but ever since, she'd been asking me if I really thought it was the right thing to do.

"Yes," I said, with more conviction than I really felt, leaning forward to make sure my mascara wasn't flaking. We'd both dressed up for the party—but luckily, I could be absolutely sure of the dress code since it was Hallie's text to her boyfriend, Ward, about this very event that had caused the misunderstanding at the pool party. So I knew it was semi-formal, but Sophie had taken it a step further and insisted we dress patriotic. Sophie was wearing a short and tight blue-and-white striped dress with red lipstick. I hadn't taken the patriotic theme quite as far as she had, but was wearing a red eyelet dress with a sweetheart neckline and a slightly flared skirt, with a pair of white flats.

Sophie frowned and applied another coat of her bright-red lipstick, but I knew my best friend, and her expression was speaking louder than words.

"What?" I asked, looking at her in the mirror. "I thought you'd be thrilled not to have to pretend to be me any longer."

"I am," Sophie said, capping the tube and dropping it in her bag. "I just don't know if tonight is the best night. Remember when I dumped Evan in the middle of that party? He was not happy, and everyone said the night was ruined."

"In Evan's defense, it was his birthday party," I reminded her. "And he spent the rest of the party in the corner, crying."

"I'm just saying," Sophie said, waving this away. "Maybe find a quieter time to do this. Not when a lot of other stuff is going on. You know?"

I thought about it as I slung my bag over my shoulder. The truth was, I was hoping it might help, to have a lot of other things going on, to serve as a buffer or distraction. Ever since Sophie had arrived, carrying on this fiction had just been too hard. I wanted to tell Josh and Hallie who I really was—and then, hopefully, I could move on with both of them. With Hallie, to a real friendship with no lies between us. And with Josh . . .

I hadn't told Sophie this, but I was hoping that after I told Josh, maybe we could move from friendship to something more. He wasn't Teddy, of course. But the more I'd thought about it, I'd come to realize that might actually be a good thing. This was the real reason I'd turned down Sophie's suggestion I wear red lipstick, too. I was hoping, if all went well, Josh and I might have our first kiss tonight. The thought of it was keeping my cheeks flushed enough that I'd been able to forgo bronzer entirely.

"I think it's time to be honest with them," I said, and with such finality that Sophie nodded.

"Fair enough," she said. "Though I was just getting used to responding to 'Gemma.'" She gave me a smile. "Ready to do this?"

I nodded, smoothed down my hair, and then checked the time on my phone. "Let's go." We headed out the front door and I let Sophie head to the car first as I closed the door and locked it. I knew when I came back everything—one way or another—would be different.

⸎

By the time we arrived, the party was in full swing. The street had been lined with cars all the way to the main road, and Sophie and I had had to park so far away that she'd ended up taking off her heels and walking barefoot. You could hear the party before you even reached it—the beat of the music mixed with conversation and laughter.

I steered us toward the Bridges' house, since that was our connection to the event, but as soon as we got to the driveway, it became clear that this wasn't a ring-the-doorbell kind of party. As Josh had indicated, the party was taking place down on the beach, covering the stretch of sand in front of all the houses I could see. There were beautifully dressed people milling about, tiki torches and twinkle lights, tables piled with food, and, somewhere, live music playing. It was like something out of a dream.

"You're here!" Reid was at Sophie's side so quickly, I had a feeling that he had to have been watching for us. "You look wonderful," he said, staring at her. "I mean, really. Just incredible."

"Oh, thank you," Sophie said offhandedly, smiling at him.

"And you look nice too," Reid added to me with barely a glance in my direction.

"Thanks," I said. "Really."

"Can I get you something to drink?" Reid asked Sophie, already starting to shepherd her down to the water. "Or eat?"

"Sure," Sophie said. She turned to look at me. "Do you want to come?"

"I'll catch up," I said. "I'm going to try and find Hallie first." I could tell Sophie knew what I meant by this, and she gave me an encouraging smile.

"I think I saw her in the house," Reid said, as he gestured vaguely toward it without taking his eyes from Sophie. I nodded and they started to make their way down to the beach.

I turned in the direction of the house—and promptly crashed into someone. "Sorry," I said, taking a step back. I was just glad I hadn't had a chance to get something to drink yet, because it probably would have been all over both of us.

"Yeah, sorry," the person I'd collided with mumbled. It was a guy, around my age, and as he looked at me, his eyes widened.

I realized suddenly that I knew him—it was Ty, the waiter at the Crabby Lobster. I opened my mouth to say something, but before I could, he was speed-walking down to the beach. I looked after him for a moment, wondering why he'd practically run away from me. Maybe he felt guilty about serving me bad lobster?

I shrugged it off and headed toward the Bridges' house, when I saw Josh, standing alone on the edge of the deck, hunched over something. I smoothed down my dress and hoped my hair was still behaving itself as I walked over.

"Hi," I said as I stepped closer to him.

Josh looked up at me and smiled. He was wearing a blazer, dress shirt, and khakis, but no tie. I'd never seen him dressed up this much before, and it brought home how incredibly handsome he was, like in a maybe-he-models-those-pants-too kind of way.

"Hey," he said. "I was looking for you."

I suddenly felt warm inside, like I'd just had a long drink of hot chocolate. "You were?"

"Yeah," he said. He straightened up and I saw what he'd been hunched over was a laptop, attached to a projector. "I was hoping to get this started before you got here." He pressed a button, and then pointed at the house. There were Westley and Buttercup, huge, projected against the side of the house. It was *The Princess Bride*, larger than I'd ever seen it.

"Nice movie choice," I said, smiling as I watched them take hands in front of a sunset, their romance just-begun and still perfect.

"Yeah," Josh said. "I have good associations with this movie from the last time I saw it."

"You mean when you were recovering from horrific food poisoning?" I joked.

"No," Josh said, his expression serious. "I meant who I watched it with."

Oh. I just looked at Josh for a moment. My heart wasn't racing, but beating steady and true, and telling me everything I needed to know about how I felt. This was Josh—who had rescued me from the pool and let me rescue him from the bad lobster. He was my friend, but he was also, in that moment, suddenly so much more than that. And I had never wanted anything so much as I wanted to kiss him.

Josh cleared his throat, then asked, "Did you want to join the party?"

"Sure," I said. Then I thought about the party that awaited us—lots of people and lots of noise—and I realized I should take advantage of this quieter moment. I'd planned to talk to Hallie first, but Josh was here, and the moment was right. I needed to tell him the truth. I didn't know what would happen, but just then, I remembered the Clarence Hall motto: *no reward without risk.* "But can we just talk for a moment first?"

"Yes," he said. Maybe it was from the tone of my voice, but he seemed to know I didn't want to keep just carrying on a casual conversation on the deck. "Let's go inside."

I followed him into the house. There were some people milling about in the kitchen and hanging out in the living room—so clearly some of the party was taking place inside. I was about to ask Josh if we could talk someplace quieter, but he must have realized this was what I wanted—or maybe it was what he wanted too—because he led me past the TV room, to a little alcove just big enough to hold a bench, but with floor-to-ceiling windows and a great view of the water.

"So," I said. We were standing closer together than we normally did, and even though I could have blamed it on the smallness of the alcove, I knew that wasn't the real reason. "I have to tell you something."

"Me too," Josh said, before I could even begin.

"Wait," I said. I was ready to tell him the truth, and I didn't want to lose my courage. "I just wanted to talk to you about—"

"Me first," Josh interrupted. I couldn't help laughing at that, and he took the opportunity to jump in. "I just wanted to say how great it's been to get to know you. I . . . feel like I can be myself around you, and I just . . ." He trailed off, took a breath, and looked down at me, right into my eyes, and I felt my knees weaken a little. "I guess what I'm trying to say is that I really like you. I didn't think I was going to be able to after everything that happened this year, but . . . I guess I fell harder than I was expecting to." It took me a moment to place these words—then I realized they were what I had said to him on the train, after I'd fallen into his lap.

He took a step closer to me and reached out slowly, carefully, like he was making sure it was okay, and tucked a lock of hair behind my ear.

"Josh," I whispered. He'd left his hand there, touching the side of my face gently. He was closer than ever, so close I could reach out and rest my hand on his chest without even extending my arm, and I was getting dizzy in the best way. I knew I had to tell him while I still had my wits about me. "There's something I have to . . ."

But before I could finish, he leaned his head down and kissed me.

CHAPTER 29

*O*h my god.

I kissed him back.

It was maybe the best first kiss in all of history.

Josh and I left all the other first kisses—me and Teddy, Westley and Buttercup, everyone—far behind. I didn't care if anyone could see us. In fact, if they could see us, they might get some useful information on what a perfect first kiss looked like.

Josh's hands were around my waist, then my hands were in his hair, then he was lifting me off my feet for a moment, and when he set me down my knees were wobbling. And still we didn't stop kissing.

It didn't start out hesitant or unsure. It was like we'd been waiting to kiss each other this whole time, and now that we were finally doing it, we weren't wasting a moment.

When we finally stopped to breathe, his arms were around me, holding me tight like he never planned on letting go. My hands were on either side of his face, and I could see his freckles clearly, and I wanted to count each one and memorize them. Josh leaned his forehead against mine and took a shaky breath.

"Wow," he murmured.

"I know," I said. I ran my hand over the back of his neck, still a little amazed that I got to do this.

He leaned back a tiny bit and looked at me. "Sophie Curtis," he said softly, tracing his finger down my cheek, saying the name like it was precious, like it was beautiful.

It was enough to shake me from my daze. I wanted him to know, right then. The next time he spoke my name in that wonderful, sweet way, I wanted it to actually *be* my name.

"Listen," I said. I reached up and brushed his soft hair back from his forehead. "I need to tell you something."

"Now?" he asked, kissing me just below my ear and weakening my resolve.

"Yes," I said faintly, trying to ignore the fact that I could feel his heart beating against mine, and the fact that his arms around me felt so *right*, in a way I'd never felt before. "Josh, I—"

BEEP-BEEP-BEEP.

We both jumped at that, and Josh cursed under his breath as he pulled his phone out of his jacket pocket. "I'm so sorry," he said. "It's the stupid phone. I can't get it to stop telling me when . . ." His voice trailed off as he looked at the screen. He glanced at me, his brow furrowed, then back at the screen again.

"What?" I asked, my tone light and teasing. "Some earth-shattering e-mail?"

"I . . ." He looked back at me, and I saw that all the happiness had drained from his face. "What is this?" he asked. "Sophie, what is this?"

I took the phone from him and suddenly it was like all the oxygen had left the room. There, on Josh's phone, was my Friendverse profile—the one you could only access if you were one of my friends. The one with *Gemma Tucker* printed along the top in large type, next to a picture of me.

"This is what I was going to tell you," I said quickly. "See . . . okay, here's the thing. I—"

"What do you mean?" Josh gave a small laugh, like he was hoping this was all a joke. "This isn't real, right?"

"Listen," I said. "I meant to tell you earlier, but . . ."

"You mean it's true?" Josh took his phone back and just stared at me. "Your name isn't Sophie?"

"Well," I said, my heart pounding hard, "technically, no. But it's like I was going to tell you, I—"

Josh shook his head. "So you've—you've been lying to me this whole time? This whole summer, you've been letting me believe that you're someone else?"

I swallowed hard. This was not at all going how I had hoped it would. "I've been me," I said, in a voice that came out shaky. "Just not with my same name."

"Oh, is that all?" Josh asked, his tone trying for sarcastic, but mostly just sounding hurt.

"Please just listen," I said, taking a step toward him. Josh took a step back, and I felt tears prick the corners of my eyes. A minute ago—a handful of seconds—his arms had been around me like he was never going to let me go. And now he was backing away. "It was just a misunderstanding at first; you saw my coffee cup, and—"

I didn't think it was possible for Josh to look more shattered, but somehow he managed it as understanding dawned on his face. "Gemma Tucker," he said hollowly. "It was you. Not that other girl. You were the one who was so terrible to Hallie all those years ago. It was *you*?" His voice broke and he looked away from me for a moment.

"Josh," I whispered. I wanted nothing more than to touch his arm, but I didn't want to see him flinch, didn't want to feel him shake me off. I swallowed hard and spoke fast, trying to get in front of the tears that were starting to gather. "It's like we talked about during the movie, remember? It doesn't really matter about my name, right? Not when two people care about each other?"

"*Care* about each other?" Josh turned to me, and I could see now that he was angry as well as hurt, a dull red flush on his cheeks. "I don't even know who you are! You've been *lying* to me all summer, and making me think that you—"

"I haven't," I said, and I couldn't stop it now, as two tears rolled down my cheek. "I do—"

"Was this all part of some game?" he asked, his voice raw. "Was I just some pawn you were trying to hurt?"

"*No*," I cried, wiping my tears away and closing my eyes for a second. Everything felt like it was moving too fast, spinning out of my control, and I wanted to go back to just a few minutes before, when I was, quite possibly, as happy as I had ever been. "No," I repeated, opening my eyes again. "I've been trying to make things right with Hallie. But you were just . . ." I looked at him and took a breath around the lump in my throat and made myself say it. "So wonderful. And I didn't want to hurt you, I swear."

"Well," Josh said, with a hard, brittle laugh, the kind I had never heard from him before, "you did."

I was full-out crying now; I couldn't stop it, or seem to get it under control. There was no way I could make things better or present the facts in a way that would make him stop looking at me like he was now—like he'd never seen me before. "I'm sorry," I whispered. "I'm so sorry."

"I think you should go," Josh said, his voice quiet and broken. "Please."

I nodded, but didn't actually think I was going to be able to move. If I left, what then? What about us? Where did we go from here?

The answer came as quickly and clearly as if someone had texted it to me. Nowhere. There was no *us*. It was all over.

I took a step away on legs that felt shaky, but before I'd left the alcove, Josh turned to me. "You know, after everything I went through last year at school, I thought with you that I'd found someone I could trust. Someone who wasn't going to hurt me just because they could. Someone . . ." He trailed off, and I just stood there and wiped my tears away as I felt the full realization of what I'd done to him. "I liked you so *much*," he whispered, his voice breaking on the last word.

"Me too," I said, feeling my chin tremble. Josh turned his head away and I backed out of the alcove, then walked across the house as fast as I could, breaking into a run as I reached the door and went outside.

I looked straight ahead so I wouldn't see what had been our movie as I took the steps down to the sand, around to the side of the house, and retreated into the shadows. The party that had seemed like a dream now felt like a nightmare. I buried my face in my hands and tried to get my breathing under control.

I was still trying to comprehend how everything could have fallen apart, and so quickly. There was no more Josh. I had ruined everything, just at the moment I'd realized how much I'd really liked him. Tears were falling again, and I rubbed at my eyes, willing them to stop, trying to force myself to breathe normally.

Because I had one more person to tell. Josh would tell her soon enough, but I wanted her to hear it from me. I was going to find Hallie and tell her the truth.

It was time to end this.

CHAPTER 30

I found Hallie standing alone at the edge of the water, separate from the rest of the guests. She was in a white strapless dress, and tucked underneath her arm was the pink clutch I'd seen in her closet. She was barefoot, and her hair was up in a knot. I realized as I got closer to her that it was the first time I'd seen her hair up all summer.

"Hey," I called as I walked up to her.

Hallie turned her head and smiled at me. "Hi," she said. "You made it." She looked closer at me in the moonlight and frowned. "Sophie, are you okay?"

"I'm fine," I said, running my hand quickly over my face. I looked around at the deserted stretch of beach we were standing on. "What are you doing out here?"

"Getting the best view," she said, glancing out to the water. "The fireworks are about to start."

I took a deep breath. There was nothing else to wait for. I'd already lost Josh tonight. If I was going to lose Hallie, too, I might as well get it over with. "I have to tell you something," I said, and Hallie turned her head to look at me, her expression calm and composed. "I'm not Sophie Curtis," I said in a rush. "We've actually met before this summer. I'm Gemma Tucker. I let you think I was Sophie because I wanted to try and make up for my behavior. I wanted to try and make things right. And I am so, so sorry for what I did. I hope that we can still . . . be friends."

Hallie stared at me for a moment, then smiled. "I know who you are," she said. "I've known from the beginning."

I stared back at her, trying to get this to make sense. "What?" I whispered. Hallie just raised an eyebrow at me. "Did you . . . Are you the one who told Josh?"

"Well, someone had to," she said. "Nice to see that you've gotten over Teddy so quickly. I thought it would have taken you longer than that."

I blinked at Hallie. Nothing in this conversation was going how I'd expected it to, and I was struggling to catch up. "What . . . what do you mean?" I asked. I hadn't told her his name, I was sure of that. I'd just called him my ex. How would she have known this?

"Oh," she said, seeing someone behind me and waving at them, "I should introduce you to my boyfriend."

I turned around and my jaw dropped.

Teddy Callaway was standing in front of me.

CHAPTER 31

I stared at him. I suddenly felt unsteady on my feet, like the ground had just been pulled out from under me. I closed my eyes for a second, but when I opened them again, Teddy was still there—looking more tan than usual, his hair blonder, wearing a button-down and khakis. I wasn't hallucinating this; it was real.

Teddy blinked at me. "Gemma?" He asked it with a half-laugh, like he was hoping the answer would be no.

"Hi, darling," Hallie said, walking toward him. As I watched in horror, she slid her arm around his back and kissed him. It felt like someone had squeezed my heart, and I found myself gasping for air. Teddy didn't pull away from Hallie, but it didn't look like he kissed her back, and his eyes kept darting to me.

"How, um," Teddy said when Hallie had stepped away again. "How do you two know each other?"

"Oh, we go way back," Hallie said lightly, looking over at me, a small smile playing around the corners of her mouth. "Don't we, *Gemma?*"

"How do *you two* know each other?" I asked, my mind still trying to catch up with what was happening before me. "You said your boyfriend's name was Ward," I said to Hallie, who smiled.

"Yes," she said. "Which is a nickname for Edward, last time I checked. Just like Teddy." She turned her head to kiss him again, and for the first time I noticed that there was something on the back of her neck. Something that looked like a tattoo.

My head spun as I tried to understand what this meant. Hallie was the neck tattoo girl? Hallie had been with Teddy this whole time? I noticed that Teddy looked pale under his new tan, absolutely terrified, more so than when he'd had to face down the bulldozer when he was trying to protect the habitat of the Marsh Warbler. And finally, a month too late, I realized what was going on.

"Teddy, did you—did you cheat on me?" Teddy opened his mouth, but no words came out. "With *her*?"

Hallie looked away, like she was trying to give us our privacy, but I could see her satisfied smile.

"I . . ." Teddy looked at Hallie a little helplessly, then back to me. "I don't think I would put it quite like that. . . ."

"So that's why you broke up with me." Shock was fading away, and I was starting to realize how angry I was. "Because of Hallie."

"I never wanted you to . . ." Teddy started. He took a step closer to me, and I noticed that he was wearing the shirt I had bought him for his birthday, the one I'd had to save up a month's worth of babysitting money for. "I didn't want you to get hurt."

I just shook my head as I stared at him. "You didn't want me to get hurt?" I repeated, incredulous. "You broke my *heart*. And this whole time, I haven't known why. I've been wondering what I did wrong. . . ."

"Nothing!" Teddy said quickly. "I just . . ." His voice trailed off, and we simply looked at each other for a long moment.

"Are those for me?" Hallie asked, coming to stand close by Teddy's side. Her voice, though light, had an edge to it.

"Yes," Teddy said, and held out what had been behind his back—a pair of heels. Very familiar hot-pink silk heels. "I thought your feet might be cold."

"You're so sweet," Hallie said, smiling at him. "I knew these would go perfectly with my purse." She leaned on his arm to step into Gwyneth's shoes.

I just stared at them, still not quite able to believe this was happening. My heart was beating hard and I was having trouble breathing properly. The part of me that could still comprehend what was happening—a very small part—wondered if this was what a panic attack felt like.

"Could you give us a minute, baby?" Hallie asked Teddy, resting her hand on his chest. "Gemma and I have some things to wrap up."

"Yes," Teddy practically gasped, looking thrilled for an excuse to leave. He headed up the beach, then stopped and looked back at me. "Gemma, I . . ." He took a deep breath. "I'm sorry. You deserved better than that." He looked at me for a moment longer, then turned away and walked up the beach.

Hallie turned to me, a smile on her face. "So how are you liking the party?" she asked.

"You . . ." I started, then had to take a breath and gather my thoughts. "You stole my boyfriend."

"Of course I did," Hallie said, like it was the most obvious thing in the world. She took a step toward me. "I have been planning this for *years*," she said, her voice low. "And I have been getting you back all summer."

"You . . . you have?" Suddenly, a summer's worth of mishaps flashed though my head. "You mean . . . the pool party and the bathing suit . . . and the babysitting?"

"I told the girls to wreck as much as they could," she said. "Pity they just got to the one award."

Things were starting to fall into place in the most horrible way. "Oh my god," I whispered. It was all starting to become clear, like a filter had just been pulled off the summer and I was seeing it for what it really was.

"And don't forget the lobster," Hallie said, smiling fondly at the memory.

"The lobster?" I echoed. "But how did you . . ."

"It helps to make friends with waiters, no matter how boring they are," she said. "Tyler thinks we're pals, and he was more than happy to make sure you got the lobster that had been sitting out in the sun for a few hours."

I remembered then why he seemed so familiar—I'd seen him talking to Hallie at the pool party. The one where she'd told me to come in the wrong clothes, given me a self-destructing bathing suit to wear, and then stolen my shoes. The summer—the truth about it—was sliding sharply into focus. "But—"

"Sometimes you made it really hard to keep believing your

little scheme," she said. "I mean, my god, you left a receipt with your *name* on it with the bathing suit. How stupid did you think I was?"

"This whole summer," I said, my voice shaking, "this whole time, you've been—"

"You were *horrible* to me," Hallie said, taking a step closer to me. Her cool, triumphant smile was gone, replaced by pure, raw anger. "And it was all just a big joke to you, wasn't it?"

"Of course not," I said. I shook my head hard. "Hallie, no. I've hated myself for doing it. I've always regretted what I did. And—"

"Yeah," Hallie said with a hollow laugh. "Sure. That's why you made certain I got your notebook, filled with details about all your plans. All the ways you were trying to hurt me. Including notes on what wasn't quite mean enough, and what you could do *better*. You sent me that so I could be sure to know just how much you hated me." Hallie's voice broke on the last word, and she looked away, bringing her hands to her face for a moment.

I swallowed hard. "You weren't supposed to see that," I said quietly, after a moment. "That was an accident."

Hallie turned back to me, and her bottom lip was trembling. "But you did all those things, right? They weren't all 'accidents,' were they?"

"No," I admitted. "I did them. And I've always felt terrible about it. But I have been trying, all summer, to make things right."

Hallie just stared at me for a long moment. "You really expect me to buy that?"

"Yes," I said, looking right at her, hoping, despite everything, that she would believe me. "It's the truth."

She folded her arms across her chest. "Why I should believe anything you say?"

"Because," I said, and I could hear my voice rising. "You know me."

Hallie let out a short laugh. "Oh, do I?"

"Yes!" I almost yelled it, and I realized that, on top of everything else, I was feeling betrayed. Everything that I'd thought we'd been building this summer had been fake, and now it was totally gone. "I thought we were friends."

Hallie looked discomfited for a moment. "What, just because we hung out and you got me in to see a band I like? We're not *friends*, Gemma."

"Well, obviously not, since you've been sabotaging me all summer." Hallie shrugged, and suddenly I thought of someone who had nothing to do with any of this—someone who was just collateral damage. "What about Josh?" I asked.

Hallie flinched, but when she spoke, her tone was tough, challenging. "What about him?"

"You wanted to get revenge on me that badly? You were willing to let him get hurt?"

"I . . ." Hallie started. She looked down and let out a long breath, and when she spoke, it sounded like she was also trying to convince herself. "I told you," she said. "I tried to tell you not to get involved with him. I was trying to keep him out of this."

I thought about Josh's heartbroken expression. I thought about everything Hallie had put me through this summer, the hoops she had watched me jump, knowing the truth the whole time. It was enough to make me feel nauseous. "I only told you I was Sophie," I said, "because I wanted to make things up to you. I was trying to do the right thing."

"And you thought I was just going to forgive you?" Hallie asked. "Did you really believe that it would be that easy?" She shook her head, the speed of her words increasing as her voice started to shake with fury. "You *ruined* my life. You almost wrecked my family. Did you think I was going to let you get *away* with it? You think I didn't see through you the minute you stepped off that train?"

She looked away, and when she turned back to me, her face was composed again. "Go home, Gemma," she said, biting off my name. "Go on home to Connecticut. I won. This is over."

She turned and walked away then, up the beach, not hurrying, not once looking behind her.

I walked to the water's edge, feeling the need to scream or cry—maybe both.

It had all been for nothing. I had tried *so* hard to do the right thing—and it had been used against me at every turn, and resulted in nothing but heartbreak. Hallie had been willing to hurt me and Teddy and her own brother, all to get revenge. There was no point in even trying to make things right with someone like that. I shouldn't have wasted my time.

Overhead, the first firework shot up into the sky and exploded, sending down a bright-red shower of sparks.

I took a deep breath and then let it out. Strangely, I no longer felt like crying. I only felt the cool, hard certainty that I'd last felt when I was eleven. The clarity that comes from knowing who your enemy is.

The last thing Hallie said to me was reverberating in my head. And as I looked up into the sky that was bright with fireworks, I knew there was one thing she had been wrong about.

This wasn't over.

It was just beginning.

ACKNOWLEDGMENTS

I am so very grateful to Jean Feiwel, who believed in this project from the very beginning. Thank you so much. I'm so lucky to be part of the Macmillan family!

Thank you to Anna Roberto, for your brilliant notes, insights, and all-around awesomeness. It's truly a joy to work with such an amazing editor.

Emily van Beek—thank you for being there every step of the way, from my initial, vague idea to the final draft. I'm beyond appreciative. Without you, there would be no book.

Thank you to Anne Heltzel, wonderful writer and amazing friend, who sat across from me in countless Paris cafes, read drafts, and shared insights, along with cookies.

Thank you to the incredible team at Macmillian: Kathryn Little, Courtney Griffin, Caitlin Sweeny, Ksenia Winnicki, Ashley Halsey, and Lauren Burniac. And thank you so much to Rich Deas for the gorgeous cover!

Thank you to Trey Callaway, gentleman and scholar, for graciously letting me borrow his last name and first initial.

Thanks and love to my mother, Jane Finn. And thanks to my brother, Jason, my first reader, who always gives me notes, whether I want them or not.

I have the best friends in the world. Thank you to Sarah, Lauren, Jessi, Rosa, Leslie, and Rachel. You guys rock. Cupcakes on me.

BROKEN HEARTS, FENCES, AND OTHER THINGS TO MEND

BONUS MATERIALS

PLAYLIST

"What Becomes of the Broken Hearted?" · Four Tops

"On Your Own" · Green River Ordinance

"This Broken Heart" · Something Corporate

"Little Secrets" · Passion Pit

"Who I Am Hates Who I've Been (Acoustic)" · Relient k

"Deer in the Headlights" · Owl City

"Bad Blood" · Taylor Swift

"Get Right Back Where We Started From" · Army Navy

"Little Lies" · Fleetwood Mac

"Secrets" · OneRepublic

"*Crosses Fingers*" · The Secret Handshake

"Nightswimming" · R.E.M.

"Dreaming" · Smallpools

"La La Lie" · Jack's Mannequin

"The Tip of the Iceberg" · Owl City

"The Good Fight" · Dashboard Confessional

"Good Arms vs. Bad Arms" · Frightened Rabbit

"It'll All Work Out" · Tom Petty & the Heartbreakers

"You and Me" · Parachute

"Don't Lie" · Vampire Weekend

"Young Love" · Mystery Jets

"Everybody Learns from Disaster" · Dashboard Confessional

"Stay Young, Go Dancing" · Death Cab for Cutie

"White Dress" · Parachute

"The High Road" · Broken Bells

"Even If It Breaks Your Heart" · Eli Young Band

"Your Ex-Lover Is Dead" · Stars

"Love Like Woe" · The Ready Set

"She Doesn't Get It" · The Format

"I Lied About Everything" · The Secret Handshake

"Fireworks" · You Me at Six

"The Best Deceptions" · Dashboard Confessional

"Better Than Revenge" · Taylor Swift

"I Always Knew" · The Vaccines

"Ruthless" · Something Corporate

"Uncharted" · Sara Bareilles

"Anything Could Happen" · Ellie Goulding

"Can't Go Back Now" · The Weepies

GOFISH

QUESTIONS FOR THE AUTHOR

KATIE FINN

What was the inspiration for
Broken Hearts, Fences, and
Other Things to Mend?
A few years ago, I started thinking
about the idea of revenge—and about
revenge cycles, and things escalating.
I thought it would be a great framework for a series, since
the stakes would get raised in every book. I also thought it
could be an interesting way to show how people change . . .
or don't, as the case may be. But I felt like the straightfor-
ward revenge story had been done a lot. When I thought
about doing a *reverse* revenge story, everything fell into
place. I liked the idea of someone trying to atone for her mistakes, not realizing that she's making everything worse in the
process.

That ending! Why did you choose to end it on a
cliff-hanger?
That had always seemed like the perfect way to end the first
part of the story—all the truths are out, and now Gemma
needs to deal with this new reality. It was also really fun to
finally reveal the secrets I'd just had to tease throughout the
whole book.

Was the story always going to end like that?
Yes! I usually don't know my endings, but I knew this one—right down to the lines the characters spoke—from the very beginning. I loved writing that final scene; it felt more like transcribing than writing, because I'd been thinking about it for so many months.

Both Gemma and Hallie do some pretty mean things in this book. Why did you choose to write characters like that?
I really loved writing both of their unscrupulous moments, mostly because I could understand where both of them were coming from. I've always liked the idea that no villain ever thinks they're a villain, because they have a perfectly rational explanation that makes sense to them and makes them the hero of their own story. And both Gemma and Hallie might be doing bad things, but have been able to justify their actions to themselves one way or another. It was much more fun to write that than someone just being mean for no reason.

Why did you choose to set the book in the Hamptons?
I knew I needed to set it in a summer community. Gemma had to be able to go under a fake identity and not get found out, which she never would have been able to do in her hometown. I wanted it to be close enough that people could get there easily from Connecticut and New York City, and it needed to be a place where people return to year after year.

I love the Hamptons, and was working on the initial idea for this book at a writing retreat in the Hamptons. As soon as I started playing with the Hamptons for the setting, the whole book started coming together. And I knew it was the only place I wanted the story to be set.

What's going to happen with Gemma and Josh?
You'll have to read book #2! There's a *lot* of drama. I can promise that much!

In the book, Gemma goes under another name. Is it true that you *also* do this?
Yes! ☺ I also write Young Adult novels as Morgan Matson. (Full disclosure—Katie Finn is my middle name.) Unlike Gemma, who finds it really stressful to go under an assumed identity, I love having two names to write under!

Do you have any writing habits or rituals?
I need to have a really great playlist, and I need to have some sort of snack within arm's reach. Otherwise, I'm spending all my time seeking out snacks, and not writing. I also need some sort of caffeinated beverage close at hand—Starbucks preferred!

What can we expect in the sequel, *Revenge, Ice Cream, and Other Things Best Served Cold*?
Drama. Secrets revealed (including some secrets that *weren't* revealed at the end of book 1)! Several new characters. Many returning characters. Lots of ice cream. Unexpected documentary filmmaking. Kissing. Anti-dairy sentiment. Revenge. Stolen identities. Impromptu protesting. Faulty algorithms. And the biggest bombshell of all . . .

Gemma's world has just been rocked by Hallie's betrayal.
Who can she trust now? Is there any hope Josh can forgive her?
And what does this mean for Gemma and Hallie?
Their friendship might be over . . . but the war is just beginning.

Keep reading for a sneak peek!

CHAPTER 1

I woke with a gasp, sitting straight up in bed. I was drenched in sweat, my heart pounding. Flashes of memories and dream fragments were swirling around in my head so quickly, it was like I couldn't catch my breath.

And the last dream—make that a nightmare—had been terrible. Hallie had known who I was all along, she'd been playing me all summer, and *she* was the reason that Teddy had broken up with me. . . .

I made myself breathe more evenly, and felt my pulse start to slow. I lay back down again, settling into my pillow. I was just about to close my eyes and try to go back to sleep when I saw the pile of clothes in the corner. There was the white dress I'd worn to the Fourth of July beach party, crumpled on the rug. The clutch I'd picked to go with my dress. There were my flats, tossed in a heap, the soles still sandy. And it hit me, all at once, that it hadn't just been a terrible dream. It had all actually happened. It was worse than any nightmare I would have been able to fabricate, and it was the truth.

I closed my eyes for a minute, hoping against all logic and sense that I could unlearn what I now knew, go back to that restful time when I was just going under my best friend's name and trying to make things right with Hallie, when Josh still liked me. . . .

Josh.

The thought of him, and of the way he'd looked at me when he'd realized my true identity, was enough to jolt me awake. I sat up and squinted at the amber-colored numbers of the digital clock on my bedside table. It was six A.M., but I could tell I wasn't getting back to sleep any time soon. I pushed myself out of bed and headed downstairs in the tank top and shorts I was wearing as pajamas.

Normally, I would have put a robe on, or tried to make myself a bit more presentable, but it seemed like a small comfort this morning that I didn't have to worry about running into anyone, and not just because it was six A.M., or that the house—the beachfront Hamptons mansion of my dad's college roommate-turned-Hollywood-superproducer, Bruce Davidson—was big enough to defy all logic and sense. The real reason was that the only people currently staying in the house were myself and my best friend, Sophie Curtis.

My dad and I had been invited to spend the summer, but I knew Bruce's offer to stay with him was only partially generous. My dad was a screenwriter who worked on a lot of movies for Bruce, and I had a feeling Bruce liked being able to keep an eye on my dad's work progress, with the ability to shut off the Internet if he thought the pages weren't coming quickly enough. But Bruce and my dad—and Bruce's longtime assistant, Rosie—were currently in L.A. taking meetings, so I had the house to myself, since I knew Sophie wouldn't be up for a few hours yet. Bruce's kids, Ford and Gwyneth, were supposed to come to stay at some point this summer, but I'd never gotten an exact date from them. And at the moment I was very glad to be alone. I needed some space to try to get my head around the fact that everything I thought I'd believed this summer had been a lie.

I crossed through the dark empty kitchen, silent except for the subtle hum of the giant silver fridge, and saw the glint of water in the distance. The beach was right outside the house. It was where I'd found myself multiple times so far this summer when I needed to organize my thoughts, and there was nowhere else I wanted to be at the moment. I plucked a sweatshirt that was folded on one of the kitchen stools on the way out—the sun was barely up, and I knew how cold it could be down by the water. The sweatshirt was maroon and soft, and I pulled it on over my sleep tank as I walked past the pool house and down to the water. I had no idea whose it was, but I breathed it in for just a moment, feeling somehow comforted by the scent—like the ocean and dryer sheets and something sweet I couldn't quite place—almost like cinnamon rolls.

I made my way down to the sand in the half-darkness. There was nobody on the beach this early, though there were a few surfers bobbing in the waves, too far away to even make out their faces—just shapes in dark wetsuits. I sat down on the sand and hugged my knees to my chest. I'd come out to this very spot when I'd first arrived in the Hamptons. It was where I'd decided I was going to go along with the misunderstanding at the train station, try to make things right with Hallie. I let out a short laugh as I picked up a handful of sand and then let it trickle through my fingers. So much for that plan.

Even though I knew the facts—knew full well what had happened last night—I still couldn't quite make myself believe it.

Hallie.

It had been Hallie all along.

Hallie had been the reason that Teddy had broken up with me at the beginning of the summer. She had known who I was from the start and had been sabotaging me every step of the way.

And something else she had said last night was echoing in my head. She told me that she had been planning this for *years*. So, she hadn't been moving on with her life, letting go of what I'd done to her when we were kids. Instead she had been plotting revenge on me for who knows how long. I shivered, even though as the sun rose, it was starting to get warmer. It was all just such a reversal of the way I'd understood things that I was feeling like I had whiplash.

Needing a distraction from these thoughts, I stretched my legs out in front of me and looked at the surfers. Most seemed to be staying behind the breakline, just sitting on their boards and bobbing up and down, but there was one surfer who was riding nearly every wave in, and doing it with panache. It was clear he was really great at this, miles better than anyone else who was in the water with him. As he paddled back out, swimming against the current like it was nothing, I weighed my options.

Did I really want to stay here in the Hamptons, where I'd made such a mess of things? Where I apparently had a mortal enemy? Did I really want to put myself through that? I couldn't go back to our empty house in Putnam, Connecticut—my mother and my stepfather, Walter, were still in Scotland. Walter was a former professional fly-fisher and current salmon expert, neither of which I had known were actual things you could be before meeting him. He and my mother were staying in a castle while Walter advised the laird on his salmon. Though my mother had made it pretty clear I wasn't invited, I knew I could call and tell her that I absolutely had to leave the Hamptons, and she'd let me come. Or I could most likely convince Sophie to go back to Putnam and let me stay with her. They were both decent options, but . . .

I dug my fingers into the sand. Somehow, I didn't like the thought of slinking back home and letting Hallie think she'd beaten me, despite the fact that she very clearly had. I knew I wasn't innocent in all this—I had put this thing in motion years ago—but I had been *eleven* then and scared out of my mind. Hallie, on the other hand, had apparently spent the last five years scheming, coldly plotting out how to ruin my life. How best to hurt me. And she had certainly figured it out. The image of her kissing Teddy flashed though my mind, and I closed my eyes tightly as though it would make the memory go away.

Seeing Teddy again—and seeing him with *Hallie*—had been more painful than I'd been prepared for. It was like my broken heart, which I'd just begun to put back together, had been shattered all over again.

I knew I couldn't just stay in the Hamptons and worry that Hallie was about to do something else to wreck my life again. I couldn't spend my summer that way. But I didn't have any other ideas at the moment. Feeling like I wasn't going to be able to make any coherent decisions until I was properly caffeinated, I pushed myself to my feet and brushed the sand off my hands. The sun was almost totally up now, and the beach was slowly starting to get populated with early morning joggers and power-walking senior citizens.

I had just turned to walk back to the house when one of the surfers—the good one—caught my eye. I watched as he rode a wave in then dove off his board and into the water. For a moment it was like the world went into slow motion as the surfer emerged from the water, slicking his hair back and reaching around to unzip his wetsuit. He peeled it down to his waist, and I felt my jaw drop. Then he started walking up to the beach, his surfboard tucked under his arm like it weighed nothing.

I suddenly wished I'd brought my sunglasses with me, even though it had been dark when I'd left the house, and it wasn't really all that bright now. But I would have liked a way to look at this guy without it being totally obvious what I was doing. Even without my sunglasses, it was really hard not to stare. It looked like this guy must surf *a lot*—or else do some other activity where you get crazy-defined abs and arms and shoulders. I expected him to head toward the parking lot, but to my surprise, the guy kept coming closer. I wasn't sure if I should get out of his path, and was just hoping he wasn't going to start lecturing me about objectifying him or something, when he dropped his surfboard onto the sand and started to run right toward me. Before I could even react, I was swept up in a huge hug, and as he set me down—though *dropped* might have been the right word for it, when I was still a few inches off the ground—I realized of course I knew who it was, and that I should have recognized him right away.

"Hey," he said, brushing his hand over the top of his black hair, and turning it into tiny spikes. He grinned at me, but his tone was light, like we were used to seeing each other daily and this was no big deal. "Morning, Gemma."

"Hey," I said in the same faux-casual way as I smiled back, hoping it wasn't obvious how hard my heart was pounding. Ford Davidson—Bruce's son, computer genius, and my long-standing crush—was back in the Hamptons.